About the Author

Mark F. Johnson loves American history, particularly the period of the middle twentieth century, from the 1950s through the 1970s when there was so much social transformation in the United States. As an American of African descent, he is particularly interested in the Civil Rights struggle that found its legs and began its march forward during this time. Also, he has an interest in international affairs and has studied the period during which many countries in Africa became independent of Europe about this same time. Mark has worked extensively in American politics including his work in the United States Senate and also for a Presidential reelection campaign. Mark has worked on the staff of one major US newspaper and he has also been a freelance writer for several local papers in both Chicago and Washington, DC. Mark is a native of Washington, DC and has lived as well in Chicago where he went to graduate school and New York City. His interests include museums, national and public parks, urban history and neighborhood transformation, touring around the world and throughout North America, news and commentary programs, social dramas and political thrillers, historical fiction and social commentary and Victorian, Art Deco and Mid-century Modern architecture. Mark is also a fan of most types of twentieth century popular music, art and culture. He is hopeful for further evolution of American political, social and cultural values in the twenty-first century as well as worldwide understanding of inequality in all its forms.

White After Labor Day

Mark F. Johnson

White After Labor Day

Olympia Publishers
London

www.olympiapublishers.com
OLYMPIA PAPERBACK EDITION

A CIP catalogue record for this title is
available from the British Library.

ISBN: 978-1-80074-114-0

This is a work of fiction.
Names, characters, places and incidents originate from the writer's imagination.
Any resemblance to actual persons, living or dead, is purely coincidental.

First Published in 2022

Olympia Publishers
Tallis House
2 Tallis Street
London
EC4Y 0AB

Printed in Great Britain

Dedication

This book is dedicated to my mother, Lillian, who passed away long before I got to really know her! But, as the years have gone by, I feel as though I understand her much better now and I can pretty much tell her story. In fact, I have to some extent in this book! She, like many "colored" women of her generation, was always aware of style, appearance and "fitting in". She was the first person that I heard the phrase "no white after Labor Day" from.

Acknowledgements

I would like to acknowledge my tenth-grade history teacher, Edna Jackson. She was my all-time favorite teacher, and was among the first African-American teachers to teach in my formerly all-white high school.

Also, acknowledgement to my former mentor, Charles Peterson, who grew up as a Mainliner outside Philadelphia. He helped me learn to navigate "majority" culture early on in life!

Only Americans can hurt America.

Dwight D Eisenhower

Introduction

It was hard! Getting out of bed came with a struggle on this early October Monday morning. He lay there, basically captive, one minute fighting and the other surrendering, to the fore-day fantasies.

For the past several weeks, in fact, Junior had felt at war both with himself and with outside forces. One battle always resulted in a happy ending! Thankfully, that was the case this morning. However, the combatants pulling him in the other direction had not surrendered. The smile brought to his face this early morning would soon be expunged once he got into enemy territory, otherwise known as Arlington High. That is, unless the friendly forces raged again, hidden behind enemy lines!

It was not that he didn't look forward to going to school. Not that at all. But he needed his feet on the ground and his head on straight to fight this battle effectively. The natives had been restless! And right now, he was defenseless and vulnerable after floating on a cloud during the night, suspended somewhere in space. And speaking of space, it was clear that his rocket had blasted off sometime during the night or early morning by the wet spot on the bed, near where he lay.

All these images of space floating around in his head, Junior realized, were so vivid because he had watched the premiere of that new television show on Friday evening with his family. Everyone at Arlington High had been talking about the coming of the *Twilight Zone* for the last few weeks! Besides, the new CBS show had been touted on the network for much of the summer.

Junior certainly felt as if he could identify with the astronaut who found himself alone in "Where is Everybody"; after all there he was, at a place where many thought he didn't belong. But instead of wishing there were people around as the out-of-place astronaut did, Junior wanted it that way! No one in Arlington could know what went on behind those stone walls, home of the Fighting Rebels! Look away, look away, Dixie Land!

There would be new challenges awaiting him at Arlington High this week. Definitely among them, the academic rigors of tenth grade at one of the best high schools in Virginia. And even more daunting, the stressful trials of being among the first colored students to be integrated into one of the Old Dominion's most venerated high schools. But Junior believed that he had the talent and the strength to overcome these two challenges. He had been dreaming about something else. That was why it was so hard waking up.

The touch he felt in his dream excited him! The hands caressing his body made him smile and brought a burst of joy! He could still feel it as he lay partially dazed although there was a part of him at full attention. Kissing and caressing Carolyn Stanley against the walls of Frederick Douglass Junior High and in the alleys and behind the trees on the way home had never had the same reaction on him! This, and this alone, could thrill him the way the Platters sang about in *Only You*!

How to be alone with Cliff Peterson again, as he had been the Saturday afternoon before and several times before that! This was the biggest challenge facing Junior as he lay in bed! This would be no easy task at a place where all eyes were on him and where no one could know what he and this white boy did! The mere thought of it and all the strategizing involved made his head practically explode!

"Get on up, Wynn Junior," Julia Mae called from the bottom of the stairs, loud enough that he could hear although his bedroom door was closed, fortunately, given what had been going on under the starched white sheets now stiffer! "You're not gon' make your father late for work." He knew she meant it seriously. She addressed him by Wynn only when she meant business. He also knew that Jeanne was already downstairs getting her hair pressed. He had heard her come out of the bathroom after her bath and close the door to her room as she got her clothes on. This was their morning ritual. As usual, at the top of the stairs, the stench of hair grease joining forces with the hot comb to do battle with the coarse ways of her hair to set it straight, was wafting in the air. He didn't need to open the door to know this.

Their father had been driving his son to Arlington High School ever since "that day", as he, Julia Mae and everyone they knew, referred to it. But now a month since "that day" a lot of the anxiety had dissipated. The fear of being attacked and beaten up or killed, the fear of having the car ambushed as they drove to the other side of town, the fear of having the house burned or bombed as they slept, the fear of Julia Mae being attacked as she walked to or from the bus stop from her job at the downtown department store, all that had pretty much subsided.

Arlington, Virginia did not lie in ruins, burned to the ground because the colored kids were now where none had ever gone before! But yes, everyone still had to be on vigil! There was that white woman back in April who had been put out of the Senate hearings on civil rights because she blared that she would kill every Negro in the country if she could. Everyone knew she was crazy, but it was also wide scuttlebutt, at least in the colored community, that "the old ofay wench lived in Arlington or Alexandria where most of her kind live".

Instead, though, after the expected protests, outcries and lines formed around the schools prompted by the Supreme Court order to desegregate public schools, the "end of the world", as many in the white community might have foreseen it, came without too much extirpation. Perhaps the constant glare of the television news cameras and the newspaper reporters those first weeks helped and certainly the continued presence of the National Guard didn't hurt! Regardless, even though the judges said that colored students must be allowed to go into the formerly all-white schools, the jury was still out as to how long that would last!

Much of white Arlington didn't like it and yes, many tried hard to prevent it from ever happening. But for many of the Negro residents, particularly older ones, this was one more step toward the *liberty and justice for all* that those very students proclaimed each day as they pledged allegiance to the flag. The few colored children chosen to be the first to go to these white schools were young soldiers in their eyes. They were making the sacrifice to integrate the Arlington school system and be on the front lines of all the hatred and resentment that would surely come their way. This was the Old Dominion, after all! Richmond, the former capital of the Confederacy, sat less than two hours away from their present-day battleground.

15

In Julia Mae Horry's mind, Junior had to get up, get a bath, get dressed, eat his breakfast and get ready to hit the battlefield. And he had to do it quickly so his daddy could get to work!

Most of his close friends, including Carolyn who was quite sweet on him, had decided to make their life easier and go to the colored high school. Although Carolyn was most disappointed in his decision to go to Arlington High, she and most of his other friends as well as their parents were proud of the Arlington Five, as they were called. But although integration was coming to Washington DC's nearest Virginia suburb in 1959, it was shuffling along instead of going with "all deliberate speed" as the Supreme Court had ordained in its school desegregation decision five years earlier. The truth is that Carolyn and Junior's other friends from Junior High couldn't go to Arlington High.

Desegregation didn't mean freedom of choice for the Negro students to go to whatever school they wanted to go to. It meant instead that a very select few would be allowed to go to the one local white, elementary, junior high and high school that was made open to them. Many factors played a part in deciding which few colored kids were chosen to enter Arlington High.

Their grades and family background played a part in the schoolboard's decision but also input from white people who knew them, mostly as the offspring of the colored people who worked for them, played a part. A few of the colored students allowed to go to these schools with white kids were the children of teachers in the Arlington County Public Schools Negro Division.

Julia Mae wasn't a domestic like some of the other mothers, but she knew many white women with some influence because she sewed for them. As much as she could, she would put one or two of those relationships to work to get her smart son who knew how to "act" into the best public high school in town, one with all the latest facilities, new textbooks and well-qualified teachers. Never mind that many of these teachers may not have wanted Junior there. Once he got there, he would know how to get what he needed out of it, she and his father Wynn Senior had no doubt.

By the time he was done with his bath it was about ten minutes till 8, on that bright, still very warm early October morning. Julia Mae had slipped his button-down plaid short-sleeve shirt and his brown slacks, both clean and pressed, on his bed.

All dressed and downstairs now, Junior and Jeanne greeted a bowl of hot crème of wheat. This was their breakfast of champions, at least during school days. Julia Mae believed strongly that a warm and wholesome breakfast was the way to start the day. That was how her own mother had started her out in her school days years before in a small Virginia town, long before she had moved to Washington, DC. That was the tradition she decided to continue in the Horry household.

Had this been a Sunday morning, however, or perhaps if she had felt like it on a Wednesday or Thursday, breakfast might have been buttered grits, scrambled eggs and bacon. To this extent, the Horry house could have been any in Hilldale. No matter whose table in the largest colored section of Arlington, grits made an appearance regularly on Sunday morning. Sometimes with bacon, sometimes with scrapple and sometimes with salmon cakes. Even if there was no meat side-lining, grits were a weekend morning staple.

Jeanne had been waiting for her brother to come downstairs so the two of them could eat together with their father. That was also the way it usually was. After breakfast the two would either get a ride to school from their father or from the parents of neighbor kids. But that was when they both went to the same junior high school, when Jeanne, two years younger was in 7th grade while Junior was in 9th.

"You look nice, Son," Julia Mae said to him. "How do the slacks fit, nice? Did I hem them right?"

"Yes, Mama, they fit fine," came the reply she expected.

She had always thought her only son to be a good-looking young man. He was tall like his father, had an athletic build from running track and carried himself well. He had a mix of her darker complexion and his father's perceptibly lighter pecan brown color. Although he had more of her facial structure with his pronounced cheekbones and sculpted warm brown face.

But she didn't just dole out praise on Junior. She was equally proud of Jeanne who was considered a pretty girl by most of colored Hilldale. At least, as many would say, "She's pretty for a dark-skinned girl." She had a magazine figure. Jeanne played softball, basketball and ran track.

Yet she found a way to be girly too and wore her pressed hair in a poodle cut, the way Pearl Bailey and Sarah Vaughan often wore theirs. Since Julia Mae did her hair most of the time, she pressed and curled it tight as she did her own. Twice a month, they would both go to the hairdresser.

Their mother was a fine-looking woman herself, most thought. Again, though, they would add the "for a dark-skinned girl". Dark-skinned colored women weren't automatically acknowledged as good looking even if they were. Their dark complexion generally had to be pointed out mostly because it made them the exception. Good looking fell under the domain of lighter-skinned women by default. Be that as it may, compliments were often lavished on Julia Mae, soft chocolate complexion notwithstanding. It wasn't surprising to anyone that she could have snagged Wynn Horry senior, a former Army infantryman in World War II that she met and married in 1944 when he had come back from Europe on leave. When he got out of the army in 1947, they moved back to Virginia from across the river in Washington and he went to work at the Pentagon. They were two very nice-looking colored people who had both come from ugly circumstances of deprivation and inequality in the south, she from southern Virginia and he from South Carolina. They both wanted to make each other better and find a better life!

Looking neat was important to her and Wynn Sr because that is the way they were raised. But it was especially important now! Her son was representing all colored kids in front of these white principals, teachers and students at Arlington High. The way they looked, smelled, laughed, talked, walked, dressed, everything about them was under microscopic scrutiny.

Arlington High held a special place in the minds of white Virginians! It was the first high school established in the county of Arlington. Its wide halls were filled with photographs of alumni who had graduated years earlier including many who had become well known and highly regarded in government, business or even in Hollywood.

In the school's Hall of Fame, there were marble busts, similar to those of Greek or Roman gods, dedicated to former Confederate generals and old Virginia politicians, atop waist-high rectangular plinths. Many of the students over the years had descended from this list of southern who's who! The Stars and Bars hovered in various places throughout the school, and tall white concrete columns still stood firm in the school's main concourse, although they had come to sustain a few cracks that were becoming visible. One of the newly arriving colored students, a trespasser many would say, had told a newspaper reporter that the school reminded her of "an old plantation"! The newspaper never used her name at the pleading of her parents and for concerns for her safety, but the colored students knew who said it.

Everyone was aware of Arlington's reverence for the Rebels. "Stonewall Jackson and General Lee would toss in their graves if this they could see," read one sign of protest posted faithfully outside the school for the first few weeks.

"Too many people are looking for a reason to get y'all outta that school," said almost everyone in Hilldale from neighbors, to church members and especially the colored teachers. "Whatever you do, watch how y'all act." Some of the older folks went so far as to admonish the kids in the way they had been told. "Don't show your race over there," they would say, fearing that the best way for the five students to carry themselves was to act "white". These older colored people knew how to smile for white people no matter what. If they were good at anything, it was putting on a face for the white people they encountered. They had done it all their lives no matter what.

Though there hadn't been any serious damage or harm, threats against the colored students occasionally came in and some white parents as well as students continued to yell, scream and stand outside the schools. The Negro population knew it must not be easy for those kids to go through all that. Even though the adults were supposedly older and wiser, hardly any of them unless they had grown up in the north or on the west coast had had the experience of being educated with whites at that age. Those who had televisions, or who worked in homes with televisions, had probably seen the tense and painful news reports of the nine colored students who attempted to integrate Central High School in Little Rock, Arkansas just two years earlier. Everyone knew how that had gone and how badly those kids were treated and for no reason since the governor closed the public school system afterwards. The Negro population was praying that would not happen in Arlington.

Besides, word was beginning to get around Arlington that something

19

had already happened with the colored kids at the high school! None of them had been physically harmed, at least as far as they knew, but something had happened that caused one of them to go missing! The fact that most in the colored community didn't know any details kept them on edge!

Arlington High was not the only school to desegregate at the start of the new school year in September. A formerly all-white junior high school had been ordered to let in four colored kids and a formerly whites-only elementary school had been ordered to do the same. No white child was asked to go to a formerly all-colored school.

However, much of the anti-integration animus had been focused on the high school. These students were older. They were soon to be adults and it was crucial that they understand and learn to function in the southern way of life. This was especially true now that the old ways were under attack. Now, the fear was even greater for what could result from the mixing of the races. Even though the few colored students that had been allowed to attend had different classes, they pretty much all stayed together when they could, especially in the cafeteria and coming to and leaving school because it was safer to protect them that way and also because they felt more comfortable.

A few of them knew one or two of the white kids in passing mostly because of their parents working for them. But of course, there was little socializing between them. Junior had met or seen some of the boys because Julia Mae had made clothes for their mothers. But he knew Cliff Peterson quite well by the time school had started. He knew his parents, his house, his little brother and he knew what his hair felt like with his fingers running through it, pomade and all, and what his partly naked body felt like pressed against his own partly naked body!

They had grown close, Wynn "Junior" Horry and Clifford Peterson, but they could never let that be known at school. Some of the teachers and the principals knew that Mrs Peterson had written a letter vouching for Junior to be admitted to Arlington High. He had been cutting their lawn for two summers at that point and her son seemed to like him quite a bit. In fact, Cliff took to Junior right away! The two were exactly the same height and were able to meet each other's eyes easily! Junior saw in Cliff a teenage version of Bronco, one of the cowboys who often captured his attention on television, and he didn't particularly like cowboy shows! Cliff didn't have the swagger and nor did he wear a cowboy hat, but with his light brown hair, square jaw, height and build, he brought to mind the gunslinger whose television theme song went show me a girl who's kissed him once, I'll show you a girl who's kissed him twice! Bronco's lips must have a powerful allure, Junior imagined.

All that first summer, Junior thought of that song every time he saw Cliff. He couldn't help but wonder if Cliff's lips had some kind of bait on them too! But it was hard to imagine that Cliff had ever been kissed. He seemed awkward and yearning. He didn't have many friends and he wasn't much like the other boys in his world. Cliff was always looking at Junior as if he had something to tell him. Or perhaps it was that he wanted to draw to himself the confidence and grit that he saw in Junior, through his eyes!

Junior couldn't help but notice and found it difficult to keep his eyes off Cliff as well. He tried to keep his mind on trimming the grass, which is what he was there for, but his interest in this boyish Bronco kept growing!

Jeanne was still a student at Frederick Douglass Jr High. She had not attempted to go to the white junior high school. Her parents wouldn't have allowed that even if she had wanted to. Wynn would not want his daughter around those white boys. The memories of growing up in South Carolina and the things that almost happened to his sister and did happen to many of the other colored girls he knew, things that were done to them by white men and white boys who were learning very early of the power and autarchy they could take over colored people, particularly women and girls. They learned early on that it was part of their birthright. By the time they had gotten to junior high school, they were well schooled in the *privileges* they enjoyed as white males.

Now that breakfast was over, Jeanne was on her own to get to school. She could ride part of the way with Wynn and Junior since Arlington High was all the way across town in one of the wealthier white neighborhoods, or she could go next door and ask Mr Raymond for a ride. That was her friend Delores' father. Delores and her two brothers, Tommy and Allen went to Douglass Junior High as well. Wynn was already running late since Junior didn't get up so early. He had to be at work by 9:30 at the latest. It was now 8:35 and Junior had to be across town by 9:00 It should take no more than ten minutes to get him to school but if there were protests and parents blocking the streets as had been the case when the school year started about a month previously, it could take longer. Wynn was a cautious man. He preferred to take few chances at anything.

"Bye, Momma, see you tonight," said Junior as he walked out to the car with his father. Julia Mae was kissed goodbye by both her men and Jeanne received a nudge on the shoulder from her father as the two Horry men left to get in the car to make their way up from South Arlington where the colored people lived to North Arlington where Arlington High was located. Few colored people lived up there, and many were live-in housekeepers, nannies or butlers.

Julia Mae was always the last to leave the house. Like most colored women she knew, she worked. She had always worked and never really imagined herself as a housewife. That title was generally reserved for the white women that she came in contact with in her couturier work. Although the colored women that she knew who worked for these white women, her sister Nellie included, were more married to the house than these women, she always thought. Their main function was to look good for their husbands and keep them happy, entertain their guests, and make cocktails.

Her job as a seamstress at the ritzy Horrschorns department store in downtown Washington didn't begin until 11am. She always had time to wash the dishes, clean the kitchen and bathroom after everyone's bath and prepare her lunch and herself for work. She usually also had time to start dinner. She didn't get off work until 7pm most nights, so the family dinner would never be served before 7:30 pm at the earliest, that is, unless her sister Nellie had stopped by from her housekeeper job in a congressman's house in North Arlington, not too far from Junior's new school, in fact. Nellie lived in the District with her husband Talley, but she drove to her job in Virginia. If her sister was running late or if she just wanted to help out, she would sometimes stop by and put the chicken in the oven that Julia Mae had left out or cut up some greens and put them in the pot until Jeanne got home from school to finish the cooking job or help her aunt in cooking.

Nellie, shorter and with a rounder face and body than her sister, had no children, so in a way, Junior and Jeanne were her own son and daughter. She didn't get married the first time until she was nearly 30 years old, although her warm and friendly disposition and face, more cinnamon to Julia Mae's cocoa, did attract a certain kind of man. Her first husband was in and out of jail, an alcoholic and eventually ran off. Later she found out that he died or more accurately, was killed in a fight in Lorton prison outside Washington, DC, where colored men went for almost any offense. She and Talley, her second husband, were usually both busy. He was the chauffeur for the Congressman that they both worked for and he also was the handyman for a couple of apartment buildings the family they worked for owned, one in the District and the other in Virginia. Working in the Congressman's house Nellie got to hear what white people talked about and what their concerns were.

"Don't worry too much about those white kids at that school," Nellie told Wynn, Julia Mae and Junior just before school was to start in September, "They will be too upset, that Superman is dead to cause y'all any trouble," she cackled and everyone joined her in the laughter. But even this attempt to lighten the family's tension for even a minute was a tough challenge and she knew it. But Nellie had to be Nellie and her joking was one of the reasons they all loved her so much. It was true, of course, that George Reeves, who played Superman on television, had committed suicide that summer. The mild-mannered *Daily Planet* reporter who shed his glasses and donned a cape when Metropolis needed a hero had apparently taken his own life in the middle of June! Metropolis, which looked a lot like New York, would be on its own to fight crime unless there was someone else around who had come into contact with the hero-making Kryptonite!

On the trip to school Wynn and Junior never had much to talk about. They did most of their talking at the table or as they watched television. They were one of the few colored families they knew in Arlington that had a television. Most colored people in DC that they knew had one, but not in Arlington. Nellie and Talley certainly had one. In fact, the one Wynn and Julia Mae had had come to them from Nellie and Talley as a hand-me-down from the Congressman. The Congressman had given Nellie and Talley the old one when they got a new one in 1956. Nellie and Talley had bought themselves a new one at the beginning of '59 and thus gave the Horrys their old one. This was the first television in the Horry household.

So the conversation in the car, as much as there was one, was about whether Junior was getting any trouble at school that he didn't want his mother to know about or whether he was being tempted by some white girl or whether they would let any of the colored boys play on the sports teams at his new school. Junior had run track at Frederick Douglass's. He was a sprinter and he was good. Wynn was a good runner himself but his love was baseball. He had always wanted Junior to love baseball more. In fact, he wanted him to be more sports-minded, period. He had always urged him to play baseball or football. Wynn figured that, as fast a runner as Junior was, playing baseball was a good way to use that talent. It was more a means to an end, in his mind, than just "runnin' for the sake of runnin'!"

The Chicago White Sox had just lost to the Los Angeles Dodgers in the third game of the World Series on Sunday. Wynn was a Dodgers fan. The Dodgers had Charlie Neal and Jim Gilliam. Although the White Sox had the most colored players, the Dodgers were the first to have a colored player! That was when they were still in Brooklyn. It meant a lot to Wynn and almost everyone he knew when Jackie Robinson signed onto the team twelve years earlier, in 1947. "I hope those Dodgers do it again. I like the White Sox," he told his son, "But I can't help but root for those Dodgers." The fourth game was later that day in Los Angeles. Wynn would be sure to listen to it at work or on the car radio driving into the District to pick Julia Mae up downtown if she had to work at Horrschorns Department Store late into the evening.

"If you picked up a basketball or a baseball, you could show those white boys what it's all about, Junior. I know you keep up with them in your studies but showing them what you can do in sports is a whole 'nother thing, man." It was one of those conversations that Junior was never very comfortable with. He just didn't have the interest in sports that his father did. Running track, he liked, but he never saw himself as a ball player of any kind.

"I understand, Pop," Junior replied to Wynn Sr's exhortation. His lack of interest in sports was particularly disappointing to his father because Jeanne played on the girls' softball team at the colored junior high school that he once went to.

Chapter 1

Wynn Horace Horry Jr was a good student. He had earned mostly As with a side of Bs throughout his time in elementary and junior high. Learning had always been important to him and he was one of those teenagers who read books even when he didn't have to. Yet there were other things about his new school that interested him more! His mind wandered during the ride up Glebe Road to Arlington Heights. He eyeballed the cafés and restaurants along the streets, ones that he might never eat at. He ogled the large homes on rolling hills and the manicured lawns. He gazed at the people on the streets carrying on as if worries, frets, disappointments and setbacks were strictly forbidden from their world, even this early in the day. He peered at the bushy trees still with their green leaves that would soon turn yellow and gold. The leaves in Hilldale would turn the same colors but to him, the rusts and cinnamons were shinier and more succulent up here! He thought it was a bit ironic that these people's lives were lived in technicolor as compared to the black and white lives of the people in Hilldale and other Negro areas.

It was only a three or four-mile trip from their house in Hilldale but no matter how many times Junior had driven up here in the past month since starting school or even before with his father driving his enterprising mother to deliver a dress she had made, for a white woman who lived in one of the fancy North Arlington neighborhoods, it always seemed as if in this world everything was always just right! This was *Mayfield* and *Springfield* and all the other television towns rolled into one. Here he wasn't just watching the perfect life, but he was actually seeing it in three-dimension!

Julia Mae had a good side business sewing for mostly white women in northern Virginia and in the District. She often brought Junior along to deliver a dress or take measurements for a new one, in part because she wanted him to see how white people lived, wealthier white people that is, to give him something to hope for. This is how he met Mrs Peterson and her son. She occasionally brought Jeanne for the same reason. They both had a chance to see inside many of these homes as they traveled with Julia Mae on evening or weekend deliveries or meetings, with Wynn always at the wheel since Julia Mae didn't drive.

Junior didn't usually get past the front door but occasionally he would get to come inside and at least stand by the door as the matron of the house went to get Julia Mae's money or as his mother waited to see if the dress fitted right or needed alterations. Sometimes the matron had other friends over who, liking what she had done for the lady of the house, wanted to get fitted for a new handmade dress. They could buy them from Julia Mae for much less than at any Arlington dress shop or certainly from any of the department stores in downtown Washington. This was especially true of Horrschorns.

Wynn never came inside but she would take Junior in with her because Wynn thought it was the smart thing to do. Junior enjoyed going for other reasons. It occasionally offered him the chance to get a passing glimpse of those people who looked like the ones he saw on television or at the movies, certainly before he started going to school at Arlington High. Those faces he saw in certain magazines sometimes held his attention for longer than he knew they should have. Just like when he'd be out in that part of town with his family or friends, his eyes would go places that he well knew they shouldn't settle.

Although, generally Junior felt safe! He knew that who he was looking at would never look back! As long as he didn't hold his stare too long, he would remain invisible to them. They would never really see him, and they would never guess how he felt as he looked at them! However, in Cliff Peterson, he had met one who did see him!

The venerable department store of limestone, the one that had employed Julia Mae since the late 1940s had sat on 14th Street for decades and catered to the wealthiest and most powerful people of Washington. Of course, colored shoppers were not much welcomed there and hardly any went. His mother often designed her own styles but would also copy a pattern of a dress sold at Horrschorns or that was out of a glamor magazine. The matron would pay for the material and Julia Mae would add her cost to the product. Definitely, she would charge more than the material would normally cost and at times she would bring some material home from Horrschorns. Colored women, especially those who worked in the homes of white people knew how to help themselves to what they thought should be theirs. So long as it wouldn't be missed by those who actually owned it.

As they drove closer to the school Wynn and Junior saw students walking towards Arlington High. "They don't look no better than you and Jeanne from what I can see," he announced to his son. This, of course, was a measure of pride for him because it meant that he was able to provide for his two children adequately. At least when it came to school clothes. Junior did have a weekend job as a dishwasher at Horrschorn's tearoom in the winter and he cut white people's lawns in North Arlington in the summer, which gave him money to buy some of his own things. Wynn provided more for Jeanne and, of course, Julia Mae made most of his sister's clothes.

"Those National Guard, friendly to y'all?" he asked his son.

"We don't talk to them and they don't bother with us," replied Junior. "I heard they may be leaving soon anyway. They just make sure that everything is okay, and they watch us coming and going and when we're in the cafeteria at lunch and stuff," he explained to Wynn Sr. A couple of times a group of white male students had surrounded Junior and Ray Williams, the other colored boy in the Group of Five. Ray was also 15, but he had a larger build than Junior and he was slightly taller.

At the start of the school year, there was a third Negro male student whose name was Jackson, but by the end of the second week of September he had been expelled. He wasn't going to the colored high school either and it was assumed that he either dropped out or went to a high school in the District. Junior didn't know him because he came from the colored neighborhood closest to the school. No one knew why he was no longer at Arlington High or, if they did, they weren't saying. It certainly wasn't because of fighting or bad behavior because Jackson wasn't a belligerent boy from what any of them could see, and he never even reacted to the taunts that were leveled at him. The colored kids had been repeatedly told not to fight with the white kids and it never came to that.

But yes, they were taunted. Particularly the two boys, and it seemed to intensify for several days after Jackson had been expelled. That was one of the reasons that Julia Mae insisted that Wynn continue to drive Junior to school. But the vitriol wasn't limited to Ray and Junior. The three girls got their share too. One of them, Shirley, a very smart, somewhat plump dark-skinned girl wouldn't much hold her tongue. Many of the white girls who would otherwise seek to vex her had learned not to. Shirley had learned the power that being smart, dark and a bit thick-bodied could have.

Whatever insults or disapproval people felt about her or her presence at Arlington High, they most often kept to themselves. She was used to being taunted for her deep brown skin, so dark that all the Artra in Virginia and DC combined would only bleach it to match the color of rich coffee with merely a splash of milk poured in. Of course, the white boys would be more vocal. They had more to prove. They talked back to the teachers even. This would never happen at Frederick Douglass Junior High or the colored high school which was called "Mercer" but the official name was John Mercer Langston, named after Virginia's only colored member of Congress who served during Reconstruction. Colored kids knew not to sass.

"The cafeteria workers and janitors look out for us too," said Junior to Wynn. "They can't really do nothing if anything happens, but we know they are watching." This, of course, was no surprise to his father. Colored people were funny! While they could spend way too much time tearing each other down when it was just them, they also knew how to guard each other's back when they got around white people. Maybe one wouldn't tell another one about a job availability he knew about even though he knew the other was out of work and able to do the job. But, if the two were downtown or on the road and it looked as if an altercation with a white man might ensue with one of them, the other would stand and watch. Besides that, colored people always greeted each other in the street, whether they knew each other or not. It was a way of saying: I see you, when they might have otherwise felt invisible!

He had seen this all his life and was happy that his son was seeing it too. In fact, almost all the colored folks in Arlington were excited for the colored kids who got to integrate the white elementary, junior high and high school, finally, in 1959. Colored kids had already been going to school with whites in the District and even in some states further south. Virginia had held out until it no longer could. When those fourteen colored students, six in the high school, and four in both the junior high and elementary schools first walked into those three white schools it was as if all of colored Arlington, VA walked in there with them!

Although he knew he was colored, how could he not, Junior, as far back as he could remember, never really felt Negro on the inside! At least, not in the way he was sure other colored people did, including his own parents. Julia Mae probably less so than Wynn Sr, perhaps. This is probably where he got it from.

As far as he could observe, most Negroes accepted the narrow confines that were carved out for them. Perhaps it was an accident at birth but Junior for some reason felt as though he must have been meant to be white! He didn't feel colored inside. Although he had to live in his Negro skin, he felt bigger than the space that skin allowed him. Negro skin only bought a minimal amount of "space" in the world he figured out long before the age of 15. But, for some reason, it was just so clear to him that, without doubt, he was meant to appropriate more space which meant that he would have to spread himself into the other world, the world that was white!

By the time Wynn had dropped Junior off, the other colored kids were all waiting to go into school. Four of them were in the same homeroom class and one girl was in a homeroom in which she was the only colored student. All five of them were freshmen. It just so happened that the girl who was in the homeroom by herself was the lightest skinned of all five. From a distance in fact, Thomasine might be mistaken for white. The other four ranged in complexion from the dark brown Shirley to tan. Junior fell near the middle but closer to the darker side, with his medium chocolate color, Ray was just a tiny bit lighter and the third girl, Luella, who was a good friend of Carolyn's fell in the dark beige category. The complexion of colored people, of course, is what defined them in the world and so often how they defined themselves!

The darker-skinned kids perhaps stood out more on account of their complexion than at the colored schools as they were surrounded by white students and teachers. On the other hand, complexion might have mattered less here than at the colored school. Whether they were too dark or not light enough wasn't so much a worry for them at Arlington High. They were all Negro! And with the possible exception of Thomasine, for all their darkness, they all blended into invisibility at Arlington High since many didn't really want them there and didn't regard them as worthy of being at this school in this neighborhood!

But everyone knew, whether they wanted to fully embrace it or not, that things were changing. It was beginning to be obvious to most Americans, no matter their race or where they lived in 1959, that the "system" they had known was slowly and strategically being challenged. No one knew how quickly change was coming or how sweeping it might be, but whites were seeing colored people slowly being integrated into their culture, on television, at the movies, in "their" music, in major sports and depending upon where they lived, sometimes in their neighborhoods. With regard to music, it was more accurate to say that white music was more and more appropriating traditional jazz and blues styles as well as the new rock and roll, but most whites didn't see it that way.

Junior's second class on Monday was civics which came after geometry! Civics was one of his favorite subjects since Frederick Douglass Junior High. The big discussion in civics class since school had started in September was the addition of Alaska and Hawaii as the 49th and 50th new states. Alaska had come in earlier in the year and Hawaii in August while students were still on summer recess. "I hope your assignments are all done," said Mr Rakowski, the teacher. "Who wants to start the discussion on what the addition of Alaska and Hawaii will bring to the Union?" he asked. Near the beginning of the school year the class had been divided up into two groups. One group of students had been assigned to write a report on what the two new states bring to the country, the other group, how the addition of Alaska and Hawaii might change the country as it had been.

Junior was in the latter group. One by one the students went before the class or stood up at their desk if they preferred; Mr Rakowski had some sensitivity to the shy students. He also had an allegiance to custom. As Junior's group went second, as the one colored student in the class, Mr Rakowski called upon him last to give his report. High school students were often called upon by their last names with Mr or Miss coming before. Many of the teachers found it difficult to call the Negro students Mr or Miss, as they had never done it before. So often they would refer to them by both names. "Wynn Horry, how do you see the nation changing as a result of the two new states coming into the Union?"

"I see the population of the nation changing to include more different types of people," Wynn Jr asserted, deciding to deliver his report from his desk rather than walk to the front of the class. "Both the Alaskans and the Hawaiians are of Asian descent. They represent different races from the European and Negro races that are here now." Other students in his group had alluded to this in their reports as well. Coming last, of course, it's difficult to come up with too much that's novel. But of course, it has a different impact when the only colored student in the classroom is the one talking. "What about the Mexican population and the other Hispanics in the country? What about them, you didn't mention them," Mr Rakowski pointed out, appearing to reprimand Junior.

"Yes sir, there are Mexicans too. I didn't mention them because they aren't as large as the white and colored population," Junior replied. To this, Mr Rakowski said nothing. "The two new states also bring different kinds of products to the economy," Junior continued. "Alaska provides oil and gasoline for cars all over the country and Hawaii gives us fruits and certain other tropical foods as well as sugar." Junior further added that the people who are native to those states add variety to the American culture through their clothes, music and habits. This was a point that none of his other classmates had made, so it made him feel good to be the only one who had pointed this out.

The topic of race was discussed widely at Frederick Douglass Jr High and not just during Negro History Week in February. But Junior had no idea whether that week ever came at Arlington High. Did white people ever talk about the accomplishments of Negroes? Did they at all care anything at all about them?

"Thank you all for the reports. Next week you will get the opportunity to meet someone from both Alaska and Hawaii who will come to speak to the class." The teacher unveiled this news proudly.

Chapter 2

Needless to say, Arlington High was the school that the kids of a few Congressmen and Senators attended as well as those who worked for the White House and other government agencies. So, it wasn't too difficult to have someone from Alaska or Hawaii come speak to the class. Junior was in the same civics class as Cliff Peterson. His father worked at the State Department. They had traveled to many parts of the world since Cliff and his younger brother were born. They had lived in Egypt and Ghana in Africa. Ghana had recently become independent of British rule and his father was one of the first to represent the United States government since the new nation's independence. They had been there working with development projects on behalf of the US State Department, working through the British government before the ties were cut from the British Empire. The Petersons had lived in Ghana until the late spring of 1957 and Cliff and his younger brother had gone to British schools in Africa. But now they were back home in the US, having left Ghana earlier than originally planned.

"Cliff is a nice boy but he's a bit shy," Claire Peterson forewarned Julia Mae when finalizing the arrangements for Junior to cut the lawn while he was a student at Frederick Douglass Junior High. Cliff, who was the same age, was going to Robert E. Lee, the nearby junior high for whites. Both did well in school, and neither was the incredibly outgoing type. "If he doesn't say much to Junior, it's only because he sometimes doesn't know what to say," Mrs Peterson tried to explain. She said that Cliff would be the one working with Junior, since she was often away doing charity work or other civic responsibilities. "And my husband is either playing golf or doing something else."

The Petersons were very civic minded, especially when it came to colored children and other disadvantaged groups particularly in

Washington, DC. Claire thought she was doing her oldest son a favor by lining up a "friend" for him. Someone for him to talk to at least before and after Junior cut the grass. His younger brother, Robby was the exact opposite of Cliff in that he was much more outgoing and assertive, even at ten. The two of them were merely brothers. The five-year age difference notwithstanding, they would never have been friends or had any dealings with each other were they not both the sons of Chester and Claire Peterson.

"Mind yourself over there! Make sure you do a good job and don't say too much," Julia Mae schooled Junior. "They are paying you to cut the grass and keep the yard nice. You are not going there for a garden party," she reminded him. "You know not to tell white people too much no matter how friendly and interested they may seem." This is what she and Wynn had always told their two children. This was one of the litanies of rules that the Horrys considered exigent for Jeanne and Junior to learn. One of the other rules was not to eat any food that white people would offer for fear that they might appear to be hungry. Since he was working outside in the summer, it was okay for him to drink a glass of water or lemonade if offered.

It was over the lemonade or iced tea that he got to know the Petersons the best, especially Cliff. They had quite a big yard at their North Arlington house that sat on a bit of a hill. The back of the house had an even larger yard. It would take Junior about 40 to 45 minutes to finish the work. He generally used the equipment of the homeowner. If they didn't have their own equipment, then Wynn would have to drive him with their own lawnmower in the car and then go back and pick him up. When one or both of the Petersons were away on the Saturday that Junior would work on their yard, and Robby was off playing baseball or swimming, neither of which interested Cliff that much, although he did enjoy tennis and volleyball, Junior would spend a little time in the house enjoying his lemonade more slowly and maybe munching on a chocolate chip cookie too. Of all the families he cut grass for each summer, he liked the Petersons most.

He could tell that Cliff didn't want him to leave when the work was done. Even though he usually had another house to go to, he didn't want to leave either. Part of it was that he enjoyed being at that house. He loved the spaciousness of it and the way the sun lit it up on those summer afternoons. He was in awe of the African sculptures and masks that the family had brought back from their time abroad and displayed on their walls and shelves as if they were prime museum pieces and not some animal head deprived of life for some white man's sport.

He loved the new and very modern furniture they had. It seemed as though the sofa, chairs and tables were floating in the air. Unlike the very heavy and old timey furniture that sat stolid on their floors in Hilldale, and took up so much space, the Petersons' furniture seemed to be from outer space. Its angles and lines were not like those he saw in the homes in Hilldale nor in the people he knew in Washington, DC. He had seen furniture like this before, in magazines and in some other homes in North Arlington. But here he noticed it more. He felt as if he was transported to the future here. The world was definitely changing, and this house was a visual representation of what would be. Here the future didn't seem shadowy and overwrought. Rather it seemed bright, light, happy and hopeful!

Junior felt guilty for what he was thinking and feeling! He didn't want to feel that these white people were better and that this white boy was special and perfect. But yet he did! He wasn't ashamed of himself, his family, his home or his color. It was more as if he felt that he himself could be Cliff and all this would be his! Why should this not be possible? Why should it not be possible for him to be Cliff but also be Wynn Horry Junior at the same time? Were white people really born to own the world? Or was there some way that a smart, polite and talented colored boy could carve out some piece of it for himself?

"What is the favorite song for the colored kids right now?" Cliff asked Junior as they both stood and sipped lemonade one Saturday afternoon in August, after he had finished cutting the grass. The house was cool, and he enjoyed the respite from the heat. Houses in North Arlington had the new air conditioning and he tried to get to feel it whenever he could although he generally didn't get to go inside. This was just before the new school year was to start and they would both be freshmen at Arlington High. Junior laughed and then Cliff laughed too. They both knew very well that the music that colored people and white people listened to was often different. They knew this to be true also for dances.

"My sister Jeanne likes 'Charlie Brown' and most of her friends do too," Junior shared. "I think it's dumb but a lot of the kids like it, particularly the youngsters," Junior continued, separating himself from the pre-teen crowd. What he didn't tell Cliff about was the song that was most on his mind about a year before when they first met. That year, Jeanne owned the hit "Maybe" by the Chantels. She played it all the time and, of course, almost everyone they knew loved the song; after all, it was sung by a group of pretty colored girls not much older than Junior. After he had met Cliff, Junior thought of him often, especially when he heard that song, and had started to change the lyrics of the song to fit him. "M--a--y--b--e if he will know how I feel if I hold his hand, maybe if I kiss his lips, he'll be under my command." Junior altered the words a bit because he knew that he had a certain power over Cliff, even early on in their meeting each other. But he had never shared this with Cliff nor would he now.

"I really like 'Smoke Gets in Your Eyes', but then again I like pretty much everything by the Platters," he went on. "I kinda like 'Sea Cruise' too, most of the kids I know like that. Who is the singer, Frankie Ford, well, he sounds colored," Junior said, laughing.

"Yes, he does," Cliff replied. "Is that why the colored kids like it?"

"What are some of your favorites?" Junior queried.

"'Mack the Knife' is my favorite right now," said Cliff. "I also like 'Venus'."

"Don't laugh," he implored of Junior, seeing a smile form on his face, which, of course, caused Junior to chuckle even though he didn't really want to. The truth is, that he sort of liked "Venus" too but he probably wouldn't have shared that with any of the friends he talked to about music and dances regularly. Instead, "'Mack the Knife' is a good song the way Bobby Darin sings it," Junior noted. "I definitely like it better than the way Satchmo did it three years ago."

"Louis Armstrong sang 'Mack the Knife'?" asked Cliff.

"Yes, his version was a big hit with colored people and jazz people," Junior asserted. "I guess you didn't get to hear it over in Africa!"

"I guess not," Cliff chortled.

"Do you like 'Dream Lover'?" Junior asked of Cliff, staying on Bobby Darin.

"Oh yes, definitely," Cliff answered, "Don't you?" he asked, to which Junior replied,

"Yes, I like Bobby Darin a lot. My mother and sister like him too."

"My parents like 'Don't You Know'," Cliff confided to Junior, as he put his empty lemonade glass down on the nearest table and moved closer to him as if being nearer to him gave discussion of the song more meaning.

"Yeah, so do mine," answered Junior a bit nervously in response to Cliff's advance. "They dance to it slow sometimes and they look happy, I guess!"

"How do they dance? Please show me," Cliff asked, looking down toward Junior's midsection because he was afraid to look into his eyes. After a few seconds of gathering himself, Junior closed the two feet of space that now stood between him and Cliff, breathed in deeply, put his right hand on Cliff's waist and cupped his left hand over Cliff's shoulder. He put Cliff's right hand on his waist and, following suit, Cliff raised his left hand over Junior's right shoulder, and he began to lead Cliff around the floor in a slow drag, one wildly beating heart pressed against another! Junior locked his right leg against Cliff's left and their groins met and fiercely strained against each other's!

Cliff rested his cheek against Junior's neck as they moved across the floor, not so much dancing as leaning against each other, tightly bobbing back and forth. Neither wanted to look at the other but after a few minutes, Cliff lifted his head away from Junior's neck and, with his eyes downward all the while, let his face introduce itself to Junior's face and trembling, he wanted so badly to have his lips say hello to Junior's. But Junior was not yet ready to find out if Cliff's lips did tender some kind of bait or not!

This was probably the fourth or fifth time they had been close like this since they met in the spring of the year before! They had touched each other, grazing arms awkwardly at first, but then more resolutely as their comfort level and interest continued to rise! But now in the heat of mid-August was definitely the most intense and the longest they had locked their bodies together. It felt good! It stirred Junior, almost took his breath away and made him tremble. This must mean that it's wrong, the thought ran through his mind briefly! But it felt good! No! It was definitely bad for the two of them, both boys, one colored, the other white, one from the poor side of Arlington, the other from the wealthy part of town, to be doing this. No one thought of Junior as a punk, and he didn't consider himself one either. But isn't this what punks do? Regardless, it felt good! And Cliff felt like the right person to be doing it with.

In this moment, the two of them intertwined together, Junior's mind drifted back to a movie he had seen a year earlier with his parents that starred Sidney Poitier and Tony Curtis. The movie, about two prisoners, one Negro and the other white who had escaped from a chain gang chained together showed this black man and white man who couldn't get away from each other even though they both wanted to be free of the chains. They had to get through some tense situations, and they had to do it together or else neither of them would overcome. By the time the movie was over, they had had their chains broken yet they stayed together. Perhaps no one else in his family thought it but Junior wondered if the two of them had learned to love each other after all they had gone through together. Why else would the black man end up sharing a cigarette with the white man while the white man was sitting on the ground between his legs with the black man's arms around him?

This seemed like the only conclusion that Junior could come to. In all his years, he had never witnessed a scene like this in a movie or certainly in real life. But it made a powerful impression on him especially because Poitier, the black man was so strong and in charge that Curtis basically melted into his arms, at least as Junior recalled it. It was clear as to who was the leader and who was the follower. Sidney Poitier defied the role that the black man should take with a white man and it caused Junior's heart to beat fast as he watched the display on the screen. He wasn't sure about the convict that Tony Curtis played, but Sidney Poitier's character was definitely a Defiant One!

This moment with Cliff and other times they had been alone together always brought that feeling back to him and it vexed him more strongly each time both with confusion and concupiscence!

About the time that he was simultaneously tormenting and

pleasuring himself, they both heard the slam of hard wood against the floor! It caused them to instantly tear apart, as if they had been ripped away from each other! Both boys wore a frightened and startled look on their face as they turned wide-eyed to the door! Cliff knew where the sound came from! As his heart pounded so hard it seemed it would burst from his chest, he wondered if Robby had seen them as he passed to go to his room and that was why he had thrown his baseball bat down on his bedroom floor. Even though this is what he always did when he came home from softball, today his routine was particularly suspect!

Neither he nor Junior said anything still, but the flushed look on Cliff's face and the strong beating in both their chests spoke loudly. Just a few minutes before, their hearts were beating full force for an entirely different reason. But now, those moments of bliss seemed so far away as the two 15-year-old boys struggled with the possibility that they might have been caught slow dancing together tightly against each other and rubbing each other clumsily but with passion! What on earth could be worse than this? Neither had ever been in this situation and both panicked as they never had in their lives.

Finally, Cliff knew he had to confront the situation with Robby. He still didn't allow his eyes to meet Junior's and Junior didn't want to look at him either. He was nervously readjusting himself and preparing a hasty exit from the room and out of the house. Cliff would be on his own with his younger brother!

Chapter 3

It was a busy Monday for Julia Mae at Horrschorns. Thanksgiving was just about a month away, and most people that mattered, which definitely included the people who shopped there, were back from vacation. Rich women in Washington and in the suburbs, were buying dresses and gowns for the fall and winter season. They needed them fitted and altered in various ways. Julia Mae, a veteran at Horrschorns for 12 years, knew how it worked. The busy period was already upon her and the three other seamstresses she had seniority over. Julia Mae had been among the first colored women hired, just after the War when many white women had quit the workforce since their husbands had returned home.

This also meant that her side business had picked up. She was known around Arlington, and even had some customers in Alexandria. Of course, quite a few of her private clients lived in Washington, DC as well, mostly in Northwest and on Capitol Hill. These were the parts of DC where the money was. However, Julia Mae had to be cautious and prudent! Never was Horrschorns to know of what she did on her own sewing machine at home in her own time.

"Do you work in a dress shop?" many of the women would ask her.

"No, I sew for people," she would respond, ever mindful of that lesson that you should never tell white people too much of your business. Those whom she had worked for longer and trusted knew where she worked during the day. In fact, for many this was proof of her abilities making them less apprehensive about employing her dressmaking skills than they might otherwise have been. But since she was tucked away in a non-public area, there was no chance that any of these women or men would see her at Horrschorns. They held a high regard for this store, similar to the way Upper East Side or Murray Hill New Yorkers looked upon Saks Fifth Avenue, B. Altman or Lord and Taylor, or Philadelphians of their ilk, John Wannamaker, or Strawbridge and Clothier.

The three other ladies that Julia Mae worked with sat quietly in the alterations room as the activity in the big department store pulsated around them. This would be the last week they would be just the four of them. A supervisor had been hired to replace Miss Ames who, after being at the store since before the 20s got Roaring, had finally retired. Since her tenure, colored women had started working in the alterations room, and Julia Mae, not only the most senior but also the best became the "supervisor" in the absence of an official one. Miss Ames had always considered Julia Mae her best assistant.

But soon a new lady would come and be their boss. She had been recommended by a customer after just moving to DC from Alabama after her husband had passed and to be near her daughter who had recently married an aide to an Alabama senator. She needed to work to get her mind off things! The colored women weren't sure what to expect from this white lady from Alabama. She didn't seem nearly as cordial as Miss Ames when she had come to look over the department before she actually started in the job.

The Beaux-Arts Nickolas Horrschorns & Co building, made of limestone, stood eight stories tall and was perched majestically at a major downtown intersection almost directly in line with the Washington Monument and a stone's throw away from the White House. Known by most everyone as Horrschorns, the building occupied nearly the entire block. To the right of the main entrance sat a major hotel from the time when enslaved servants lived in the nation's capital. Or perhaps they more endured than lived! The Tibor Hotel held that block-long spot, on 14th Street as it sloped downhill toward the Monument, on a route that Julia Mae traveled every day back to Virginia, since the days that enslaved Negroes worked in homes in Washington, DC and in Georgetown. On the other side of the hotel, newer office buildings that were home to insurance companies, accounting firms, association offices and other shopping stores had sprung up.

People came and went on the department store's eight floors, the first level being the grandest in Washington. Chauffeur-driven limousines appeared and disappeared, as cash registers rung sales, a bell on the register announcing each new purchase! Salesgirls served customers under tall ceilings with beautiful mosaic tile inlay, intricate plaster carvings and dangling crystal chandeliers that sparkled, while they stood on floors of plush carpeting gently folding items in white tissue paper the consistency of linen! They then placed these acquisitions in gold paper bags with blue trim or gold boxes with blue ribbons and white piping, remembering to add sales slips containing the name, address and phone number of the buyer.

While ceremonially-dressed doormen eased the entrance and exit of shoppers and elevator men ascended and descended in their steel cases, the three ladies sat at their sewing machines and made things right for those who were wealthy and well placed and who would take nothing less than perfection.

They also talked as the sewing machines hummed and whirred. They talked about the people they encountered, mostly those for whom they were doing the alterations. They talked about the heat in summer and the cold in winter. They talked about cooking and clothing. They talked about church, their families and their kids. And they talked about how things were changing.

"That colored woman in Virginia and her white husband moved down the street from my sister this summer," one of the women revealed. Everyone knew who she was talking about not only because the marriage of a colored woman and a white man was news making. The two had married a year before in the District and then moved back to a small town in Virginia together as husband and wife. This was news enough. But their last name, which was Loving, made the story that much more salient! They had been run out of Virginia where the marriage was illegal. Now they were back in DC and almost all of colored Washington had heard about them.

"Why she would marry that white man in the first place is beyond me," said Julia Mae's co-worker, an older, heavy-set dark-skinned woman. "They done run 'em out of Virginia and now they living over there near the Howard Theater. Lord knows it IS like some kind of show if you ask me," she imparted as the other women, including Julia Mae, chuckled. "They got a little half-white baby running 'round, my sister

41

said and looks like she pregnant again."

"She married him because he white," said another seamstress, one closer to Julia Mae's age and close to white in color, herself. "She probably feels she can get further with him than with a colored man."

"Well, neither one of them is gon' get too far in Virginia," Julia Mae added. "They were about to go to prison for marrying each other in the first place. Living in that crowded area up there off 7th Street is better than prison."

"Well, they can't live in the white neighborhoods, so they ain't got too much choice," the first woman concluded. "Lord have mercy on them."

"Pretty soon Junior gon' have himself a white girlfriend with that new school he's goin' to," this woman joked. "Then y'all gon' have to move back to the District too." This time laughter and foot stomping could be heard above the sewing machine noises as all the women chortled at what had been said.

Julia Mae was laughing too. But a part of her had silently wondered if this could happen. She would never tell these women but that was, in fact, a fear of hers.

"Lord ha'mercy, I'm gon' see your letter to Martin Luther King on what to do about my son and his romance with the white girl at school," the other woman shot out laughing so hard she could hardly get the words out. Of course, this brought out more giggles and foot stomping in the room. They often got a kick out of some of the letters sent in to the Advice for Living column authored by the young minister in *Ebony* magazine when they read the letters to each other when things were slow in the alterations room and there was no one else in there but them. But of course, this was probably going to have to change when the "bama lady", as they called her, came in to take the office by the window.

Chapter 4

That evening after work, Julia Mae took the streetcar down Pennsylvania Avenue to Georgetown. She would be meeting her family there and they would have dinner at her sister Nellie's house. This would normally happen on a Sunday evening, but it was happening on Monday because Nellie had to serve a dinner party at the Congressman's house the night before. She had in fact stayed over in Arlington since the party ended late and had come home in the middle of that Monday afternoon to rest and prepare dinner. Wynn Senior, Junior and Jeanne would drive over together later that evening. After dinner on Monday nights, they usually watched *Make Room for Daddy*. They had loved the show for years since Louise Beavers played the maid who was also named Louise. But this would probably not happen tonight since they would be at Nellie's house.

Wynn Senior wasn't such a big fan of these shows but then there wasn't much on TV that he did like to watch. Since they took the *Nat King Cole Show* off in '57 he had been on the outs with television. Except for sports, there wasn't much that appealed to him. The Horry family and pretty much everyone they knew watched the *Ed Sullivan Show* on Sunday night. Ed Sullivan frequently had colored guests on the show. That wasn't their only reason for watching it but that helped. But otherwise, Wynn and Julia Mae were not big television watchers. Jeanne and Junior, however, had quite a few shows that they liked. Junior knew for a fact that he was hooked on the new science fiction program *Twilight Zone* since its first very recent episode.

Nellie was preparing fried chicken, collard greens and candied yams for dinner. This was Junior's favorite meal, as she well knew. This was the dinner that either his mother or she would prepare on his birthday, quite often if not every year. Once he knew this was the menu, he couldn't help but feel that this dinner involved him somehow. It wasn't his birthday because that had already passed. Hmmm, he thought in trying to come to some explanation for the meal on a Monday night in October. He knew that he was the guest of honor but the question in his mind was, "Why?"

Wynn Senior arrived at home about 6:45 that evening. Junior and Jeanne were both doing their homework although Jeanne had just started hers about an hour before. She had been outside with a boy from her school that she had been spending some time with. He didn't live in Hilldale, rather another colored area of Arlington, further up north, closer to Arlington High. It was a colored area surrounded by white people but it wasn't as if they were a part of the same community. The colored neighborhood was separated from the more middle-class white people by a six-foot tall brick wall that ran between them for about three blocks. They could sometimes hear the whites and the whites them, but they couldn't see each other, and they definitely didn't talk to each other.

Sometimes the adults went to work in the white people's houses, but they had to walk around the wall to get there. This boy, like many of the other kids in his neighborhood, rode his bike down to South Arlington to go to Frederick Douglass Junior High. He and Jeanne had known each other in passing since they had both been at the school. But while they both liked the way each other looked, it was only since the beginning of the school year in September that they had started to talk and decided to go together. Her father did not know about this and she wasn't ready for him to.

Junior was complicit in keeping her secret. He had a few of his own. He had been trying not to think about that time at Cliff's house just before school started. Although he saw Cliff pretty much every day at Arlington High, they had not been able to have a close encounter since. Cliff wanted to, Junior knew and Junior longed to be close to Cliff again, Cliff knew. But where would it happen? It was nearly November, and the grass was beginning to lay low for the winter. So, he had no reason to be at the Petersons' house. Cliff could probably have come to his house in Hilldale, but that would have caused lots of questions. Houses in Junior's part of town were not big, and they were fairly close together. Somebody was always home and there were always eyes on everything. They couldn't go to any of the after-school hangouts in North Arlington. The colored kids had their own soda and hamburger joint not far from Junior's house, but again, that wasn't the solution. What would he be doing at Fat Jack's with Cliff and how could they hold each other tight, feel each other's heartbeat and get their hands on each other's parts that no one else got to see??

The thought of this laid hard and heavy on Junior! He heard the boys talking in his neighborhood and the white boys at school talking about their petting. He wanted to feel Cliff next to him too, to rub his hair and his body and to put Cliff's head on his shoulder. He wanted his hands on Cliff and Cliff's hands on him. One afternoon, just before the start of fifth period, the final class of the day, Junior had the idea to sneak into a janitor's closet with Cliff. Junior knew most of the janitorial staff, after all; they were all colored and most lived in Hilldale. He knew that often the doors to the room which held brooms, mops, pails, ladders and such, were not locked. They could be each other's squeeze for at least a few minutes before going to the last class of the day. No one would be hurt by it and Junior's heart would be less heavy. He needed his heart and mind to be lighter and being alone with Cliff could make this happen.

It was nearly Homecoming season. Everyone's attention was on getting ready for the football game that would determine if the Arlington High Rebels were the number one team in Northern Virginia in 1959. They had a maintained a good record since football season started in late September. The Rebels weren't known for their football prowess like some of the other white high schools. Arlington High was generally full of smart kids who didn't care so much about sports. They had never won a football or basketball championship ever. They had won a baseball championship twice but both times were years earlier.

However, this year things were different. Not only were there five colored kids going to the school for the first time ever. But suddenly, the all-white football team was actually showing some talent. One joke making its way around town was that the Group of Five, particularly the two boys, gave the football team more incentive to run faster and tackle harder. They were using the presence of those Negroes as incentive to kick butt on the football field, went the joke. This was one of the few social jokes that made its way through the colored and white parts of town equally.

"Hey y'all," said Wynn Senior as he walked into the house. "You two start getting ready to go to your aunt Nellie's? Make sure you finish your homework first," he admonished his kids. "We'll be there late so you won't have any time after we get home, and you know your mother wants to make sure it's all done."

But even as he tried to focus Junior and Jeanne on getting ready for their trip into Georgetown to be with their mother's sister. Wynn was in no rush, himself. He wanted to relax a bit with his favorite Johnny Walker on the rocks before heading over to Nellie's house. It would be a long evening. "So, what happened at school today anyway?" he asked sincerely, looking at them one after the other.

"Nothing special happened, Daddy," Jeanne responded first. "It was just a regular day at school. We have a field trip to the Lincoln Memorial next week," she announced.

"Did the white kids kick y'all out of the school yet, Junior?" Wynn asked his son with a smirk. Junior knew his father was just being Wynn Horry senior.

It was his more lighthearted way of asking his son if everything at Arlington High was still okay… at least as okay as it could be. He and Julia Mae had stopped being too worried about their son at the new school. But they knew there might be some things Junior would never tell them for fear of worrying them or making them frightened of him attending there. The family had never talked of taking him out and enrolling him in the colored high school and he had certainly never even thought about leaving Arlington High. But he knew there could be a breaking point for his parents.

"No, we still get to go back, Pop," Junior confirmed with a wry smile.

"What happened at work?" Junior asked to divert the conversation, knowing his daddy would never take the question as an invitation to enlighten his children on his day-to-day undertakings as a chief electrician at the Pentagon. He was the kind of man who did his job quietly and went on his way to the next challenge of wiring an office, tending to electrical shortages or checking the power on several pieces of machinery in and around the Pentagon. The Defense Department was in a bit of a growth spurt due to concerns about the Soviet Union and therefore the Pentagon was seeing new offices added all around the building. Sometimes he even went to neighboring military bases to do work because he was good at what he did. This had been his job in the army during the War. When most colored men worked in the kitchen or did clean up, Wynn got to work on establishing electricity where it could be established. He worked at base headquarters and this brought him a certain power. Not too many enlistees, colored or white, had his skills.

"Oh, you know, I don't do nothing but help people see the light!" That was usually his answer to the question. Of course, it was to deflect from any serious or deep conversation about his work, but he also found it humorous.

"Aww, Daddy, you always say that," Jeanne interjected. "You need some new jokes. Hurry up and finish your whiskey because I need to help Aunt Nellie," she instructed her father.

Wynn went upstairs to change out of his uniform which he had worn home from work this time. Usually he changed into street clothes, but knowing he was going to his wife's sister's house for dinner he wanted to be in clean clothes. Julia Mae had already laid his clothes out on their bed before going to work. A short-sleeved blue check shirt was pressed, as were a pair of black slacks. Black loafers were polished and clean socks were rolled up inside. All he had to do was take a bath and get ready. The kind of work he did often left him dusty or smelling of burned electrical wires. Julia Mae wouldn't want him going around people like that.

On the trip into Washington, Jeanne sitting next to her father and Junior in the back, Wynn searched around on the radio to find some evening news, especially sports news, although there wasn't so much in the way of sports that interested him at this time of year. His Los Angeles Dodgers had already won the World Series a few weeks earlier. Before he could settle on a station his children called upon him to let one of their favorite songs play… The autumn leaves of red and gold… since you went away the days grow long, and soon I'll hear old winter's song, but I miss you most of all, my darling, when autumn leaves start to fall.

Their mother loved Nat King Cole and the family used to watch his show on television until it went off two years earlier. But they still played his albums and "Autumn Leaves" was among the favorites. The ride across the bridge covering the Potomac River which separated Virginia from Washington, DC was quick on the Monday evening. There was never that much traffic coming into the city after dusk anyway. Rush hour had now become the cocktail hour for much of Washington, so the streets were not too filled with cars or even buses. They would soon be driving up 14th Street near Horrschorns Department Store, following the route that Wynn took often if he drove into the city to pick up Julia Mae to save her from a bus ride into Arlington if she had to work late at the store. But she wouldn't be coming along for the ride since she had already taken the streetcar into Georgetown to Nellie's house.

After all, it stopped right outside Horrschorns and she wanted to get to Georgetown early to help Nellie with the meal. Getting there ahead of her husband and children also gave her time to talk with her sister about things she probably wouldn't want to discuss in front of Wynn and the children. Sisters, especially those as close as these two, always had things they preferred to talk about privately. Not so much that they had secrets to keep. But more as if their conversations were a box of treasures that only the two of them could open and enjoy. This was true even if they were just gossiping, which they very often did.

Chapter 5

As a housekeeper to a Congressman, Nellie heard and saw a lot. Of course, she had a front row seat on the goings on among many of the Congressional wives and sometimes the Congressmen themselves. She would hear them talk about politics. Nellie was most interested in the issues of civil rights and economic rights, the two often going hand in hand. One time she had served a party at the Congressman's house which Senator John F. Kennedy and his wife Jackie had attended. It was exciting to see him in person and if she could vote he would definitely be getting her vote for President next November if he decided to run as it was much bandied about that he would. In fact, there wasn't a colored person alive, at least as far as she or husband Talley knew, who would be voting for Vice President Nixon. But, residents of Washington, DC were not allowed to vote!

Kennedy, as a Democrat, as a northerner, as a younger man and as a Catholic, just seemed like the kind of President that would help colored people. He was unlike anyone who had been in the White House for a long time and he offered hope to a whole lot of people. "That man will be good for us," she told her sister and Wynn, her neighbors in Georgetown and members of her church. "His wife will make a gorgeous First Lady and they will bring some class to Washington." Most colored people seemed to feel that way. They felt that the Kennedys might be the ones to break Jim Crow's back.

Eisenhower and the Republicans had not done themselves any favors with Negroes. It was bad enough a few summers back that the boy from Chicago had been savagely beaten, shot in the head and then dumped in the river with a hundred pounds drawing him down to the bottom of that Mississippi river! Everybody all over the world knew about it! But then when his poor mother was refused a meeting by

President Eisenhower after the two white men who admitted to killing her son got off and even bragged about the killing to a magazine, well, colored people all over the country, and many whites too, had no more Like for Ike. Eisenhower had found the time to deliver a goodwill message to the whole world from a satellite, making his the first human voice to be heard from outer space. Yet he couldn't find a minute to console a grieving mother in Chicago whose son had been murdered, his body sunk to the bottom of a river in Mississippi. From that point on, the D Day victor was dead to them! Things were changing in the country and, of course, they wanted someone in the White House that wouldn't stifle progress but instead spur it.

Her nephew was going to school with white children, for God's sake, and in Virginia. This was certainly a sea change from her time. But this is also what she wanted to talk to her family about. This was why she had called for them to come over to dinner.

Julia Mae had arrived shortly after Nellie got home from North Arlington. She generally got home at about 7pm after preparing dinner for the family she worked for. But they were at home in the district the Congressman represented, having left that very afternoon. They were gone for a week, which meant that Nellie could take two or three days off. Talley had gone to drive the family home, so it was just her at their house in Georgetown, a small two-story brick house that peeked out at a colored playground across the street. It was originally a colored park, but whites had been using it for years since there was no designated park for them nearby. Still, this was the Negro section of Georgetown. Julia came wearing a beige cotton dress with a white collar and a blue ribbon that hung down between the two sides of the collar. The dress had three-quarter sleeves, it was belted at the waist with a shiny black sash of leather and came down just below her knees with a surge of pleats.

Of course, it was one that she had made. As it was late October, evenings in Washington were cooler than the hot and humid summer evenings the city suffered through. For that reason, she had arrived off the streetcar wearing a deep mustard pleated shawl. It was a fine look for a woman who knew how to put a stylish and classy outfit together. The white gloves added that final touch.

But by the time her family would see her, these symbols of colored woman respectability would either be removed or covered up by one of Nellie's aprons so that nothing would get messed up in the process of preparing dinner. When Wynn, Junior and Jeanne had arrived, Julia Mae was wearing a white and blue apron with a big pouch in the middle that had been given her by her sister. The fried chicken, collard greens and yams they were preparing for dinner would be introduced to the apron before they would meet her new dress. The single strand of costume pearls she wore, which matched the pair of real pearl earrings, remained.

Finally, the 1955 Black Buick carrying Julia's family turned onto Nellie's street, after traveling down Pennsylvania Avenue past the White House where Ike and Mamie Eisenhower were living out their final year. By now the radio station that had played Nat King Cole had finally been switched to the news. As they went around Washington Circle, up Pennsylvania Avenue past the hospital for women and several new apartment houses and small hotels, they eventually rolled onto M Street heading west.

Then suddenly a blitz of small shops and liquor stores appeared. Although, if one didn't want to actually buy booze, on a windy day, they could just stand on the street and wait patiently for a free whiff. Surely a strong gust could stir up the lingering aroma of barley and hops that had been turned into beer at the old brewery which stood a few blocks away, even though it had closed three years earlier. Many people, colored and white, were coming in and out of these shops and pouring onto one of the main business strips leading into Georgetown. Finally, they crossed Rock Creek Park and although it was getting darker, they could make out Nellie's house on the right before turning the car in its direction. Just as they found a parking spot a few doors down from Nellie's house, Wynn turned off the radio midway in the news report.

The colored radio stations were still talking about former Brooklyn Dodger Jackie Robinson's confrontation at the airport in Greenville, South Carolina at the beginning of the week. The Greenville airport waiting room was whites only. The colored baseball legend had been asked to leave the waiting room. It was South Carolina after all. A crowd of fans, colored and white, gathered to watch what would happen! Jackie Robinson was loved by many around the world and, of course, many white people in America revered him as well. The confrontation ended without arrest or violence, but still colored people all around the country felt the sting. Jackie boarded his fight to New York and Jim Crow went back to life as usual, though, with one more blow to its already increasingly flagellated and forlorn frame!

Junior had been anticipating his aunt Nellie's fried chicken so much that he honestly believed he could smell it on top of the stove all the way back in the kitchen as he walked up her front porch with his family behind him. He knew her front door was unlocked, so there would be no formality involved in getting in. He was determined to do his best at rushing the pre-dinner conversations along so they could eat.

"Hi, Momma, hi, Aunt Nellie," he chimed as he then hugged both in the same order. Of course, Jeanne was as happy to see her mother and aunt and greeted them both with a hug and kiss! Wynn kissed his wife on her lips and put his hands around her waist at the same time, drawing her into his kiss. For Nellie, the kiss was delivered on the cheek as his left hand extended out to touch her arm between the shoulder and elbow.

"Go on and watch television, dinner is almost ready," said Nellie, completing both thoughts in the same sentence. "What y'all want to drink?" Everyone knew that Nellie and Talley always had sweet iced tea on hand. Regardless of the season that is what they usually drank. Hardly did they serve alcohol at dinner. Usually if there was a scotch or whiskey, it was served as a digestif, although they wouldn't have used this word at her house; she knew it from her years of working for white people.

Not too long after arriving, Wynn and Junior had settled in the living room in front of the television. Nellie and Talley had a cheap version of French Provincial furniture and they called their sofa "Louis". It was no secret that they imagined themselves as the king and queen of their little castle in Georgetown's colored section. Jeanne was helping her aunt and mother by setting the dinner table just before Nellie announced that dinner was ready. All the food was on the table! The collard greens were in a glass bowl that was fogged up as steam rose from the top. The candied yams were in a rectangular glass Pyrex dish. The rolls, just out of the oven, were in a round basket and covered with a clean cotton hand towel to keep warm. The fried chicken — legs, arms, breasts, thighs, sat on a meat platter in the middle of the table! The golden-brown bread-crumb-coated entrée looked and smelled as it usually did. That was to say it looked juicy, crispy and delicious! If "delicious" had a smell, this was it!

Nellie always assigned seats. This is something she was used to doing from working with the people who employed her. When he was there, Talley sat at the head of the table and she at the other end. Wynn sat to her right and Jeanne to her left. Julia Mae sat to Talley's right and Junior to his left. With Talley absent tonight, Junior sat at the head of the table. After all, the dinner was called primarily to talk to him.

With everyone seated, Wynn was asked to say grace. Colored people just didn't enjoy a meal before the Lord was given his due for providing it. In fact, colored people, particularly those from the South and those who had known what it was like to be without, were not too shy or too proud to show their gratitude to God for pretty much everything good that came their way. "Thank you, Jesus, for this and everything you provide," Wynn started his prayer! "We are blessed by your grace and care to have this meal before us. Thank you for caring for us and providing for our wants and needs, thank you for family and thank you for giving us the strength to make it through each day. Thank you for Nellie and Julia Mae," he continued, "and make us worthy of the gifts you provide including this beautiful meal for the nourishment of our bodies as we go from this table to do things that are pleasing in your sight, Father God. Thank you for loving us and blessing us each and every day."

And with that longer than usual Wynn Horry prayer, previously bowed heads were upright and eyes focused on what would go on the plate first. Five pairs of hands were reaching all over the table as the fried chicken was passed first, and then the yams on one end, and the collard greens and rolls on the other. "The chicken came out fabulous, Nellie," said Julia Mae of her sister's famous recipe.

"Yes, Nellie, always love your chicken," Wynn noted, and Jeanne weighed in with a "ummmm um" as she chewed her chicken and yams at the same time. Nellie and everyone else at the table looked at Junior, waiting for him to stop his chomping long enough to give his food review, although they all knew what it would be.

Looking up, he finally managed to say between bites, "You know I like it, Aunt Nellie, I always do."

"Thank your Aunt Nellie again," said his mother. "Remember she made this meal mostly for you and it ain't even your birthday." Despite the chewing and gnashing of teeth, everyone broke out in laughter. It was true that Nellie made an effort to prepare both her nephew and niece their favorite birthday meal every year, at least since they were old enough to realize what their favorite foods were. Their mother rarely endeavored to make a meal for such a special occasion and certainly not a birthday cake. Julia Mae had the talent of sewing and making clothes. But Nellie was the one in the family with the cooking talent. There was nothing she couldn't prepare. Between the two of them, their family often joked, they would always stay employed. "As long as there were white people who wore clothes and ate food these two would have a job," they jabbed.

Nellie could have easily been employed as a cook, that being her only duty. But being a housekeeper who also cooked provided her certain advantages that someone who stayed only in a kitchen would not have. She became more familiar with and thus indispensable to her "family". "Knowing what people like to eat is power," she would say with a wink. She got paid more, received better gifts and was always getting items like clothing, sometimes furniture that the white employers no longer wanted. Many times, these items were nearly new. Several times a week she got to bring food home. She did the food buying and very often she would buy more than the Congressman and his family needed, even though they did lots of entertaining. Much of that food came to Georgetown to feed her and Talley. This was the way it was done. This was the way, colored people who worked for rich white people, had managed to get by and in many cases "get over" for years. It was definitely a reason to want to work in a white person's house. Or at least it was a benefit thereof.

Another benefit of domestic employment was exemplified by the reason they were there in the first place. Housekeepers, nannies, butlers, and even cooks and gardeners often got to hear things. White women, and white men too, talked a lot, just usually about different things than what Negroes talked about! And they often talked in front of their colored workers without thinking most times that they were listening or even cared about what was being discussed. But, in these days when things were changing as much as they were, colored people were usually more attuned than they might have been in the past, although there was never a time when many were not listening and planning and plotting based on what they heard. These household workers were good at being in the room with their ears and eyes fully engaged while appearing as disinterested and as obtuse as possible. Many Negroes held in slavery helped themselves to freedom after all, because of what they overheard when it was thought that what was being said in their presence had actually escaped them!

These days white people often felt under siege. The world that they knew was changing before their eyes. Many were scared and most were at least unsettled. They talked with each other generally openly about what was going on in society. They talked about how things might never be the same, as it was all coming to an inflection point. They talked about how the people who were pressing for all this change in society were not ready for it and that society was not ready for it and how it wasn't necessary because things were fine the way they were.

Sometimes the conversations were tinged with hatred, animosity and anger. But much of this reaction was based on fear! White people didn't know where this would all end and how it would end. What was beginning to be clear for them, though, was that the world they knew would probably not be the same world they had grown into. The world their children would know as adults would almost certainly be "different" and to them that generally meant less great. They felt sorry for their children. They felt they would be deprived of their legacy, the legacy their parents had left them and their grandparents had left their parents, and generations before them. It was a feeling that left a hole in them. As much as they wanted to control it, they felt as though in the long run, they might not be able to. While they were busy winning the game, somehow the rules were suddenly changing as they played. This was a very disquieting and unsettling feeling for them. After all, they owned the game and the table it was played on!

Colored people were not used to seeing white people afraid. For their entire lives Wynn and Julia had never been in a position where the cards might fall more fairly. And hardly did they ever dream of such a day. Why would they? What in their past would have given them a clue that there would ever be any kind of racial equity? But it looked as though things could possibly be at least a little more balanced for their two children. In a way, colored people were as afraid as whites were.

Neither side, the adults among them at least, knew how to live in this new way. Their children would learn, become comfortable and perhaps teach them how to deal with the change. But the fear was different between the two races. While many white people feared for what their place would be as things changed, many colored people were afraid that they didn't know how to be equal to whites. Yes, they were ready to walk into this new world, but many were afraid of this unchartered path. Most colored people, particularly older ones had simply not seen a path laid out for them as they grew into their lives, where they would walk side by side with whites and see their children go to school with them and perhaps become friends.

So, these were the conversations that Nellie overheard among the friends and neighbors of her employers. It wasn't that Julia Mae was unaware of how the changes were being perceived among the white women that she sewed for or her bosses at Horrschorns Department Store. But she wasn't in their presence the same way that her sister was every day. Wynn too knew that whites talked to each other about what was going on. But most of his interactions were with men and military men at that, in and of itself, enlightening in many ways. But men didn't show their fears and concerns as openly as women and besides, military people were more used to integration, the military having been integrated for just over ten years, starting about three years after the end of World War II.

However, Nellie's vantage point was the best from which to hear what rich white people with power were thinking and talking about. She gave them good food, a clean house, good and loyal service, and that comfort that you couldn't put your finger on, but that colored women among all others, brought best! Historically, it was colored women who offered comfort, support and strength. Nellie gave this to these people she worked for. In return, she got "gifts" and information. The irony was the white people usually didn't know they were giving either!

Much of the dinner conversation concerned people they knew in common either in Arlington or in the District. They talked about Talley's trip back to the Midwest with the Congressman and his family and how he was looking forward to getting back. They talked a bit about the upcoming 1960 Presidential election and how Nellie had enjoyed serving the Kennedy couple at a party the Congressman's wife hosted. "She looks a little bit like a white Dorothy Dandridge," Nellie joshed to her family. Jeanne idolized Dorothy Dandridge. Junior liked her too, so Nellie knew the two of them would reward her quip with laughter.

Finally, after about 45 minutes dinner was done and it was time for chocolate cake. But that would have to wait until the table was cleared of the dinner dishes, which would be done by Nellie, Julia Mae and Jeanne while the two Wynns would wait for sweets until after the table was cleaned and prepared for the cake and iced tea. Hardly anyone wanted coffee at this hour and, because of the kids, none of the adults would have a drink. And besides, the Horrys had to drive back to Virginia.

Nellie had made the cake the night before at the Congressman's house. She had made two cakes, in fact, and had all along planned to bring one home. It was a yellow cake with her thick and buttery dark chocolate frosting spread all over it. After a dinner of fried chicken, greens and candied yams, a slice of chocolate cake could find little room in anyone's stomach, yet no one would dare allow it to feel unwanted. Jeanne cut four good-sized slices and put them on dessert plates and then handed them to her father first, then Julia Mae, Junior, and served herself last. That is the way she had been taught by her aunt Nellie when she was a little girl. No one ate before all had been served. Nellie was still in the kitchen getting glasses of iced tea ready to bring out, but Jeanne knew not to cut her a slice of her own cake. Her aunt hardly ever ate dessert but if she did, it was only once a week, usually on Sunday.

Nellie knew the cake was delicious. She had been making it the same way for years. And besides, she had been tasting the batter and frosting along the way as always. By the time the cake was on the table, or any other dessert for that matter, she was usually done with it, unless it was a Sunday or holiday in which she would join others at the table and eat. The slices of cake that were left, Jeanne had cut eight, would go to Talley once he got back home. It would still be good by then. Maybe Nellie would have a slice with their Sunday dinner in a few days.

As everyone was pretty much full at the time the cake was served, the family didn't eat so quickly this time. But that doesn't mean they didn't enjoy what they were eating, Nellie was certain of that! It was nearly 8:30 as they sat mostly in silence eating their cake, a little small talk here and there.

Junior, still in suspense over what his aunt wanted to talk to him about, was now calmer and more tense at the same time. They had come through an entire dinner without anyone looking at him strangely or seeming agitated, confused or disgusted. That let him know that it couldn't be about the worst of his fears — that they wanted to talk to him about what went on in private (at least he hoped it was still private) between him and Cliff Peterson. So, figuring that this wouldn't be the subject matter definitely made him more at ease. But he still didn't know what it was that seemed this urgent that a dinner had to be arranged on a Monday night instead of the usual Sunday.

"Junior, we wanted to tell you about something we have been thinking about," finally his mother said, breaking the silence as she put down her empty dessert plate that had once held her slice of chocolate cake. "Your aunt Nellie and me have been hearing a lot of talk about colored kids planning boycotts and picketing at the stores in Arlington." There was some growing backlash at the way Negro shoppers were often treated for a long time.

But the discontent had bubbled up more strongly now since the firing of a colored boy who worked at one of the stores for what everyone who knew him considered to be trumped-up charges. He had been accused of something that involved a white woman that everyone knew wasn't true but because of it he had lost his stocking job. He also got to make deliveries when one of the white boys was busy and that is what caused him to lose the job.

They were talking about Jackson, Junior realized! The mystery of the colored boy thrown out of Arlington High was no longer a mystery to most of colored Arlington. Junior had met Jackson only once and that was early on when he was part of the original Group of Six. They never really got to know each other since he was not there for a full two weeks even. All the other Negro students knew was that he was no longer going to school with them. His family had said nothing and shut themselves off from the rest of the community. Later, they disappeared all-together!

"We are thinking how much we would like to participate in

something like that to do our part to make changes," she acknowledged to her son.

"We old folks know how hard it is for y'all youngsters goin' to that school when so many white folks don't want you there," Aunt Nellie interjected. "Y'all inspire us to want to do more. But even though our hearts are there, we old people need to worry about our jobs," Nellie sighed. "It ain't easy for us to go protest outside the store or sit at the lunch counter and run the risk of getting fired just for trying to eat some hamburgers," she kidded, shaking her head. They all laughed til their full bellies ached, but everyone knew that Nellie's point was a serious one. "The only one who might be safe is your father and he can't be taking off work to do that kind of thing."

"You young people, see us now that we are grown and you think this is how we always were... worried about paying bills and making ends meet," Nellie lamented, as if she were providing a retrospective on her life. "But believe me, children, we had our moments of being tired of how we were being treated and how we were denied. We knew it was wrong and as young people especially, there was many times we thought we couldn't or wouldn't take it one more day," she went on.

"In those days there wasn't much we could do except go someplace else," Julia Mae interrupted, "and everywhere you went you still knew you were colored." But their mother went on, "Thank God in some places being colored wasn't as much a sin to these white people," she said nodding her head as if to relieve it of the burden of her painful memories.

"Son, we know you gon' be hearing about this from the young folks around our way if you haven't already," Wynn jumped in taking his cue from Nellie. "They may want you to join in but please understand that you already doin' your part by goin' to that school. If you join any kind of demonstration, that could get in the way of your staying at Arlington High. Not a one of us wants to see you get thrown out of that school."

"Let the other kids do that protesting. You stay in that school and keep your head down," advised Aunt Nellie. "Don't get thrown out like that other child did," she admonished her nephew. "I know it was wrong what happened to him but that's even more reason for you to stay in," she added.

"You got to stay there for both you and him," his mother and dad

59

said almost at the same time.

The truth is that both Jeanne and Junior had heard some of the kids in Hilldale making comments about the businesses in North Arlington needing to treat colored customers better. This sentiment among black Arlingtonians was nothing new. But what was new was the amount of power the colored community was beginning to realize it had. Restaurants in the District had begun to serve colored patrons and even a few across the line in Maryland were doing so as well. Department store lunch counters and Five and Dime lunch counters in downtown Washington had been slowly beginning to integrate. And, equally surprising, a few had begun to hire colored salesgirls. That had not yet happened in Arlington.

And, adding to the already incendiary situation, Jackson, one of their own, had quickly been burned at the stake even though no one believed he was capable of any of the things he had been accused on, whether they knew him or not.

Horrschorns, still hadn't hired any colored sales staff. But everyone knew that place would be a hold-out for as long as they could resist that kind of change. That is where the "head *crackers*" had control as many in the colored community referred to them. Southern members of Congress, or more specifically their wives, shopped there along with other government officials, the ones who just couldn't bear to see the world as they knew it come to an end. It wasn't even as if Negroes were banging on the door to get into Horrschorns. They had known they weren't welcome since the doors first opened years and years ago.

"I haven't really heard many of the kids talking about it," Junior lied to his family. He did this in part to assuage their fears that he would get himself mixed up in something that could cause him to be put out of Arlington High. Jeanne nodded her head in agreement to support her older brother. But the fact is that she was more aware of the talk than even he was. It was the kids and to a great extent, their teachers at the colored junior high school that had been discussing the issue here and there. The teachers weren't encouraging the young students to protest but they could hardly not discuss the subject of equal rights and equal access to the youngsters at a time when so much was changing around them. These people went across the river to Washington and had to be served in many places that a few short years ago would not have served them. It was only a matter of time before they would expect the same in Arlington.

"Well, just don't get y'all selves mixed up in things like that," Aunt Nellie admonished one final time. "Things will continue to change without us!"

"Everybody can do what they can do and keep on living the best they can like we always done," Julia Mae added.

"Well, Jeanne, let's help your Aunt Nellie clean up these dishes and get on home," she directed her daughter.

"Thanks," Nellie replied, "but y'all go on home, I can clean this up." Jeanne insisted that she and her mother would help wash the dishes before they left.

As the women went to the kitchen with the dishes, Wynn had been directed to wrap some slices of cake for him and the children to take home. Talley wouldn't be back for a few days and Thanksgiving wasn't far away. Nellie didn't want to have too much food sitting around the house. After all, they would see each other again in a few weeks, skipping their usual Sunday get togethers for the annual Thursday feast! The two sisters and their families were traveling down to southern Virginia for Thanksgiving to visit their brother who had just lost his wife a few months earlier. He had three children without a mother, and they wanted to cook them a good holiday meal and take presents. They would be gone for only a couple of days. Nellie could only be gone away from the Congressman and his wife as long as they were back at home in their district visiting their family. His wife did not enjoy flying, so they would need Talley to drive back out and bring them back to Washington just a few days after Thanksgiving.

Besides, Julia Mae and Wynn had to get back to work as well and, of course, Junior and Jeanne were due back in school. This was a busy time for Julia Mae as Christmas approached. She was always busy at this time of year working on dresses for Christmas and New Year for her private clients in Arlington and the District. Fall was her second busiest time of the year because of the upcoming holidays. Spring was usually the busiest, though. Between her full-time job at the department store which was definitely busy too and her private work, she stayed at a sewing machine. These women's holiday wardrobe was quite important to them. They had all expected their dress, suit, coat or evening gown to be done in time for the Christmas holiday. This often meant a long December for Julia Mae and her crew as they worked many times late into the evening. And likewise, a long night for Julia Mae at home after she left the department store. Listening to holiday music, particularly their old favorite that Nat King Cole sang about chestnuts roasting and flying reindeer, she took the reins on her sewing machine, steering a new outfit to completion through the night. And once Wynn and Junior got around to putting up the Christmas tree about a week after Thanksgiving, sewing amidst the sparkle and the colored lights actually gave her energy and motivation to finish all the orders. The money that she would then collect would certainly help make for a Happy Holiday for the Horrys.

She had a very special order to work on as well! Julia Mae had promised Jeanne her first fancy formal dress! Jeanne wanted it to be white, a very popular color du jour for young ladies, especially for evening wear. "You're not supposed to wear white after Labor Day, young lady," Julia Mae several times instructed her daughter in the age-old clothing rule practiced particularly in the south. But Jeanne always countered that white was a color like any other that should be appreciated whenever.

"Snow is white," she would say. "It comes in the winter." At first the comment burned Julia Mae up, but she learned to brush it off.

"And look at how snow looks after it gets dirty," she countered. "Is that how you want to look in your white in the winter?" She realized this didn't make a lot of sense, but it was something to say to her daughter who was getting much too wise too quickly.

Julia Mae preferred a gold or emerald green for her daughter, also popular for dresses. She thought it would look better against her skin. But everywhere she looked she saw white dresses — in the magazines, on television and certainly at Horrschorns. Her customers wanted white. Princesses wore white and that's what they all wanted to look like. Jeanne was her princess so, she finally convinced herself, why shouldn't she as well?

Chapter 6

For all her ability to adapt to all kinds of different situations and people, Claire Peterson was really a perfectionist! She had been brought up to always expect the best of herself and those around her and to always make a spectacular presentation! When she was growing up, her family in Rochester, New York entertained a great deal. Her father ran one of the city's smaller architectural firms and thus, clients and other businessmen and their wives were often at their house. Her mother, a Canadian, had studied music in New York City where she had met Claire's father. She often gave music recitals at their house, a Craftsman built early in the century, on a wide tree-lined street with many families not unlike Claire's.

So, preparing for Thanksgiving guests including her parents who still lived in Rochester, though not in the city neighborhood in which she had grown up, a brother who lived in Chicago who was single and an aunt and cousin of her husband Chester and, of course, their two sons, was causing her a minor amount of stress.

When they lived in Africa for all those years, they never got to see any of their family. That is, unless they traveled back to the United States. So, now that they had returned home, they wanted to see their family, and their family, particularly the grandparents, wanted to see them and the two boys. Besides, their beautiful house in "the Heights" with all the gorgeous new furniture was always primed to be shown off! Now that Claire was done with all the diplomatic abodes that they had been living in while posted abroad, she no longer had any kind of appetite for heavy, and ornate furniture. After all, growing up in the 1920s, her family's house was filled with the new Bauhaus style of furniture.

Her architect father loved the clean lines and simplicity of the then new German design, and the house he had bought for them, in a neighborhood full of beautiful homes built for up-and-coming families when the new century was still a moppet, was just right for that style. Her love and embrace of the new Modern furniture probably grew out of what she had lived with growing up. After all, the clean lines and simple good looks were similar. But she also loved the current Space Age look. It wasn't exactly the style she had grown up with. It was a newer and more current version!

Holiday meals were carefully planned in her family. Her mother and both grandmothers had always given more than a month of planning to the menu, who would sit where, how the table would be dressed and, of course, how the house would look. Claire had inherited this love of planning even though she had been unable to do much about it for all those years they lived in foreign countries. After all, no one visited them in West Africa for the holidays or any other time of year. They would often travel to Europe during holidays, if they had opted not to come back to the States to visit family.

This penchant for planning way in advance led her to the purchase of the new Danish dining table she had bought just after Christmas the previous year. That year they spent the holidays with Chester's family in Palm Springs, California. They had just recently retired to the new community, coming down from the hills of San Francisco. Since she was planning to do more entertaining in their new home in Arlington, it was clear that the Petersons would need a larger dining table. Much of the furniture that they had previously owned had either been sold or given away. Now that the boys were older, they would have more company and needed larger and more comfortable furniture. A diplomat family was always called upon to entertain.

This new, larger table that she had bought in Washington would seat their family of four quite comfortably and, with the help of three leaves inserted in the middle, would expand to host a dinner party of eight to ten. The dining table and chairs, all of reddish teakwood, were upholstered in black leather, nicely matched the new sofa that Claire had bought also. It was long, sleek and also Danish-made of teak that had been cut from Thai trees. The sofa looked as if it floated in space and could carry four to five medium-sized bodies suspended in midair. The blue-green wool tweed fabric was warm in winter yet still comfortable and soft in summer and spring. Since no one sat on it unless there was company at the house, it continued to look new even though now it was just over a year old.

The house in Arlington Heights had four bedrooms and three baths. So, there was just enough space for the guests who had arrived for the holiday. It meant that Robby and Cliff would need to share a room for the time the guests were there, but they had lived in smaller houses before where they slept in the same room all the time. Claire's brother Peter would have a room to himself and Chester's aunt and cousin would as well, this way. Claire's parents stayed out in the guesthouse, a separate dwelling on the property that had originally been a carriage house but years before had been converted into a place for guests to stay instead of horses and buggies.

Robby's rambunctious and outgoing personality had always come in handy when family visited. Claire was engaging to an extent, she was the wife of a diplomat after all, and knew what was expected of her. Chester, too, was able to step into the role of host or conversationalist easily as he had been doing it professionally for years. But though he tried to make it seem that he was always engaged and enjoying himself, he was mostly at work. And since he took his work seriously, he put in all the energy and interest that was necessary when he was around people. Cliff was a much different story.

He frankly didn't enjoy company that much and made only the obligatory efforts to be convivial. Claire had tried to teach him since he was Robby's age to at least act interested when company was around and people wanted to talk to him, as adults seemed to love to do with children. Cliff was a cute little boy which, of course, gained him more attention from others. Of all the people in his family, Cliff was the most like his Uncle Peter. Claire's brother was a bit shy as a kid too, and like Cliff, he was quietly very driven and very accomplishment-oriented but not many people knew it. What they saw, as with her son Cliff, was a young man with a quite retiring personality.

But, as a man now in his late 30s, Peter had grown out of his reclusiveness or at least he had learned to camouflage it better. A sharp wit had become his armor. Peter worked in advertising in Chicago and his sharpness and cleverness were quite useful to his firm. She saw a lot of Peter in Cliff. It gave her hope that her son would also learn to be more outgoing. Although neither she nor Chester wanted for their son to be single, without a family as his uncle. But Peter was introverted. It was easy to explain his lack of a close relationship with anyone who might have become a wife on that. Also, despite his attractiveness, his bite might have also struck women the wrong way. This at least is the reason Claire and Peter's parents had concluded that he might never marry and have a family.

Holiday dinners always began with drinks and hors d'oeuvres for Claire's family. While her parents and brother and her husband's aunt and cousin sat in the living room, she was in the kitchen putting final touches on the Thanksgiving meal they had all come for. The food was cooked mostly the day before by their housekeeper, Gussie, who had also set the table the day before. Claire generally didn't like to ask people who worked as domestics in her house to work on holidays or days that were of special significance in their lives. It is what she thought of as egalitarian and she did the best she could to see the people who cooked and cleaned and guarded their family while abroad, as people themselves, worthy of as equal treatment as possible. That is, as equal as possible for people who did work that by its very nature, declared their subalternate status.

Needless to say, there would be no possibility of the people who had worked for the Peterson family to ever be people that they would run into at a party or at church or at a restaurant or living in the house next door or around the corner for that matter! So, they were not equal in that sense. But it wasn't in her nature to think of these people who were almost always of a darker skin color as unequal. She had tried to teach her two sons to think this way too and Chester agreed.

Even so, it was obvious to the two boys that colored people and Mexicans and other darker people weren't treated the same as them or given the same clearance to move through the world! So, what it meant in practicality is that they made efforts to treat these people with some respect and not with the indignity that many other white people treated them. They would recognize that they had something to offer, especially as it related to sports, music, dancing and cooking and cleaning up after them. Her family would be kind to this group of people. They served their role after all. Many proved that they were worthy of being treated kindly.

The Petersons could see what was happening maybe more clearly than some they knew. Colored people were now showing whites in America and around the world to the extent that the world was paying attention that they, in fact, wanted more. They wanted a bigger slice of the pie, as it were. Just as many of the countries in Africa that Chester had worked in and they had lived in as part of the American Legation, that were ruled by whites, wanted their country back and to regain the sovereignty to rule themselves. And so, it was that back at home in the United States, this group of people whom most white Americans wouldn't invite to a meal in their home, even though they were often the cooks, also suddenly wanted a place at the table!

"It's time to eat turkey and stop talking it," Claire chuckled as she came out of the kitchen carrying a large, beautifully tanned turkey garnished with roasted onions, green peppers and squash, on a platter to the dining table. She was followed by Chester's cousin who was carrying two casserole dishes, one in each hand. Claire's mother was still in the kitchen pouring gravy into gravy dishes and scooping freshly mashed potatoes into a dish, but she would soon be following with more holiday food to be thankful over.

The men and boys as well as Chester's aunt who had continued to sit in the living room with them drinking her cocktail and eating little crackers with cheese and duck pâté on small slices of bread as she awaited dinner, listened as she prognosticated that they would soon be in the decade of the unknown. "The world is going to be so different as it turns into 1960 and beyond, I'm afraid," she forecasted to her pards. "This country does not know what it is going to look like from here on out, just watch."

"Yes, things are changing, Mother," said the daughter. As they were finishing this conversation about the future of the United States, Claire herself was changing, that is she was taking off her apron, checking her face and outfit in the powder room, and spraying on a fresh mist of Arpège, the perfume she had learned to love on trips to Paris. Claire had always been an attractive woman and unlike many couples they encountered in their Arlington Heights neighborhood, she and Chester matched in looks. That was often the case for diplomatic couples.

The State Department generally had its pick of tall, square-jawed men usually from the North-east who had gone to good colleges. They usually married woman from the same social setting who were nice-looking, charming, graceful and functioned well in social settings that called upon them to look good, know how to entertain and disarm with their charm and wit. Generally, among the people the Petersons encountered in their neighborhood or at church, the women were often more attractive than the men. But when they were around fellow diplomatic couples, there was generally more parity. They had certainly passed on their good looks to their two sons. Cliff was already nearly as tall and broad-shouldered as his father with his light brown hair color. Robby would probably grow tall too but with his mother's even lighter hair. He definitely showed more of Chester's more outgoing personality, though, if not his more Nordic angled features.

The long trip back to Arlington from Danville, Virginia on Friday was made a bit quicker and easier because hardly anyone was on the roads. Everyone was still resting in place from the previous day's Thanksgiving feast. Wynn and Julia Mae had driven their own car with Junior and Jeanne in the back and a few gifts and provisions for Julia Mae's brother Horace and his three newly motherless children. Horace's wife had passed a couple months earlier from diabetes. The Horrys and Lesters drove down from Arlington at the same time but Julia Mae and Wynn came back a little bit earlier than Talley and Nellie. As the older sister, Nellie thought it her duty to spend more time with her brother and his family. She would leave them with meals to last for another week or two, depending upon how much the kids ate. Also, she and Julia Mae helped clean the house and Julia Mae had brought the children their Christmas presents early. She had made clothes for them. Their brother worked on the railroad and didn't get much time off for the holidays. They probably wouldn't see each other again before the year was over unless he had a trip to New York or Boston and arranged to layover in Washington for a few hours. The kids would stay with their mother's mother or a single woman that Horace knew, when he was off serving the passengers on the Baltimore and Ohio railroad.

Also, Wynn didn't particularly like driving through small towns in Virginia when dusk was nearing. He made sure the car was full of gas before leaving Danville and waited until everyone had used the bathroom after breakfast before they departed. Nellie had made sandwiches and put some bottles of Coca Cola in an ice chest for the trip. But since there were many places that would not allow coloreds to buy gas and certainly not use the toilets along the way, Wynn, and Julia Mae as well, wanted their family to get home as quickly and safely as possible. White people in small Virginia towns were at unease a lot of late as colored people pushed to desegregate schools and ride in the front of public buses, sitting next to white people. There was much anger, fear and resentment among the white population and often, the nearest "nigger" that crossed their path paid a price, as if that would help restore their sense of their place as white people.

Like many colored men, Wynn traveled through the south with a pistol hidden, but nevertheless just a reach away if necessary. He did not go back to South Carolina often to see his own family but when he, Julia Mae and the kids did go, "Black Ben" traveled with them. Many colored men gave a name to their guns because they were often their best friend as they drove through small southern towns. But, as this was not a long trip and the roads were pretty empty, no one expected anything to explode. After all, this was the weekend after Thanksgiving, not some hot summer night when passions were on the rise!

Their car, even though it wasn't new or fancy, was at least well kept. Their clothes were not tattered, and they didn't dress like most of the Negroes in the towns they passed through. In fact, they might have looked to some like white people who had somehow fallen into a big vat of chocolate at the local candy confection company in town.

But this in itself could make many local whites even more angry. The Horry family were better dressed than many of them and that wasn't expected or appreciated from Negroes. For this reason, most colored people driving through the south from up north would never wear their nicer clothes. They would take them in suitcases and keep them undercover much as they did their rage or in many cases, fear!

Jeanne and Junior were due back in school on Monday and neither had finished homework assigned to them over the Thanksgiving holiday.

Both Wynn and Julia Mae had to return to work on Monday as well. Coming back on Friday freed up space in the small house that Julia Mae's brother shared with his three children as well as his two sisters and their families over the holiday. Coming back on Friday also gave them some time to relax a bit before going back to work and to begin to decorate for Christmas. It also gave Junior the opportunity to watch the weekly episode of *Twilight Zone* later that night.

The show had in a few short weeks become a hit with teenagers. Many parents, though not the Horrys, had complained to the Columbia Broadcasting Service, the network that carried the show, that their kids were staying up too late to watch it. But the other way of looking at that was, kids who didn't have a date or a party to go to on a Friday night at least had another appointment to keep!

Besides, the Horrys had another surprise for Junior. They had planned to take him and his sister to see the new movie *Take a Giant Step* playing at one of the colored theaters on U Street in Washington. The film seemed particularly apropos as it revolved around a young colored teenager going to school with white kids in New England. It also starred Johnny Nash who Jeanne and many of the colored girls were overly sweet on, since they saw him on *American Bandstand*. Those who had televisions, that is.

As for Junior, his thoughts were focused on Cliff. They had not had much time to spend together over the fall since the grass at the Petersons' house had taken a winter break from growing. They hardly talked much at school. The four colored kids rarely talked to the white students unless they were working on an assignment together. And even then, conversations were short, often terse and awkward, especially since the entire class was looking on.

The desire to touch each other was still strong for the two boys! But the opportunities were hard to come by. There were the times in an empty boys' bathroom that the two would go into separately if no one was watching, and over in a hidden corner they would fondle and hold each other for a minute or two. But that was never safe at a school that was usually full of coming and going. Junior had become friendly with some of the custodians, all of whom were colored except their boss. Many of them he would see at church or out in the neighborhood.

He would often chat with them around the school as they checked on him and the other colored kids. Since they didn't want to be seen by the white people talking too much, he would spend a few minutes with them in the basement surrounded by mops, brooms, pails and an assortment of other cleaning tools that stood around them in silence. His favorite was the one everyone called Old Papa. At least, that is the name Bertie Henley was known by in Hilldale, and among the other colored workers at Arlington High.

A dark brown-skinned, slender man in his late sixties, Old Papa was a grandfather to some kids that Junior knew fairly well. They went to his church and lived not too far away. He was a friendly man who walked with a slight limp and he was slightly stooped over. Old Papa never said much but generally had a smile on his face. The white people called him Bertie and he had been at Arlington High for about ten or fifteen years, keeping the school clean and in order.

There was no fear of being overheard or spied upon, Junior felt, when he talked to Old Papa, or any of the other custodians. No white person other than the custodial captain would ever come to the basement where they kept themselves, unless they needed something. That is except for Cliff Peterson. Since they were both afraid of being seen with each other in the bathroom or in a locker room or in an empty classroom, Junior had started to bring Cliff to one of the janitors' closets every now and then when he knew that no one would be there since the janitors performed their work on a schedule. Here they could do things with each other that they wouldn't feel safe to do in any of those other places.

Junior was missing this, and he longed to be close to Cliff in one of their secret places! Cliff reminded him so much of the men he saw in the magazines and on television ads. Cliff looked like the young men in the newspaper ads and on the movie screen. When he pressed his more athletic and stronger body against Cliff and put his limber brown fingers over Cliff's quivering face, arms and legs, longing for his touch, he felt larger than usual! There weren't many ways for a colored boy to feel more powerful than a white boy. Unless it was on the basketball court or on the race track, there weren't many opportunities for colored boys of fifteen to feel their manhood vis-à-vis a white boy. But the way that Cliff submitted to Junior, there was no doubt about who was in charge!

71

Junior was certain that what went on between him and Cliff had gone on with other boys at school... other white boys. It was a large school and he saw how a few of them looked at each other, particularly in the showers after gym! The way Cliff talked about some of the boys he knew when they lived overseas, the boys who worked for his family and other diplomatic families in the countries they lived in in Africa, it was clear in Junior's mind that Cliff had been fascinated by many of them and probably had become "close" to a few.

Junior had never been this close to another boy before. He had noticed a few at Frederick Douglass Junior High and he had had his eyes on one or two on the track team. But he would never have considered touching any of them. He didn't know of colored boys touching each other. Many girls liked him, so it was easy for him to caress one of the many who wanted to pet. The girls liked to stake their claim on who they considered to be the best boys, in junior high school. This practice continued, of course, in high school when many were making decisions on whom to marry. This is, of course, how he got to know Carolyn Stanley, a pretty, toffee-colored girl with long, wavy hair that did not need to be processed to lay down. Many of the colored boys chased Carolyn but she had set her sights on Junior and kept them there since their sophomore year at Frederick Douglass Junior High. Junior high school was the time that boys discovered girls and that was no less true at Frederick Douglass Junior High.

There was always lots of secret and sometimes not so secret occasions of fingers unbuttoning blouses and hands going up skirts in stairwells, under the bleachers, in empty classrooms, in the cafeteria and pretty much anywhere a boy and a girl felt they could get away with it. And this wasn't always only between Negro boys and Negro girls. When they saw a white boy in Hilldale, or any of the other colored neighborhoods, they could often assume why he was there if it was clear he wasn't wearing a service uniform or delivering furniture. Even though the colored boys didn't like it and often ran a white boy away, they knew that one of their neighborhood girls had probably been on the receiving end of his visit.

Peter was the first to leave after the Thanksgiving break. It was clear that he was getting itchy and ready to be back in his own realm. For the most part the seven of them had spent the entire Thanksgiving holiday at the house together. However, the Friday after the fete, Peter suggested going into the District to see *A Summer Place*, a movie that had just come out the week before. So, he, Claire and Chester, Chester's cousin and Cliff all piled into the car and headed to the Ambassador Theater downtown to see this movie about teenage sex, staring Sandra Dee and Troy Donahue. At least, that was what Peter had told them it was about. "You will enjoy it, Cliffy," he told his nephew. Chester's aunt and Robby stayed at home. Later that evening, after bringing everyone home, Peter decided he wanted another crack at DC and headed back over into the city in the dark November night.

When it was finally time to head back to Chicago, his and Claire's father had driven him down to Washington National Airport Friday afternoon, to get his flight back to Chicago. Although the airport was just about four miles from Claire's and Chester's house, it gave the father and son a chance to talk a little. At least it allowed them more privacy than they had had over the holiday at a house full of family. His father could ask the questions he might not have asked around the other family.

"So work is good?"

"Yes, Dad, I think I have been given more and more accounts to manage at the firm. I think I'm on the road to becoming a partner," Peter announced to his father.

"Great... that sounds great, Peter.

"Did you know that Chicago-style pizza was trying to gain a foothold in New York?" Peter quizzed his father, laughing. "Noo, no, Son, I didn't know that," his dad replied twisting his head from side to side and grinning. "I don't even know what Chicago-style pizza is" the elder Mandyk declared.

"It's a thicker version of what we have on the East coast," Peter explained. "It comes down to a perception problem as it turns out. People in New York and other cities out here find the deeper dish thick pizza to be inferior," Peter chuckled. He told his dad that a good bit of his time would soon be spent in New York and Philly doing market research. The idea was to engender a taste for the thick pizza among large Italian populations used to the thinner style and once it had their blessing the sky would be the limit!

"I have never had pizza," his father acknowledged. "But are you sure your way of thinking about developing a taste among East coast people for thick crust is not pie in the sky?" his father quipped.

"Are you as busy in your social life as you apparently are at work? Anyone special taking up your time?" his father asked once the laughter died down.

Of course, Peter expected this question. However, usually it came from his mother. His father rarely showed much interest in his personal life. He assumed it was because he had hardly had an "interesting" personal life since he was in high school. He had friends but few of them were girls and there was never a "steady" girlfriend to introduce his family to. Many girls had liked Peter because of his looks but, as near as his parents could tell, he was never serious about any of them. Once he had left high school and headed to college at Northwestern University, his family had somewhat lost interest in his personal life and he never had anything to share with them.

"I hardly have much time for a personal life, Dad," Peter said, rousing a smile to his face as he turned his head towards his father from the passenger's seat. "But I do go out every now and then and Chicago does have its share of beautiful women, so I don't have to go out alone unless I want to," he said, with the bit of laughter he was able to summon

"I suppose that's true," his father replied. "A city like Chicago would probably have a lot of beautiful women. I suppose the advertising firm hires some of the most beautiful in town, huh?"

"Yes," answered Peter. "But paying too much attention to a girl at work can bring about its own problems. It's better to plow in slightly distant fields, y'know!"

"Yes, I know, Son. I know."

"So are you even close to retiring, Dad? Can you ever leave the firm?"

"Well, your mother wants to travel more, in fact. She feels much happier now that Claire and the boys are back home," his father acknowledged. "Grandchildren have a way of making grandparents want to stay put," his father stated, looking at him as he said it.

"Yes, I suppose that's true," Peter replied, his head turned toward the window as he could see them nearing National Airport. "Well, thank you, Father for the ride. Please give Mother another kiss for me and tell her I will call her next week."

"Yes, Son, I will! You have a safe trip back and it was very good to see you!"

Now, at the airport, sitting in the waiting room for his late afternoon flight to O'Hare, Peter could relax as he had not done since he had come to Washington to be with his family for the holiday, except perhaps for the previous Friday night when he decided to cruise back over to Washington. A cigarette in hand, one leg crossed over the other, his eyes darting back and forth at the people walking by, he contemplated a strong cocktail aboard the flight back to the city with broad shoulders. Chicago was definitely his kind of town. Every now and then, the wind blew something good his way!

Chapter 7

"You can't keep a lovely girl away from a pretty pinafore!" At least, not according to the headline in a recent issue of *Ebony* magazine that showcased some party dresses that a debutante could don for the holiday season. Julia Mae knew the headline was indeed accurate because Jeanne had been begging to see how much of the white dress that her mother was making for her for the mid-December formal had been finished. This white dress that Jeanne insisted on was taking shape even though its color was still a thorn in Julia Mae's side.

Besides, the dress wouldn't be white — white! Julia Mae had already told Jeanne that she would not allow her to wear a stark white dress in the winter. It would be more of a silvery white! It would have pouf shoulders with a bit of lace at the end, a cinched waist and a full but not too full skirt. Two petticoats underneath would be enough. But teenage girls loved full skirts and probably all of them at the party would be wearing a skirt that, to some extent, floated in the air. A layer of lace with flecks of "snowflakes" would rest on the lace, making Jeanne look as though she had just waltzed in from a light snowfall.

Her daughter would be beautiful with her soft dark brown skin and white costume pearl choker and matching costume pearl earrings. The earrings that she and Wynn had bought for Jeanne were off-white and dangling. They planned to give them to her as an early Christmas gift to wear with her new dress at the Hilldale Winter Cotillion.

Junior would be going too but she was not making him a tuxedo. Instead, they were renting one from a shop just off U Street in the District. He would be escorting Carolyn Stanley who would no doubt be looking like a Sepia version of that new Barbie doll that was all over the store shelves for the holiday season. Although it was getting cold out, Barbie was wearing only a bathing suit!

By Sunday late afternoon, Nellie was back at home in Georgetown. Talley and she had driven back up from Danville. He had dropped her off and was headed out to the Midwest to pick up the Congressman and family who wanted to be back in Washington. The kids needed to be home in Arlington to start back at their private school in Washington, and even though the Congressional session had ended in September, the Congressman wanted to be on the Hill for a few more weeks at least. Although they would soon be headed back home for Christmas and New Year.

Take a Giant Step was a highly promoted movie among the colored population in many big cities around the country as it tried to capture the mood of the times with the subject of school integration and Negroes intersecting with whites at its core. Everyone thought Junior and Jeanne too would like it and besides, it had that lovely Ruby Dee whom Julia Mae and especially Wynn, had loved as the wife of the baseball player in the Jackie Robinson Story which had come out about ten years earlier! Wynn, as a Robinson fan, was thrilled that the movie starred the "Colored Comet" as himself. At least, that's what the Canadians called him. Ruby Dee was popular, in fact. She was starring in that new play on Broadway about a colored family moving into a white neighborhood. Colored people were definitely doing new things! If you were colored and standing still these days, something was wrong. This was the time, the Space Age, and coloreds were shooting for the stars too.

They had brought lots of leftovers back from Danville, or at least Nellie had, so they would all meet at her house for the final remnants of Thanksgiving dinner since she was invited to join them for the movie and Talley had to head back to the Midwest to pick up their boss. On the way to the theater, Wynn drove them across P Street, around Dupont Circle and up New Hampshire Avenue to U Street where the colored restaurants, night clubs, soda fountains, shops and theaters were. Now Negroes could go downtown to white theaters too, but practically everybody still went to U Street to one of the four or five theaters there. If they wanted to see a colored movie in Washington, that was the only way to do it.

Junior had actually thought about asking if Cliff could come along to see the movie with the family. He would probably like the story as well. It did involve high school friends, both colored and white. He wasn't sure, however, how his family members would feel about having him along. Besides, he had snuck over to the Peterson house the previous night! He was anxious to see Cliff and knew that they could figure out some way to have a few minutes alone together since Claire and Chester Peterson had taken the train up to New York City earlier on Saturday for a party on Saturday night, leaving Cliff and Robby home with their grandparents who were staying until the parents returned on Monday afternoon. Junior continued rewinding that evening in his mind even though he had already decided against inviting Cliff.

Yes, the whole thing had weighed heavy on him! The big concern for Junior was how he would get out of the house and get up to Arlington Heights at night. There was no place they could meet, and they didn't want to meet in public anyway. However, the only possible venue for the rendezvous was on the football field at Arlington High, under the bleachers. No one would be there and, although not the most favorable of circumstances, they could have some time to themselves in the dark.

As it turned out, Junior had been invited to a friend's house party who lived in that colored neighborhood up in North Arlington. Cliff would come up with some excuse for his grandparents who would probably be asleep anyway and besides, they were in the guesthouse, so even if Junior had come to the Peterson house after dinner, they wouldn't have seen him. Robby would have, though, and perhaps some of the neighbors too. Once Cliff was sure Robby was in his room and ready for bed, he could sneak out for a bit and say he had gone for some ice cream or to meet a friend which would actually have impressed both his parents and grandparents! Everyone who knew him knew he didn't have a circle of friends as one might expect from a prepossessing young man of 15.

The plan was that Cliff would meet Junior at the bus stop at Glebe Road and Washington Blvd and they would walk to the schoolyard from there. There were plenty of reasons why a colored boy would be in that neighborhood on a Saturday night. For one thing, it would probably be somewhat quiet, given that it was the weekend after a big holiday. But also, there were a number of restaurants and bars nearby and teenage colored kids often worked as dishwashers or they cleaned these establishments. So, the fact that he was up in Arlington Heights around 8pm on a Saturday evening wasn't too astounding.

By the time the bus rolling up Glebe Rd had arrived at Washington Blvd, Cliff was waiting and, as Junior stepped down off the bus from the rear door, Cliff walked on ahead toward the school and Junior followed behind him, neither saying anything to the other. There were other people around, other white people, but everyone went about their business either heading toward one of the shops that was still open or turning down a quiet street that led to stately homes in the neighborhood.

As they neared the school field and the bleachers, they could hear sounds indicating that others were about on the field too. Since they didn't see anyone, they assumed that the clandestine meetings were of the same order that they themselves had planned, except they were most likely between boys and girls, all of them white. Neither of them had imagined otherwise. This discovery made them falter and for a minute, their excitement to be together waned a bit. Cliff suggested going instead to nearby Adams Park which made Junior a bit uncomfortable. He wanted instead to go to a school yard at Mercer, the nearby colored high school that no one would be at and he would feel safer. Mercer was much further away than the park, however. On the other hand, the school was closer to the party that he had been invited to and he could get to the party more quickly after he left Cliff.

"It will be okay in the park," Cliff assured, breaking the silence between the two boys as they walked away from the busy bleachers at Arlington High. "There won't be anyone out there tonight, I'm sure." The park was fairly big, with picnic tables as well as a baseball lot where Robby often played. There were park benches and pole lights, but the benches were hardly filled, and the lights weren't so bright that they washed all the dark areas of the park away. There were many bushy areas and paths far from any houses and besides, those areas were mostly dark. There were other people about in the neighborhood but as far as the park was concerned, it seemed to be empty. People were mostly in their homes. The smell of burning firewood emanating from fireplaces and television images coming from nearby living rooms testified to that. Besides, no one would know who they were even if they had seen them, although it would be odd to see a colored boy in that park and anyone could raise an objection if they wanted to. It was a park for white people.

The two boys found a dark and quiet spot behind some tall trees far away from any houses and there they fell onto each other as they had not been able to do for weeks. They caressed each other's face, grabbed, hugged and, as both pairs of blue jeans went down and Junior's favorite burgundy suede bomber jacket fell to the ground, they did other things that they enjoyed doing with each other. Their temperatures rose even though the air was chilly.

This was the first time they had ever done anything like this together out in public and both were a little apprehensive about it. So much so that Junior had wanted to keep his burgundy wool cap on for the illusion of anonymity, at least, but it prevented Cliff from touching his hair the way he liked to. Nevertheless, they spent nearly 20 minutes alone together in that park. How "alone" they weren't completely sure as they could hear the occasional sounds of other people nearby. Although they were sure that no one had seen them. If anyone had seen what they were doing with each other, they would surely have yelled something that neither of them would have wanted to hear.

The other kids at school had their *seven minutes in heaven* as Junior heard the white boys bragging to each other about their exploits with girls at parties. But that was in a dark closet. He had just spent twice that much time in a dark park with Cliff where no colored boy should be, to say nothing about what they were doing. Once they had finally torn themselves away from each other, pulled their clothes together and gotten out of Adams Park, Junior went in one direction for the long walk to his friend's house and Cliff turned toward home. But none of this before they heard some man screaming as he seemed to be running toward them!

That Sunday evening at the movies on U Street, Junior and Carolyn Stanley sat together, two rows in front of his family in a crowded theater. Lots of people had wanted to see *Take a Giant Step*! Julia Mae suggested that he ask Carolyn, and she was not sure why he hadn't thought of it himself. She had mentioned to Carolyn's mother a week before the holiday, on the bus into DC that they were going to see the movie. She said she hoped it would be okay if Junior asked Carolyn to come along. Carolyn's mother worked in the cafeteria of one of the government office buildings in Washington and sometimes they took the bus together if

Julia Mae was going into work earlier than usual.

Junior reached over for Carolyn's hand to hold as they watched the movie. That's what the other boys did and often they tried to do much more with a girl they went to the movies with. At least this was what they told each other afterwards. But Junior had done these things, done them the way he wanted to at least, with Cliff the night before up in North Arlington in a dark park that he really shouldn't have been in and certainly not doing the things they were doing. But he enjoyed it, Cliff enjoyed it and their joy of being with each other was evident throughout their time pressed against each other in the dark and quiet November night. Junior could recall the excitement thinking about it as he sat in his seat next to Carolyn, shifting a bit to get more comfortable and make his excitement less evident. But once again he was also reminded of the exhilaration and downright fear that came from practically being chased down the street as he and Cliff were headed toward Glebe Road after their after-dark assignation.

Carolyn might have thought his squiggling and shifting was due to her being so close and to the handholding and finger dancing they both did with each other. But that wasn't it. There was the part that Junior had really wanted to block out, but he knew that it happened. He knew that he heard someone yelling, "Get away from here, you black jungle bunny, and don't come near my wife anymore!" He knew Cliff heard it too because he turned and looked at him as they were running toward the main street. The man doing the yelling and chasing wasn't that close to them and he had stopped mid-way as neighbors began to open their doors and look out. But even in the dark of the evening, he could see the red in Cliff's face caused by what they had heard from the screaming man!

This was the scariest time Junior had ever had in his life! There he was in a white neighborhood at night with a white man chasing him. The fact that he was with Cliff made it a little bit less daunting but if it had turned bad, what could Cliff do? And how would he explain what they were doing there in the first place? He wasn't sure how much help Cliff would be in a situation like that and actually, having him as an accomplice would probably exacerbate the situation.

But, and had this happened before the Thanksgiving holiday instead

81

of immediately after, the fact that he escaped that situation without being caught, would have been his biggest reason to be thankful! That he had managed to get to the house party he told his parents he would be going to, and to meet up with one of the other colored boys he said he'd be out with, was definitely a reason to be grateful.

He had told Wynn and Julia Mae that Ray from school would be at this party. In fact, it was Ray who invited him. Ray lived in that neighborhood and these were his friends who lived in the walled-in colored neighborhood in North Arlington. The boy who was Ray's friend was having some friends over to play records and dance. Wynn was picking him up at 10:00 that night, so he had to make it to the house, and he had to look and act as though nothing had practically scared him to death just an hour or so before.

As he watched the movie, basically the story of a colored boy about his age in New England, the only Negro in his high school, he was more reminded of how tormented he was going to Arlington High and having to be in that white neighborhood. Like the lead character in the movie, no one really understood him, and it was clear that many of the teachers just didn't feel right having a Negro student in their class. The friendship between the white boys and the colored lead character made him think of his relationship with Cliff. Except in the movie, the friendships didn't involve touching each other's face, unzipping each other's pants, rubbing each other's heads and pushing up against each other in a dark park at night! While it made him feel good, the way his heart raced when he was alone with Cliff made that clear in no uncertain terms, there was also an unease.

He knew it was wrong; they both did! He would never do with a grown man what he did with Cliff; after all, he had seen the film *Boys Beware* in Frederick Douglass Jr High admonishing him not to. But that was about the dangers of perverted older men who ran after teenage boys. There was no mention of teenage boys who went after each other! Was this perhaps some indication that what he and Cliff did was not so abnormal? No doubt there were other boys who did it too. He had never seen any going at it, but once again, he definitely had his suspicions since being at Arlington High.

But he also thought about what the boys at Frederick Douglass would call him if they knew! Is this why he always felt someone was seeing what they did? Something this wrong surely can't remain between just the two of them, Junior often lamented. He felt this less when they were at school in the janitor's closets but, being out in the open, even though it was dark, there were at least a few people walking on the park's periphery and getting in and out of cars parked on nearby driveways. In fact, as they were coming out of the park the previous night, before the man started screaming and running toward them, he could hear a car radio nearby.

It was either parked on the street or in someone's driveway, he wasn't sure. "I don't have love to share, I don't have one who cares, I don't have anything since I don't have you!" The song had been out about a year, but it was still popular and played often on white radio stations. But it was one of those rare songs that both white and colored kids liked about equally! The colored kids called the singing group the white Platters because it was clear that they loved the way colored singers, sang! Junior liked the song and agreed that the lead singer was trying to sing like a colored crooner!

Yes, that action-packed night was definitely one of the most exciting nights of his life. On the one hand, he was in heaven for a few minutes, but after that, he had to walk through that hell, that one brief period of damnation that reminded him at the age of 15 of what he was and would always be, at least to these people, that is to say, a jungle bunny! But at least he knew that whatever that white man thought of him, he had never been with anyone's wife!

The '55 Buick carried the six home as comfortably as it brought them to the movie, after it was over. Besides, the car carried the sextet only as far as Georgetown and Nellie's house, which was only about a mile or so away from the theater. After they had said goodbye to her, Jeanne got out of the front seat, sandwiched between her parents, and into the back of the car next to her brother with Carolyn on the other side of him. Everyone had school on Monday, after the week-long Thanksgiving holiday and, of course, Wynn and Julia Mae had to go back to work. While things wouldn't be "normal" until after the next holiday at the end of December, at least they would be routine with the busyness that came with holiday preparations, for the next few weeks.

The Winter Snow Ball was coming up in two weeks and they would all see Carolyn again then. Junior was her escort. Julia Mae had not completely finished Jeanne's white dress for the dance. While all this sudden interest in being a princess was new to her, she was determined to please her child and be the kind of mother who could accept the choices her children made!

Chapter 8

Claire Peterson had enjoyed the weekend in New York City, perhaps more than Chester did, even though the couple they were visiting had been friends of his since college. At least the husband was. He had gone into banking and he and his wife, a finishing school girl, but not a college graduate like Claire, lived in an exquisite apartment on the East Side. It was their tenth wedding anniversary. He was 30 when they married, having been a Wall Street bachelor for a few years and she was a secretary for a publishing house located near Grand Central Station and 23 years old at the time of the wedding. The Petersons stayed at a small, stately hotel in Murray Hill not so very far from their friend's apartment, just off Park Avenue in the upper 40s. It was the kind of small hotel Europeans who came to New York felt at home at.

Most of the wives were younger than their husbands by at least a year or two. Many of the women in this crowd had gone to college, to one of the seven sisters even, but, of course, not all. Regardless, they had all achieved the same honor in the end and that was their gray flannel suit-wearing blond, brunette or red-haired husband who was a live version of the men they saw in magazines, on television, in the movies. They were the ones who ran everything. They, who made the decisions and who provided, prevailed and prospered!

The party was fabulous, and their friend's large apartment had never been so full of people, nor had it ever looked so swell! The wood-paneled apartment with lilac-colored wallpaper displaying tiny multi-colored flower petals, art in and of itself, was full of paintings on the walls, flowers, and antiques that had been passed down in both families for hundreds of years. It looked like a spread out of *Vanity Fair*!

Claire wore an evening dress she had bought in Rome the previous spring when she and Chester had gone on vacation. The boys were visiting their grandparents at the time because they were out of school for the spring vacation. At the soirée, Chester had got the opportunity to catch up with more than a few friends from his East Coast college and their wives. He heard about their jobs, their children and their vacations and they asked him about Africa and what he thought of all these countries full of black people becoming independent nations all of a sudden. Most didn't ask because they thought it ridiculous but because to them it was curious.

How they would be able to govern themselves was more the driving force for the questions. And for a few, there was the nagging question of equivalency. Was all the recent outcry for equal rights and equal access to things that had been all-white since America began, related to what was going on in Africa? Was the plea to Uncle Sam for integration and equality in accommodations borne of a long-broken but still extant familial tie to African cousinry? "Do you think Negroes will soon want their own part of the country once they find out that we're all a bunch of drunks and hardly any of us is satisfied with our own lives?" asked one friend, primarily in jest but himself slightly inebriated.

"Those that work in our homes already know that we're drunks and constantly complaining," interjected the wife of another friend involved in the conversation as a burst of laughter broke out. She couldn't help but laugh herself.

Claire chuckled a bit herself but it was with some unease because she was uncomfortable when the conversation revolved around colored people! She herself was turning a bit red, but this could also have been due to the vigor of the vermouth in the Manhattan!

Both Claire and Chester loved Manhattan enough to have stayed at least a few more days. But the two weekend nights were about all they could manage given that they had to get back home. Her parents needed to leave to return to Rochester, Chester needed to get back to work and both of them needed to get back to being parents. It had been a busy weekend in New York with the party, seeing old friends, shopping for Christmas presents and even sneaking in a movie, a British one at that, but it was time to head to Pennsylvania Station where the *Senator* would bring them back to Washington.

Besides, they would be back up for Christmas with the two boys.

The apartment their friends lived in would be theirs for the Christmas holiday as the couple, who had no children, would be off to South America until after New Year. They had planned to go to Cuba but the recent rebellion in that country had made it impossible. Their American friends, hotel owners in Havana, had fled back to the States earlier in the year. They were headed to Rio de Janeiro and perhaps Caracas, to see what other real estate buying opportunities might await south of the border. They had heard that Brazil might be building a new capital city soon. It would need hotels, especially ones that Americans and Europeans would want to stay at.

The goings on in early December in Arlington Heights were about the same as they were in Hilldale or anywhere else. Except in Arlington Heights there were probably more tony Christmas parties, more Christmas lights, outdoors and inside, and more Christmas pageants in the churches, community organizations and private clubs.

But in Hilldale many of the teens and, of course, their parents, were preparing for the Snow Ball where they would crown a prince and princess! Although it had not even snowed by that second Friday in the month, the night the party was held. No one knew it at the time, but there would be no more than four inches of snow for the entire month in Arlington. That was of no concern, though. The Snow Ball didn't require actual snow on the ground. The storm of white dresses in the basement of Mount Calvary Baptist Church where the dance was held was more than enough white. And on top of that, there were the flakes of white confetti that fell like snow over the teenage couples from time to time as they danced around the wide, polished basement floor. The church basement was festooned with a big green Christmas tree adorned with large colored electric lights, bright and festive glass ornaments and colorfully packaged gifts underneath. In addition to the tall green Christmas tree, there were a few silver trees as well positioned around the basement, also with colorful bulbs dangling off them. The aluminum trees were the new thing and not many people had actually seen them except on television or in the magazines. But Mount Calvary had them for the party, paid for like all the other decorations and food and beverages, from the proceeds of the cost of attending the party.

These were not the Jack and Jill, boys and girls! The preponderance of dark-hued girls made that clear! Despite the nightly rituals that many practiced of rubbing bleaching cream deep into their face and neck, they would never beat the paper bag challenge. Besides, their parents were not the doctors, lawyers, business owners or college professors, most of whom lived in the District anyway, that was typical of Jack and Jill parents. Yet these mothers and fathers — government workers, teachers, maids, cafeteria workers, handymen, garbage haulers and chauffeurs — were willing to pay to have their daughters and sons attend this "ball" and were proud to do so. They loved seeing their girls, hair pressed and shined, dressed in white and wearing white gloves and their sons in black suits, bow ties, shined shoes and hair parted on the side, or made wavy with a nightly do-rag pressed tight on their head, accompanying these well-turned-out young ladies.

However, Jeanne Horry was the only girl there wearing a Julia Mae Horry design! Of course, Julia Mae, also in attendance, donned an evening dress that she had made. It was a silver-white sheath dress which she wore with a pearl choker and mid-length gloves which matched in color. She and Jeanne looked lovely, no doubt, but to her mind, her son Wynn Junior was definitely the handsomest boy there! Jeanne's fella did not go to the party. He wasn't the type for that kind of thing nor did his parents want to pay the money. Instead, her escort was the boy next door who she had grown up with. He liked her that way, but she saw him as a regular Joe.

Just as in Jack and Jill, the ages of the partygoers ranged from thirteen to sixteen. It was thought that anyone older than 16 would hardly want to attend an event with a thirteen or fourteen-year-old. Part of the rationale was that younger teenagers needed to see slightly older teenagers in social settings in order to know how to properly conduct themselves. They weren't adults, so patterning too much like an adult may be the wrong strategy. But a boy or girl two or three years older was just right. And, the thinking went, they all needed to be under the eye of adults, particularly those who knew how to conduct themselves properly in social settings. Most of the party organizers were the teachers in the colored schools who happened to attend one of the three churches that sponsored the Ball, as they liked calling it. The teachers were the people in Hilldale and all the other Negro communities that were most looked up to. They had been to college, at least most had.

These organizers chose to hold the Snow Ball in Mount Cavalry's basement because it offered the most space and was the most suitable in terms of appearance. The Horrys were members of Mount Cavalry. Julia Mae sang in the Cavalry gospel choir and Wynn Senior was a deacon. Almost all the colored population of Arlington and nearby Alexandria belonged to either a Baptist church or an African Methodist Episcopal or Episcopal Zion church. A few were Catholic as well. But everyone knew Mount Cavalry as the largest colored Baptist church in Arlington. It competed with some of the churches in Washington for Sunday morning crowds.

Carolyn Stanley didn't belong to Mount Cavalry, but she was known there. Her mother was an occasional attendee although she went to church in Washington where the man she was involved with, lived. Carolyn was looking very beautiful in a white evening dress her mother had been paying on for her for months from a store downtown. The Jewish-owned stores in downtown Washington would allow for what they called layaway purchases which let customers buy merchandise by making payments on it over time. Usually, the entire payment was made within six months, sometimes sooner, sometimes later. Carolyn's mother had been able to purchase the dress within three months with the help of money from her father who she was still married to but separated from. He lived in Fredericksburg, about an hour further south and worked as a caretaker at a women's college there. He did not see his daughter in the dress but would have agreed with his estranged wife that she did look beautiful if he had!

Of the older girls there, close to 40 in all, Carolyn was definitely among the five or six that stood out most. The same could be said of Jeanne when considering the younger ladies in attendance. There were about 25 of them. And, of course, each girl had an escort, so all in all, there were close to 130 teenagers in that basement. And with the teachers, some of the mothers and fathers and a few church officials also present, the total number in that basement was about 150, including the four-piece band that had been hired for the event. The band was composed of local musicians, many from the church, who mimicked the favorite tunes on their instruments which, of course, included a piano and a horn.

After dancing the "Cotillion Dance" as they had known it, otherwise called the Waltz, which they had practiced for an hour or so the Saturday afternoon before the Ball, the kids also got to Bop, Stroll and Twist, dances they were much more familiar with and didn't need any lessons in. The Twist had just come out earlier in the year, but everyone knew how to do it. It was probably the colored kids' most popular dance. Most white kids didn't know about it and they wouldn't find out here in Mount Cavalry's basement. Although, some of the church ladies didn't really think the kids should be doing that dance in church, after all Hank Ballard sang all those racy songs. But they couldn't really keep them from wanting to dance it. It was a shiny new thing and it had to be played with!

Beyond the dancing, Junior got to talk to a few of his friends from Frederick Douglass who had either gone to the colored high school in Arlington or were using someone's address to go to school in the District.

"So how many peckerwoods have you had to pop already at that school, brother?" asked one boy whom Junior didn't know real well but had had a few classes with and raced against in gym class.

"None so far," Junior responded with a smirk, "no rumbles so far."

"I hear those pasty faces get shook up sometimes at y'all being there," said another. "My cousin is Shelly," he added, naming one of the three colored girls among the Arlington Five. "She says that it ain't as bad as it was at first, but they still look at y'all like you ain't supposed to be there."

"Do you talk to any of them?" one of the girls who had come over to talk to Carolyn, asked.

"Yes," replied Junior, "we sometimes have to talk if we're doing an assignment together. At other times there's one or two that might say something probably because they want to seem hip."

"They made us watch a movie a few months ago called *What About Prejudice!*" Junior told them. "Ever since then more and more of them manage to spit out a hello," he added with a wry smile on his face.

To more laughter, Rocket, a fellow he had run track with in junior high, asked, "Did any of 'em take notes?" They imagined that the film probably showed scenes of Little Rock High two years earlier as well as focusing on the lynching of a colored man earlier in the year in

90

Mississippi. But in fact, the movie *What About Prejudice* which was filmed at a high school in Kansas and being shown around the country as an educational tool, didn't even mention colored people at all really. Simply, it focused on a group of white teenagers at school who were suddenly confronted with a boy whose face was never shown but the viewer knew that he was not white. Anyone watching it could easily conclude that Bruce Jones, the boy's name, was a colored kid, though. Anyone, that is, who was aware of what was going on at high schools and even junior high and elementary schools in parts of the country. Bruce Jones was certainly a Negro; Junior knew for certain. Although all he could see in the movie was Bruce Jones' legs and feet, he knew that he walked in his shoes.

"Everyone was pretty silent during the movie," Junior recounted to the group surrounding him and Carolyn. "The civics class teacher didn't say anything either." Carolyn asked him if everyone was looking at him during or after the movie and Junior looked a little bit ill at ease for the first time during the conversation.

"Yes, many of them were," he answered her. "But I kept looking at the screen, even when the movie was over. I didn't want to see their faces and certainly didn't want anyone feeling sorry for me."

"For you?" asked Rocket. "Those crackers should be feeling sorry for themselves!"

To this, everyone laughed and, as the band was beginning to play the Stroll, all scurried back to the dance floor area. Carolyn had taken hold of Junior's hand and led him off while he and the others were just ending their laugh session. Heading toward the floor all knew what to do. The boys and the girls separated and formed two lines facing each other with a wide bit of space between them. The one boy on the end closest to the band stepped out toward the center as did the girl facing him. They then began to stroll down the aisle as if they were lovers out in the park on a Sunday afternoon.

After about thirty seconds, the next couple followed the same routine and the two strolled down the aisle putting their own particular spin on the dance. It was a while before either Jeanne and her escort or Junior and Carolyn got their turn. But as he waited on his side of the divide, Junior knew that this pretend stroll in the park would be nothing like the one he had had a few weeks ago in the dark in the white part of town with Cliff.

When the dance was nearing its end around 8 pm, it was time to crown a Snow Princess. The teachers and church members, all women, of the participating churches had all nominated girls for the title. The girl with the most nominations usually got to wear the crown. Partly because she was among the Arlington Five, partly because of her family's financial support of the Snow Ball and partly because of the way she looked, Thomasine, the lightest-skinned of the girls chosen to attend Arlington High, was crowned princess of the first Snow Ball.

Her family, the mother a teacher in a colored elementary school in Alexandria and the father, the owner of a colored taxi service that served Arlington and Alexandria, was generally liked by most. They didn't act like most light-skinned, better off colored people. Still, some of the mothers felt slighted when the tiara was put on Thomasine's head. But through it all, they realized how proud the community was of her for being one of the three girls chosen to integrate Arlington High and they knew she was a smart girl. They also knew of the contribution her father had made in terms of providing taxi service to and from the event for those who didn't have another way of attending.

But they also felt that this was the one opportunity for a pretty, brown-skinned young lady, like Jeanne or Carolyn, to finally wear a crown. All things being considered, it was not too much of a surprise to anyone. At least her date had been a fine-looking dark brown-skinned boy. And since Thomasine had been crowned Snow Princess, as her date, this boy automatically became Snow Prince.

In the end, the Snow Ball was a success if for no other reason than for the money it raised for the community. It helped to support youth activities for the colored kids in Arlington and everyone agreed that was a good thing! Everyone walked out into the not-too-cold-for-December, snowless night, leaving the fake snow on Mount Calvary's basement for the volunteer cleanup crew to sweep away. Christmas was two weeks away, and that was exciting for most to look forward to. Soon it would be a brand-new decade and that too held out a lot of promise. The way things were already changing, it was hard to even imagine what great things awaited in 1960!

But even more exciting to Junior this evening was a new episode of *Twilight Zone*. It would give him and Cliff something to talk about if they got a chance to sneak off somewhere on Monday during the school day. They did manage to talk as well as other things during these stealaways.

Chapter 9

The days before Christmas were characteristically hectic for the Petersons. The four of them were spending the Christmas week at their friend's apartment on the upper East Side of New York. Claire's parents were planning to take the train down from Rochester and they would stay in a hotel near the apartment. Peter had said he'd be joining friends in Hawaii for the holiday. He and his friends were anxious to be under the sun and what better time than the winter holiday. Anyone who could, wanted to get out of Chicago for a few days in December. When Claire asked who he'd be spending the holidays with he never provided any names but said that it was a combination of friends from work and so on. "We will be staying in Honolulu through New Year," he told his older sister. His Chicago advertising firm had done some work for one of the country's major canned fruit companies. The canning industry in Hawaii was beginning to dry up after decades of bringing pineapple especially to the mainland and the rest of the world. His firm had been called in to help keep America's taste buds set on the sweet and succulent taste of pineapple, most of which came from the island state.

Anyway, he and some of his colleagues had spent a fair amount of time in Honolulu and other places on the island and had made some new friends who invited them out for fun in the sun and sand and mele kalikimaka! While his family would have a white Christmas and the glitter of Manhattan in December, Peter Mandyk would have Diamond Head with the brown boys in the sand!

The last several days of school at Arlington High, before the start of the holidays, were filled with exams, socializing and gift exchanges among the students and the teachers and parents giving the teachers their Christmas present. Claire had picked out a nice cigarette case for Cliff's homeroom teacher, Mr Aikens. She knew from past encounters that he smoked. The custom of giving the teacher a gift wasn't so much expected in high school as it was in elementary school, but Claire did like George Aikens' efforts to get her introverted son positively involved with his peers and not so much the object of their jokes and pranks. She was on the school's PTA social committee and had known many of the teachers through her volunteer work.

None of the parents of the five colored kids at the school were on the PTA and needless to say, it would have been a surprise if any had sought to join! Most of them, however, Julia Mae included, were involved with Frederick Douglass Jr High activities. Of course, Julia Mae still had a daughter attending there, but regardless, she would have been as helpful to the school as possible. After all, it was in the neighborhood or at least not too far from their house; she knew many of the teachers because they went to church together or they lived not too far from the Horrys. Hilldale and even the other Negro communities in Arlington were really like one extended circle. Chances are you knew someone from your church or another church, from a social organization, or from your kid's sports or social group, or they lived in your neighborhood or had friends who did. Julia Mae also knew the regulars that she rode the bus with or passed her unused DC Transit bus transfer off to or received an unused one from to ride the bus without paying an extra fare. Colored people did these things to help support each other. They realized they were all each other had!

Amid all the gift-giving, Cliff had something for Junior. The Friday before Christmas was the last day of school for 1959 since the holiday was the following Friday and families needed time to prepare for the holidays and any upcoming travel. Cliff and Junior managed to meet each other in the basement of the school one final time for the year and it was at that point that Cliff gave Junior his gift.

As they hugged each other goodbye and petted a little too, both boys would be traveling with their families for Christmas, Cliff pulled out something from his pants pocket. It was a small box with Christmas wrapping paper on it and a little bow tied on top. Cliff figured he had better wrap it himself because no one else would have done so except his mother and she would certainly have not expected her son to have a Christmas present for Junior. After all, she and Chester had already given him an envelope containing a Christmas card with a dollar bill inside as a Christmas tip, a dollar less than they gave their paper boy who delivered the news every day of the week. Junior cut the grass only from the middle of spring until the beginning of fall.

But Cliff had his own present for Junior, which Junior was not expecting. The final time together before Christmas vacation and the arrival of a whole New Year, and new decade, was enough for Junior! "What's in this box?" he demanded of Cliff with the same smile that would come across his face exactly one week later while he was with his family and his grandparents exchanging presents in North Carolina. Junior shook the little box from side to side to see if any sound that would come from the shaking might tip him off to what was inside. He could hear some sliding around but nothing tell-tale. "Come on, tell me," he once again asked Cliff as he smiled at him widely while looking alternately at him and the red box with gold ribbon he held in both hands.

"Open it, nerd," Cliff answered, "That way you'll know."

"Okay, spaz, I'm opening it," Junior shot back, using a term he had heard often around Arlington High from the boys joshing with each other.

Inside was a coin that Junior didn't recognize. It was about the size of a half dollar coin and about the same color but Junior knew that it wasn't a half dollar just by looking at it from a distance. "It's money from Ghana," Cliff explained. Junior could see from the inscription on the coin that it was a shilling coin minted a year earlier in 1958. He knew from school and from talks with Cliff that was the year the West African country that the Petersons had lived in became independent. "This is their new money," Cliff explained to Junior. "Now when you go there you will have something to spend," he added with a glint in his eye.

"What will a shilling buy me in Ghana?" Junior inquired, smirking.

"I don't know… but you can buy some food and go see a movie with it," he posited. Both boys laughed and Junior thanked him for the gift. He realized that he would probably be the only person in Hilldale with currency from the new nation of Ghana and probably one of a few in all Arlington, with the exception of the Petersons and perhaps other residents who worked at the State Department or for a bank dealing in international currency.

"I don't have anything for you, sorry," he told Cliff, "But maybe after I get back from visiting my grand momma and poppa in North Carolina." Cliff assured him that it was okay and that he wanted him to have the coin.

Finally, the two boys, saying goodbye and about to leave the janitors' closet, heard some footsteps by the door. Junior thought it was probably Old Papa or one of the other janitors returning to the closet after cleaning up after the faculty Christmas luncheon. So, they decided to be quiet and remain in the closet awhile hiding in a corner behind a wall. After a few minutes of huddling together, the door never opened and nor did they hear any more sounds. Junior quietly walked over to the door and listened to the silent hall. He then tiptoed back over to Cliff, still hiding, and reassured him that it was okay to come out now before someone actually did come back to the closet.

Junior opened the door slowly, and, neither seeing nor hearing anyone, pulled Cliff by the arm, neither of them saying anything. Both walked out of the door quickly into the quiet, dim and still passageway and each went in a separate direction down the hall to the closest stairwell that would lead them up to the first level where each would leave the school building from a different exit. On his way out, Junior thought he heard someone in one of the closed doors of a utility room but, since no one was hardly ever in a utility room, he figured he couldn't have heard what he thought he did. At least not on a Friday after school was officially closed for the year-end holiday!

"That ol' cracker woman is trying to make us all crazy jus' cos she ain't got nobody to spend Christmas with," said Julia Mae at Sunday dinner with her family and Nellie and Talley. "She wants at least two girls on duty up through Christmas Eve. I told her that most people are done with alterations at least three days before Christmas because so many of the customers are going away," Julia Mae explained, obviously frustrated, "but she just keeps on telling me that we got to be prepared for last minute changes and that I don't know what I'm talkin' 'bout! I've been there for almost fifteen years and not once have we had a rush on alterations on Christmas Eve," she continued. "I can see keepin' one person on duty for at least a half day on Christmas Eve, but not two for the full day!"

"Well, y'all are still leaving on Wednesday, ain't ya?" asked Nellie.

"Is she making you stay till Thursday evening?"

Julia Mae replied that the other two ladies, both of whom were staying in Washington for the holiday, would stay at the department store, although one of them had wanted to be off on Christmas Eve to be home when her daughter and grandchildren arrived from New York City for Christmas. "If they couldn't both stay, then we would've had to leave on Thursday night or early Friday morning 'cause I would have had to be there," she explained.

"Sounds like she thinks she's still in Alabama," Wynn responded as husbandly commiseration with his wife.

"Well, that biddy will soon find out where she is when she's sittin' in the alterations room by herself," Julia Mae chuckled. "I for one have got too much outside work to put up with that old-time mess."

By now, everyone was sitting down to dinner and talking about how busy their week would be as the Horrys prepared to go to North Carolina to Wynn's sister's house, a house she shared with her husband and their three teenage children. Wynn's parents had moved in with his sister Leeta, from their small town in South Carolina. They were getting old and the father, especially, needed some looking after as he could hardly walk owing to so many years of hard physical labor. His mother had continued to work cleaning some of the homes she had cleaned for years but her employers kept her on mostly out of loyalty and because their children, all of whom she had raised, had pretty much demanded it. She took care of their young children too. Wynn and his sister had convinced them to move to Charlotte, but their mother insisted that she find a domestic position for at least three days a week which allowed her to take care of children. She wanted to be able to contribute to her daughter's household since her husband couldn't.

They left their ramshackle house near Conway, South Carolina with all their furniture, for their middle son to have a place to live. He was an alcoholic and hardly ever had a steady job. He was also father to at least four children and, even though he went from the home of one of the women who had a kid of his, to another, he really didn't have a place of his own. Wynn and Leeta, in an attempt to help him, told him to keep an eye on their parents' house, the house they had all grown up in, and in exchange he could live in it. As far as they knew, the house was still standing, at least as precariously as it was when the parents left.

While the Horrys were away, Nellie and Talley would have the Christmas holiday together. They hardly had time off together, but with the Congressman and his family back home in the Midwest until after New Year they would have time to themselves until Talley had to drive back out to pick up the Congressman and his family. But this wouldn't be until after the New Year. So, they would have the week between Christmas and New Year to themselves. Of course, Talley might have to take care of an emergency problem, possibly with the heat or hot water at one of the Congressman's apartment buildings but otherwise, he'd be free. Nellie's brother had promised to visit for New Year's Eve. He would take some vacation time from the railroad to spend with his children since he preferred to work during the Christmas holiday for the pay. Besides, the Horrys would be back at home for New Year. They would be in Charlotte from Thursday, Christmas Eve only until the Saturday after. Both Wynn and Julia Mae would be back at work on Tuesday before New Year's Eve.

"What night do we have theater tickets for?" Claire whispered to Chester, after lowering the telephone from her ear and then holding her hand over the phone's mouthpiece, "Is it Friday or Saturday?" Chester was bent over the suitcases on the bed arranging neatly folded and freshly laundered dress and casual shirts and sweaters into a belted compartment of his dark blue Samsonite with marble swirl. "Mother wants to know so they can plan something for the boys," Claire explained.

"I don't remember for sure," Chester replied with a quick shrug of his shoulders, "but I think they're for Saturday."

It surprised him a bit that Claire had asked him since she was the one who had made the reservation at the Broadway theater months ago. She was always good at remembering things and keeping everything in order. It wasn't usually his job to remember these kinds of things. But he did recall that it was difficult getting tickets for any night, even months in advance because *Raison in the Sun* was so popular among New York theatergoers!

"I believe it's Saturday night, Mother," Claire said into the phone, "At any rate, I will check my calendar to be certain and call you immediately if it's Friday." After a few more minutes of chat, Claire hung up the phone and turned to Chester to help him with his packing. It was the day before the four of them were to board the train for New York. She had yet to finish her own packing and to help Robby and Cliff with theirs.

"Mother and Father want to take the boys to see *Ben Hur* on the evening that we go to the theater," she told her husband. Chester nodded his head, signaling his approval of that plan.

"I think that would be a fine idea and I'm sure they'll enjoy it," he added. "I would like to see that movie myself. We should have already taken the boys ourselves to see it downtown," he told Claire.

"It's only been out a month and we did have Thanksgiving and now it's Christmas," Claire noted. "Besides, this will give us all something to talk about at Sunday dinner," she japed at Chester with a wink. He chuckled in reply, fully realizing that it was true that the four of them did often have little to discuss over dinner. Cliff and Robby didn't often have much to say to each other and neither of them were too much interested in what had happened at the State Department that day or what was going on around the world.

After helping Chester with packing his bags and beginning to work on her own, Claire checked her engagement book and confirmed that the theater tickets were indeed for Saturday night, December 26. Two tickets Belasco, left center orchestra pick up at will call, was the full entry, in fact! After reading, she called back to Rochester to let her mother know for certain. They would tell the boys later that evening at dinner about the movie with their grandparents. But there were other things to be concerned about as far as the boys went. Should she and Chester give them their Christmas presents before they got on the train to New York which meant that very day, as they were leaving on Christmas Eve? At least, thought Claire, the bigger toys they had bought for Robby would be better unwrapped at home. Surely, he wouldn't want to wait till they got back after New Year. They had decided to pack only the gifts that would easily fit into a suitcase.

Chester was good at coming up with plans. His suggestion was to give Robby and Cliff their larger gifts at breakfast on Christmas Eve. They didn't go to Union Station until 1 pm, so they had time if they got up early enough. "Yes," Claire agreed, "that's a good plan, but it will mean I need to pack both their bags tonight because I doubt anyone will be focused on doing it tomorrow morning after breakfast and early gift-giving!"

Robby loved Union Station. The big rounded white structure which sat on Massachusetts Avenue facing the Capitol and across the street from the main Post Office called a train to mind just by its very architecture. When Cliff was younger, before they left for an overseas post the first time and they lived in the District, Claire would bring him down to Union Station to watch the trains leave. He loved the Roman soldiers that stood guard high above the main waiting room and watched as passengers scattered for their northbound trains on the same level or descended downstairs to get a train going south.

It was so cavernous that the chatter of hundreds of conversations would rise to the top and all the noise would hover in the air. If only those Roman soldiers were real and not carved from stone, Cliff imagined all that they would hear and see in that hall, standing high above it all. How many lovers had said goodbye to the loved one they were leaving behind and how many incriminating confessions might have been shared and international secrets exchanged? How much intrigue had they seen and how many furtive glances had they witnessed over all those years, between those who would be petrified if anyone other than the glancee had noticed? But still, the stone soldiers had stood there and kept silent!

Cliff loved the hanging iron light fixtures and the beautiful wooden benches in the waiting room also. He loved standing at the gates and seeing the trains come and go. Claire had noticed that Robby too was fascinated by Union Station and the coming and going of all the people. If they love this, she thought, wait until they get to Pennsylvania Station in midtown Manhattan! When she was younger, she had danced to songs played by big bands that heralded Pennsylvania Station!

Chapter 10

"Is everything in the car?" Julia Mae asked of Wynn and Junior as they returned to the house after carrying what she thought was the last batch of Christmas gifts and suitcases to the trunk.

"Everything but the chicken and biscuits," her husband quipped, receiving one of her eye rolls in return.

"The food's not all ready yet, Daddy," Jeanne yelled from the dining room as she was bringing out hot freshly fried chicken and putting the pieces in shoeboxes lined with tea towels to make sure the golden goodies stayed warm. The smell of fried chicken was unusual at 8:00 in the morning but they wanted it to be fresh and warm for the trip. Julia Mae and Jeanne were frying the chicken, but Nellie had made the biscuits the day before and dropped them off. It was bad enough that the men weren't getting Nellie's chicken, although, truth be told, Julia Mae's and Jeanne's wasn't half-bad either, but they insisted that Nellie make some biscuits at least. She had surprised them by making a dozen cupcakes as well.

"Y'all need something fun for the trip," she winked at her niece and nephew when unveiling the unexpected chocolate treats. This, along with some apples and oranges, would fill the food boxes as the kids had renamed the shoeboxes full of food when they were young. They were used to packing food for the car trip down south. The ritual since they were toddlers was to try to make sure they had completed all their business in the bathroom before they left, that Wynn had safely packed away an extra amount of gasoline even before he had filled the tank to the brim before departure, and, of course, the food!

In all the years that Wynn Horry had been driving back to the deep south to see his or Julia Mae's family, he knew that none of those highway "comfort" signs applied to him or his family. They could not "eat here" nor sleep at any of the places that advertised on the new interstate highways that got them to their destination and certainly not on any of the less-traveled or backroad routes. Now that the Interstate system was being constructed to take travelers from cities in the north to the south, Negroes felt a little bit more secure traveling through the south because it kept them off backroads more. Finding a place to get gasoline was often just as difficult, though, and, unless you traveled with a copy of the Green Book, getting a room for the night or a place to stop in for a sandwich was near impossible unless you wanted to go to a window counter or the backdoor of a place that served white people only inside.

Most colored people had their own private Green Book even if they didn't buy the published one. If they had driven those routes often enough, they knew where to get off the road to find the colored sections of town where someone was always renting a room for the night or serving up some fried chicken or fried fish, okra or corn on the cob and cornbread or biscuits for dinner. Many colored women in these towns and even in larger cities made their income this way. They weren't fancy hotels or restaurants. Most just offered a bed and a washroom, but they were cheap, clean, comfortable and safe places to stop and almost always, the food was good!

Wynn, as usual, wanted to be on the road by no later than 9 am that Wednesday morning. He figured they would get to Charlotte by at the latest, 6 pm that night, most likely earlier. Leeta's husband, "Brown" (his real name was Harris, but everyone called him by his last name), would be home from work by then. He was called Brown also as a joke because he was a yellow-skinned man with short-cropped curly black hair speckled with gray. He was taller than Wynn by only a few inches and much portlier. Brown had a deep voice and a strong laugh. He didn't have a lot to say to most people, but he was devoted to his family, especially his kids. This, he and Wynn had in common, although Wynn was a generally more outgoing person. Brown and Leeta had met when she came to Charlotte to attend Johnson C. Smith University during the War. She was an attractive young woman of medium dark complexion, and he was a soldier on home leave.

After her graduation from college, Leeta became a teacher in one of the colored high schools in Charlotte and, after having a child shortly after her college graduation, she and Brown got married on one of his home leave trips back to Charlotte. When the War was over, Brown moved back to Charlotte and worked for various local businesses as a loader or truck driver. He had just a month before Christmas started as a route supervisor for the new food company Harris-Teeter, based in Charlotte after ending a two-year driving position with Food Town, about an hour away in Salisbury.

The trip from Arlington to Charlotte took the expected eight hours that Wynn had forecasted. Traveling from I-95 to the new I-83 which they picked up around Petersburg, the trip was fairly easy even with the increased number of holiday travelers on the highway. They had made only two bathroom stops the whole way out, and both at Esso gas stations because Esso was known to be more amenable to colored travelers, and the gas tank had held enough fuel to get them to Cherry, the neighborhood that Leeta, Brown and their children, Asha, Harris Junior, known as BJ for Brown Junior, and Ashton, lived in. Asha had graduated high school in the spring and was on her way to college but was working as a housekeeper at one of the downtown department stores to help earn money. She was headed to Johnson C. Smith where her mother had gone. BJ was a year older than Junior and still in high school and Ashton was the same age as Jeanne.

"Hey brother, y'all made it safely," said Leeta, extending her arms widely enough to bring Wynn in for a hug after she had opened the front door when seeing them parking in her gravel driveway.

"Hey, girl," Julia Mae said to her sister-in-law while waiting for her hug after Wynn. "We are glad to get off that road and get in this house," she declared.

"Any problems along the way?" Leeta asked as first BJ and Ashton came into the living room followed by Asha down the stairs.

"Nope, not a one," answered Wynn. "We saw some boys pulled over up around Nutbush, but it didn't look too bad from what I could see. We slowed down to watch." Wynn used the term that Negro men often used to refer to each other, but it was not the same way that white people used it to refer to Negro men! "Otherwise, it was pretty smooth sailing," he added.

"Let me look at my niece and nephew," said Leeta walking over to

Jeanne and Junior who had gone over to greet their cousins. Jeanne had a hug for all three while Junior shook hands with Ashton and BJ and hugged only Asha. He quickly left Asha's embrace and hurried to his aunt, arms opened wide again and this time with lips pursed for a kiss on the cheek. "Hi, Aunt Leeta," he said, "it's good to see you." Leeta replied that it was good to see him too, adding that he had gotten taller and way more handsome since the last time she had seen him about two years earlier.

Next it was Jeanne's turn for a hug and kiss on Aunt Leeta's cheek. "Hello young lady," her aunt said. "Aren't you becoming a dish," she said with a smile in her voice and a wink of the eye. "How old are you now, thirteen or fourteen?" asked Leeta. Jeanne replied that she was thirteen and in 8th grade at her school. Her niece knew that, as a high school teacher, Leeta was always interested in where people were in school and how they were doing.

"You're still at the colored school, right?" Leeta asked. Jeanne replied that yes, she was at Frederick Douglass Jr High.

"I don't want her at that white school," Wynn interjected, "You know what those white boys do to colored girls," he scowled, looking at his sister as if to remind her of some deeply buried revenant of the past.

Losing the smile on her face Leeta looked at him with narrowed eyes and then quickly turned to Junior, saying, "I want to hear all about your experiences at your new school," trying to bring enthusiasm back to her face.

"Okay, go bring in your suitcases and take them on upstairs, y'all. "Brown will be home soon, and we can eat dinner," she announced. "BJ, go help your aunt and uncle bring their stuff in from the car." With that, all had turned to do as instructed and Julia Mae, Jeanne, Asha and Leeta went upstairs to see their rooms and where the grandparents were waiting.

The Browns' house was only slightly larger than the Horrys'. It was on a quiet street of modest homes full of everyday colored families. Normally, the trees on the street would be leafy and forest green but now they were bereft of leaves, providing an unobstructed view of rooftops, some with patches, and windows, some with curtains that didn't match and others with sheets nailed across them to maintain some privacy. The colored population in Charlotte was fairly large, so there were other colored neighborhoods than Cherry. But, once you had seen one, you had basically seen them all.

Although the Brown house had one more bedroom than the Horrys' for a total of four, there still weren't enough for all the guests. So, the arrangement was that Jeanne and Asha would sleep together and Junior would share the room with BJ and Ashton. Wynn and Julia Mae would sleep on a rollaway bed on the sun porch which his father would sometimes nap on. It was never too cold on the porch so even in December, it was comfortable enough to sleep there with a heater and blanket.

"Hey, Pop how are you feeling, hi, Momma, I'm happy to see you," Wynn said to his parents who were downstairs sitting in the living room by the time the men had finished bringing everything in from the car. His father, Janney, never had much to say but he did muster a weak, "Hey Son, how you go," in response to Wynn's greeting.

"Hey, baby, good to see you, baby," said his mother, followed by "you hungry?"

"We gonna eat as soon as Brown gets home, Momma," Leeta pointed out. "Don't worry," she added.

"Wynn, you and Julia and the kids keep company with Momma and Daddy, while me and Asha get the food ready," she requested. "Brown will be home any minute and I know he wants his food on the table."

"You're a good wife, sis," Wynn said in reply to this. "A man sure do like his food on the table when he get home!" He uttered the last statement with a smirk on his face while looking at Julia Mae.

"That same man can find the kitchen and the stove and get his own food and his wife's too," Julia Mae responded with a roll of the eye and love in her voice as everyone chuckled, except Grandpa and Grandma. Grandpa probably didn't hear or understand her remark and Grandma probably didn't agree with it, especially since the man in question was her favorite son. Julia Mae, knowing how much "Mama Essie" loved her boy, chuckled to herself as she flashed a warm but slightly devilish smile at her mother-in-law.

Chapter 11

Shortly after the Petersons had arrived by cab at their friend's Murray Hill apartment at around 5:00 in the evening that Christmas Eve, Claire phoned the Drake Hotel located nearby on Park Avenue to see if her parents had taken their room yet. She knew that her mother would want a nap after a six or so-hour train ride down from Rochester to Manhattan. They had promised to join them for cocktails at about 6:30 but not for dinner. Her father had many former architect colleagues in New York, most of whom were retired and many of whom didn't see their grown children for the holidays.

They were having Christmas Eve dinner with two such couples at the home of one who lived in a splendid apartment on Park Avenue near 68th Street. They had moved into this apartment just after the Crash and managed to hold onto to it through the bad times until it became one of New York City's highly sought addresses again.

"Hello, Father," said Claire into the beige princess phone in her host's bedroom. "How was the train ride down?" After discovering that her mother had picked up a mild headache on the trip down and was taking her regularly scheduled nap, she ascertained from her father that they would be meeting as planned at 6:30 at the Drake for cocktails. The boys would stay in at the apartment by themselves for the hour and a half Claire and Chester would be gone and they would have dinner and dessert at a restaurant and then have a walk around Manhattan to see all the activity in the streets and all the Christmas lights and decorations, at least until they all got too tired. They had had a long day that started with getting up early and unwrapping some of their gifts and then heading to Union Station after lunch for the trip to New York. But this was Santa's big night and they wanted to experience jingle jangle in the Big city!

Christmas Eve in New York City, like in Washington when they left, wasn't particularly cold and there was no snow. It wasn't warm but it was about average for winter on the east coast. And they would dress for the weather, which for Chester meant his wool overcoat, gray wool fedora and a plaid wool scarf. For Claire it meant a mink coat and matching hat over a gray wool suit with a tight belt at the waist and black leather gloves. Cliff and Robby would wear wool car coats with scarves and caps for their jaunt around Manhattan after their parents had returned.

The maître d' at Shepheard's showed Claire and Chester to the table where her parents were waiting. After hugs, kisses and handshakes they all sat down, and Claire and Chester ordered their cocktails as her parents were already sipping theirs. It was always a sidecar straight-up for Chester while Claire generally went in for an old fashion. Her mother had been enjoying a Sazerac and dad his trademark gin gimlet. They toasted to the holidays and to the beauty of the Big City! Claire's father could never get enough of Manhattan and had worshipped the city all his life. He would have wanted his architecture firm located there but for all the competition. There was much for the eye to see all around them as the restaurant, much like the rest of the lobby area of the Drake, was lavishly decked for the holiday season!

"Isn't it just amazing about that family in Florida," Claire's mother said as the conversation about how beautifully the hotel was decorated and how she felt much better after her nap had died down.

"Yes," answered Chester, "and apparently they still have no suspects a week after the murder." Almost everyone was talking about the murder of the Walker family a week before in a small town near Sarasota. Both parents had been murdered on the previous Saturday and the wife was raped beforehand.

The husband, whose name was Cliff, which spooked Claire even more, was murdered when he returned home with their two small children, a boy and a girl. The boy was shot and the girl was drowned, although probably shot also before the drowning. The Walker murders got a lot of attention around the nation because of the gruesomeness and because they happened around the Christmas holiday. There were wrapped presents around the tree when police entered the home. As far as most people knew, this was an unusual crime in America and an awful way to end the year.

108

"Oh my, we have to talk about something happier," Claire interjected looking at her father who sat quietly shaking his head at the conversation. "I hope you're looking forward to dinner tomorrow night," she beamed, projecting over the tall poinsettia plant with its lively red and green leaves that maintained a prominent spot at the center of their table.

"Oh, did your friend's maid make a nice meal?" her mother asked.

"Yes," Claire responded. "She made everything I asked for and I think you will love it." Her hostess's maid, at Claire's request had come in on Christmas Eve before they arrived at the apartment and made an entire Christmas dinner for the Petersons and Claire's parents. She would be back on Monday afternoon to clean the apartment after the Petersons had left for their New Year's trip to Palm Springs. Claire had already sent a check up to New York for the purchase of the food for their Christmas dinner. But she would, of course, leave a tip as well before they left.

After cocktails, the Petersons returned to the Murray Hill apartment they were staying at to find their two sons dressed and ready for dinner. As they could have predicted, the boys were rapt in front of the television in the living room, Robby on the floor and Cliff on the sofa. One of their favorite television shows had just ended and the two brothers, without talking, were watching the commercials but not really paying attention to *Bat Materson*, which had just begun its episode. It just wasn't a cowboy show that most boys identified with. *The Law of the Plainsman*, however, was another story. It had just ended on channel 4, as their father was putting the key in the door. The two boys rarely agreed on much but they both did like this program, however for different reasons. Robby liked it because, unlike all the other Westerns, Sam Buckhart, an Apache Indian, was in charge. Cliff liked some of the cowboys who appeared on the show, but also liked that Sam was the hero. It surprised him that Robby did too.

Chapter 12

Christmas Eve at the Browns' had passed with a gust of activity. Brown had to work to make sure that food delivery trucks were loaded so that shoppers could get their last-minute grocery needs met before the holiday. He would be home probably a little earlier, though, so the family could eat dinner and then wrap last-minute presents. Leeta and Julia Mae and their kids also had some last-minute purchases to make downtown although the Horrys had come with a car loaded full of gifts for everybody. Julia Mae wanted to see what Janney and Essie Mae needed, though, before she bought anything, so after arriving in Charlotte she would get a better sense of what everyday items they could use. She had already made a housecoat for Essie Mae and a robe for Janney. Wynn thought it would be nice to get some grooming items for them as well to go with the clothing Julia had made.

The Brown house was always neat but with seven people living there regularly and four extras for the holiday, it took an extra effort to keep things tidy. There was only one bathroom in the house originally, but Brown had put in a toilet and sink downstairs for his father who had lived with them before he passed on. Still, the only bathtub, a white cast iron one with claw feet, although one foot was nearly all chipped away, was upstairs and everyone in the family took a bath every day, so this made it extra necessary to come up with a schedule. Leeta, being a teacher, couldn't have seen any other way around it. Brown went first, she second and then Julia and Wynn and afterwards the grandparents. The five kids took turns in the bathroom the night before so that all they need to do was wash their face and brush their teeth in the morning. If baths started at 7:00 every morning, then all six adults should be clean and dressed by 9 or 9:30 at the latest and this would be just in time for breakfast.

The house in Cherry looked festive, dressed for the Christmas season! The Christmas tree stood about five and a half feet tall and was trimmed with ribbon, bulbs and colored lights. It sat in the living room by the window on a white sparkly blanket-like cloth that covered the base and also made for a pretty place to lay all the gifts. Brown and Leeta, like Wynn and Julia Mae, loved their children and wanted them to have the best of everything. Their money couldn't afford the best, so they always gave them the best of what they could afford, and the children never knew what they were missing because they always had what they needed and most of what they wanted.

Since both Asha and BJ worked after school and in the summer, they earned their own money, although their parents still bought them gifts at Christmas and, of course, the food they ate. Asha saved her money from housekeeping at the department store mostly for college and for everyday items that an 18-year-old girl wanted like grooming products, stockings or maybe a new dress or coat or hat if she could sacrifice the money. BJ, who worked a concession stand and sometimes the ticket booth at one of Charlotte's colored theaters, spent his money usually on clothes, records, radios or sports equipment.

Both Leeta and Asha knew they would be getting a new dress from Julia Mae, but the men of the family could only assume they would unwrap a necktie, shirt or sweater or possibly something they hadn't thought of. Julia Mae knew what sophisticated white people in Washington wore and what they accessorized with and she wouldn't see her family members looking as if they had just come out of the fields.

The Brown house, like the Horrys', had older, heavy dark furniture. Junior wouldn't see any of the modern, floating furniture here that he saw in Cliff's house or other homes, all white, that he might have visited in Arlington or DC with his mother. They had a television which they had just bought about a year ago to help entertain Janney while he was at home by himself while Leeta and Brown and Essie were working and the children were at school. It took many extra shifts for Brown to make this happen, but it was worth it because all the family had come to enjoy watching a few hours of television in the evening. They had even begun to enjoy *Twilight Zone* and other shows that Junior and Jeanne had suggested, particularly BJ and Ashton. There were few paintings on the wall but there were family photographs and pictures of Jesus and places they would like to visit around the world.

There was probably too much furniture for the size of the rooms, but they also had brought in much of Janney and Essie's furniture from South Carolina, the antiques that Essie had been given by white families that she had worked for over the years. They brought them to her daughter's house to keep her wayward son from selling them. She loved these pieces and knew that they actually had value to a buyer. She had been given dressers, tables, buffet lamps and lots of dishes and silverware from these assorted South Carolina families flush with plantation money. The nicest of these pieces were hauled away to her daughter's house for safe-keeping and, actually, during the holidays with extra guests in the house, many of them came in handy.

Now that the two ladies and their children were bathed and dressed, it was time to face the downtown Christmas Eve crowds for last-minute shopping, department store window display-gazing and meeting some of Leeta's friends later for a late lunch at a restaurant that was owned by the husband of one of the teachers at Leeta's school. There weren't that many colored-owned nicer restaurants in Charlotte but this one was fairly nice and Leeta wanted to show Julia Mae what Charlotte had to offer to its better colored population.

Of Charlotte's sizeable Negro population, you wouldn't usually see many downtown, at the department stores. Christmas was a special time with all the store windows dressed and the way the stores themselves looked and smelled during the Yuletide. But for most of the other 360 days of the year, most Negroes stayed away because of the way they were treated. They weren't able to try on clothes or eat at the cafés or get waited on until all the white customers had been waited on. This treatment wasn't limited to Charlotte, as it happened at most stores in the south and sometimes even beyond the south. Julia Mae, of course, witnessed this same behavior at the store she worked at in Washington.

But despite all this, Julia Mae, Leeta, Jeanne and their combined three sons headed uptown to Invers, perhaps Charlotte's finest department store. It was the one that Asha worked at. They didn't expect to see her; housekeeping was called out only if needed, but they at least knew she was there. They recalled the run-in they had had at that store eight years ago when the Horrys were visiting for the holidays and Junior was seven years old. They had gone to the toy department with all the children as a reward for their being good. Junior had seen a red truck; a 1951 Chevy pick-up truck that he went to play with on the floor of the toy department. Julia Mae, feeling uneasy at this, told him to put it back up on the display shelf.

"The store is crowded, baby, you better leave that truck alone before you run into somebody," she said. Junior decided he wanted to roll it around a little bit longer before putting it back and at that time, a young white boy, about his age, walking with his mother, came into Junior's path as he quickly yanked the toy up from the floor to avoid hitting the boy's foot.

"Look at this girl with her unruly child about to run into my boy," yelled the woman to the nearest clerk loud enough for probably everyone in the large and crowded boys' toys section to hear.

"I'm sorry, ma'am, he didn't mean to hit your boy and in fact he didn't hit your boy," Julia Mae blurted out, a bit nervously but nevertheless with a protective motherly overtone, Leeta standing by her side holding her two sons, one on each hand. By this time Junior had put the truck back and was standing with his mother and sister. Julia Mae had grabbed both their hands and was holding onto them tightly. Jeanne and Junior might have felt her sweaty palms, but the moisture had been captured inside her brown leather gloves.

"Junior, let's leave now, we have to go," Julia Mae announced while the woman with her son stood there scowling and other customers in the toy department looked on, some making comments quietly and shaking their heads. Julia Mae and Leeta assumed these hushed comments were in solidarity with the complaining woman and others just looking on as they walked off.

Finally, the clerk yelled, "That truck isn't damaged, is it? If it's damaged, you will have to pay for it or go to jail." The clerk was certain that this would appease the other customers who might be looking to her for some reaction. None of these other customers were colored. There might have been one or two other colored customers but they had all steered away at the first sign of any confrontation.

"There is no damage to the toy, miss, and we're getting out of your way," Julia Mae announced over her shoulder as she pulled off with her kids with her sister-in-law and nephews following closely behind. Leeta was fastening the buttons on her coat as she scurried, which she had unloosened during the heated encounter.

"Thank you, miss, and sorry for the trouble," Leeta called back adding, "Merry Christmas!" The six of them found the nearest stairwell and hurried down the steps to the main floor and then somewhat quickly out of the building. They didn't want to walk so fast that they would be accused of having stolen something.

"Lord, this is that same store," Julia Mae chuckled over to Leeta as they came up on the entrance to Invers.

"Yes, it is, girl," Leeta answered back. "Now, Junior, you leave the cars alone and don't get us locked up out here," his aunt chuckled while Julia Mae shook her head mumbling, "peace be still!" Everyone chortled as they stepped up to the store windows behind the crowds that had already gathered to see the Christmas window display that had adorned several of the department store's large windows. But all these exhortations for Junior were, of course, unnecessary. This was eight years later, and most likely people were thinking a little bit differently now, Junior thought. He was going to school with white kids and he was grabbing onto a white boy and instead of rolling a toy car into a foot, was crashing into him with his body!

Besides, his aunt's exhortations aside, these days, he was less interested in looking at and playing with trucks than the ones who might drive them. What was catching his eye mostly as he looked around at the uptown crowds were the guys who reminded him of Cliff or the faces that populated the magazine or newspaper ads. He figured that there were other friendships similar to his and Cliff's even here in Charlotte. He looked around at those he saw and wondered who might look back at him the same way. Who might be a part of one of those friendships, or wished they were?

Christmas dinner was a joint effort at the Brown household, and all involved in roasting the turkey, baking the ham, cooking the collard greens, baking the macaroni and cheese and stirring up the sweet potato poon graciously accepted the credit lavished upon them! Mama Essie took the lead in meal preparation and she alone made the pound cake and the sweet potato pie. Leeta took charge of the turkey while Asha handled the macaroni and cheese with her mother's supervision. Julia Mae baked the ham remembering how her sister Nelly always does it and she and Jeanne took dominion over the collard greens.

The baked goods had been made on Christmas Eve night while members of the family wrapped gifts, drank and held court in the living room. The turkey went into the oven early on Christmas morning and the ham had been started after Julia Mae, Leeta and the boys got back from lunch with Leeta's co-worker and shopping in Uptown. They had had a fun afternoon, and everyone joked at how nice it was not to be arrested or more accurately threatened with arrest, at a department store on Christmas Eve this time.

After Leeta had put the turkey in the oven, she, her husband and three kids went off to visit Brown's family for a little while and take them their Christmas gifts, leaving the Horry women in the kitchen to get their dinner contributions prepared. The macaroni and cheese wouldn't take too long to bake, and Asha would finish that once they got back home. It would still be late afternoon and therefore plenty of time to finish preparing the Christmas meal.

Later, with everyone back at home, it was time to open presents just before they sat down to eat dinner. That was the tradition at the Brown house, whereas the Horry clan opened their gifts after breakfast on Christmas Day when they were at their home. They normally spent the afternoon visiting as well and preparing for their contributions for the Yuletide meal which was normally taken at Nellie and Talley's house in Georgetown.

Everyone seemed happy with their presents from each other and Leeta and Asha, in particular, loved the dresses that Julia had made for them. They had given her a bottle of perfume they knew she liked and a pair of gloves. Wynn would never go to buy perfume for Julia Mae, so he would ask his sister to do it when they were visiting. This time, Leeta did it on her own.

"Lawd, my grandchirren sho don' growed up," said Mama Essie as everyone was sitting in the living room eating dessert, which was either her sweet potato pie or pound cake with vanilla ice cream, or both, as in the case of Junior, Ashton, BJ, and their fathers.

"Yea, they have," Papa Janney chimed in in his slow low gurgle which was often hard to understand. "I'm proud o' erry one of 'em!"

"So how do you like the new school?" Aunt Leeta asked Junior holding her plate of pie and cutting a slice with her fork before putting it into her mouth. "I been wanting to ask you since you got here." Before he could answer, she took advantage of his chewing his pound cake and continued, "I haven't heard any horror stories, so I assume things are not too horrible."

"No, Aunt Leeta, we haven't had any serious things happen. Some of the kids are jerks," Junior told his aunt. "They do little things to try to annoy us and sometimes to pick fights but for the most part things are okay. Some of the teachers try to ignore us or find a lot wrong with our assignments sometimes," Junior lamented, the frustration showing clearly on his face. Leeta asked him if there were any teachers at all he could talk to and Junior replied that there really weren't that many but every now and then one or two of the teachers, usually a music or art teacher, would show some amount of concern if something was said or done that seemed extraordinarily harsh or insulting.

"He knows two or three of the white boys," Julia Mae added in an attempt to make the situation not seem so hopeless. "I sew for their mothers and one in particular he's quite friendly with."

"Junior cuts the grass at some of their houses in the summer," Wynn explained, "and even gets invited inside every now and then," he chuckled as the family all laughed.

"Well, I guess that's good," Leeta concluded, "better than getting run off with a gun or a baseball bat."

"Better than getting strung up on a tree, is what you mean to say," Mama Essie bemoaned. "Too many colored boys, done gone to heaven hangin' from a tree."

"That's right, Grandma," replied Asha and BJ almost at the same time, both in an effort to acknowledge the gruesome image Essie had conjured on Christmas night and to move the conversation along.

"I don't know if y'all heard about Dorothy Counts here in Charlotte," Leeta directed to Wynn and Julia Mae in particular.

"Who is she, Aunt Leeta?" asked Jeanne.

Clearing her throat after a slight pause, Leeta explained that Dorothy was a colored girl who had attempted to integrate a Charlotte high school two years earlier and, after getting in as the only colored in the school, was run out within a week. "She was 15 just like you, Junior, but those white children called her all kinds of names, spat on her, threw everything they could at her and the teachers did not a thing," Leeta explained.

"After all that, her parents told her she had to get out of that school," Brown stated, getting into the conversation. "Ain't no Negro been in that school since 'less they came in there to clean or serve the food," he added, shaking his head.

"Things got so bad for them they moved to Philadelphia," Leeta noted. "So, if you're not dealing with all that hatred, I guess things aren't so bad up in Arlington."

"That's right, Leeta," Wynn jumped in. "We keep hoping for the best, but I tell you one thing, Jeanne won't be going to a white school. I don't want her dealing with all that and I certainly don't want her around no white boys," her father concluded sternly.

'I don't know if it's quite like that these days, brother," Leeta said to Wynn. "I don't think white boys follow colored girls like they did back then."

"Well, I ain't about to find out with my daughter," Wynn declared. "Besides, there's a colored girl in our neighborhood who is pregnant right now from some white boy that is always following her around."

"She's about to have that baby in a month or less," Julia Mae told her sister-in-law, jumping into what had been a one-on-one between Leeta and Wynn. "Her parents don't want anybody to know but all the kids at school know."

"Jeanne is friends with her brother, and he told her, and besides we all see the white boy from time to time sneaking around the house," Junior added.

"Those white boys ain't changed," Wynn asserted narrowing his eyes and shaking his head from side to side. "They still go after whatever they want when they want it. But if a colored boy looks wrong at a white girl, they ready to come for him."

"We tell Junior to keep his eyes to himself at that school because we don't want no trouble like that," his mother Julia Mae said with all the sternness she could summon.

Leeta had turned her face away from her brother. He knew why and he also understood the look of consternation on her face. When they were

117

children outside Spartanburg, South Carolina Leeta had been chased by a white man on a bicycle once when she was about 13 years old. She had been coming from visiting a friend who lived not far away; it was a Negro section of the town. On an early Sunday evening, it was in fall, the white man was riding his bike through their neighborhood. There was no reason in particular for a white man to be riding through a Negro neighborhood but usually when that did happen it was because he was in search of a colored girl. Leeta was aware and astute enough to hide from him. As he circled back after spotting her walking she stiffened and realized that she might be in some danger.

After summoning her legs, she ran and hid behind a tree in the yard of a family she knew, waiting there for several minutes until she believed the man had given up, before coming out of the yard and running home. Her father asked her why she was so out of breath and she told him that a white man had been chasing her,

"Well, what was you doing?" her father asked.

"I was walking home," she replied, "I wasn't doing nothing!"

"Well, don't be out there bothering no white people," her father replied. "Sometimes you too smart for your own good." This had incensed a young Wynn at the time and, every time he thought about it, it sent a wave of wrath through him.

"It ain't her fault," he told his papa at the time.

A hard slap across the face with no accompanying words was the reply from Janney! Wynn knew even as a young child that this meant that no one questioned what a white man did. No matter if it came to the harm of his sister, he wasn't to question it. These were the rules of his father and probably many Negro men who had grown up at his time, particularly in the south. A young Wynn knew even then that it would be hard for him to live this way!

Soon after dessert and all this tense conversation, everyone either took their Christmas gifts up to their rooms or replaced them neatly under the tree in the boxes they had been wrapped in. All torn wrapping paper had to be thrown away, though. Leeta wouldn't have tolerated the trash left on the floor all night. She had learned after all those years to take control of what she could take control of! It was enough that she, Asha and Mama Essie would be up after everyone else had gone to bed, washing dishes and putting away whatever food had been left over after

Christmas dinner.

The Horry family had a long drive back to Arlington ahead of them on Saturday. They had taken their gifts to their suitcases for final packing in the morning after they had finished breakfast with their family and put away some of Mama Essie's leftovers, in the shoe boxes they had brought Nellie's fried chicken and biscuits in, to nosh on for the return trip home.

Chapter 13

The Belasco Theatre on West 44th Street was quite crowded on the Saturday night after Christmas and Claire and Chester had wonderful orchestra seats for *Raison in the Sun*! The seats were several rows back but pretty much directly in the line of center stage. It was a full house that night and the diamond earrings and tiaras scattered throughout the theater sparkled almost as loudly as the pre-curtain chatter crescendoed.

Under the Tiffany lights of the intimate theater known for its murals and wood paneled walls sat a rapt almost all-white audience awaiting a practically all-colored cast starring in a play about integration of a formerly all-white neighborhood in Chicago. Like Claire and Chester Peterson, these people could enjoy and perhaps even appreciate a play revolving around the first colored family to move into a modest white neighborhood. After all, it was just a play. Probably no one in that audience would have been faced with the same issues as the white people of Clybourne Park!

Probably there were others who had been confronted with a few Negro children integrating their kids' schools but, for the most part, probably very, very few had to face the idea of living next door to a colored family. And while this was New York City and there was definitely more racial mixing than in Arlington, for the most part, it was either the very poor or the working class that lived within proximity of colored people. The middle and upper middle class of which most of the audience was composed on average did not have to face this issue. Even though things were changing, for most of them they hadn't changed that much on the block they lived on. This was a play, a very popular play and also a timely play. But it was a piece of theater that was not a fact of life for most at the Belasco Theatre at 444 West Broadway that night or any other night since it had been running!

"Wow, it was great to see that Sidney Poitier up close and I have always enjoyed Ruby Dee, she's so beautiful," Claire told her parents after returning from the theater. "It's an interesting piece," she acknowledged. "Both hopeful and tragic at the same time."

"But it's nice to see colored actors on the stage in a play about their own lives," Chester added.

"I guess it is," said Claire's father.

"I don't know anything about their lives," said her mother. "I'm surprised that many people would be interested enough to want to see a play like that. But things are changing, and it just might be that there's more of this kind of thing to come." She shrugged her shoulders, not in a dismissive way, but in the way of someone preparing themselves for something that is in the offing that they don't understand but nevertheless are hoping to be prepared for.

"Claire has always had a fascination with colored people," her father intoned. "I remember how she lamented over the skin color of our first colored maid when she was a little girl."

"Oh, my word," said her mother. "She thought she could wash off the color at first. That woman, I forget her name now, would let her scrub her arm and hand thinking she could wash the brown off and never said a word," Mrs Mandyk recalled. "I told her; dear, it won't come off! That is how they are and that is how they are supposed to be, I guess," she added. "Finally, Claire understood but I believed that she ended up feeling like something was wrong still. She seemed to continue to believe they should really be like us," her mother went on. "Sometimes I feel like Claire continues to think that way," her mother concluded. Turning to look at Claire with a warm smile on her face, her mother said, "I believe she somehow feels like something went wrong with the Negro race and they were really meant to be like white people but for this error at birth. She has continued to try to fix it, my beautiful dear daughter."

"Oh, mother, please," Claire contested. "You know that isn't true. You know I'm the one who accepts things as they are and tries to make everything work out right. It's your son Peter who has never been satisfied with things as they are and has always wanted to make everything over."

"Yes," Mr Mandyk, concurred. "That is my boy!" Everyone had a laugh but not at Peter nor Claire's expense.

"Didn't you see a British movie about a colored girl wanting to marry a white man the last time you were in New York?" Claire's mother queried.

"That's right, it was called *Sapphire*," Claire replied.

"More accurately, it was about a fair-skinned colored girl passing as white and being engaged to a white man before her secret was discovered and she ended up dead," Chester explained.

"Well, if that's the way those things end," Claire's father chided, "is it worth any of this effort to bring these disparate worlds together?"

"What kind of thinking is that, Dad?" Claire asked, rather in jest but hoping to drive home a point. "Does that explain why *Madame Butterfly* is one of your favorite operas?" Everyone chuckled at this except Chester who was no longer in the room. He had gone in to peek on Robby who was sound asleep after seeing the four-hour movie *Ben Hur* with his grandparents and brother. By the time he came back into the living room, Cliff was telling his mother about the movie and all the adventure scenes. Cliff had especially liked the Roman soldiers but that wasn't part of his retelling.

Chapter 14

Like the trip to Charlotte, the eight-hour drive home to Arlington was without incident although there were many more travelers on the highway. Lots of Americans were still discovering the new interstate highway system and because of it, more people were taking to the roads and especially during this time of year when folks were visiting relatives and friends during the holidays. Colored people liked Interstate 95 which brought them in and out of the south, quite a bit because it took them off backroads where nefarious encounters with police or nigger-hating locals were more likely to happen! Leeta, Brown, their boys and Asha had all promised to come to Arlington to visit them in the new year, but they knew it would be hard to get them all there at the same time. Leeta could come only during school breaks and Brown hardly got any time off from work since he was in a new job and also worked as much overtime as he could since the family could use each penny of extra income it could get.

"Send the kids up next summer," Julia Mae implored as they were saying their goodbyes on Saturday morning.

"That's a good idea," Leeta and Brown replied, "these kids don't get to go anywhere much except down to South Carolina and going up to Washington would be nice for them. Things are so different there and I want them to see that." The Browns knew that they were welcome at the Horry house anytime and the Horrys knew the feeling was mutual in Charlotte. Neither family had a lot of space to spare but with the kids coming alone that made it easier for accommodations.

Sunday, December 27 was the last Sunday of the year, in fact of the decade, and Julia Mae wanted her family to be in church. It was important to end the year in church on the last Sunday and to start the new year in church on the first Sunday. The fact that this was the last Sunday of 1959 and that January 3 would be the first one of 1960, well, that made it even more crucial to her!

"Everyone will be in church with all their Christmas clothes on," Jeanne joked.

"That's right," answered Wynn, "and the collection plate will be light when they get done passing it because nobody got any money left after all those Christmas clothes."

"Be quiet, Wynn," Julia Mae scolded her husband. She didn't want her children to think that the Lord wasn't still owed his due just because it was Christmas and, indeed, most folks' pockets were flat. She had to chuckle at his comment, though.

Most definitely, Mount Calvary Baptist was packed that Sunday and as forecasted, many members had on what looked like new togs, particularly the women and children. Mothers and daughters were resplendent in new dresses, hats and a smattering of furs. Julia Mae, one of Arlington's best-known seamstresses, had a fox fur draped over her shoulders which matched her fox fur hat. It wasn't cold that Sunday, but new coats and hats still got to see the light of day, even though there wasn't so much light due to the fog and off and on rain. Colored people didn't often wear their "Sunday best" outfits when they could get wet, but the Sunday after Christmas was different. Nearly everyone had something new to wear, play with or use and they wanted it known! But it wasn't only the congregation that was resplendent. The church was too! Mount Cavalry was still wearing its Christmas best also. There was a giant green wreath on the large white wall behind the altar with a big red bow at the bottom. Green garland was strung along the side walls underneath the stained-glass windows, running the length of the church. And silver angels who sparkled and glistened in the afternoon light were scattered throughout, heralding the birth of the new Savior.

"I know many of you will understand this reference right after Christmas," said the minister from the pulpit as he quieted the church to begin his sermon. "I want you all to think how much the holidays can be like an instruction manual for how to put your life together! For example, think of Christmas and the New Year as a time to give birth to a new you and to a new direction for the way you want your life to be. What new world awaits us or what new existence can we give birth to or create? We can be or own newborn Savior," the Reverend told the hushed church in his sonorous preaching voice, which was more singing than talking.

"As we go into a new year, a new decade, we can rise from the cradle of what was to what is to become!" To shouts of Amen and Hallelujah, the minister bellowed as he walked down the steps from the pulpit and through the center aisle of the sanctuary, "We can be our own joy to the world as we seek to change things for the better." Likewise, the minister offered to the congregation, "We can have no more silent nights as we proclaim to the world the dawn of redeeming grace!" Foot stomping, hand raising and more shouts of Amen and Halleluiah let the pastor know that he was reaching his congregation with a message that they could feel! Colored people needed to feel things! You could talk to them all you wanted to but if they didn't feel what you were saying, you weren't really reaching them. Most Negro ministers knew that! And so did most organists in Negro churches. The organist spoke with the organ and the congregants heard the message in their souls!

Things are changing for the colored race, the minister preached. "This is now the time to celebrate this new birth of opportunity, hope and yes, change! We don't need to be afraid of it, because this is the gift we have been waiting for almost a century now," he announced. "We have been free for nearly a hundred years, but we are now just beginning to live in freedom!"

"Praise the Lord," "Yes, Jesus, yes," "Speak on it, Rev," were all among the responses yelled back at the preacher from a worked-up Mount Cavalry.

"Don't let Christmas get you so warm and fuzzy that you forget the lessons that lie underneath all the pretty wrapping and bright and colorful lights," the pastor interjected to his fired-up congregation and sensing a good time to lighten the mood a bit. "After all, Rudolph the Red-Nosed Reindeer is really a song about acceptance." Laughter broke out throughout the church at this comment, delivered by the pastor with a twinkle in his eye. Who had ever thought of the traditional children's Christmas song as having any kind of reference to social change? He waited a bit for the levity to die down before putting the tinsel on the tree, so to speak. But it was true that Rudolph was different. He had to show his worth to the others for them to realize his value!

"We have heard the angels on high, congregation," now with a trembling voice the Reverend told his rapt Christian flock, "And they are saying that a new day is on the way, not just a New Year, but a new day, I tell you, when all God's children will dance in the freedom garden and be bombarded by the balm of victory!!!"

Now almost the entire church was on its feet, save a few of the elders and many of them, with the help of family and nearby congregants, rose to their feet as well! Everyone was looking forward to 1960 and what it had to offer. It was pretty clear to most that a change was coming and, as the minister had preached, even in the dead of winter, people could sense a sweet smell in the air. It was as if the long winter of darkness was giving way to a new, brighter light and that the weight of injustice and denial was slowly lifting and the shoulders of those who had borne that weight for so long were suddenly beginning to stand straighter and stronger!

This new year that was only four days away had a lot riding on it! "The countdown to tomorrow," as the change in the decade had been dubbed, was an encouraging phrase that probably meant different things to different people. To colored people, it was encouraging, hopeful, auspicious! To white people, it probably connoted the advancements in science and technology that were surely taking place. But everyone knew that what was coming was hugely different from what they had known up till then and the thought of the unknown could induce delight at one moment and dread the next.

After a long church service and visiting with church members afterwards, the Horrys drove over to Georgetown for dinner with Nellie and Talley. They hadn't seen them since before the trip to Charlotte and they had some catching up to do about how they had spent their respective Christmas holidays. Plus, there was more food to eat since Nellie had made a nice dinner for the four of them, careful not to repeat any of the dishes they might have had over Christmas. But even if there had been some repeats, it wouldn't have mattered because the way Nellie cooked, it would be like it was the very first time they had ever tasted whatever the dish was, anyway!

Chapter 15

The cab ride to Idlewild on that Monday morning for an early flight to Los Angeles was expected to take more than an hour. That's why Claire wanted to have the family leave the Murray Hill apartment by 7:30 am at the latest. Not being used to New York City rush hour traffic, she wanted to make sure they had enough time to get over to Queens in order to make their 9:00 am flight. As expected, getting to the Midtown tunnel took perhaps the most time as morning rush hour was at full tilt on Manhattan's East Side.

Traffic was stop and go inside the tunnel and also on the Long Island Expressway by the time they finally reached it at about 8 am but the Checker taxicab moved fairly at pace along the Grand Central Parkway and it was somewhat smooth sailing to Idlewild thereafter. They arrived at the airport around 8:35 in good time to board the United Airlines DC8 flight. They had not had time for more than a glass of orange juice, a cup of coffee for Claire, and a piece of toast and a banana each before leaving the apartment. But they knew they would have a full and complete breakfast on board the flight. In fact, in the seven hours of airtime, they would have non-stop food at their disposal, they knew. They hardly had time to relax in the United terminal when it was time to hand over their luggage and walk out to the flight.

This was a family that was used to flying and they knew how to fly well. They all loved air travel and knew they would be fed nicely. In addition to breakfast, they would get a full lunch with dessert and several other food offerings in between. Even though they would arrive in Los Angeles around lunchtime on the Pacific coast, the Petersons would already be full, and Claire and Chester would have already had an afternoon cocktail or two. Claire would have smoked at least three cigarettes by the time they landed, and Chester would have smoked at least one cigar, if not two. Robby would have filled out his postcard to his grandparents in Rochester, the ones he had just spent Christmas with in Manhattan, slept, talked to other passengers, asked to go into the cockpit and ate as much as he could. Cliff would have perhaps finished a book in the flight time. He would have walked the carpeted walkway as much as necessary to break up the boredom.

He would have wanted to write his postcard to Junior but he would not. Instead, he would save it to give to him once back in Arlington after the first of the year. Otherwise, he too would have eaten a lot but most likely wouldn't make any efforts to talk to other passengers. The stewardesses would all try to talk to him. His handsome looks always brought him this kind of attention, but he wouldn't have much to say back. That kind of attention was uncomfortable for him. One particular stewardess, Anne, petite of course, dark haired and in her twenties, seemed to have chosen the Petersons as her personal charges, showing particular attention to Cliff and Robby, but mostly to Cliff who got as much ice cream as he wanted, iced tea and coca cola too! He would have a window seat while Robby sat next to him in the middle in the three-across arrangement seat.

His parents would be in front of them. They would make this trip in tourist class. They had flown first class before when traveling for the State Department. But really, tourist class was fine. The seats were wide enough, and they could recline when they wanted. Chester would take off his suit jacket and perhaps loosen his necktie just a bit. Cliff and Robby would probably leave their ties tied up all the way, but Claire would definitely remove her hat and probably her shoes as well.

Perhaps the food was a bit fancier in first class but really, there wasn't that much difference! Everyone was eating well on flight 232 during those seven hours to Los Angeles International Airport.

Not long before landing, Chester and Claire had imbibed their last cocktail which came shortly after their "dinner" of cream of broccoli soup, roast beef, roasted potatoes, corn soufflé and crescent rolls, followed by lemon jello and butter cookies for Claire and pineapple upside-down cake for Chester. Instead of just plain ice cream, Robby chose a banana split and Cliff too had the pineapple upside-down cake but with vanilla ice cream. Anne had insisted. At the time the flight had landed in Los Angeles, and all the passengers were lined up to depart the aircraft, Anne was standing at the door just above the stairway that the passengers would descend into the LA afternoon. She made sure to hand Cliff and Robby an extra postcard and saluted her two favorite passengers, goodbye.

Chester's brother, Gray would be waiting for them outside the airport, after they had picked up their suitcases from the skycap, at least if everything was going as planned. As they knew from experience, waiting in line to point out your luggage to the skycap could take longer than expected especially as so many passengers confused their luggage for someone else's, particularly after several cocktails on board. Suitcases in hand, "Uncle G", as the boys called him, would pack the four of them into his car to drive them to Palm Springs, about two hours away, to his and Chester's parents' place, the home they had retired to from San Francisco, four years earlier.

It was a typical afternoon in Los Angeles for late December. The temperature was in the high 60s, nearly 70 degrees in fact, and there was plenty of sunshine! It was perfect to drive from the airport eastward into the desert in Gray Peterson's 1959 convertible Chevrolet Impala. He had bought the car just before Thanksgiving the previous year at the "Go See Cal" Worthington showroom in Los Angeles and it still looked new and shiny with its glossy black body and white canvas top which was, of course, down for the ride. Worthington, whose whacky television commercials Gray's film company helped bring to the Southern California market, was one of his best clients and one of the most popular car dealers in Los Angeles.

Westerns were, of course, popular at the movies and on television and his company produced a few of them. Gray Peterson and his company would be a natural for the Los Angeles ad firm to seek out to do a Western-inspired TV ad campaign featuring Cal in a white Stetson hat. Gray's company had nothing to do with the new local television hit *Cal's Corral* which broadcast country music live from the dealership to the LA viewing audience, but the success of that show every Friday and Saturday night made the advertising job his firm came up with that much easier.

The long drive through the desert to Palm Springs was quiet and at times lonely. A car, bus or truck was not unseen but the new highway leading from LA wasn't nearly as busy as the interstate highway that took them from Arlington to Washington, DC or up north to New York when they drove. They hadn't seen Uncle G in quite some time and in fact, he had gotten a little bit fatter since they had last seen him. Yet, that Peterson profile remained and although his face was a bit fuller, he still retained a somewhat keen German-English structure with his prominent and narrow nose. He looked a lot like his older brother Chester, as they both had blue eyes and sandy brown hair although the California sun had brightened Gray's so that he now appeared to be a blond.

Their father was taller and, even though six years older, was still better looking but both brothers could be called handsome. Seeing the two of them together it was more obvious that Robby took more after his father's English and German side while Cliff with his angular features, took more after Claire's with his more distinctive Dutch and Danish looks.

"What year is this car?" Chester asked Gray once he had settled in the front seat next to him.

"It's a '59," Gray replied.

Before he could say anything else, Robby proclaimed, "Cool car, love the fins!"

"I can just imagine my younger brother going into the dealership last year asking to see something cool in a 1960 model." He looked over smiling at his brother who was smiling back as he shifted the car into first gear and let the clutch up slowly as the car moved on its way out of the airport. "When they said, 'why sir, uh, we don't have any 1960 models in yet', Gray must have said, 'OK, so can you get one or two in by next week for me to choose from.'" Now both brothers were laughing and Gray, looking over his clip-on Ray Ban shades, counterpunched his brother.

"You think you know me so well!"

"Oh boy, this will be a long drive, I can already tell," Chester chided, as he mussed his brother's hair which had been neatly parted and combed to the left and formerly held in place by a sweet-smelling hair balm.

Sitting in the backseat with their mother who had by now exchanged her hat for a headscarf, the two boys were only sporadically involved in the conversation the adults were having about work and family, particularly about Chester and Gray's parents.

"So how was the flight, boys?" Gray asked over his shoulder later along the desert ride hoping to engage them as they looked out on the barren and stolid desert. "Jeff and Julie haven't flown yet, but we might take them to Hawaii sometime next year," he announced, referring to his own two children who would be joining them later in the week when he came back from LA with his wife just before New Year's Eve.

"How are Jeff and Julie enjoying the new neighborhood?" Claire wanted to know. The family had just recently moved from View Park to Ladera Heights, closer to Culver City where the film studios where he worked were located.

"Everyone is happy there," said Gray. "A few of the other families that got out of View Park since things started changing have moved into Ladera, so the kids know a lot of their schoolmates."

"How is the new house compared to that nice spread you had in View Park?" Chester wanted to know. Gray replied that Ladera houses were mostly newer, many of them including his having been built since 1950 compared to the 1930s house he sold in View Park. "Meg loves that the house is newer and that the shops and restaurants are closer, and I am a happy Joe since my drive time to work is shorter."

Once the conversation had lulled a bit, Gray turned the radio up and Cliff could hear the beginning of "To Know Him is to Love Him," a tune from last year that he still loved. The girl who sang it had a soft, sweet voice and he imagined that she might have felt about the guy she sang about the way he felt about Junior, when he let himself acknowledge his feelings for Junior. "To know, know, know him is to love, love, love him, just to see him smile makes my life worthwhile…" Cliff imagined the two of them dancing in his bedroom with his head on Junior's shoulder and each with their arms wrapped tightly around the other. He imagined that no one would walk in on them and they could dance, caress, and explore each other the way they had done on their brief opportunities when both were titillated and timorous at the same time!

Wouldn't it be fun to be alone with his colored boy in the California desert right now, where they could be unseen and undisturbed, Cliff imagined? Just as his mind was drifting to a concocted desert interlude, he chuckled to himself when the tune on the radio suddenly interrupting his sand dune rapture was "Lonely Teardrops", a hit from earlier in the year that Junior loved. Apparently, Claire heard him laugh. She turned and looked at her son and could see, through her cat eye sunshades, that he had an uneasy smile on his face.

Just as they were pulling into Palm Springs, they were coming upon The Comet which was a popular drive-through restaurant with a cool Space Age shape that really caught Robby's eye. The place was basically a silver diner with a long, extended comet-like shape which rose high above the ground making the restaurant look as if it was shooting across the sky. It hadn't been that long since they had taken their last meal on their transcontinental flight but, seeing Robby's excitement, Uncle G suggested that they stop for a soda before heading on to his and Chester's parents' place. His own kids liked coming to The Comet, so this was a stop he was used to, and he had almost figured out what made the hamburgers so juicy and the French Fries so tasty. He had concluded that they must be adding sugar along with salt! They all climbed into a booth, a chrome diner table with a white and blue shiny pattern on it which sparkled like the stars separating Claire, Chester and Cliff from Gray and Robby who sat on the other side.

Chapter 16

The week after Christmas both Wynn and Julia Mae had returned to work. Jeanne and Junior were old enough to be home alone and besides, both had work to do to keep them busy. Junior had picked up some extra shifts in the kitchen at the Horrschorns tearoom which was extra busy during the week between Christmas and New Year. He worked from noon until 4pm from Monday until Thursday, New Year's Eve. Jeanne was needed at home to help her mother with the final touches on dresses and gowns that she was hired to make for her private clients. Jeanne didn't share her mother's talent for sewing and making clothes, but she had been taught early on how to sew on buttons and bows where needed and also how to iron and press. At 13, Wynn wasn't thrilled with leaving her at home alone but many of the children in the neighborhood at her age were taking care of younger brothers and sisters while working parents were kept away from the house.

Jeanne enjoyed the rare pleasure of staying at home on a weekday and it also gave her the opportunity to see her boyfriend since everyone was out of school for the Christmas vacation. Although she was not to have him or any other visitor at the house without her parents or older brother there, the boy did visit once or twice that week, but Jeanne was not one who would do anything that her parents wouldn't want her to do. She and the boy had kissed and petted but that was as far as it went. He never pressed and she never teased.

One day her neighbor and friend Virginia who was one year older than Junior came to visit with her newborn baby, the baby that she was told by her parents that she had no choice but to take to a home in Washington, DC. Washington was where the homes for colored babies born out of wedlock were located. She begged her parents to let her bring the baby home for a few days, but she knew it couldn't live with them in their house in Hilldale. The nearly white baby, a girl, was named Arlene and she was a small, smiley baby who squirmed a lot.

Arlene had been born on Christmas Eve at Carver Hospital in the District and it would have been hard to drop her off on Christmas Day at the home just off North Capitol Street, not far from Armstrong High School. Her parents had arranged for the newborn baby to go there in the hopes that she would be adopted by someone. A half-white girl would be highly sought after and there was no question that Arlene would find a home with a colored couple who couldn't have their own children or desperately wanted a pretty, good-haired fair-skinned daughter. Virginia, who was herself a pretty girl, with skin the color of a pecan shell, had sworn that the white boy who gave her the baby loved and wanted to marry her.

Although he had seen her hardly at all during the pregnancy, she preferred to believe they might still continue a relationship. After all, she was hardly around much after she got pregnant because her parents put her in the high school for pregnant girls in DC and she wasn't allowed to be at their grocery store much in case someone would see that she was carrying. Virginia, although everyone called her "Gin", knew that he was going around with a girl from his high school, one whose father his father did business with.

Perry, the father, was the son of the man who owned the building that her parents ran a neighborhood grocery store out of in the colored section of Alexandria, near the railroad tracks. Gin worked in the store after school since she was thirteen along with her older brother and younger sister, at least once her sister was old enough. She had known Perry since she was 14 and he was 15 when he started to come to the store with his father and they would do work on the property or collect the rent. He was a tall, skinny, brown-haired boy, about 17. He wasn't bad looking and had a round face and wore his hair in a buzz cut.

Perry Cocceli had always preferred colored music and colored girls. Although it was bad enough for his parents to tolerate the first preference, they definitely did not tolerate the second and so he had to keep that one quiet, although it was still no secret to anyone. Italians were often even more splenetic when it came to Negroes than other whites. They felt that they were the stepchildren of the white family, with their often olive-

134

colored skin, energetic mannerisms and more unbuttoned way of life. They thought they had to fight hard to keep their place in a family which generally preferred more buttons buttoned.

Perry went to one of the other white high schools in Arlington, where he played on the basketball team. He was popular, especially with the girls at his school, yet Junior would occasionally see him in the neighborhood where he would visit Gin at her house when her family was all at the store. She would say she needed to work on schoolwork and, if anyone in the neighborhood looked suspicious at Perry coming or going from her house, she would say he was her tutor. It wasn't so surprising that a white kid would tutor a colored in Arlington, even before the two races had started going to school together. However, everyone knew where her head was buried when he was at her house and it wasn't in a book.

"She is a pretty child," Jeanne declared after Gin had given her Arlene to hold. Perry had said that too, after he finally saw his daughter at Virginia's house a couple days after Christmas while her family was all at their grocery store. Virginia could tell, though, that he wasn't complimenting the baby girl in the way that a proud father would but more because she had so many of his features. He was basically complimenting himself on making a pretty half-colored baby, Gin knew deep down inside.

"She will have a happy life and you should feel good knowing that she will be taken care of."

"I can take care of her myself," Gin countered, "but I know it will be better this way. I will be 17 in 1960 and I can get married," Gin noted, "but it will most likely be too late to get Arlene back."

"But then if you get married you can have as many children as you want," Jeanne reminded her friend. "You will have a name and so will they."

"Anyway," said Gin, "we have to leave now because I want to get her to the home before too late. I just wanted you to see her and how pretty she is."

"Well, she really is pretty," Jeanne confirmed. "She will be on the cover of *Jet* or *Sepia* one day for sure," she predicted, and thanked her friend for letting her see her newborn daughter just as she was about to give her up.

"How is Junior?" Gin asked as she was taking Arlene out of Jeanne's arms. "Is he getting along well at Arlington High?" Without waiting for Jeanne to reply, Gin went on to acknowledge that things were opening up and pretty soon being with someone white "would be more regular".

"I don't know," replied Jeanne. "I don't think Junior is going to be with a white girl. I don't think Carolyn Stanley would see it that way." Each of them laughed at this and they hugged each other before Gin left with her baby. Jeanne did wonder for a minute, though, what would be possible in the future for a half-white child born in 1959, almost 1960. It just might be that they would have all the opportunities in the world from here on out!

With her friend gone and her parents and Junior at work, Jeanne had the house to herself for about another hour before Junior got off the bus from downtown DC to come home. As she was done with all the chores Julia Mae had asked her to do with the newly made clothes for her clients for that day, Jeanne settled down on the living room sofa to watch *As the World Turns*, a soap opera that her Aunt Nellie had watched and talked about all the time. She watched it while doing the ironing or starting to prepare dinner at the Congressman's house with the lady of the house when she was home and by herself when she was not. Many domestics throughout the country learned how to act like fancy white women by watching those soap operas. Many also learned to hate themselves and their own lives. For many of the others, it reinforced what they were seeing played out right in front of their eyes every day, and that was how incredibly troubling these white people's lives could be!

As he did every day during the week when he worked afternoons washing dishes in Horrschorns tearoom, Junior stopped by the alterations shop to say hello to his mother, although they both knew the "old pale lady", as Julia and her crew called the new supervisor, didn't much like it. Julia Mae had just wanted to make sure her son had had a decent day and had not been confronted with any of the attitudes that many of the Negro men had to deal with at that store. Junior being young might be seen as an easy target. However, there was a waiter in the tearoom who had taken a shine to him. He was a blond-haired white man, probably no more than ten years older than Junior, if that.

This golden-haired garçon smiled at him all week and would find excuses to come into the kitchen just to make a casual glance at him. It wasn't typical for the waiters to talk to the dishwashers, almost all of whom were colored or Spanish. But this waiter who came on duty about the same time that Junior did had found a way to start a conversation with him that didn't make their communication seem overly conspicuous. He had told Junior that if he wanted a cigarette one evening after he got off from his waiter shift at six, they could go to his apartment up on 16th Street.

Junior imagined that this apartment up 16th must have a green door. He smiled, at least to himself when he thought of how he might carry on once he got behind that door, remembering the song from a few years earlier. Departing from his usual serious and precocious self, Junior let his mind wander when he allowed that door to open.

He had never expressed a strong interest in visiting this man's apartment, but he did wonder what it would be like to be alone with a tall, slender, attractive and grown white man who smiled at him a lot and always looked at him in a certain way. After all, this smiling Joe in the black slacks and crisp white shirt with the black bow tie was a grown man who didn't live with his parents and Cliff was a lil bit square except when he had his arms around Junior and his hands pulling at this or that. Then he was a tiger! Suddenly, Junior remembered the film *Boys Beware*! Be that warning as it may, he felt more curious about this man than he did cautious! The idea of going off with him didn't seem quite so sinister as it was supposed to, at least according to the film shown to boys his age in gym class.

Chapter 17

"Beautiful, just plain lovely!" Claire exclaimed as they pulled up to her husband's parents' new house in the old Tennis Club neighborhood near downtown Palm Springs. "Such a modern place and look at that mountain view," she added. Gray had sounded the horn just as they pulled up and out came the two elderly people who lived in the new and thoroughly modern house that the three adults would refer to as Mom and Dad, and Robby and Cliff as Gran and Grandad!

"Oh, how was the trip, welcome, welcome come on in you must be tired and ready to relax," said Gran all in one breath. She reached to hug her two sons, Chester first, then Gray and Claire after him. "These two handsome young men are all mine for the next few days? Well, how lucky am I." Gran beamed as she ran to hug both Cliff and Robby at the same time. She had not seen any of her east coast visitors, since three years earlier when they were still living in Ghana and traveled to London for the holidays. Gran and Grandad, whose names were Elsa and Chester, had flown to London to see them and spend the holidays together. Chester had been the first name of three generations of Peterson men. The one who owned this gorgeous three-bedroom ranch house with sloping roof in the California desert was Chester the II, making his son who had just arrived with his family, Chester the III. Number III had always been called "Sonny" in part because he was the son and in part because of his sandy-yellowish hair. Other than when he was with his parents, "Sonny" would never be used.

The house that Elsa and Chester moved to in 1955 had been newly built. It was part of an explosion of construction in Palm Springs. The two of them had loved the desert town since first coming to visit back in the late 1930s when things were just beginning to really develop. At the time, Chester worked for a bank in San Francisco where he had moved to from New England after college on the east coast. His mother had come from San Francisco but moved east where his father's family was from. An only child, upon her death, he came to take over his mother's house in Pacific Heights, a beautiful San Francisco Victorian, built right after the 1906 earthquake, that overlooked the Pacific Ocean. He started work with one of the biggest banks on the west coast, headquartered in the downtown Financial District, a bank that his family had had years of ties to.

But, after years of working in the bank and being part of civic society in San Francisco, he and Elsa, whose health would better favor an arid climate, decided to move to Palm Springs as they had loved it for years. The house they moved to was one of many newer ones built in one of the oldest communities in Palm Springs. They had been visiting what was called the Tennis Club area for years because of its popular tennis courts and because of the resorts that had formed around it. Lots of money was pouring into Palm Springs and Chester's bank had grown richer and richer as a result of the development boom.

This new house, "the polar opposite of the Beaux Arts on Baker," as Chester II called the house his sons grew up in, was all one single level, with floor to ceiling windows, dirt and gravel landscaping with snatches of greenery here and there including three tall palm trees, hence justifying the name "Three Palms" that Elsa had dubbed it. The house had a gorgeous crescent-shaped swimming pool in the back and a casita with two smaller bedrooms with a bath designed as a smaller replica of the main house.

"Father would love it also," said Claire. Her architect father thought of modern architecture as "fun and future fantasy" and had never designed many modern structures in his years of work but nevertheless appreciated the simplicity of the style. Definitely, the interior was to Claire and Sonny's liking as well with the tile floors, subtle colors of lime, mustard and aqua and gleaming silver appliances and fixtures. She had suggested some furniture designs to her mother-in-law before they moved into the new house and Elsa had hunted the shops of San Francisco and Los Angeles to find just the right pieces to populate Three Palms.

139

She settled on Paul McCobb, Jens Risom, Borg Morgensen and, Heywood-Wakefield for a few of the bedroom pieces. This combination of American and Scandinavian designers appealed to her because of the lines and styling of the furniture. Also, it mimicked her own pedigree. She wanted pieces, thanks to Claire's suggestion, that modeled the lines of the house and its design angles. A minimalist style did not mean that walls had to be bare either. Elsa had chosen several strategically placed bold paintings, mostly oil abstract paintings, on white canvas with lots of colors. There were a few of faces and of landscapes and buildings but even these were nearly all abstracts. Chester had always had a thing for bridges and there they were on the walls throughout the house. Bridges in front of towering skylines, bridges over water and bridges standing tall and alone. "We need something to remind us of San Francisco," Chester would always tell anyone who commented on the number of bridge paintings that floated on walls throughout the house.

Similarly, the lanai furniture was as well thought out. That large, white concrete tiled area needed to be a launching pad for spacecraft that could be lounged on while enjoying a swim or looking up at the stars. Elsa commanded three Salterini black flying saucer chairs, two with detachable chaise and drink table, a Bertoia table with six chairs including two diamond chairs and a white Woodard sofa. All the outdoor pieces were made of wrought iron and would withstand the hot desert heat.

"Wow, Mom," said Gray, "you got most of this patio furniture since I was last here."

"Of course," Elsa replied. "We had Sonny coming for New Year's Eve along with your family and we needed it."

"In fact, we're waiting for more pieces to arrive tomorrow," Chester acknowledged. "Your mother just ordered a new sofa from the Knoll shop in San Francisco which is supposed to arrive tomorrow," Chester said with a smile at the same time shaking his head back and forth.

"Don't forget about the Bertoia patio loveseat as well," Elsa piped in. "Too bad we couldn't have bought those pieces in Los Angeles but there is no shop there. I believe they're opening one next year, though," Elsa added.

"Yes, I heard that in New York over Christmas," Claire offered.

"They said their new west coast showroom opens in 1960."

"But we couldn't wait another few weeks or months," Chester concluded. "We needed to have these pieces now," he stated walking off toward the pool house with his grandsons. "Are you boys ready to see your room and take a swim too?"

By the time Chester, Claire and Cliff had awakened from their nap in the pool house, Robby was still doing laps in the pool and alternately resting on the Salterini chaise which Elsa had covered with a plastic cushion, Gray had left for the drive back to LA. He preferred not to drive through the desert once it was too dark. It was now 5:00 and it would start to get dark soon. Elsa had prepared to have cocktails and appetizers on the lanai with ice tea and lemonade for the boys. The dishes and glassware at Three Palms were not the same as the ones they had used in San Francisco. Gone were the heavy crystal wine glasses and bone china. Elsa's updates were replete with new and modern patterned glassware in colors of teal and aqua and solid color dinnerware to match. They had left their beautiful Edwardian furniture and also accoutrements like silverware and dinnerware in Pacific Heights. Only a few of their favorite smaller personal pieces made it to Palm Springs. Elsa liked to joke to friends that they had "left their art in San Francisco". Over the years, they had amassed quite a collection of Impressionist paintings and Elsa had a thing for French figurines from the 19th century.

After cocktails, with lemonade for the boys, they would go out for a meal although it was probably not likely that the East Coast Petersons would want to eat much after all the food they had been served on the long flight. In fact, they could have just stayed by the pool, but Elsa and Chester were anxious to show them Palm Springs after 5.00 and in fact, the East Coast visitors were curious to see what so many loved about the desert town. For Elsa and Chester, it was the way the sun went down in the mountains and cast a warm and friendly shadow over the prickly Saguaro cactus trees! It was the way a sultry day turned calm and cool at night and the stars came out proudly against the black sky as if they were celebrating the sun's retirement for that day. Also, it was the beauty and relative simplicity of the architecture compared to the ornateness and grandeur of their San Francisco neighborhood. If asked at that moment what they liked about the desert landscape, her grandsons might have said the *swimming pool*.

Who might they see from Hollywood out and about just before New Year's Eve? Claire and Chester knew that at least two of their favorite entertainers were in town because they were scheduled to see them perform on New Year's Eve at Palm Springs' hottest resort nightclub.

Chapter 18

Nellie had a big pot of collard greens boiling on the stove by noon on New Year's Eve. Even though she and her family had planned to be at a party at a nightclub on 11th Street, just off U Street in NW, they would still eat dinner before they arrived and would need food for the New Year's Day ritual of collard greens and black-eyed peas. Of course, Nellie being Nellie, she couldn't leave it at greens and peas, but she had to put a sweet potato pie in the oven as well. In fact, she also had made a pecan pie only because she had made several to sell and had some extra pecans left over. Nellie made pies and cakes to sell about five times a year. Certainly, always around the Christmas and New Year's holiday, but also for Thanksgiving, Easter and fourth of July. She also took orders for birthdays but only in the fall, winter and spring. She didn't like to use the oven too much in the summer. The hot summer sun in Washington, DC did enough baking for anybody!

"We'll be over at about eight this evening," Julia Mae said to her sister as she hung up the phone on Thursday early evening, the last day of 1959. She had left the department store at 4 pm to catch the DC Transit bus going across the Potomac to Arlington. Wynn was getting off from the Pentagon at 4pm also and would probably beat her home since he only had a few miles to drive. Nellie had a few days off because the Congressman and his family were still in the Midwest, but Talley would have to leave on Saturday, January 2 to bring them back to Washington. They wanted to be home by Sunday afternoon on the third. The second session of the 86th Congress was to begin on Wednesday, January 6 and it would be a busy year because of the Presidential election.

Nellie would need to be at the house in North Arlington on Sunday morning to make sure everything was ready for their return and to have lunch prepared for them. She would also make dinner too before she left to come home. Since they were missing watch night services to bring in the new decade, Julia Mae, Wynn, Junior, Jeanne and Nellie would all be at church on the first Sunday of the year. The Horrys, of course, at Mount Calvary in Arlington and Nellie at Florida Avenue Baptist, near 7th Street, where the two sisters had lived together since first coming to Washington in the late 1930s. They had come to live with an aunt when Julia Mae was about sixteen and Nellie soon to turn 21. Nellie had preferred to go to New York but their aunt, who was ailing, needed them to help her run her boarding house on 5th Street. They would have a place to stay, food to eat, which Nellie cooked and fun places to go where Negroes could stomp and strut, forget their troubles and get happy!

Jeanne and Junior were going to a dance in Washington with Jeanne's boyfriend and Carolyn Stanley. There was a social club at the church near Nellie's house that was sponsoring a young lady and gentleman's New Year's Eve party that would begin at 8:00 and end at 11:00, leaving time for parents to pick the young people up and still be somewhere by the stroke of midnight.

"Let me see how that dress looks on you so I can do any alterations before I start to get ready," Julia Mae said to Jeanne as she poked her head in her daughter's room after hanging up the call with her sister downstairs.

"It looks fine, Momma, I tried it on twice already."

"OK," replied Julia Mae, "if you say so, but I won't have any more time to work on it before we leave." Julia Mae had made a forest green party dress with a semi-full skirt due to the crinoline slip, lace collar and quarter-length sleeves for Jeanne for her last birthday but Jeanne had gotten a little "more ladylike" as her father described it over the year necessitating a slight alteration in the bust.

At 13, Jeanne was looking more like the attractive young woman she would clearly become. She and her boyfriend would drive with Wynn and Julia Mae to Georgetown and Junior and Carolyn would drive with Carolyn's parents. Since the two Horry children would need to come back to Nellie's house by 10:00, their respective dates' parents had to pick them up from the church social. Jeanne and Junior needed to care for their young cousins while the adults would be reminiscing to the tunes of Billie Holiday at the King's Court on 11th Street. Their mother's brother, Horace, was in town with his two young daughters and his girlfriend. Billie Holiday wouldn't be there, since she had passed away back in the summer, too soon many thought, but her music still lived on through the vocals of some gal who sang like her and even resembled her a bit. James Brown and the Famous Flames were said to be in town and many times big stars would make a surprise visit to the King's Court, and what better night than New Year's Eve?

The King's Court, like the Bohemian Caverns and all the other clubs on and around U Street that night, was packed with plenty of primped and preened colored people. People who always enjoyed a good party and an opportunity to show up in nice clothes and drive nice cars and drink good booze. But this New Year's Eve was even more special! It was more than the turn of another year, it was the turn of a decade.

Whether they said it or not most of these people had never felt more hopeful for themselves, their children and their place in this world as 1959 gave way to 1960. The pig was finally being done in by the rat. At least, that's the way the Chinese saw it! The pig was slow, sloppy, lumbering and oafish! That's the way pigs were perceived by those who had grown up around them, particularly in the south. The rat, on the other hand, for all his dirty ways, was a sleek and fast city slicker who knew how to get into places he wasn't wanted and get what he came for and scare the hell out of anyone who encountered him in the process!

The sky was the limit everywhere you looked and, even though some may have been afraid to say it too loud for fear of a dream going up in smoke, almost everyone wanted to soar high above the barriers that had been keeping them down. Perhaps that is why the ceiling of King's Court was full of red, white, yellow and bright green balloons and there were lights strung across the ceiling that mimicked twinkling stars. A big sign on the back wall of the stage that read "High Hopes for 1960", a take-off of Frank Sinatra's popular song that everyone was still singing since its recent debut in a movie.

They would let the good times roll, roll into a new decade and a new way of life! Nineteen sixty had been dubbed the world of tomorrow!

By the time Carolyn's father had come to pick her up from Nellie's house it was nearly 10:30 pm. Traffic coming across the bridge from Virginia was heavy because lots of people on that side of the Potomac had planned to greet 1960 somewhere in Washington, DC. Jeanne's boyfriend had been picked up by an older cousin from the church youth party, a cousin that lived nearby in Foggy Bottom at a house where the young man would spend New Year's Eve with his family and friends. The small cousins were already in bed and Junior and Jeanne were playing records with the volume low while the television was on in the background. The kids had been dancing to Chubby Checker, Sam Cooke, Fats Domino and the Platters and, of course, the adults were dancing along with them pretty much all evening until Junior and Jeanne returned home. By then, it was time for the small cousins to go to bed, but the adults promised them that their cousin Junior would wake them up at midnight.

While the adults were out at the New Year's Eve show in Black Broadway, which was never totally Black because there were almost always white men with white women, white men with colored women and white women with colored men, Junior, Jeanne and their Uncle Horace's kids would be watching Guy Lombardo's New Year's Eve 1959 television special *All Eyes to the Future*.

Chapter 19

The second day of the New Year in Palm Springs was a bit cool as the Petersons piled into Gray's car to head back to Los Angeles International Airport for their tourist class flight back to Washington National. It was a 12-noon flight which meant that they would arrive in Washington around 9 or 10 pm with the time change. Despite the temperatures in the low 50s Robby pleaded with his uncle to put the top down as they drove through the desert for the two-plus-hour trip back to L.A. for their flight. No one complained about this because the dry winter air in the desert just smelled so appealing.

They had said goodbye to the family they were leaving behind in California, which at this point was Chester's mother and father. Gray's wife and kids, who had been in Palm Springs for the New Year's Eve celebrations, had left on Friday to go back to L.A. Gray drove them back and had promised to come back early on Saturday morning to take his brother and family back to the airport in order to save their father from the long drive back and forth. His eyesight wasn't so great anymore and he got tired quickly these days. While the two sons were headed toward L.A., Chester and Elsa would lounge on the newly arrived patio furniture and reminisce about all that had happened thus far in the new year that they had brought in together. As the sun was beginning to rise in the desert, these memories would warm them even more!

Claire had timed the departure to be at the airport when her brother Peter's airplane landed from Honolulu. Peter and his friends had arrived the evening before, but he wanted to spend the night in Los Angeles before his onward flight to Chicago. His friends had boarded an earlier jet to O'Hare, but he waited to see his sister, brother-in-law and two nephews at the Pan American terminal before his 1 pm flight headed east.

"Well, I certainly can't say enough about 1960, so far," said Claire from the backseat of the Impala on the way back to L.A. "And I really liked 1959," she added with laughter.

"Yes, it was great to be out here with Mom and Dad and the rest of the family," her husband agreed, over his shoulder from the front seat. "Seeing Gray and Meg and the kids was just super!"

"That New Year's Eve show at the Barracuda Club with Frank Sinatra, Peter Lawford and Ella Fitzgerald was just a dream," Claire gushed. "I so love the way she sings Skylark, and their duet of The Lady is a Tramp was pretty schnazzy too."

"Was it like they did it on the TV show?" Cliff asked.

He had enjoyed watching the *Frank Sinatra Show* with his mother and sometimes his father would watch too. Ella Fitzgerald was one of the few colored singers who would appear on the show, but it was clear that she and Frank enjoyed performing together. She had put her arm in his several times throughout the performance and he hugged and kissed her cheek often. They even duetted together. That was rare. A colored woman and a white man singing together for an all-white audience. Never would it be a colored man singing with a white woman. It was likely, the Petersons imagined, that Ella had stayed at Sinatra's house in Palm Springs since they weren't sure as to whether any of the hotels would host even her!

"Yes, that evening was a great way to bring in the New Year," Gray agreed, joining the conversation, "and the champagne and Baked Alaska was pretty good too." A smile was breaking out on Chester's face even before his brother had finished his New Year's Eve memory. "I thought Mother would pass out from that champagne just as Peter Lawford was heading over to our table to kiss Claire's and Meg's hand." Everyone in the car got a good laugh as they recalled the moment at the Barracuda Club that came just after the stroke of midnight when the new decade made its debut in the desert.

"Mother was truly among the stars in more ways than one by that time," Gray acknowledged, laughing as hard as he could while talking at the same time. "I was so happy you were sitting next to her, Sonny, otherwise I think she might have fallen face first on the table just as Peter Lawford reached for her hand."

No one was listening to the radio during the beginning of the trip to the airport because they were having so much fun talking about the New Year's Eve week in Palm Springs. Even Cliff and Robby had something to say about the festivities. They had watched Guy Lombardo on television. The band leader was too old for Robby but both he and Cliff did enjoy the scenes from Times Square as the show shifted from the Roosevelt Hotel to the throngs of people waiting for 1960 in Times Square. It probably wasn't very cold that Thursday night for those thousands of people, Robby thought as he watched. It hadn't been very cold the entire time they were in Manhattan. But even if it was cold, it wouldn't have nipped the excitement! People either went to Times Square for events like this already excited or they got excited by what they encountered when they got there. More than likely, it was a bit of both!

The two boys pretended they were still in New York as they watched the ball drop, in Times Square on the Magnavox television at Three Palms. A year, but not just a year, a decade had come to an end! Those thousands of people would walk away onto a blank slate. They would be able to take hold of this new piece of clay called 1960 and shape it into anything they wanted!

"Will Uncle Peter have Christmas gifts for us from Hawaii?" Robby asked his mother.

"We'll need to wait and see once we get there, won't we," Claire replied giving her youngest son a gentle side eye glance.

"Of course, he will, silly," Cliff chided his brother. Cliff rarely got an opportunity to make Robby look naïve even though he was nearly six years older. Robby seemed to almost always be a step ahead of Cliff and there were times when Cliff wondered if Robby knew more or had seen more than he let on. Just the thought of this made his heart race a bit but it also put thoughts of Junior into his head. They were the usual thoughts, of the two of them being close to each other, touching, groping and feeling each other's heartbeat up close.

Thoughts of them pulling at each other's clothes and of hands reaching for parts of each other that no one would ever believe that they'd allow the other to touch. Unless Robby of all people knew that the two of them had touched those parts of each other. Cliff's heart beat even faster the more he thought about it. He had to turn his attention to the desert as if to bury his excitement in the sand. For Cliff, the drive back to Los Angeles seemed longer than the drive out as he tried to keep his thoughts of Junior down so that he could fully appreciate the last hour or so in the desert.

"Hey, there's Uncle Peter," Cliff pointed out to his parents, having seen him first in the Pan American terminal. Peter was sitting in the waiting room smoking a cigarette and talking with a husband and wife who, as it turns out, were waiting for a flight to Washington. The husband worked in the White House on Vice President Nixon's staff. Peter found out earlier in their chat that he had been with the Vice President ever since he was a senator from California.

"Uncle Peter, we're here," Cliff hollered, much to Claire's dismay.

"Be quiet, Cliff, Peter is talking with people. Please don't be rude!"

But, by that time Cliff, and Robby too had run over to their uncle, Robby more because he was curious about the shopping bag that lay next to Peter's legs. "Oh, it's my two nephews and they brought my sister and brother-in-law," Peter explained to the couple. "They live outside Washington over in Arlington and Chester works for the State Department. You all should meet."

By this time Claire and Chester were walking over to the black Naugahyde four-seater tandem bench with chrome base that Peter was sitting on with the couple, although by now he was standing up. "Hello, Sis, Mele Maliki Maka!" He said this as he reached out to grab Claire in an embrace as he kissed her cheek.

"Mele Maliki Maka to you too, whatever that means," Claire responded.

"It means Merry Christmas in Hawaiian," Peter explained. "I don't know how to say Happy New Year, otherwise I would have said that instead."

Chester laughed as he extended his hand to his brother-in-law and said, "Whatever it is, I'm sure it sounds more exotic than Happy New Year!"

"Peter, do you remember my brother Gray?" Chester inquired. "He just drove us all the way from my parents' place in Palm Springs and just had to see the new Pan American terminal before heading home to his wife and family." The two brothers-in-law shook hands as they hadn't seen each other in years.

"Well, it is a beautiful terminal, in fact the new design of the airport is pretty spectacular," Peter noted. "This, of course, is just since the jets started flying in and out of L.A. at the beginning of the year!" Peter corrected himself. "I mean, at the beginning of last year! Anyway," he went on, "Claire and Chester, you should meet your some-what neighbors," Peter quipped turning to the couple he had been talking with who had been sitting quietly and smiling at everyone in between brief exchanges between themselves. "This is my sister Claire and her husband Chester," Peter told the pair. "I don't think we ever exchanged names ourselves. As you may have heard, I'm Peter."

The couple introduced themselves to everyone and told Claire and Chester that they lived in Dupont Circle, just off Connecticut Avenue. The Petersons knew the area well as a few of Chester's colleagues from State lived around there. "Yes, I am familiar with the neighborhood," he acknowledged. "We get over there for parties from time to time."

"In fact," Claire acknowledged, "we lived over near Columbia Road off 19th Street when we were first married." It was a wonderful neighborhood, she went on. "We were there until our oldest son started school and then we moved over to Arlington. He loved playing in that park, in fact."

"Yes, such a peaceful place yet close to shops and restaurants as well," Chester noted. Claire had offered to tutor some of the children at the nearby colored elementary school when they lived there. From time to time, she got to help them with their reading and writing. Although there were some colored parents, as well as other white ladies, who offered to help as well.

Uncle Gray, in the meantime, had been saying goodbye to Cliff and Robby as he was preparing to get back to his car to leave having seen what he came to see. "Well, Claire, Sonny, I will leave you in the hands of Peter and the swankiness of the Pan American Airways terminal now and bid you a wonderful trip back home. It was great to see you all after so long and next time, me, Meg and the kids will need to show up in Washington."

"Bye-bye, Gray, and thanks so much for the chauffeur service,"

Claire said, hugging her brother-in-law. "It was so lovely to see you all again after so long."

Chester chimed in similarly shaking his younger brother's hand and then bringing him in for a goodbye hug. "We will hold you to the promise to come visit soon. Don't let Cliff go off to college and you still haven't shown up."

"Well, don't you run back off to Africa before I do show up," Gray admonished with a smile as he headed off, waving.

"So what's in that bag, Uncle Peter?" Robby couldn't hold himself back from finally asking. Peter was a bit distracted as it was clear the couple was preparing to head toward the jetway to board their flight to DC but not before the husband had exchanged business cards with Peter and Chester.

"Perhaps we can all meet for cocktails at the Shoreham or some place," the Nixon aide suggested.

"Perhaps we'll be working for the same boss next year so you can give me some tips," Chester joked as the couple was gathering their suitcases to leave. Definitely it ran through both Chester and Claire's mind that, if Nixon became President later in the year, this could be a very valuable contact. Even for an advertising man like Peter this was true. So, with these two possibly beneficial but also nice "near neighbors" about to board their flight, Claire got to ask her brother, without any interruptions, "Yes, so what is in that bag?"

Peter had neatly wrapped a stash of brightly colored packages in the shopping bag for his two nephews and for his sister and brother-in-law. Claire asked her sons to wait until they got on board their flight to open their gifts so that there wouldn't be wrapping paper all over the terminal floor. She reminded her brother that he would have a package or two waiting for him once he got back to Chicago. She had mailed off a couple of gifts for him from New York while he was off in Honolulu with his friends. She was careful not to ask too much about the friends because she suspected that he would be judicious in his responses. She knew that he had traveled with a male friend that he worked with and a girlfriend of theirs.

They had to leave for their flight soon and they had to get to the United terminal to find it. But they all wanted to hear about Hawaii and to see some of Peter's Polaroids. He wanted to hear about Palm Springs too and Claire and Cliff couldn't stop talking about Frank Sinatra and Ella Fitzgerald. Never mind that Cliff wasn't actually at the Barracuda room that night. Peter had taken a number of Polaroid photos of the beach and the rock formation known as Diamond Head. He showed them several photos of young surfers near Diamond Head as well as the hotel they stayed at and some local Hawaiian luaus that they got to attend. Claire managed to see his friends in a few of the photos and thought that his male colleague was handsome, as handsome as her brother. The girlfriend was attractive, she thought, but didn't appear to match his colleague in looks the way she and Chester did. She kept those impressions to herself, though.

"I hope this is something to eat in here," Robby warned his uncle.

"Don't worry, I think you'll like it," Peter replied. "You too, 'Cliffy'," which was his nickname for his favorite nephew. He tried not to show his favoritism but Cliff, and Claire too, knew it.

"Well, if we stay here too much longer, we may as well go home with you," Chester joked looking at Peter. "It's about time we head over to our terminal and get ready to fly back. Maybe Anne will be on this flight too, Cliff!" Cliff brought a slight smile to his face and his cheeks became a little flushed because of his father's comment.

"Did Cliff meet a girl on the flight?" Peter asked.

"Oh, it's not a girl, it was a stewardess who showered him and Robby with attention and ice cream," Claire interjected. "I doubt she'll be on this flight."

"Well… it will be nice to see her if she is," Cliff mustered.

"I'm sure it will," Peter retorted. "If for nothing other than the extra ice cream!" He winked at his nephew who seemed to blush even harder at that point. "Don't forget to call me tomorrow to discuss that school project you mentioned to me before Christmas… if you're not too overcome from the flying experience. I liked some of your ideas and I am curious to see what you came up with so I can help you sell it to the teacher and class."

"Will do," Cliff confirmed with his uncle, "I will call you on Sunday."

"We better get going, now. We don't want to miss the flight," Chester admonished his family. "Besides, Peter probably wants to scour the waiting room to see who else he can strike up a friendly conversation with."

Peter looked at his brother-in-law with a grimace and after clearing his throat, replied that he had probably talked to just about everyone there was to talk to already. "Besides, I will need to save my lungs for at least two cigarettes on the flight and out-talking who ever my chatty seatmate might happen to be."

Claire chuckled, kissed her brother goodbye and grabbed her husband and youngest son to head off to the United terminal for their flight back to Washington National Airport. The January 5, 1960 *Look* magazine that she took from Elsa and Chester after it had just arrived in the mail was under her arm and would be the object of her attention for the beginning of the flight, probably before and after the lunch was served. The cover showed a rocket ship about to blast off and the headlines offered a story about Americans' hopes and dreams for "the soaring 60s"!

Claire, like many people that she knew, had been thinking about issues like this and was curious to know what the nationwide poll of other Americans would say about what people were thinking as the decade turned. What better time, she thought, to ponder these questions than while floating high in the sky for hours while the problems down below seemed to be buried under the big, white clouds that obscured any of the dismalness that might lie below on the surface.

Certainly, many people's thoughts were turning toward space and what existed beyond earth. Of course, for other people, the focus here on earth was on gaining more space! They wanted to expand beyond the borders that had been "established" for them. For those for whom much access was denied, there was more concern about what was going on right here on the ground.

Chapter 20

The holiday assignment for civics class was to come up with a "hero" for the 1960s that almost every American could rally around. The hero was to be unveiled to the class on the Wednesday of the first week after Christmas vacation. Junior had spent a good bit of time over the two-week holiday thinking about his "hero". He had decided that it would be a sports figure, probably a baseball player, and figured his father would be happy with the opportunity to help him with this assignment. He and Wynn had talked about it many times over the holiday, particularly over the long drive back and forth from Charlotte. In fact, everyone had taken the time to offer their suggestions and advice during this time and Junior was pretty sure he had his assignment planned out. He would spend the Saturday and Sunday before school started to put his hero creation on paper and write up the "news story" on who this hero is and why he is the Great American Hero of the early 1960s.

Cliff was in the same class and therefore had the same assignment. Junior wondered what Cliff would come up with but, owing to the fact that it was the Christmas holiday and Cliff had been out of town since before Christmas, the two had not spoken. He was certain, though, that Cliff wouldn't come up with a sports hero since he was no good at sports. Not that Junior was an All-American athlete either but at least he had a father who could help him out. From what little Junior had seen of Mr Chester Peterson, almost always in his starched white shirt, striped tie and dark suit with black shoes always shined until they gleamed, some colored man working in the basement of the State Department must be responsible for that, Junior figured, no image of an athlete popped into his head.

But how would a baseball player be the kind of hero he wanted to portray, Junior thought? After all, even though all the Major League Baseball teams had one colored player on the roster, and this, only within the last five months, what message would a baseball player send that he wanted to get across? Even the hometown team, the Washington Senators had only at the beginning of the year signed their first colored player, at least their first colored American player! Unfortunately for many, the Cuban guy signed in '54, although "black as coal" didn't count. He was not home grown.

But, with further thought on the matter, Junior had heard a bell ring in his head! He had his hero and 1960 was the perfect time for him to dance into the spotlight! Brick Springfield would emerge as the "knockout" hero of the upcoming summer Olympics in Rome! As envisioned by Junior, Brick is a tall, strong blond boxer from Philadelphia, the City of Brotherly Love, who would knock out a Russian boxer in the first round of their match, earning him a gold medal as a light heavyweight. The fact that he knocks out a Russian, who, at the time, was touted to be the best young boxer in the world, makes him a hero, certainly an American hero! America needed a win against the Soviets, and nothing said victory better than a Russian on his back seeing stars flashing before his eyes. It was far more victorious than having one soaring among the stars of outer space in a rocket. The US was having much trouble getting a rocket ship into space! But the Soviets weren't.

True, the US had launched Pioneer 4 back in March and that had made it *near* the moon but the Russians had gotten even closer in January with their Luna rocket! But Junior wasn't thinking about going off into space anyway. No one in his family, church or neighborhood was talking about that.

Most of the invention of "Brick" came from Junior. Wynn suggested that he make his boxing champion a Negro because, since his childhood, Wynn had known only colored boxing champions. It was one of the few arenas in which Negro men excelled. Jack Johnson was a champion at the time he was an infant. Joe Louis was the champion during his teens and twenties. "Many would call Sugar Ray Robinson the greatest fighter right now," he told Junior. "Why do you need to make your hero a white man?" Junior, like every other colored person in America, was aware of the legacy of Negro boxers. But he also realized that a colored boxer would not be considered a hero at Arlington High School. Even if some of his classmates could accept it, his civics teacher, Mr Rakowski would not swallow it. His hero had to be *portrayed* as white. He had to have blond hair. He had to be unmistakably white! In his heart and soul, though, Junior dreamed of Brick as a Negro!

But, thought Junior, and he let Wynn in on the joke, he would give his hero the last name of Springfield because it was the hometown of Abraham Lincoln. Besides, there were thousands of Springfields throughout America, and it was a name that white people recognized and felt comfortable with. "I see, mister, make the whites feel comfortable," said Wynn. "I see what you doing!"

Wynn reminded his son that the young fighter Cassius Clay was likely to go to Rome in September and would likely come home with that medal that he was putting in the hands of Brick Springfield, to which Junior nodded his head in agreement. They laughed at this and so did Julia Mae who had listened in as they were plotting out the assignment. "This way it will make it easier to accept the reality when they are sucker punched into the fantasy that they need to believe, Pop." Junior smirked.

"See, I told you." Julia Mae chuckled. "My son is gon' lead us to a new day! Go ahead and make Brick as white as he needs to be, boy! We all know the truth and it shall be revealed soon enough."

"Yes Momma, you're right," answered Junior. "Now I just need someone who can draw to sketch Brick Springfield on the page."

Chapter 21

The United Airlines flight back to DC was much like the flight from New York to L.A. There was all the food, the drinks and the constant attention to every comfort of the passengers by the stewardesses. Both Cliff and Robby liked their postcards but not as much as the ones they got en route to Los Angeles. After all, they lived in Washington, or the nearby suburbs and they could drive by the White House, the Capitol or the Washington Monument anytime they wanted to, so the postcard of a United jet flying over the Washington monument, meant less to them than one of the same jet, flying over the sign painted in big white letters and nestled into the hillside announcing Hollywood!

But nevertheless, they thought they would put the postcards to use by, at their mother's suggestion, writing thank you notes to their grandparents Elsa and Chester for the Christmas gift of a ticket to California, which was no cheap gift. They would write their Uncle Peter on regular stationery to thank him for the Aloha shirts that each received and the candy too. Peter had given Claire a lovely necklace and there was a handsome cigar case for "Sonny" carved from monkey wood, not that Chester needed another one.

By the time they arrived home from National Airport late that evening, in a taxicab they had heard the news that Senator John Kennedy had announced his run for President earlier that day from a Congressional hearing room. It was a Saturday and only the second day of the new year but it was nevertheless newsworthy. Claire Peterson smirked as she recalled the ad for the new Plymouth that she had seen in the *Look* magazine aboard the plane. "Suddenly… it's 1960," it read. Yes, it was indeed! In fact, that ad had been appearing in the magazines for at least three years, Claire remembered. It was to serve as a drumbeat telling all that the future was almost here and it was going to be one filled with big changes. Well, here it was and undoubtedly the big changes were right around the corner or perhaps, up in the air!

Upon hearing the news of Kennedy's intention to run, she and Chester both chuckled as they recalled the couple they had met through Peter at the airport in L.A. and imagined what they must be thinking. The husband who works for Vice President Nixon would highly likely have a busy year on his hands. Nixon hadn't announced yet, but everyone knew he was running on the Republican ticket to succeed his "boss", Ike.

Right now, there were two Democrats running for their party's nomination since Senator Hubert Humphrey had made the announcement on the day before New Year's Eve. Surely, Nixon would be announcing soon. At this moment, Claire and Chester's money would go on Nixon over Kennedy or Humphry. They liked much of what they knew of the young senator from Massachusetts, but like many in and around Washington, especially those involved in government, the thinking was that Nixon would most likely succeed Eisenhower as President.

"Let's not toss his business card away," Claire admonished her husband regarding the Nixon aide who had given him his contact information at L.A. X. "We just might want to give a dinner party sometime this spring and invite them over."

Cliff was up early on the Sunday morning before school was to start for the first day of the new year. He had already tried on his Hawaiian-made Aloha shirt that he got for Christmas. In fact, he would soon call his Uncle Peter to discuss his work assignment for civics class that was due on Wednesday. But, given that it was an hour earlier in Chicago, he thought that he would wait until after breakfast before doing so. As he wrote the text for his Hero of 1960 character, he thought of how Junior might look in that new shirt. It was exotic and so was he! Of course, it wasn't African; Cliff knew African clothes very well, but that didn't mean that Junior's medium chocolate skin wouldn't look good in this shirt, with all the palm trees, boats and blue sky on it. The color of blue would definitely go well against that chocolate brown skin, Cliff thought.

He wondered at what point he would see Junior at school on Monday. They had two classes together and one of them, the civics class, met on Monday, Wednesday and Friday. So he would see him in there just before lunch and maybe then they could plan to meet in the basement after school. He was certain that Junior had wanted that as much as he did. Arlington High was a big school with lots of students and it seemed easy to move around without being noticed as a result.

In fact, Cliff was surprised that the boys and girls that everyone knew fooled around with each other didn't go to the basement to do it. But then again, they could always go to the park, to a car or perhaps to the home of one or the other if the parents or housekeeper wasn't around to see it. There were other boys who probably fooled around with each other too; Cliff had been eyed by a few of them since he had been at Arlington High, but it was different for them. They could go to each other's house and each other's room without anyone suspecting anything. Even though Junior had been at his house many times, it wasn't really the same thing, and both knew the difference. Junior was never really a guest in Cliff's house. He was there to deliver a service.

"So have you decided on a name for your astronaut hero?" Peter asked his nephew during the phone conversation later that morning.

"What do you think about Whitey Powers?" Cliff asked, proud that he had thought of that on his own.

"Hey, that sounds great, sounds like a real astronaut and definitely the name of an American hero," said Peter approvingly. "Can't you see him floating in space looking for Martians and other aliens?"

Cliff laughed at this and said, "Well, part of his story is that he gets lost in space and can't be found for about a week while he just floats around. Finally, Space Control locates his rocket ship and brings him back to Earth. In the meantime, he has made all these discoveries and put American flags on as many planets as possible."

"Well, of course," Peter retorted, "that's what makes him a hero. I think that sounds great, young man. You're onto something here." Peter asked Cliff how he envisioned Whitey looking and told him about some magazines he could check to get some ideas. "I see him as looking a bit like you, Uncle Peter, underneath his space helmet, that is, kind of tall, All-American-looking!" Besides, everyone in Arlington had seen the introduction of the Mercury 7 astronauts back in early April on the evening news. The story also made the front pages of major newspapers on the next day, a Friday morning. Part of Cliff's introduction of Whitey

160

would be that he was one of the astronauts introduced to be the first to be launched into space as part of the new organization, the National Aeronautics and Space Administration's ambitious plans to conquer the moon and the stars!

"Well, what an honor that he looks like me" his uncle replied. "I guess going through Whitey is about the only way I'll ever get into outer space. By the way," Peter said before ending the phone conversation, "I would have brought you a surfboard from Hawaii instead of an Aloha shirt, but it wouldn't have fit on the plane."

Cliff laughed at his uncle's parting comment. "It would have no problem fitting in a rocket, though," he answered before hanging up.

Back at work on Monday morning, Chester observed that things were moving at a quick pace at the State Department. He had been on vacation since before Christmas and lots had been happening on the Africa Desk. Cameroon had become independent of France on the first of the year and it was more than likely that a string of French or British colonies, particularly on Africa's west coast, would be fighting for independence as the year wore on. Chester had done a great job as an American attaché in Ghana, his superiors thought. Up until he and his family left Accra in 1958, about a year after the country became independent of Great Britain, he was on a list of Foreign Service Officers being considered for higher positions, especially in the wake of the growing independence movements in colonial Africa.

He knew that this could mean a position as Deputy Chief of Mission for one of the new countries. The only issue was having to move back to Africa at a time that his boys were growing up and one would soon be going to college. Besides, America was on the move too and we were heading into outer space! Was this the time to move the family away to a region that was so lacking in the very things that his boys needed to be around at this time? He and Claire had been talking about this and how he would respond if asked to move away. They could ask one set of grandparents to look after Robby and Cliff for a few years while he and Claire went back off to Africa, more than likely Claire's folks in Rochester. After all, this would be an excellent opportunity for his career and one day it undoubtedly would facilitate his promotion to ambassador. He didn't doubt he would do a good job as Deputy Chief of Mission.

Claire, of course, could have stayed behind in the States. Many diplomat wives did. But he knew his wife would have wanted to be with him. She helped him in many ways and, he needed her! Certainly, he depended on her! She "directed" his life as she had confided to many friends over the years. He never disagreed. It was how they were both made, and it worked for them just as it had for his mother and father and probably on and on before that. It also worked for many of the couples they knew. The men were at the helm but that didn't mean they were keeping things afloat, necessarily!

Despite all the thought they had put into it, Chester and Claire had not come to a decision. At any rate, they wouldn't be moving anywhere before the end of the school year. Chester's two-year stint back in Washington was about to be over before the new year ended and even though he could stay in Washington since his knowledge of Africa was useful at headquarters in Foggy Bottom, his career might be further advanced by going back abroad, the nagging thought came back. But now, things were further up in the air! Cameroon had just become independent. It was a French-speaking country and he had worked mostly in English-speaking places. Although Chester spoke French quite well, dealing with the French government officials during the transition from colony to independence was different from dealing with the British. At least, this is what he had heard from his colleagues at State. But, come the next break for independence of a former British colony, and everyone knew that Nigeria, one of the largest colonies in Africa, would soon be marching to independence, his star could soon be on the rise back in Africa, just as America itself was reaching for the stars!

Chapter 22

The first Monday of the new year was cold in Washington, DC. It was the kind of weather that made some colored people feel that their bones were aching whether they were or not. The summer weather "soothed" bones while the cold made them cross!

Two of the ladies in the alternations room aside from Julia Mae had spent some time in the south over the Christmas holiday and the conversation couldn't help but turn to how cold it was outside and how much they enjoyed the warmer holiday. One of them had brought in a copy of a women's magazine that showcased the new spring styles for 1960 and the women all took turns leafing through the issue as if looking at the short and three-quarter-sleeved dresses and suits would make them feel warmer!

"Which one of these dresses are you gon' copy first, JH?" one of the women asked, with laughter.

"Whichever one they want," Julia Mae replied without missing a beat. "I sew to suit," she quipped.

"Hey, that could be your slogan when you open your own shop," the woman said winking at Julia Mae.

"I have no plans for that now and I certainly wouldn't talk about it here," she acknowledged. Their boss had happened not to be in her office at the time as she had gone to the café to get a muffin and cup of coffee. This is the reason they were talking so freely. Since she had arrived the previous fall, their conversations were not nearly as frank or as fun unless she was away.

This did make their work less enjoyable than it was before she came to be their boss, but the ladies managed to make it work. When she came back into the vicinity of their conversation, the topic would switch back to the weather and how they had spent the holidays until she had the need to talk with them about some work instructions.

Arlington High was abuzz with excitement on that first Monday back to school! The teachers seemed to be as animated as the students and everyone wished each other a Happy New Year and expressed high hopes for 1960. Junior was certainly rising with excitement as second period approached. The glow on his soft chocolate brown face almost matched the sheen on his cordovan loafers that had come as a Christmas gift from his Aunt Nellie and Uncle Talley. He wore them with a pair of brown wool slacks cuffed at the ankle and a green wool cardigan with a marigold button-down shirt peeking through. As with most of her son's outfits, Julia Mae had orchestrated this "look".

Civics was usually among his favorite subjects and, despite how much he felt ignored by the teacher, he still liked the class and what he learned. Besides, this was the first time he would see Cliff after two whole weeks. Even though neither had arrived at class yet, he could already see Cliff in his mind. He would probably be wearing a plaid flannel shirt with a well-ironed pair of blue jeans and either a pair of shined black brogans or his brown penny loafers with white socks. His hair would be rising on his head in a pomaded crown and his blue eyes would be sparkling.

They didn't sit that close to each other; both sat near the back but not in the same row as Cliff sat to the right about two rows ahead. Junior could always see him from behind as he did this morning now that they were both in class. He smiled to himself as he realized how right he was about what Cliff would be wearing and how he would look. And as usual Cliff turned around as if looking at something on the back wall but really beholding the brown boy that made him beam each time he saw his face, even though their eyes met each other's only for a few seconds before both withdrew their glances. Cliff felt his heart beat faster for those few seconds and Junior wondered if anyone else could hear the pounding in his chest as he looked at Cliff for that flash of time that had to make up for a fortnight of vacancy.

They sometimes spoke quickly at the beginning of class but usually no extended conversation. There were other boys who spoke in passing with Junior but for the most part, he had no real friends in that class. None of the other colored students were in that particular class. One of the girls had transferred to take a home economics class that she had been encouraged to take since it was being dropped later in the day when it had originally been scheduled for.

Cliff did have classmates that he was friendly with. One of them, Pamela, he knew liked him in that way that teenage girls like teenage boys. She always smiled at him and made an effort to engage him in that class and in the history class that they were both in. Pamela didn't live too far from Cliff and often saw him on the school bus that picked them up in their fancy North Arlington neighborhood and dropped them off at high school. But there were a few fellows too that Cliff would be friendly with although he never invited any over to his house or went to the home of any of them, a fact which distressed his parents because they wanted him to socialize more.

There was a family in the neighborhood that the Petersons were close to who had a teenage son and daughter that Cliff did visit and who came to the house to visit him. These kids went to private school in Washington. They were pretty much the only two whom he cared to be around and opened up to, aside from Junior, of course. Although Pamela and one boy in his civics class tried hard to gain his friendship. It was as if these two had decided that Cliff was worth the work and they would one day conquer him.

The boy, Richard, a pale, freckled skinny boy with reddish-blond hair, looked at him the way Pamela did. He recognized the look. Cliff knew that if he could see himself in a mirror, this was probably the same way he looked at Junior. At no time did he look at either of them the same way. He was friendly with them, but he suspected that if he got too friendly it would encourage both of them to try to get closer and, frankly, Cliff just didn't know how he would deal with this. He wasn't good at dissipating people's infatuations with him or expectations of him, so his best defense, he thought, was to keep them at a manageable distance.

Just before the end of second period and the start of the lunch period, Pamela came over to Cliff to ask him about his holiday. She was wearing a burgundy sweater, white blouse underneath and a plaid skirt with colors of burgundy, green and gray on a white background. It was tweed and pleated and gave her a sophisticated look. She was an attractive girl, about five feet and three inches tall with dark brunette hair. She wore a bit of rouge on her cheeks as did many of the girls in high school. She also wore short-heeled shoes like many of her female classmates.

"Oh, me and my family spent Christmas in New York and New Year out in California," he told her with a slightly blushing smile.

"Oh cool," Pamela replied, "my family went to our new cottage in West Virginia!" Pamela continued to explain that there were many fires in the fireplace and toasted marshmallows during the stay, not to mention hiking with their dogs and visits to nearby small towns and lots of shops, as she brushed her hair back from her face. It was curled but loosely so and sometimes one or two curls broke from the bunch.

"Sounds like fun," Cliff replied. "We got to do some swimming in my grandparents' pool in California, so I guess that gave us the same exercising you got while hiking." Cliff thought this might have sounded a little competitive after he blurted it. But he couldn't think of anything else to say at the time.

At this time, Richard had come over and tried to enter the conversation. As usual, his clothes were ill fitting since he was so skinny and he had that "golly gee" look on his face, his standard countenance. "Gee, I would have preferred either of your vacations. My grandparents came to visit and all we did was stay home." Both Pamela and Cliff smiled at him, trying not to say too much in reply which might encourage him to talk more. Cliff wanted to catch up with Junior who had walked out of class already. They had stolen glances at each other a few more times while the two other classmates were holding court with Cliff but there was no reason for Junior to hang around. No one was talking to him and it would look odd for him to hang behind.

Cliff knew that Junior would be sitting with the other colored kids in the cafeteria and always felt he shouldn't go over to them during lunch, although he did walk by every now and then to say "hello" as did a few of the other students. But, thought Cliff, he could walk over and say something like, we should talk about the civics assignment later to Junior, as he passed. This, he figured, would be a sign that he wanted to meet him in the basement so they could wish each other their own special Happy New Year! The thought of this plan brought a smile to Cliff's face as both Richard and Pamela droned on. He hardly paid much attention to them and finally Mr Rakowski, the teacher suggested that they all run off for lunch before the third period began.

At lunch, Junior sat with the rest of his usual "gang of five" as they jokingly called themselves, while the newspapers had referred to them as the Group of Five. He was situated between Ray and Louella while Shirley and Thomasine sat on the other side of the table. There was a white boy that often sat near them, as close to Thomasine as it felt comfortable, with a few of his friends but he had been admonished by a few of the white girls and hadn't sat with them since before the Thanksgiving break. Although he and Thomasine still talked in the hall in between classes when they had the chance.

"My pop and momma played Billie Holiday records all through the holiday," Ray told the group, making it clear how bored he became after the first day of this.

"Yea, mine too," Shirley announced, "everybody was surprised about what happened to her."

"We went to see *Porgy and Bess* with our family from Memphis," Louella reported, "otherwise we stayed around the house and ate, although we did go up to Philly on New Year's Day to visit our cousin." Thomasine was always the quiet one. The group thought that she always had secrets that she couldn't or wouldn't share. All four had on some new piece of clothing undoubtedly, but Junior wasn't sure in every case what was new.

Thomasine always looked nice and dressed quite nicely for a high school girl of any race. Her hair, slick and shiny, was always pulled back in a ponytail. And she often wore a jumper with a blouse or sweater and saddle shoes or loafers. As Junior noticed more carefully it was clear that Shirley had on a new blouse and skirt. The blouse was the color fuchsia. The full skirt was purple and made her look slimmer and the beige scarf around her neck gave her a softer, more feminine look. Ray looked handsome in a Shetland sweater, something he wore to look more as if he "belonged" at Arlington High along with a pair of navy-blue slacks, also cuffed. Instead of loafers, he wore a pair of black lace ups. Junior thought that Ray was a nice-looking boy before this but couldn't help being impressed at this new look of his.

Very light-skinned people like Thomasine and her family often didn't associate with darker Negroes, so some of the gang might have thought that the explanation for her quietness but they all knew her family and knew they weren't so much like that. They were all light skinned, yes, but they didn't seem to separate themselves from the rest of their community. It was just Thomasine being Thomasine, they had come to conclude. Not that they thought about what it must be like for her at Arlington High, looking so much like them but yet being colored. She was at once the one considered more "acceptable" particularly by the boys but also a few of the girls.

Of all of them, she was the one that seemed to get the best treatment from the teachers. But at the same time, Thomasine was held at a distance too. It was as if she was invited to their party but never got much past the front door. This might be different, it was clear to them, from the attention that she got from some of the white boys, if it happened to be a party for two. But Thomasine never seemed to give those white boys too much of her time. She knew they found her attractive, but her interests were in a colored boy who lived in the District. In fact, Thomasine had said at one time when she was particularly talkative, that she might transfer to a school in the city next September. That school, also an integrated high school, was the school this boy went to. Someone in his neighborhood would allow her to use their address so that she might be able to attend school in Washington.

"Did anybody go to any sock hops?" Junior asked with a smirk. They all chuckled. Colored kids didn't too often take off their shoes to dance because it was a style as much as they did because it helped them to do their dance moves with more skill and swiftness. They certainly didn't refer to this undertaking as a sock hop! The five of them were learning a lot about white culture up close. What they saw on television made more sense to them since they were going to Arlington High. In a way, it was as if they were a part of the Cleaver family. Or more likely, they worked in the Cleaver household and got to see them up close every day. They laughed and talked about their observations and tried to help each other understand as foreign exchange students might in their new school in a new land.

But the gang of five was suddenly jolted from their cocoon of privacy! "Hey, Junior, have you finished your civics assignment?" the plaid shirt-wearing Cliff asked as he stopped in front of his friend while passing by on the way to lunch with Pamela and Richard. Junior was caught a little off-guard because Cliff didn't usually talk with him in the cafeteria and certainly not in front of the other colored kids. But, nevertheless, blushing although no one could discern, he replied to Cliff's question; after all, he knew what must have been behind his effort to communicate. They had not seen each other since before Christmas and undoubtedly Cliff had thought about him as much as he had thought about Cliff.

"Yes, I'm pretty much done with it," Junior answered, "what about you?" Cliff stopped in front of him for a minute while his two lunch companions walked on.

"I just got it all put together yesterday," said Cliff. "My uncle in Chicago helped me bring it all together."

"Good for you," said Junior. "My pop gave me some ideas too."

"Anyway, good luck and see you around," Cliff added as he was about to walk off, trying to sound aloof. He figured Junior would know what the "see you around" part meant. Since they hadn't been able to plan a meeting after school in their civics class, he had to let Junior know that he was anxious to meet him in their usual spot to show him a little New Year's cheer. Since both boys were thinking the same thing, there wasn't any more that needed to be said.

Ray and the girls had all stopped talking during Junior's brief chat with Cliff but once he walked away, Ray asked Junior why he didn't ask Cliff if he had gone to a sock hop over the holiday. Junior chuckled while Ray and the girls turned in a full belly laugh. They laughed so hard that Cliff and his two companions had to hear them as they were walking off. Junior thought about that and tried to bring the laughter to a halt. "Oh, you funny, brother Ray, you funny!"

"Sorry, man. I don't mean to insult your boy, I know he's your good friend." Junior might have been intimidated by this comment had a white boy said it, but he knew how Ray meant it or basically how any Negro boy would have meant it. It was the way, colored boys jostled with each other. It was nothing for him to worry about. No one at that table or anywhere in that school actually knew how much Cliff was Junior's boy. He was fairly sure of this.

At Mount Calvary Baptist Church there was a young assistant

minister who had just joined the ministry from New Jersey. He had moved to Arlington to live with an aunt because he said he was getting tired of the life in Newark and wanted to be in a quieter community so he could hear the voice of God better. Besides, his aunt, who was old and growing feeble, needed someone around to take care of her. This new member of the clergy had quickly become good friends with the slightly older gospel choir director, a handsome and talented young man who everyone knew was *funny*, but they loved him and his music, nevertheless. He tried to dispel any rumors about his lack of interest in women by going out with some of the young women in the church but, maybe aside from a few of the women, no one took it seriously. He would always say that God wouldn't approve of any kind of unchristian relationship between him and the young women of the church and, of course, all the young women had to agree with this or else they would be chastised.

However, his fast friendship with the new assistant minister was never questioned. They were considered to be good friends by many and why wouldn't they be? Both were close in age, single and working for Christ! But there were many in Mount Calvary who might have thought their brotherly love was more than Christlike! Younger people, Junior and Jeanne among them, might have seen beyond the façade. He knew what it looked like to other people when men who were friendly were imagined to be more than friends. In his mind, there was no doubt that he and Cliff did not leave any of these traces behind. He definitely did not want to risk leaving any notion in anyone's head about himself and Cliff and how they reached for each other behind closed doors, in empty rooms and in dark parks when they were certain no one was watching!

Chapter 23

As fate, or mechanical error would have it, Americans were searching for a real-life hero on the morning that the civics assignment was to be discussed in class! The Wednesday morning news broadcasts were reporting that a National Airlines flight had exploded in midair killing all 32 aboard. According to the news, it was a suspected bombing. Perhaps there would be a survivor who knew who the bomber was and would bring him to justice. But it didn't look as if anyone would emerge alive from the wreckage of the flight which had departed Idlewild Airport in New York the night before, bound for Miami.

"Settle down, class," Mr Rakowski scolded. "Yes, the plane crash was a tragedy and definitely an ominous occurrence so early in the year! But the year is way too young to predict bad things on it because of this," he went on. "Besides, with," and he fell momentarily silent as he made a quick count of the class attendance, "with 25 heroes about to be unleashed on America, we are bound to have a good year and I'm sure this will have been the only emergency situation that we have."

With this, the class laughed, although one or two girls said in low voices that they didn't think there was anything funny about all those people dying on that plane. "There will always be death," the teacher said in response after asking one of the girls to repeat what she had said. "And there will always be new life and new opportunities to make things better." By now, everyone was quiet and ready to get onto the business at hand. That business was unveiling the year's new hero and thus, unleashing him on the world!

"Who would like to go first? Or do I need to draft someone?" the teacher asked. With that, several hands went up, most of them boys but Pamela, who sat in front of Cliff raised her hand too and Mr Rakowski chose her to go first. "Pamela, who is the biggest hero of 1960?" he asked. Pamela proudly got up and as she headed to the front of the class, a few of the boys snickered and one made the comment that it will probably be some housewife who discovered a way to cook an entire meal in five minutes. Those closest to the boy who heard the comment laughed but this was limited mostly to the boys.

"My hero of 1960 and probably beyond is Dr Spencer Cooper who has just discovered a vaccination for the measles," Pamela announced to the class. "Everyone here has had the measles probably, so I think all Americans will welcome this new vaccine and the opportunity to eradicate yet another disease that confronts many children and causes discomfort and misery." Pamela had written up a news story of Dr Cooper and how he had come to discover a vaccine for measles as well as how it would be administered throughout the country.

This was a fairly easy sell to the class because of the recent discovery of a vaccine for polio. Probably most of the students in Mr Rakowski's civics class had either been given that vaccine over the year or certainly their parents had gone to the doctor for it. Mr Rakowski complimented Pamela's work but pointed out that it wasn't usually doctors who discovered cures, but scientists. Regardless, it was timely and well thought out, he concluded. People like them had certainly either been vaccinated against the dreaded polio virus or were definitely planning to in the near future. But measles was another story! The virus was still raging and especially among people his students' age.

This was the kind of hero one might expect from a girl, the teacher thought. It was reasonable and practical, although it probably wasn't as exciting as the slew of cowboy heroes that were to follow for the next several minutes. But vaccinations would surely save lives!

How a cowboy could be a national hero in 1960 took a lot of explaining, Mr. Rakowski thought. However, in almost every case, the student who proposed a cowboy hero, all of them male, defended his choice by citing an Indian uprising starting in the west that had killed hundreds of Americans and threatened more and more lives as various Indian tribes around the nation decided to join in on the insurrection. Most of the class seemed to enjoy these various accounts of cowboy heroism, probably as much as they did the television shows that they watched at home during the evening or on the weekend.

Other than cowboys, a couple of the boys chose soldiers to be their hero. After all, soldiers were always popular, and there was a conflict still going on in Asia. Of the two or three army men heroes, one stood out, thought the teacher. H was a soldier who had led in a defeat against the communists in North Vietnam thus ensuring a free Vietnam which soon became the nation's 51st state. This gave the US a major presence in Asia close to China, one of its largest enemies anywhere and certainly the biggest one in Asia. Americans loved that the red, white and blue was spreading all over the world. They were excited about the stars and stripes being firmly planted in outer space as well!

Finally, Cliff raised his hand and headed to the front of the class. Mr Rakowski liked him a lot and knowing that he was shy and reticent about speaking before the whole class, quieted down the noise from the laughter over yet another cowboy hero. Cliff was certain that Whitey Powers would take the excitement level much higher than any cowboy or soldier could.

"What makes Whitey a hero?" he asked, having been coached to do this by his Uncle Peter. "He is an astronaut who volunteered to be the first American to explore outer space solo and to discover new planets and solar systems. While in outer space," Cliff continued in explaining Whitey's story, "he gets lost for a while and could not be communicated with at Space Command." Everyone in class appeared to be giving their full attention to Cliff as he recounted the outer space exploits of Whitey, including Junior, who sat in the back of the class but was directing his gaze straight ahead.

"How long is Whitey lost in space?" asked Richard in the middle of Cliff's delivery.

"He's lost for nearly a week," Cliff answered, having already planned this out in his storyboard. "While he's out of touch with Space Command, he is exploring other planets and traveling between the stars."

"What planets does he visit?" asked another boy whose name was Clayton, but most flippantly called him "ferret" because they thought he looked like one.

Clayton had probably thought he might catch Cliff off-guard and perhaps win some points with his classmates whom he knew were no big fans of Cliff Peterson, and probably held him in only slightly higher regard than they did Cliff. But Cliff had worked this all out beforehand. Perhaps it was having a favorite uncle who was an advertising man help him think it through completely or perhaps it was his own attention to detail, but Cliff was quite prepared to respond to Clayton's question. "Whitey landed on Mars and got to meet some Martians," Cliff replied. "He was even allowed to bring back some artifacts from Mars to show us back on Earth." Suddenly so many in the class had questions for Cliff that the teacher had to reestablish some order. Many wanted to know what kinds of artifacts Whitey brought back to Earth and wondered if they included an actual Martian!

No Martians were brought back, Cliff explained. But, perhaps answering a few questions before they were asked, gave a description of the typical Martian. They are not green as many believe, Cliff professed. "They are a mix of colors like people on Earth and they range from a deep purple to a deep gray with light graduating shades of light and dark in both colors. They walk upright like Earth people except they have talons instead of fingers and they have a much bigger head with bigger eyes, nose and mouths." Needless to say, this was funny to the majority of the class and many of them augmented Cliff's description of Martians with their own projections. Mr Rakowski seemed to be enjoying this exchange, perhaps because he favored Cliff so much but also because this was definitely one of the presentations that received the most attention and engagement from the class.

Cliff held the best part out for last, as his uncle had told him to build up to the most exciting part! "Before leaving Mars, Whitey was allowed to plant a US flag in a town square as a memento of his visit." He had, of course, taken photos of all this and Space Command had provided them to every television station around the world and newspapers all over the world had published them. "Whitey wasn't really lost; he was simply enjoying his time among the people of Mars and was discovering their planet and telling them about ours."

As Cliff gathered up his storyboard and prepared to go back to his seat, his friends Pamela and Richard started to clap and a few others joined in, causing Cliff to blush as he proceeded to his seat, clearly embarrassed by the reaction. "Why didn't Whitey stay on Mars?" one boy yelled out, "Were the girls not pretty enough up there?" the boy followed up, answering his initial question. This wise crack precipitated much laughter and noise from those banging on their desks in apparent enjoyment of the question. The laughter went on until after Cliff was back at his desk, without having answered the question. Mr Rakowski finally called the class back to attention before Richard came up to give his presentation hoping he could capitalize on Cliff's glow.

However, his hero, a fighter pilot who intercepted and detonated a Soviet missile headed for New York City, didn't seem to have quite the same fun factor. Also, or so one might surmise, the class had praised one nerd already. It was unusual that Cliff, Richard and a few other students ever got a favorable reaction to anything they had to say. And Cliff, or more accurately, Whitey Powers, had managed to garner all of it for probably the rest of the month!

Finally, after everyone had gone, it was Junior's turn! As he sat patiently in the back of the class listening to everyone else's presentation, he had convinced himself that it wasn't so bad to go last. In fact, as he considered, by the time he went to the head of the class with his storyboard to tell them about his hero, everyone would probably be too tired to focus on him too much and certainly to give him any grief. He imagined, as he walked to the front of the class, that everyone thought his hero was some kind of singer or dancer who brought the nation to its feet with some new song or dance. He had never even fathomed the idea himself, but it seemed likely to him that others might have figured that would be what he came up with.

Standing before the class, Junior waited for the teacher to ask him the same question he had asked everyone before him. "Who is your hero of 1960, Wynn Horry, Junior?" Mr Rakowki finally spoke the words to his only colored student. Gathering his courage to speak before the class, Junior, turning to Mr Rakowski and away from his classmates, cleared his throat a couple of times and told the teacher, seated at his desk and staring hard at him, that his hero of 1960 is Brick Springfield. "Brick Springfield is a young boxer from Illinois who has been setting boxing records all around the nation and even overseas and wins a gold medal in Rome at the 1960 Olympics." His mention of the Olympics was enough to get the attention of most of the class since the games wouldn't start in Rome until the summer. The prospect of the summer games made what Junior was about to say more interesting to his classmates.

"Since he burst into the ring, Brick has been undefeated in all his matches both in the United States and abroad," Junior told the class. "He easily made the Olympics boxing team due to his undefeated record and also because of his All-American looks," Junior went on. At that point, he unveiled his storyboard to show Brick Springfield, a blond-haired young man, about six feet tall and weighing about 175 pounds. Brick was posing in front of a boxing ring wearing white satin boxing shorts with a red stripe down the outside of each leg with red boxing gloves on his hands which were positioned in a peek-a-boo stance. The class was quiet, but Junior could tell that they liked the image of Brick and it was clear that they accepted him as an All-American. If he wasn't a boxer, they could envision him as a Hollywood actor, one who probably got leading roles and played opposite beautiful heroines.

In the popular style for movie posters, Brick would be the strong and tough guy wearing only a pair of shorts that served as a swimsuit, standing over a young woman who looked as though she was longing for him, straddled on a beach wearing a bikini that was getting wet owing to the raging waves that were sweeping over her! His muscles would be glistening from the sun while the girl who reached out for him would be wet! Her hand would be reaching for him, but Brick would seem a bit indifferent and stiff. Still, he would give her the impression that he wanted her too in his own way and that they would probably end up in each other's arms lying down together on the beach as the waves wrapped over them!

"'Beat Boris red, white and BLUE' is the chant of the American fans who look on as Brick delivers a left hook that takes the Russian boxer down," Junior told the class. "The Russian boxer went to the Olympic games touted as the best in the world," Junior explained to his audience, "It was not expected that the American boxer, even with his undefeated record, would knock out the Russian boxer in the first round. But when he did, it made American fans as well as anti-Communist fans around the world go crazy, particularly those in Europe, and also in Asia and Latin America!

"'Beat Boris red, white and BLUE' would become the chant heard 'round the world all the rest of the summer and into the fall as a result of that knockout punch," Junior explained as he was about to end his presentation. "Brick was the greatest," he concluded! "He was the great American hero of the 1960 Olympics in Rome and he also appeared with Senator John F. Kennedy as he campaigned for the Presidency across the country. Brick Springfield appealed to younger people just like Kennedy did, but he also appealed to everyone else as the quintessential American hero! America was on a big beat the Soviets campaign and Brick had done just that, literally!"

At the end of his presentation, Junior got some applause from his classmates, coming sporadically from around the room. Cliff was among the loudest of the hand clappers but others in the class clapped too and one girl even yelled, "Beat Boris red, white and BLUE!" Junior, who was nervous the entire time but tried to mask his anxiousness, walked back to his seat with his storyboard tucked under his arm, a good bit less timorously than he had advanced to the class only five or six minutes earlier, although it seemed to have been about 15 minutes or twenty minutes that he was up in front of the class introducing them to Brick Springfield, who single-handedly restored the reputation of American power!

Shortly after Junior had returned to his seat, the class was still full of chatter about the plethora of paladins that had been paraded before them by their classmates. But Mr Rakowski soon interrupted the many conversations by thanking the class for the work and creativity they put into the assignment. The teacher explained to his 10th grade hero-makers that the point of the presentations was to get them to think about how ordinary Americans could influence society. "The greatness of our country is really in the hands of ordinary Americans who do extraordinary things," said he. "We are at the very start of a new decade and there is so much opportunity and challenge ahead of us and if each of us pushes himself to exceed the limits of what we think we're capable of, we might just become a hero in our own right."

Chapter 24

By now, everyone was preparing for the next period as the bell was about to sound. But nevertheless, Mr Rakowski managed to quiet them down enough to give them a new assignment which was to write a speech for either of the two Presidential candidates to deliver to concerned and worried Americans about air travel given the fatal airline crash that had happened that morning. "If you were their advisor, what message would you write for Vice President Nixon or Senator Kennedy to deliver about the future of air travel especially as so many Americans are focused on going to space? Remember," added Rakowski, "we can't keep American enthusiasm high for eventually going to the moon if they are afraid to fly a few hours away to see Grandma for summer vacation."

While Mr Rakowski thought he might get a laugh, no one was saying anything about what he had announced as they prepared to leave the classroom. But Junior figured that many of the other students must have found it to be an interesting assignment as well. He believed he would never fly in an airplane as Cliff had done just a few days earlier, but nevertheless realized that the fact that people could fly in airplanes was itself a sign of progress. In his teenage mind, he wrestled with that notion that older colored people always have to negotiate. That is, that American progress isn't a sign of progress for them! Nevertheless, it is still an indication that America is the land of pioneers who travel to the far reaches and these days, the far reaches are the outer reaches of space and the universe!

He was lost in this thought walking out of the class hoping to catch up with Cliff who he thought might have written a note to him about meeting up later, as Cliff sometimes did. But he managed to notice one of his classmates lagging behind and looking at him intently. This boy had never ever spoken to him and Junior didn't recall him ever looking at him before. He thought, though, that it might be because of his presentation and that this classmate liked it but couldn't find a way to tell him that. At any rate, he didn't give it too much thought as he passed this boy's desk even though he still felt his eyes on him as he walked by. His classmate had not moved the whole time. What was on Junior's mind most was to catch up to Cliff. This boy staring at him did not stir him anywhere near as much as did the thought of him and Cliff looking into each other's eyes in some quiet and secluded place at Arlington High later that day!

The note was waiting for him at his locker. It had been stuck through one of the vents in the light green locker #6704, which belonged to Junior. All the colored students had lockers grouped together, so for Cliff to put a note through Junior's locker meant that he might be seen in the area where those five lockers were located. In and of itself, that wasn't such a telltale caper. But, mostly at Junior's urging, the two of them tried to be extremely careful about their communication and contact with each other while at school or anywhere else in public. Cliff was certainly aware that there were some eyes on them when they interacted with each other, but Junior was definitely the most concerned about who saw them talking together and concerned wasn't too strong a word for it! It went without saying that he would have been horrified if anyone had seen what else they did together!

"Meet in the usual spot," was all the note said. Junior had trained Cliff in being laconic and discreet in their public conversations and in any written notes. "No signatures ever," he instructed. It wasn't that Cliff couldn't have figured out himself that this was the more advisable way to conduct any exchanges between them, but it was that Junior felt that he did not want to risk any laxity on Cliff's part. The rest of the day went pretty quickly and at the end of school on that Wednesday afternoon, Cliff and Junior had found their way separately, of course, to the basement and to the janitor's closet that, amidst the brooms, mops, pails and cleaning supplies, held their dirty little secret!

Although they did not know it at the time, while their hands were all over each other in the basement, Will Glenn, the boy who had stared at Junior earlier in the day at the end of their civics class, had had his own rendezvous with their teacher, Mr Rakowski. "He is that colored boy who was chasing my neighbor's wife, I'm pretty sure," he told his teacher. "I

179

saw him walking away from Adams Park one night a few months ago and my neighbor saw him too and chased him down the street." He was with Cliff Peterson too, Will acknowledged, "I think they might be smoking weed or maybe even muggles."

"Now, now, Mr Glenn," responded the teacher at this revelation that his student thought himself to be making. "Let's not get too far afield here. I don't believe that Cliff Peterson is smoking marijuana and I would find it hard to believe that he even smokes cigarettes like some of the boys," he added. "However, I'm not entirely sure what influence the other boy might have on him and why Cliff and he would be walking together coming out of a park in North Arlington at night. I don't even know why that boy would be in a park around here at night since it isn't a place that he belongs in."

However, Mr Rakowski went on, "He is not the colored boy that was having relations with the woman in your neighborhood," he informed the plisky Will Glenn. "We know who that boy is, and he was not allowed to attend this school after we found out what happened. That boy goes to the colored high school and he can no longer even be in this neighborhood. So, the colored boy, Wynn Horry, Jr is not that boy that used to work at the Lee Market that attacked that woman in her home."

"Okay," said Will, "but I know I saw him coming out of Adams Park with Cliff Peterson at night back right after Thanksgiving, and then my neighbor chased him down the street and yelled 'stay away from my wife you lil nigger! Besides, I know that he and Cliff Peterson sneak off together here at the school!"

"Well, as I said, Mr Glenn, I don't believe it is the same boy. Why he was in Adams Park with Mr Peterson is another story," Rakowski argued. "Maybe Mr Peterson is teaching him how to be a better citizen," claimed the teacher. "Okay, off to your next class, young man," Rakowski instructed. He suddenly seemed consumed with his thoughts and had no more desire to continue this conversation with the student. "We will just keep this to ourselves," Mr Rakowki declared, hoping that he had made it clear to Will Glenn.

Quentin Rakowski was used to keeping things to himself! He had, in fact, kept secrets to himself for all his life! He had no doubt in his mind what Cliff Peterson was doing in the park with that Negro boy. Years earlier he had found himself in similar situations at his high school, although not with Negroes because there were none there. He didn't understand why Cliff, a smart and attractive young man from a good family, would want that either! Spending that time in Africa must somehow have reconfigured some of his wiring, Rakowski had concluded. He had apparently lost the eye for the appealing!

"I wish I could rub your head like this at my party," Cliff said to Junior slyly, as he ran his hands over Junior's close-cut, tightly curled very black hair shortly after the two boys were behind closed doors in the janitor's closet later that afternoon as directed by the note.

"Oh no, we can't do that," Junior protested a bit nervously!

"I know we can't do it, you crumb, I'm just saying." Junior then lightly play-punched Cliff in the abdomen after being called a crumb and Cliff responded by battering Junior back with play punches all over his torso and then followed it up with tickling which he knew would make Junior laugh, at least a little. However, he also knew that tickling him too much would cause him to get a little testy. After more rubbing, tugging at clothes and hands going here and there in the quiet, dark place in the basement closet, the boys thought they heard a noise outside the door! Both Junior and Cliff got stiff and quiet as their attention turned toward the door to see if someone was coming in.

Junior, being Junior, had already rehearsed in his mind what he would say if one of the janitors had come back to the janitor's closet unexpectedly while he was there with Cliff. He made sure they never got too indiscreet, although belts, shirts and slacks did get undone to an extent while they were in the closet. Junior knew that the custodial staff liked him and that they wanted to see him succeed. He had decided that he would tell them that he and Cliff were talking about a school assignment together because they didn't feel comfortable doing it in front of the other students. He figured that Old Papa or any of the other workers would believe him and wouldn't find it too questionable for them to be in a darkened basement closet together. He was pretty certain, at least, that they would never suspect that he and Cliff were up to dirty business, amongst the brooms and mops!

"Am I the only colored kid invited to your party?" Junior asked as they reassembled themselves in order to leave the closet once they determined it was safe to go outside. Whatever noise they thought they had heard was no longer discernable.

181

"No," replied Cliff, "my mother invited Thomasine also. She knows her mother and father from some of her volunteer work and she likes them and her."

"Oh great, so there will someone there for me to dance with," said Junior, somewhat sarcastically.

"Who else is coming to your sweet 16th?" Junior asked with some latent concern in his voice but also with a tinge of persiflage.

"My mom invited some of the kids from school and a few of the kids in the neighborhood, plus some of the kids of my dad's office colleagues. Everyone will be nice, don't worry," he attempted to reassure Junior. "Besides, she will probably be wearing a dress that your mother made so you should be there to see it," Cliff quipped hoping to further allay any concern that Wynn Junior might have about being at this party in Arlington Heights with all these kids that would probably not have anything at all to say to him.

"Well, I will have Thomasine to dance with at least," Junior reminded himself. "Maybe I have met some of the Joes and Janes from your neighborhood with my mother if she was delivering some clothes. I hope you play some records that we can dance to," Junior appealed. "I am not certain me or Thomasine want to dance to any Conway Twitty or Everly Brothers!"

"Don't worry," Cliff replied with a slight smile on his face in response to Junior's snarky comment. "I love a lot of the same groups that you do, so I'm sure you won't be disappointed."

"Well, maybe I should bring my Fats Domino records or some James Brown or Ray Charles, just so we can see what the other guests can do with that," Junior said laughing as he pushed Cliff against the wall, pressed his body on his one last time, and mussed his pompadour.

The two always followed the same ritual before parting from their tryst. They had to make sure their clothes were neat again with no indication that shirttails might have been pulled out of pants or that belts might have been removed and flies unzipped. After they were once again "presentable" they got quiet to make sure there was no noise out in the hall or no one walking around. Cliff always went out first. Junior stayed behind for a minute or so because he was the one, of course, who could "explain" his presence in the closet.

Chapter 25

At the Horry house, the beginning of February was marked by the celebration of Jeanne's birthday. She was going to have a party and had been pleading with Julia Mae to allow her to play Sixteen Candles for her birthday, even though she was turning 14 during the first week of February in 1960. But, since the song had been among the most popular of 1959, and she and all her friends loved it, she really wanted to play it and Wynn didn't see anything wrong with it. He loved his little girl and generally wanted to please her. "It's just a song, honey," he told Julia Mae. "Everyone knows she's 14 and not 16 but if they like the song so much, why not?"

A week before the party was to be held, Julia Mae had not relented, although she did promise to consider Jeanne's feelings. But she was usually just as exact in how she lived her life, as she was about the seams she sewed, in the clothes she made. "Why not have the party and the music fit you?" she asked of her daughter. Of course, Jeanne's reply was as could be expected. "Because when I turn 16 the song won't be popular any more, Ma," she wailed to her mother!!!

Jeanne was looking forward to the party! Not too much happened in February. It was usually cold and bleak and for the most part there wasn't that much to do. All the sports Jeanne was involved in were mostly outdoor, although she had begun to develop an interest in basketball at her father's urging, since he couldn't seem to interest his only son in it. But the one thing Jeanne was most looking forward to was that she would now be old enough to work as a candy striper at Carver Hospital, the colored hospital in Washington, DC near the baseball field. Her family was well aware that Jeanne wanted to be a nurse! She had told them that since she was eleven or twelve years old. Wynn and Julia Mae had worked with one of her teachers to see if it was possible for her to get one of the candy striper volunteer spots at the hospital. Based on her grades and her interests and poise, Jeanne was likely to be selected, her parents had been told. Quite possibly, she would be able to start at the hospital in the spring after some training!

His sister's actual birthday was on Tuesday, but Junior suggested, that she have her party on Saturday evening, the 13th, the day before Valentine's Day so that it could double as a birthday-Valentine's Day party. That way, he could invite Carolyn as his date, but then still have Sunday, February 14th free. What he hadn't figured out but was still working on, was how he would get to spend any time with Cliff on Valentine's Day if that were possible at all.

The best he could come up with is that they could both tell their parents that they were going to a movie in the District in the afternoon and perhaps hold hands in a dark theater. Junior wanted to see *The World, the Flesh and the Devil*! Although his parents loved Harry Belafonte, the movie's star, they had not seen the flick, preferring to see *Porgy and Bess* instead, which had come out recently. Surely, he could talk Cliff into seeing this movie, still playing on the weekends at one of the colored theaters on U Street. He knew that Cliff liked Harry Belafonte also. Since the movie had been out for a while, the two of them could see it without too many people around and they would have more privacy. The film centered around a forbidden relationship! Surely that subject matter should hold their attention, Junior thought.

Junior, although definitely one of the more popular and likeable Joes in Hilldale, had not had a party to go to for two weekends straight, ever! The night of Jeanne's party was exactly one week after Cliff's birthday party. He thought it ironic that Cliff did turn 16 and couldn't play Sixteen Candles, since it was a song about a girl turning sixteen. At Cliff's party he most wanted to dance with Cliff! But Cliff danced with his friend Pamela mostly and a few of the other girls from his neighborhood as well as the daughters of his father's colleagues. He did not dance with Thomasine mostly because she was the only one who would dance with Junior. Gussie, the Petersons' maid, was the only exception. She was always happy to be with Cliff and Robby and always enjoyed a party.

Gussie loved Cliff and he liked her back. She was a tremendous fan of James Brown and the Famous Flames. She and Junior did a bop to their recent hit Try Me! The other kids watched to see their dance steps and tried to match them. One boy did ask Thomasine to dance with him. He was a Latin American boy, the son of a diplomat, whose family the Petersons were close to. She and Paulo danced to the James Brown record and he tried to slow-drag her. He had not tried that with any of the other girls. After the James Brown records, Cliff also wanted to play, Please, please, please which he had learned to like, through Junior. It was basically a message between the two and both knew it but, of course, neither could acknowledge it openly. In private, Junior had danced with Cliff to this record and they both enjoyed the mood that James Brown put them in!

After the soul session, the Petersons tried to cool things down a bit! "Why don't you play your new French record?" Claire suggested. One of the diplomat daughters, one who had a crush on Cliff, had brought a copy of a new Elvis Presley-style singer who was singing as Elvis sang, in French and also moving as Elvis moved and this needed no interpretation. "His name is Johnny Hallyday and he's dreamy," said the girl, directing her comment to Claire, but wanting everyone else to know that she knew of this new French singer who no one else in the room was familiar with. She and her family had recently completed a stint at the US Embassy in France, the oldest of any US mission abroad, on the Place de la Concorde. Benjamin Franklin and, of course, Thomas Jefferson had walked those halls but none of that was too important to this girl. What she remembered most from the Paris years was the fun and most recently, the swiveling hips and bouncing blond bouffant of the singer who had just released a song about leaving the girls, before her family had come back to the States. A few copies of his new record had been given out before its big release and she had gotten her hands on a few of them!

Claire saw in this girl a future diplomat's wife. No big surprise, though, since she had grown up in a diplomat family. She recognized her perfume as the other Lanvin fragrance called My Sin. Claire Peterson recalled a time in Paris when she would visit the perfume counter at Samaritaine to sample the various fragrances. That was when she decided that Arpège would be her scent. That was the favorite Lanvin of most of the fancy mesdames that would sashay down the perfume aisles wearing their capes or minks and pillbox hat or wide sun bonnets in summer and enthrone themselves at the fragrance counters of the department stores of Paris. What a grown-up fragrance for a 15-year-old girl, Claire thought, but then again that's typical of French girls or girls who grow up in France, she opined. It was obvious to her that she liked her son in a way that girls like her like boys like Cliff. But this would not be an affair to remember, Claire had already determined. It, she had come to grips with, might never happen because Cliff was clearly the wrong man! Chester and Claire had seen the movie version of Tennessee Williams' *Cat on a Hot Tin Roof* when they had returned to the States in '58! The movie resonated with them even then as they thought about their eldest son, at that time about to turn 14. Their experiences with Cliff and some of the boys that worked for them in Africa were still fresh in her mind.

"What is he saying?" Cliff asked as the record was spinning.

"Yea, what's it about?" wondered Pamela and some of the others including Richard who tried to stay by Cliff's side as often as possible throughout the party.

"He is pretty much saying don't get stuck on girls," Robert answered.

"Well, it's more than that," the girl who had brought the record for Cliff retorted hastily. "He is also saying how difficult it is to forget all these pretty girls." Robert could not quickly come back with a response although his mastery of French was rather good. Besides, at that point, Claire, hoping to change the tenor of the conversation, stepped in to make sure that no arguments broke out.

"Come on and let's enjoy the record," she admonished. "What a nice gift, Cliff, and probably only two of you in Washington have this record. Isn't that something!"

Chapter 26

Julia Mae had saved a big piece of her daughter's birthday cake which, of course, had been made by Aunt Nellie. Yellow cake with vanilla frosting and buttercream edging was Jeanne's favorite birthday cake and that was what her aunt had made her. It was a three-layer cake, measuring about eight inches around, and was intended to serve up to 14, depending upon the way it was sliced, of course. Julia Mae had added 14 yellow birthday candles. Everyone at the party had a good-sized slice and there were cookies too, chocolate chip with peanut butter as Junior had requested and his mother, with Nellie's careful instructions, had baked herself. She was proud of her youngest child and was happy that Jeanne was growing up at a time that seemed easier for colored girls to dream of bigger and brighter futures than she could have at that age.

It was on a cold Sunday in February that Wynn and Julia Mae learned some news that sent chills through them. It concerned their oldest niece in Charlotte. During their weekly phone call with Leeta and Brown, at least it was usually weekly, although sometimes an event at church or another family affair would preempt the Sunday late-afternoon call, they got news that Asha had been involved in a lunch counter protest demonstration downtown! As the story was recounted, Asha, along with many other students at Johnson C. Smith University where she was studying, had decided to sit down at the lunch counter of a five and dime to protest the fact that Negro shoppers were barred from eating there.

These students had decided to challenge the policy that only white people could be served at the lunch counters. They did this by just sitting down in empty counter seats and asking to be served! This wasn't something that had been done before in Charlotte, but it had happened about a week before in Greensboro, a few miles away for the very first time! That act of defiance was done by a group of Negro college students as well.

Leeta and Brown did not know what to think about this. As parents they were proud of their daughter. But as colored parents who had grown up in the south, mostly they were scared. "I'm worried about my child," an anguished Leeta admitted during the call. No one had been hurt during those first two days of lunch counter protests, but everyone knew that they would continue, at least that was the plan according to the students, and the Negroes in Charlotte were of different minds on this. "Please talk to your niece," Leeta urged Wynn. "Tell her that this is not wise and not safe."

Wynn replied to his sister that she shouldn't expect her children to be as silent and as deferential as the two of them had been, although he didn't use the word deferential. "These children ain't gon' take what we took off them whities and we really shouldn't expect them to. Right now, every day when Junior goes to school with them, I make sure he remembers that he's just as good and just as smart as they are. He's not there to shine anybody's shoes, he's there to shine."

As a teacher, Leeta, of course, believed this and agreed with it. But right now, she was thinking as a mother! "Those crackers will never change," Leeta lamented on that Sunday phone call. "I don't want to see my child hurt or disappointed over this. But, at the same time," she went on, "I am glad these young people are trying to do something to make things different."

By now, Julia Mae had taken control of the phone. "These kids today are not going to sit down and let all this go on," she observed. "They are determined to make room for themselves in this world. And we need to be proud of that and encourage them. Let Asha do what she feels is the right thing to do and y'all stand by her and see that she's safe and protected." It didn't occur to Julia Mae that she had just recently dissuaded her own son from doing anything similar if asked. If questioned about it, she would likely say there was a difference between being 15 years old and in high school and 21 years old in college.

"The only thing is, you can't be next to them all the time to protect them," Leeta replied. "That's the fear. These crackers are evil and they don't want a Negro to have one bit of peace! Lord, one day things will change, though, you and I both know it," said the voice coming through the phone from Charlotte.

"This is about to be that day, chile," Julia Mae announced. "This is about to be that day!"

As this conversation came a day after Jeanne's 14th birthday party, Julia Mae couldn't help but reflect on a life that would lie ahead for her daughter. Jeanne was a determined child, always had been, her mother remembered. She knew what she wanted and always seemed confident that she would achieve it. Julia Mae remembered her own self at Jeanne's age growing up in rural Virginia with no sense of her own strength or power. She felt as if she was a piece of paper that was blowing in any direction the wind would go. No heft, no weight, no ability to stand on her own!

Black girls and boys were always at the mercy of white people, either because they controlled their parents' employment, where they lived and where they could go and just generally, the society that they had to function in. They tried to move within the world at the pace, and in the places they were allowed to, but it was never really within their control. There were parameters for them clearly outlined with bold black lettering that said Colored!

These kids were making an effort to take some control of their own lives which their parents could not do. Julia Mae understood this, and it even brought a reticent smile to her face. That smile would have been boastful and showy if it weren't for the fact that she shared her sister-in-law's concerns for the safety of their children as they tried to make their way through this new world they were creating. But the fact that the youth were creating these new horizons for themselves, well, that should have made every colored person smile, most of them beaming with pride!

As Jeanne sat at lunch on the Monday after her birthday party, she enjoyed that last piece of cake for dessert. It was the last act for that yellow cake with vanilla frosting. It followed a baloney and cheese sandwich on white bread with mayonnaise. But as much as she enjoyed savoring that final piece, she was actually in a rush to get back to class at Frederick Douglass Junior High. It was Negro History Week, and her next class was history and they would be discussing the life of Harriet Tubman! The creator of the Underground Railroad had been a hero of Jeanne since she was about ten years old and first learning of Tubman's

189

efforts to free people held in slavery throughout the south and even into the north, by leading them through a route, a safe route that she had created over several years, into freedom!

It impressed Jeanne that, first of all, this was done by a woman, and second of all, that Tubman continued to do this over and over again, even in the face of death, not only her own but also all those who had gone along on this journey to live their lives as free and unchained, a life they had never known for as long as they had been alive! What a person this must have been and how much power I can have as a woman, Jeanne had thought! Early on it had become clear to her that she needn't be stymied by the fact that she was a colored girl, nor was her being a Negro a reason to be compunctious! For some at Frederick Douglass Junior High, this second week of February was merely an extension of what they learned from parents and grandparents at home or what they heard in church. But for many others, it was basically akin to the discovery of some ancient artifact that had been buried in the ground! It was something they had never known, seen or heard about, nor was it likely to pop up in everyday discussions that might occur in their world.

And this was definitely true for many at Arlington High! By the end of the week, Junior's tenth grade history class had not only studied the Underground Railroad, but they had also learned about Reconstruction and the integration of the armed forces and Jackie Robinson becoming the first Negro to play major league baseball. Of course, most of Junior's classmates as well as most white teens around the country knew that colored sports players, at least a few of them, played with white players in some sports in some cities around the country. They knew that there were colored actors and actresses and that there were many, many colored singers and dancers. They also knew a bit about the civil rights efforts to equalize education and public access; there they were in class together after all. They knew about these other efforts to the extent they were reported in the news mostly as agitations to the white citizens in the south.

What many whites did not know was about the murders and deaths of innocent colored people primarily in the south but in other parts of the nation as well. Many may not have been aware of the separate but equal doctrine which still applied to accommodations around the country and certainly to interstate trains and buses traveling through the southern states. Many knew that in their own state of Virginia, some school districts had been closed for nearly half a year rather than to integrate public schools as Arlington had back in September of the previous year.

They also knew that a colored man had been looted from his jail cell in Mississippi, locked up on charges of raping a white woman, beaten, then shot to death and thrown into a river about twenty miles away in Louisiana. That was in April, which was less than a year earlier, so most of the class knew about it! But while they might have known that these things were real, it was questionable if they were ever discussed, considered or renounced at any of these kids' dinner tables, or at the church, offices, social clubs or private parties of their parents.

That same month, on a Saturday, Martin Luther King, Jr and other Civil Rights leaders held a rally in Washington, DC near the Lincoln Memorial, urging the integration of schools. Nearly 26,000 attended the rally according to the newspapers, including Julia Mae and her two children. Nellie came from Georgetown to attend also. Perhaps there were some other students from Arlington High there with their families but probably none or very few of the whites. At the time of the April 18 rally, the Horrys were hopeful that Junior would get chosen to attend Arlington High but it hadn't yet been confirmed.

Chapter 27

Just as class was about to end, there was talking outside the classroom door and it was clear someone important was outside judging from the teacher's reaction. She was looking out of the door at the same time she was giving instructions to the class. She was clearly distracted! Perhaps it was the principal, Junior thought. But as he sat near the back of the classroom, he wasn't able to see what was going on at the door at the front of the classroom just opposite the teacher's desk. "Next week we resume our discussion of the Civil War and talk about the Battle of Chancellorsville, the greatest Confederate victory. It was fought not too very far from here in 1863."

"This weekend's assignment is to read the Red Badge of Courage," she instructed amid the noise of opening and closing desktops, chatter and shuffling around as students moved about preparing to leave the classroom. By the time Junior was about to leave the classroom, through the backdoor, the people who were talking outside had come in and were standing at the front of the room talking to the teacher. As Junior had surmised, the principal was among them.

"Oh, yes, Mr Wilson, I understand, yes of course... oh my!" he heard her exclaim. His head down, books folded under his arms, Junior was about to turn towards the back door to leave the class when he heard his teacher say, "Wynn, would you come up here, please?"

"Yes, ma'am," he replied, unable to move at first because the whole incident came as a shock. Why are they here, he wondered? But finally Junior had been able to make his legs move. Although shakily, he began to walk toward the front of the class, still with his head mostly down. That was how he noticed that another student had come back into the room through the backdoor as he was walking toward the front. He managed to lift his head up a little and look over his left shoulder to see that it was Will Glenn. The two of them shared this class as well. He wondered why he had come back into the room as he continued his slow trek up to the front where his history teacher, homeroom teacher and school principal were waiting. Silently at that moment, Junior prayed to God to strengthen him for whatever was coming next. He realized this threesome up ahead was not a *holy* trinity!

Standing before the triumvirate, books clasped tightly under his shoulder with beads of sweat forming around his head and under his arms a stream of sweat was slowly staining his shirt. He could feel this but didn't want to look toward his underarm to confirm it. Junior tried to tame his racing heart. He didn't want any of them to hear the nervousness in his voice when he spoke. They could already plainly see that he was shaken by the beads of perspiration on his forehead and the deepening wetness of his shirt around the armpits, running like a river whose levee was no longer secure. He knew he would have to speak because they would no doubt be asking him questions.

Obviously, someone or perhaps many people, had seen him and Cliff touching each other and pulling at places that generally remained out of view except in post-gymnasium activity showers! But how could they have seen it, Junior pondered trying to remain as present of mind as possible? Or perhaps they had heard them squirming making sounds that two teenagers make when alone together!

But they were so careful to make sure no one else was around! It made him sweat even more and breathe ever harder as he rewound the tape in his mind, trying to piece out what exactly might have been overseen or overheard. But, too late to worry about that now! What Junior had assumed to be hidden in the janitor's closet or in a deserted boys' bathroom, had clearly been drummed out of the darkness and was now being held under a harsh and hateful bright white spotlight! He had no reason to think anything else!

Will Glenn was Arlington High's own *Peter Gunn*, it must be! He had done the undercover detective work, no doubt shocked by what he had discovered but not too much to report his expose, Junior figured.

"Wynn Horry, please walk with us," commanded the principal, looking stone like and standing legs akimbo across from Junior. At that moment, he felt like a wilting blade of grass about to be mowed down by the sharp blade of the encroaching grass cutter. This was imagery Junior knew well enough and how ironic, he thought, that it would occur to him now since this was undoubtedly about him and Cliff and their splendor after the grass! He knew that he had no hope of surviving this and at this juncture he could only pray that it would be as painless a skiving as possible. He did not ask why he was being escorted to the principal's office, which was clearly where they were headed, but instead, followed behind this man and his homerun teacher as they turned to leave. They left behind the history teacher as well as Will Glenn both of whom he knew had eyes set on him the entire time as if they were watching a creature from some forbidden place finally meet his doom among the good people who wanted him dead!

In fact, Junior at that moment did feel like a trapped animal or perhaps an accused criminal being dragged off to some ordeal which he didn't yet know the conclusion of but clearly knew it would not end well!

"We have learned that you have been bringing marijuana cigarettes to this school and giving them to one of our students," said the principal once they were in his office behind a closed door. "Something like that is grounds for suspension from this school." Mr Rakowski had joined along with Junior's homeroom teacher. At this point, all Junior could think of was an episode of the *Twilight Zone* that hadn't been made yet!

"Sir, I do not have marijuana cigarettes and do not smoke marijuana," Junior managed to counter in his own defense, and he was the only one coming to his defense, it was clear! Despite not knowing how he could get the words out owing to his catatonic state there in the principal's office. Just about ten short minutes earlier, he was sitting in history class during a discussion of the Civil War with thoughts of meeting up later with Cliff. But now, here he was on trial! Here he was about to be sentenced even though he had no idea what evidence existed against him!

Suddenly, as if on cue, Mr Rakowski spoke up. "I have seen you going into the janitor's closet downstairs and I have stood outside the door and heard you smoking marijuana. I know that you have been giving marijuana to another student. It isn't right for you to corrupt our students with all that," he added. "We are not used to that up here." How anyone could hear someone smoking was beyond Junior, but he realized nevertheless that he and Cliff had been caught in their clandestine closet capers.

"Mr Rakowski is correct," the principal interjected. "I cannot tolerate behavior like that, so we will have to remove you from this school." Through all this, Junior stood silent and still! He knew none of this was true but how could he respond? How could he explain what was going on in the closet? How could he even speak about the closet? So much was going through his head at that time. What could he say to these men? Had they asked Cliff about this? Did they know more than they were saying? As all these questions were going through his mind, Junior was at the same time struggling with what he would say.

He knew it didn't much matter *what* he said because he was in a trap and he knew it! "We were not smoking marijuana, sir," he managed to proclaim. "We were smoking cigarettes." Everything was already going up in smoke so why not fan the flames in a different direction, he decided.

Chapter 28

Dinner party conversation at the Peterson house on Friday night switched between the colored student sit-ins that were occurring in North Carolina, the fact that Jack Paar still hadn't returned to host the *Jack Paar Show* after walking off the show the night after a joke got cut from the taped broadcast, to the Soviet claim that they would be going to Mars in the next few years. This last topic took up much of the conversation, since they were reticent to talk too much about politics given that their dinner guests were the couple they had met at the airport in Los Angeles at the beginning of the year. The husband, after all, worked for Vice President Nixon and Chester was leaning to supporting Senator Kennedy in the November election. Claire was still undecided, although she found herself falling in love with Jack as many Americans like her were, and his wife Jacqueline too. They liked Hubert, no doubt, but didn't feel as though he could pull it off. He was seen as a little weak.

"I have heard that Kennedy is considering promising a man on the moon as part of his campaign," their guest announced with a chuckle sitting in the living room on the teak sofa that was getting some use for the first time in the fledgling year. "This is designed to show that we can keep up with the *Russkies* who keep beating our ass in space," he went on. "I'm not sure how that is going to work or if anyone will actually believe it," the Nixon staffer continued.

"Well, maybe his daddy can pay for a trip to the moon for him," his wife chided. "Let's hope he gets stuck up there and Nixon wins the election by default."

"Wouldn't that bring into question Nixon's validity as President?" Claire asked jokingly but at the same time with an honest concern.

"Not any more than Kennedy's probable placement as middle man to the Vatican," the wife replied.

"Hmmm," said Claire, not wanting to get into a debate with her guests about widespread, though unfounded concerns in her mind and Chester's too, about the religion of the likely candidate of the Democratic party.

Besides, she was concerned about Cliff. He had been in a sullen mood for the past week, although he wouldn't say why to either her nor his father. She had asked him if things were going okay at school and he said yes, so it was difficult for her or his father to imagine what would deflate his usually upbeat mood to the point that he had clearly been let down. Nevertheless, Claire thought to stoke the dying embers of the conversation by mentioning that she had started to read *The Manchurian Candidate*, quickly on its way to becoming a bestseller after its recent release.

The *New York Times* had called it "wild, vigorous, curiously readable mélange", but Claire was finding a novel about a wealthy political candidate scion suddenly becoming a killer who is "remotely controlled" by the Soviets a bit hard to swallow. Admittedly it was funny and probably a little too closely related to the reality of the 1960 election. Kennedy was from a prominent family, yes, but no one had accused him of being a communist stooge. At least from all outward appearances, he was determined to match the Soviet measures on land and in space, toe to toe.

"A thriller it is," Chester piped in, admitting that he had been reading a bit of the 300-plus page novel himself. "Funny how timing works," he added. "To think that the protagonist could remind one of John Kennedy even though he isn't a candidate for President."

"Well, maybe that means that Kennedy has a dark side," uttered the wife, "but I don't want to start that conversation again," she stated with a smirk on her face. "My husband is too obsessed with going to space to read a book like that. He's been reading a new novel called *The Enemy Stars* about humans going to the moon, or something like that."

"Who is the author?" Chester asked, between sips of his cup of decaffeinated black coffee.

"Someone named Anderson," the husband replied, "I forget his first name, but it starts with a P. I first learned of him by reading one of his essays where the Soviets have won the Third World War and conquered the entire Earth as part of their victory." But, he went on, explaining the essay, the resistance still has some hope, because space flight is still possible. "By the end of the piece, the dissidents have established themselves in another stellar system and live there for years and years but eventually their descendants build an army and set out to free the Earth from Soviet domination."

"Wow, that's quite a story," Chester chuckled. "Aren't we all just overly obsessed with outer space these days. To think that we could come to a place that we have been conquered by an enemy and are now launching a resistance battle to free ourselves. How wild a thought that is?" Chester concluded.

"Well, on that note, I think we should end this while we're still hopeful," the husband declared, looking very matter-of-fact as he walked behind Claire to the hall closet to take his wife's coat and then his own. It was a cold but not too cold Friday evening in March. A warm coat came in handy.

The couple had a relatively short drive back to Dupont Circle across the Key Bridge and then along M Street through West End. Friday night in West End was always busy with colored residents going to and fro. Even though the windows were up on their 1957 Ford Thunderbird, they could still hear music coming from houses and night clubs once they crossed into DC. Colored neighborhoods were always lively, and people were in the streets, standing on street corners, sitting on porches or walking in groups and often talking and laughing loud enough to be heard before they were actually seen.

Cliff and Robby had finished their homework while Chester and Claire were entertaining their guests. They had been given their dinner upstairs in their rooms, but Cliff had been invited to join the guests for dessert. He was quiet during most of the conversation, which was not unusual for her introverted son, but he did seem more despondent than she knew him to be around company. The wife, especially, had tried to make conversation with him, asking him about school, sports, music and movies.

He responded to all her questions with usual politeness but made no effort to extend a conversation. "What do you guys do with the chickees these days, still go to parties and dances and steal kisses behind the bleachers?" the husband had asked during dessert. "Forgive me, I don't know for sure what pretty girls are called anymore," he followed up. "I have a younger brother who just started college and that's what he says."

"Yeah, I've heard that term before," Cliff replied, trying to stir up a smile.

Just about that time, Claire looked at her son. "Cliff has a few of the pretty girls after him but he decides to hold them at arm's length," she joked. "I suspect his father might have been like that too at his age," she giggled, cutting a side eyed look at Chester.

"Oh, of course," her husband replied, picking up on her banter. "We Peterson men don't fall easily." Cliff managed to pick his head up and muster a smile at his father first, and then his mother and the guests.

But now that everyone had gone, he was focused on the weekly episode of the *Twilight Zone*, trying to take his mind off his sadness. Interestingly, the episode was about two astronauts traveling to Mars, the subject matter of much of the dinner and dessert conversation, although he had heard only what was discussed at dessert. The title of the evening's episode was "People Are Alike All Over". This made him think of Junior. Despite what the other kids thought about the Negro students, he knew that they were really all just alike… for the most part at least.

He also knew that Junior was probably watching the show as well. That made him feel closer to him even though they had not seen each other or talked for a few days. For the first time in his life, Cliff had a pain in his heart that kept stabbing at him and he was certain that nothing could take it away except being with Junior. But Junior had been taken away from him. By now he knew that Junior had been expelled from school for bringing in marijuana. He also knew it wasn't true, but he had to accept that smoking marijuana was a better explanation for their clandestine meetings than the actual truth!

As he watched the episode of the show and saw the astronaut being caged by the Martians and put on display after the spaceship had landed there, Cliff felt more hopeless and alone than before! More than ever, he needed to be with Junior because he was the only one who understood him and could make him feel better. Junior could make him feel safe! But the powers that be had taken Wynn Horry Junior away from him and there he was, on his own against the masses!

"Cliff, are you okay?" his mother's voice rang out gently as she was entering the living room.

"Yes," he shouted back to her although not turning to look her way. "Just watching the Martians repress the Earthlings." It was just an episode on a television show, but it did make Cliff think. Why are we so anxious to go into a world that we know nothing about, he asked himself? Why can't everything just be okay the way it is, he wondered lying on the floor in front of the television, on the cinnamon, tan and brown wool rug made in Sweden, his head on a pillow borrowed from the sofa. A heart filled with pain seemed to produce a head full of thoughts.

Chapter 29

A friendly face was hard to find at Arlington High that afternoon that Junior had been expelled. Finally, he found one when his Aunt Nellie arrived at school. She had been listed as his emergency contact; after all, she worked in the Congressman's house not too far away from the school. When the principal's secretary called the house, Nellie answered the phone and was glad she did. She wasn't glad to get the call to come pick up her nephew from the school because he was being expelled, but she was glad that she was the one who answered the phone and not the Congressman's wife! This is not something she would want her to be the first to find out! Once Nellie got over her shock, she put on her coat, got into her car and drove the few short blocks to the high school.

Hardly ever nervous or out of sorts, Nellie was shaking the entire time. From the time she put the phone down, found the Congressman's wife in the study reading her *National Geographic* magazine and told her she had to rush over to the high school, but she would be right back, she was shaking so hard and her nerves were so on edge, she could hardly speak the words.

"Why do you need to go to Arlington High School?" her lady asked.

"It's my nephew," she muttered. "Something has happened. I don't know what, but I have to go get him." As she rushed out of the front door headed to the street to her car, she managed to let the Congressman's wife know she would be back as soon as possible. She heard her say that she hoped nothing had happened to him as she was rushing out, feeling her blood pressure rise! "Thank you, ma'am," she hollered back while running toward her car, not sure how she was able to get those few words out! Nellie was nervous also for another reason.

She had never walked into a white school before. And yet, there she was hoping to penetrate this beautiful but incredibly imposing stone fortress that built strong minds and created leaders, sending one-time tenderfoots marching out of its mighty portals armed with the knowledge to dominate as those before them had done. Did she have to go through a back door, a side door? Where could she park her car? How would she find the principal's office? It was hard enough that her nephew was being expelled from this school, probably because they were doing all they could to get the colored students out, but now she had to deal with these uncertainties in addition to this news. "Lord Almighty walk with me," Nellie uttered to herself as she drove, hands shaking on the wheel when they weren't wiping away the sweat on her forehead caused by her nervousness and dread!

This had all transpired a few days earlier, but it still seemed as if it was yesterday! At least that was the way Junior felt. Soon it would be Easter break, and school would be closed anyway. But that didn't really make what had happened any easier to stomach. Junior already felt crucified!

Julia Mae had taken it the hardest! Her smart son who never had gotten into trouble in his life, was all of a sudden thrown out of school! This would have been completely unfathomable at any point for either of her two children. But this was Arlington High. Junior was a good student, getting good grades those first months of being there, not for a colored student but for any student. But yet he was expelled for smoking marijuana! When did her son ever smoke a marijuana cigarette and where would he ever get it? No one they knew smoked marijuana cigarettes. The only people that they could think of who would even have it would be some musicians over on U Street or on 14th Street, but how would Junior get it since he didn't know any of them or hang around them? Did he get it from the kitchen staff at Horrschorns on the weekend?

Julia Mae and Wynn had questioned their son on this ever since that evening that Nellie brought him home. He had assured them that he did not have marijuana. What he told them was that he and Cliff were smoking weed. Plenty of kids smoked cigarettes, so that would be easier for them to swallow. But he knew they would never accept that he smoked reefer! No way would anyone in his family want to hear that and besides, no one who knew Junior would even believe it!

But he did wonder if Cliff had been questioned. Did he tell them that the colored boy gave him marijuana cigarettes, Junior thought? This he quickly dismissed believing that he knew Cliff better than that. Still, he had always been instructed not to trust white people and perhaps the adults knew what they were talking about. Maybe Cliff had caved and agreed to whatever they wanted him to say. He was in no danger of being put out of school regardless, so why not just say what they wanted to hear?

This was the day of the Pioneer 5 blast off into space which everyone had been buzzing about earlier on that fateful day at Arlington High. He, on the other hand, had just crash landed and he wasn't certain if he would survive the fall! Surely the talk at Arlington High now was how another colored student had bitten the dust!

Junior could never know for sure what the talk was since he had no more ties to the school, but he did keep in touch with Ray and Thomasine who were still there. Besides, his mother had gone to see Old Papa to find out from him what was going on before she and Wynn Sr went to the school. They had made a date to go next week when she could get off from her job. Wynn would drive up in his lunch hour. The principal's office had told her not to bother to come. "It's a done deal," they said. "We do not condone smoking in this school, and we certainly don't want marijuana cigarettes on our premises which your boy brought here."

"I doubt very seriously that my son has any marijuana cigarettes," Julia Mae protested as gently as possible so as not to offend the principal too much. But at the same time, she wanted to press her case. "He told me that they were smoking weed, I mean cigarettes," she corrected herself, to sound more educated. Young people referred to cigarettes as weed but adults called them cigarettes. Since Junior had told her that it was Cliff he smoked with, Julia Mae mulled over whether or not she should try to talk with Mrs Peterson about it. After all, Cliff's mother, and a few of the other North Arlington ladies that she sewed for were actually helpful in getting Junior into Arlington High in the first place. It had been two days since this happened and Mrs Peterson hadn't called her. Julia Mae figured she was either too disgusted, disappointed about the whole thing or perhaps she didn't know. Since they all figured that no action had been taken against Cliff, maybe there was no reason that she would know.

Julia Mae hadn't told Junior that she was planning to go to North

Arlington to visit the Petersons. She had discussed the possibility with Wynn, but he asked her what it would prove. "They prolly don't want to see us," he pointed out. "Why put yourself through that? We both know they would do all they could to get the colored kids out of that school," he went on. "I just don't know why the hell Junior would give them ammunition. I just don't know what that boy was thinking," he grumbled simultaneously shaking his head.

But Julia had decided she would go to North Arlington and Nellie had encouraged her to. The same day they were scheduled to visit the principal's office Nellie suggested that she try to see Claire Peterson first. "Take the bus on up to her house and I will meet you there," Nellie assured her. After all, as she noted, "I was the one who was at the school to pick Junior up. I heard what they said about him and I believe him when he said he wasn't smoking marijuana cigarettes and didn't give anybody else any."

"Besides, it's gon' help you to show up with your sister 'cause you don't know how to work white people the way I do." Nellie chuckled when she said this and so did Julia Mae, even though Junior's mother found it hard to laugh these days. But she agreed that it might be good for her sister to visit. And going to see Mrs Peterson before she and Wynn met with the principal might be advantageous. Nellie helped her to understand that expelling another colored student from Arlington High, particularly a good one, could come at a cost for the school district. Integration was court ordered, she reminded her. They couldn't just throw the colored kids out willy-nilly!

"Wear that navy blue suit with the two buttons on the jacket," Nellie instructed her sister. "That will make you look like you belong in North Arlington."

"I don't want to go looking too good because you know how that might upset those white people," Julia Mae countered. "You know crackers don't want to see Negroes looking too smart."

In response to that concern, which in all honesty, Nellie couldn't discount, she suggested that her sister wear a pair of ballet flats. "You look good in them."

"Oh, my pumps would be too much for them, huh," Julia Mae chided.

"Well, you're tall already and you don't want to look too uppity."

"Well, at least the ballet slippers are patent leather," Julia Mae chided.

"Wear the wool tweed coat with the hood," said Nellie through the phone, remembering how she liked that coat on her sister. "And put on the white pearl earrings and beads. I want you to look better than I did when I ran over there the other day in my uniform. Junior belongs there as much as anybody and you ought to look like it," Nellie professed with increasing conviction in her voice.

"But you just said I shouldn't look too uppity," Julia Mae reminded her, laughing a bit. "Now you want me to go in there looking like Pearl Bailey?" Julia Mae had a smirk on her face although her sister couldn't see this through the phone, but she could hear it in her younger sister's voice, nevertheless.

"Chile, you know what I'm talkin' 'bout," she replied. "Dealing with white folks is like walking on a tightrope, you have to walk it just right!"

"I will wear the long black wool coat instead," Julia Mae declared. "That tweed one is the kind of coat you wear with heels."

"The funeral coat?" Nellie intoned both asking a question and making a statement. "We're not going to bury Junior."

"I will wear it with a red and green scarf," said Julia Mae, "two strong colors!"

"Girl, Christmas is over," Nellie contended.

But her sister countered that perhaps a red and green scarf would put Mrs Peterson is a cheerful and giving mood. "Let it be Christmas all over again, if that's what it takes!" The two sisters fell into laughter on their respective ends of the phone. Had they been in the room together Nellie would have grabbed Julia Mae's arm and Julia Mae would have jabbed her in the ribs.

The jesting with her sister took some of the stress off Julia Mae. Nellie knew this and was happy that she could be of support. It was quite difficult for Julia Mae and Wynn Senior to be going through these last few days with Junior being expelled from Arlington High. If it was that hard on them, she imagined how hard it must be for her son who had always loved school so much! Junior had always looked forward to going to school and learning. She could see how troubled and out of sorts he was during those days since he had been told by the principal that he could not come back to Arlington High, watched over as he cleaned out his locker and escorted to the door with only his aunt Nellie by his side as she walked with him to her car. He was shocked and sullen the whole while and she was concerned about her nephew and eager to comfort him but at the same time doubtful about the charges and disputatious about the indignancy that he had just been party to!

Chapter 30

Wynn's plan was to immediately enroll him in the colored high school. "That will put an end to all this," he argued. But when Julia countered with the argument that Junior wouldn't receive the same kind of education at the colored high school, Wynn also remonstrated that Junior would at least have a more peaceful experience in the colored high school. "He won't need to look over his shoulder all day for whatever is coming next," he bellowed. Neither parent, nor Jeanne had believed the accusation that Junior was smoking marijuana cigarettes. They knew him better than that. They had trouble believing that he was smoking "weed" either. They had never seen him smoke a cigarette even though Wynn smoked on occasion as did Julia Mae, although less frequently. At no time had either noticed a cigarette missing from a pack that they had opened. If he had started smoking, it was owing to the influence of the white kids that he was around at Arlington High, rather than the other way around!

Besides, there was countervailing evidence that Junior was not smoking in the janitor's closet as alleged and certainly not marijuana cigarettes. Julia Mae, playing detective, had sought out Old Papa, the janitor at Arlington High that lived not too far from them in Hilldale and also went to Mount Calvary Baptist Church. Old Papa had always liked Junior and Jeanne as well and did his best to look out for him at school. He was as interested in talking to her as she was to him. His daughter, about Julia Mae's age, had urged him not to get involved. "Don't get mixed up in that," she had told him. "Those niggers don't belong up there in the first place and them whities know it," she contended. "If you get crossed up in that you will lose your job after all these years and that boy's family won't be able to do nothin' for you!"

Old Papa knew that he could lose his job if it was known that he had tried to help the Horry family, but he also realized that he could talk to them on the sly. Julia Mae suggested that he come over for dinner one evening, a few days after Junior had been expelled. She knew it was better for him to come there than for her to go to his house with his daughter and wife who also lived there, trying to persuade him not to talk and making the situation more tense than it already was. She wanted to arm herself with as much information as possible before going to the school and before talking with Mrs Peterson, if that was even going to be possible. Old Papa had informed her that he couldn't stay for dinner but that he appreciated her offer. "My wife ain't gon' let me miss out on her food but thank you just the same," he said with a smile on his face after Julia Mae had approached him one day.

At that meeting, held one evening after Wynn had gotten home from work and before the family sat down to dinner, everyone got an earful if not a stomach full. Old Papa, or Mr Bertie as Jeanne and Junior had always been instructed to call him, was happy to see Junior as he opened the door. Julia Mae had suggested it because she wanted to see Old Papa's reaction to him early on. He was instructed to invite him to come into the living room, which the front door opened into, and come sit on the sofa. Wynn was upstairs with Jeanne but would come down once Old Papa had come in and Julia Mae was in the kitchen getting some iced tea with cheese and crackers to bring out. She didn't want to spoil anyone's dinner, but you couldn't have someone over to your house in the evening, or anytime really, without offering them something to eat and drink. This was how she had been raised.

Once Old Papa was on the sofa and Junior was sitting next to him, Julia Mae came out of the kitchen to say hello and Wynn and Jeanne came downstairs, Wynn heading directly to the sofa to shake hands with Old Papa. "Nice to see you again," he said to their guest. "Thanks for coming over to help us get to the bottom of this." Though he might not have seemed it, Wynn was uncomfortable. First of all, he wasn't one to want company in the house much at all. Secondly, the whole affair was difficult for him to come to terms with and Wynn wasn't one to express his feelings too well. In fact, he didn't really want to pursue the whole thing too much.

While he was angry about Junior being expelled and he believed it was all trumped up to get him out, he didn't see what dredging it up would solve since "they are not going to take Junior back into that school", he kept telling his wife. But, of course, he knew that Julia Mae would not leave it alone. He knew that she wouldn't be satisfied until she felt that she at least had confirmed that she was right that Junior had been dismissed unfairly and that he had not done what he had been accused of. He loved his wife for this, but he also hated that she put herself and her family through it!

"Old Papa, how you been, man," said Wynn as he bent over to sit on the sofa where their guest sat with their son. Old Papa, still seated, stretched out his hand for Wynn to shake it.

"An old man like me ain't gon' get no better but I thank my God that I ain't g'tting no worse," Old Papa laughed. Wynn always heard his father say some version of this when asked the same question, so he kind of expected a response that was at once jocose and genuine. That was the way, colored people bantered with each other, and older ones always did it best!

"I hear ya, my man, I hear ya," Wynn replied. "We appreciate you comin' over to help clear this thing up. My wife has had this on her mind since it happened and she just wants to get some peace," Wynn added, as if to offer a defense for what was going on.

"As she indeed should," Old Papa shouted out before Wynn could finish yelling into the kitchen for Julia Mae to come out.

"This boy ain't done nuthin' he shouldn't been doin'," Old Papa argued, his voice shaking a bit, "…other than bein' colored at Arlington High. In all the years I been workin' there I never thought I would see a colored face other than on a janitor or a gal in the cafeteria," Old Papa continued. But then when they let these six black children in I 'bout cried but somethin' told me right then, that they was gon' try to find a way to get every one of them out," he said shaking his head. "They done already got rid of one boy sayin' he was after some white man's wife and now they done did the same thing with Junior claiming he smoking them marijuana cigarettes. They know that ain't true. If that was true, I woulda smelt it and they woulda smelt it too."

By now, Julia Mae had come out of the kitchen and placed the platter of cheese and crackers on the coffee table in front of Old Papa. Wynn was seated in his favorite chair directly across from the television and Jeanne was sitting in the chair usually occupied by her mother. Julia Mae was still not sitting. She had hardly moved after putting the plate of appetizers down and she had become a little bit emotional after hearing what Old Papa had to say. "Well, I know my son never did that and I am so happy to hear you say it, sir," Julia Mae stated, her voice full of emotion. "But for the life of me I just don't know why Junior would be in the janitor's closet in the first place with a white boy. I know they know each other well and are friends but why the closet?" she went on, shaking her head.

Finally, Junior spoke up, practically cutting Old Papa off as he was about to say something too. "We were just talking, Mama, I told you that. We can't really talk in front of the others and we just wanted to talk."

"I was just 'bout to say, all I heard was talking," Old Papa interjected. "I didn't hear no arguin' or fightin', just talkin' and I certainly didn't smell no marijuana." Old Papa, falling back on humor once again, acknowledged that he knew what marijuana cigarettes smell like. "They ain't new! We smoked 'em back in the day when times was real hard," he told the Horrys. "They make hard times get better quick!!" Everyone chuckled, including Old Papa, and realized that they had gotten what they had all hoped to get out of this visit. Nevertheless, Wynn felt to ask his son what he and Cliff had to talk about down in the janitor's closet that they couldn't talk about quietly someplace else, outside the school building or something.

"And why would you say you were smoking cigarettes if you were just talking?" Wynn wanted to know, although he and Julia Mae had gone over this already.

Junior was ready with an answer, having anticipated the question. "Pop, if we want to talk about a class assignment or just talk about music or movies or something, going outside to do it would look more odd, than just going somewhere where no one will see us in the building. Besides," he added, "it's been cold outside. They cornered me so fast claiming that I was smoking marijuana that all I could think to say was that it was cigarettes," he further explained, hoping his story made sense to his father. Wynn, who had no reply to this, dropped his head and once he picked it up shortly after, looked over at his wife and said that he guessed there wasn't much more they could do at this point.

"Lord, have mercy," Julia Mae uttered. "Can you believe it's better to lie about smoking cigarettes than to admit that you were talking with a classmate about an assignment, at that school?" she asked in amazement, not necessarily to anyone in particular.

"Well, we glad to have you here, Mr Bertie and I just want to make sure you can't stay for dinner, 'cos we would be glad to have you and got plenty," Julia Mae ascertained, hoping to sound more respectful by using his given name.

"Yes, feel free to stay, sir," Junior proffered to his guest and star witness for the defense although there would never be a trial, most likely. He at least hoped not, because the truth, the whole truth, could never see the light of day, so help me God, Junior said over and over to himself.

"So where's this child gon' go to school?" Old Papa asked. "He need to be in school."

Wynn acknowledged that they had been figuring that out. "I want him to go to Mercer and finish," his father admitted. "At least he won't have any of those issues there."

"Yea, that's what they want us to do to keep the coloreds out of the white schools," Julia Mae asserted. "And that's exactly the reason why my son won't be going to Mercer." Feeling as though she had to make clear that she had nothing against the school, Julia Mae explained that her feelings had more to do with not wanting to leave the decision of where her son went to high school in the hands of those who wanted to limit his choices. "I want him to go where he is going to get the best education and we all know that is going to happen at a white high school."

"I will be going to school in the District," Junior told Old Papa, attempting to circumvent any argument that might break out between his parents. God knows there had been enough heated conversations about this over the past week since his expulsion. "I will use my aunt and uncle's address in Georgetown to go to one of the high schools in Northwest."

"One of the integrated high schools," his mother pointed out. "Just make sure you don't run off into no closet with no white boy," Julia Mae declared! "Will we see you at church on Palm Sunday and Easter, Old

Papa?" Julia Mae asked as she walked their guest to the door.

"I'm not so big on Palm Sunday but I wouldn't miss Easter if the devil hisself came up and blocked the front door," Old Papa declared. "I will see y'all looking bright and beautiful on Easter!"

This was a hopeful note on which to end the visit of Old Papa. After all, they had got what they all came together for. Easter was about two weeks away and that was always a happy time for the Horrys as the rebirth of Christ had a way of making anything seem possible! Julia Mae was satisfied. Old Papa felt he had done his duty. Wynn was glad it was over! But the one who had the most to gain or lose from it was left in a state of mild shock!

Junior was surprised that Old Papa said all he heard was talking. He didn't realize that anyone was outside listening but if they were, the sounds they would have heard, although low and muffled, would not have been talking! Nevertheless, he was glad his friend Old Papa was complicit in wanting to defend him. But he didn't want to let his mind consider what Old Papa, or any of the other janitors might have really heard because he couldn't allow himself to imagine what they would think about him if they knew, and how they could ever look at him again without disgust and disdain! But why would Old Papa lie, Junior couldn't help but ask himself? Could it be that his hearing is bad or he is just too old to figure things out, he wondered? Whatever the answer, it looked as though his greatest fear of being found out would not be realized and this was a great relief. He didn't want that for him or for his family, it went without saying.

He hadn't talked to Carolyn much since this had all happened, although she had sought to spend time with him several times since and her family had expressed their support as well. Everyone in Hilldale knew what had happened and most were disappointed and angry because they continued to be proud of those students, the first ones to integrate a white school. But needless to say, there were those who never thought it was the right or prudent thing in the first place. Regardless of all that, all he could think was that perhaps it was time to seek the company of Carolyn Stanley.

Of course, he hadn't forgotten Cliff. But his feelings for Cliff, and incidentally Cliff's feelings for him he had no doubt, couldn't stymie the need to act prudently from here on out. It was imprudent behavior, after all, that had caused this near cataclysm in the first place. He missed touching Cliff's face and hair, always full of pomade, having their arms around each other and their bodies pressed together. He missed the loud and strong sound their hearts made when they were with each other as it almost beat out of their chests. He longed for the excitement that grew and grew the longer they were with each other and how comforting it was to feel the joy that he gave to Cliff and that Cliff gave to him! Even though it was usually in the dark, he could close his eyes and still see the bright smile he brought to Cliff's face and he certainly knew the joy that exploded over him! But he had to get over Cliff now! At bare minimum, he had to contain his excitement for him after the way it had all blown up in his face, not Cliff's face!

Chapter 31

"I'm not sure this is what I want for our family," Chester affirmed loudly! "We've been through this before. I'm not saying we should just run away from everything, but we do need to come to a decision about what we're going to do about it." Chester didn't usually talk with this much conviction. There was no doubt that he was serious about what he was saying!

Sitting on the bed listening to her husband as he tied his navy-blue necktie with gold and red rep strips around his starched white shirt, Claire was clearly stressed, her head alternately turned toward Chester standing in front of the Drexel "Declaration" dresser and giving himself the final once over before turning away and declaring himself suitable for work, and down toward the bedspread as if she were considering every strand of thread on it.

"I know, Sonny," she was finally able to reply. "I know how much another move abroad can mean for your career. But like we both said," she added, "this is an interesting time to be at home. There's so much going on now, the Presidential election, all the scientific advancements, for God's sake, a man could go to the moon any day now and we would be in Africa and not see any of it on television. With the boys growing up as fast as they are, do we want them to miss out on this new and great America?" she asked rhetorically.

"Well, you're rehashing all the points we've already discussed," Chester answered her. "We know all that and we agreed that one solution would be to leave the boys here. Cliff will soon be in college anyway, so it might be better to leave him put." By now he was heading down the steps toward the kitchen where his coffee, although cold at this point, was waiting for him along with an English muffin waiting to be toasted, and his dark brown attaché case.

Claire was in pursuit. "Yes, I know that's one solution. The boys can go live with my parents in Rochester or yours in Palm Springs, but I'm not sure I want to leave Robby." This last part she whispered in her husband's ear because the boys too were getting ready for school and she didn't want them to overhear too much. They were already downstairs eating their oatmeal and toast and drinking their orange juice which she had prepared for them while making coffee for her husband.

The truth is that Claire had mixed feelings about leaving Robby back in the US if they had decided to go to Africa to take up an appointment as Chargé D'Affaires for one of the new African nations, very likely Nigeria or Ivory Coast, both of which would be gaining independence very soon. This would be a definite promotion for Chester. She thought that a boy Robby's age should be with his parents. The idea of separating her two sons killed her inside but it was true that Cliff would soon be getting ready for college and therefore it was best to leave him in a school in the United States. Arlington High had an outstanding record of students getting into great colleges, but clearly, he couldn't stay there if they had moved away. She preferred Rochester for him to live because there were excellent schools there and it was a great neighborhood her parents lived in. But her parents were getting older and she wasn't sure it was the best for either of them. She thought of having him live with Peter. They clearly were each other's favorite nephew and uncle, so from that standpoint it would work out.

But Peter's lifestyle as a bachelor might not be the best fit for her son. He needed a normal family life to model and Peter couldn't offer that, at least not currently. It was also clear, however, that it wasn't a good idea to take Cliff back to Africa! The behavior that they learned of him to be having with the houseboys and guards was troubling. They thought he was becoming too friendly with these African boys and they knew that some of his playing around with them was untoward. Claire and Chester never spoke about it but they both knew that the discovery of Cliff's behavior hastened their return from Africa!

Most of this behavior had transpired when Cliff was a pre-teen, at least as far as they knew, but still both she and Chester had figured it probably hadn't changed. This issue with Junior, which he had finally told her about, had definitely renewed her concerns. She knew they had been spending time together but figured things would be different now that they were back home. American colored boys wouldn't be like African boys! There would be none of that with them! Junior didn't work for his family, depend on them. He was not at their mercy for a basic subsistence. He had no reason to be led down Cliff's rabbit hole!

Yet her son and Junior had become close and she now knew about their discovery together in a janitor's closet! Neither she nor Chester believed that their son would be interested in marijuana cigarettes or any kind of cigarettes, but they had to come up with something to explain the behavior. They settled on the fact that perhaps it was better for a white boy and a colored boy to keep their friendship private at Arlington High. Maybe it was best that no one see them talking too much or got the impression they were too familiar with each other.

But, although Claire was unaware, that had already been Junior's defense of why he and Cliff were in the janitor's closet in the first place. He had already admitted to his mother and father that they were simply trying to find a place to be friends without the glare of all those other students and teachers who would look down on their friendship. Claire, of all people, couldn't peddle the excuse that a white boy and colored boy should not be flaunting their friendship openly at school. Hadn't she been the one to help get the colored kid into the school and didn't she also encourage her two sons to be judicious in their regard for people who might be less fortunate than themselves?

At any rate, she saw how withdrawn Cliff had become since Junior had been ousted from the school and it was crystal clear to her that Junior's friendship meant a lot to him. She wanted to do something, but part of her thought that perhaps it was best for them to be separated. Chester had agreed!

She thought about what she would say to Julia Mae who was coming over later that day to talk with her about it. "Maybe it's better for both of them," she would say. But for right now, she wanted to turn her attention away from all of it because it brought back memories that she preferred to forget and thoughts that she wished not to have! Claire and Chester did have a White House State dinner invitation to get ready for in about a week. She already had a convenient excuse to divert her attention away from Cliff and Junior's closet covertness.

Chapter 32

"Just because it seems like it's dead, don't mean it can't come back to life. That is the message of Easter and I am here to tell you that God is alive," the pastor at Mount Calvary shouted from the lectern at the top of the pulpit. He shouted it so loudly that the lectern bobbled a bit before returning to a still position. It seemed to be as agitated as the congregation who shouted back to the pastor as usual when he gave them a message that moved them!

"Hallelujah and praise the Lord!" screamed members of the congregation.

"Christ is alive, and all is renewed," shouted others.

Mount Calvary Baptist of Arlington was adorned with Easter lilies on the pulpit and there were flowers on hats, lapels, dresses and even some behind women's ears throughout the church on that bright Sunday morning! The sun shone through the stained-glass windows of the beautiful old church and the organ played spiritedly to match the moods of the large, happy congregation who had come to verify that God was alive and all was well!

"Children of the Living God, today is Easter but I don't want to bring you the traditional Resurrection Day message," the pastor told his flock. "As I look out on this church full of happy, beautiful and hopeful faces on this gorgeous Sunday morning, as gorgeous as all of you are in your marvelous hats, dresses, suits and ties, I am so happy to know that God is truly alive, and he is with us as we take every step! As we take every step in our own private lives and in our lives as a people," he went on, now pacing back and forth on the pulpit, his hands folded behind his back.

"We all know by now how Jesus rose out of that tomb on Easter Sunday after being crucified on that Friday. We all know how he died for our sins, but he ascended back up to heaven so that we may have everlasting life. We all know that the Easter egg we color with bright colors is a symbol for the new beginning that breaks forth when we observe the Resurrection of Christ," the pastor went on. "But do we all realize that we are being witness to a new crucifixion?" he asked the hushed church.

"What you mean, Pastor?" several congregants shouted at almost the same time.

"Is Christ being crucified again?" someone else asked.

"Nooo, Christ is alive and well," the Reverend replied. "It is hate, injustice and discrimination that is being crucified! It is being crucified in Greensboro, Montgomery, Birmingham and probably very soon right here in our own backyard. It is being crucified by the young," he acknowledged. "These young college and high school students throughout the south and around the nation are the modern-day Pontius Pilate." By now, Mount Calvary was no longer quiet. Instead, more shouts of halleluiah and praise God for these young folks, emanated from the full church. They won't take it no more, said many, their arms raised to the sky with palms open as if to catch the goodness of God!

"These modern-day Pontius Pilates are not on their crucifixion quest with pettiness and malice as was the case when they nailed Jesus to the Cross," the pastor continued, making his case. "Instead, it is with passion," he announced with a chuckle, acknowledging his own pun, "it is with a passion for justice and the rights they deserve, in fact that we all deserve as the children of God. Make no mistake, God is alive, and he is with us! He is giving us the power and the right to crucify injustice so that we can all find the way to God's love and let his will of loving our fellow neighbor as ourselves be fully realized here on earth!"

"Didn't my Lord deliver Daniel?" the preacher asked, prompting the gospel choir to offer the stand-by Negro spiritual. "Didn't my Lord deliver Daniel, deliver Daniel, deliver Daniel... didn't my Lord deliver Daniel then why not every man," the choir belted out from the choir loft rocking back and forth as many in the congregation did also! At the end of this sermon, everyone in the church rose to their feet, greeted each other with smiles and hugs and exchanges of Happy Easter or Happy Resurrection Day!

But Julia Mae had a smile on her face for another reason. She had confided in the pastor about her concerns over Junior's dismissal from the formerly all-white high school. He had assured her that she should not stress over it, that all would work out in the end. However, Julia Mae was still unsure as to when "the end" had truly come. But she didn't dwell on that too long. The Horry family had to share their Easter greetings with members of the church, say a word to the pastor, then get home to change clothes and head to Georgetown. Nellie and Talley would be preparing to serve them ham, macaroni and cheese, collard greens and apple pie for Easter dinner. Nellie never made an apple pie before Easter and never after Thanksgiving. That was a spring and summer treat!

"Hey, Junior," the note started. "Haven't talked to you in a while and wanted you to know that I am thinking about how you are doing. I would like to talk with you about what has been going on. Can you meet me at 4:30 on Mason Blvd on the median across from the old bus depot? I hope to see you there!"

It went without saying that Junior was happy to get the note that Cliff had written him, put in a sealed envelope and given to Thomasine to deliver. He knew the spot, on Mason Blvd, that Cliff had referred to because Junior had told Cliff that he sometimes walked up there from his house which was just a few blocks away, to look at the old DC Transit buses that had been retired to the big lot, many of them still with their destination signs emblazoned across the front. The two of them had shared their like for buses at one time. Junior had told Cliff that as a boy, he had wanted to be a bus driver at one point. Although he later realized this could not happen as no bus drivers were colored. But still, he liked the shape of buses. The way they looked like bullets with their long and curved design. Cliff had confided to him also that the shape of buses excited him also. "I can imagine myself wearing a bus driver's uniform and cap and giving you a big smile when you got on my bus," he once told Junior over a lemonade when they were alone at his house on a hot Saturday afternoon after the grass had been cut but their thirst was still on the rise.

"Thanks, Seeny," Junior had said to his friend using her neighborhood nickname. Thomasine was still at Arlington High and she and Cliff were still friends. It was a natural that he would ask her to deliver a note to Junior. He knew that she wouldn't read it and even if she had, nothing he would write would betray anything about their friendship. Junior had taught him that. In fact, Junior was sorry that he hadn't thought of sending Cliff a message through Thomasine.

But really, shouldn't it be Cliff who contacts me, he thought whenever he had an inkling to talk with him, which was often! He still didn't know Cliff's place in all this that happened at school, but he did know that Cliff was still going to Arlington High. Or at least he had no reason to think he wasn't. It was now going on two weeks since they had been in contact with each other. Junior wanted to think it was as hard for Cliff as it was for him! He thought of Cliff almost all the time and it was so incredibly frustrating not to be able to be with him. Instead of withering, his depression and longing seemed as though it would never end! How could Cliff stand it, he often wondered?

Had Cliff found someone else to touch that way? Someone that his being friendly with wouldn't cause so much attention, Junior wondered. He found that hard to imagine, since there had always been others who seemed to show an interest in Cliff and yet, he shared those parts of himself only with Junior, it was obvious. Junior was certain that the enthusiasm that he showed during their time alone together he couldn't possibly have shown to anyone else. Cliff just wasn't made that way!

Chapter 33

Claire had come to a decision herself, not knowing that her son had already made plans to meet up with Junior. She had decided that instead of having Julia Mae come to Arlington Heights, she would drive down to Hilldale. The afternoon that Julia Mae was to visit, she called her and told her that she would be busy after all and that she would contact her in a few days to arrange a time to visit her at the Horry household. When Julia Mae explained that she wouldn't be able to get off work at just anytime to have the meeting and that it was important to talk with her before going to Arlington High to see the principal, Claire realized that the situation might be orbiting out of control and that the best thing might be to abandon ship.

"Julia Mae, I don't believe that you going to Arlington High is at all the best way to handle this," she said into the phone. "They will not take your son back in the school. They have already decided that. It is probably best for you to just let it go. We knew at the beginning that this was an experiment and that there would be challenges in making this work. So many were against it in the first place and many were not committed to having it succeed." Claire had practiced this speech, as she thought she would be delivering it in person. But she was glad to have abandoned that plan and actually thought it better to say these things over the phone instead. Why prolong this or make it too personal, she had convinced herself.

"If you want a letter on behalf of Junior, I will be glad to help but I think it better for him to go to the colored school for now and just let this all blow over for a while. There are only a few months left in the school year anyway, so it might be hard to get him anywhere else." Julia Mae remained quiet while Claire went through her argument. At first, she thought it was best to contain herself because she was afraid of what she might say to this woman who she felt had decided all by herself what was best for her son and her family! But, as she knew, it was advisable for her to hold her tongue. Much depended on it, not least was her future as a dressmaker to women like Claire and, of course, Claire herself. Besides, weren't these the same arguments that Wynn had made? It wasn't as if she hadn't heard all this before. "Just put Junior in Langston Mercer and let him finish out the year there," Wynn had said time and time again. "Then, over the summer, we can decide what to do with him for the fall semester."

"My son was not smoking marijuana cigarettes," Julia Mae managed to attest once Claire Peterson had stopped her speech to take a breath. "I don't want that on his record because it isn't true. He told me that and I believe him."

Claire, took in a deep breath, and paused for a minute after exhaling not for dramatic purposes but more as a way to show Julia Mae that she sympathized with her. "Cliff has told me the same thing and I believe him as well," she stated. "I will speak again to the principal and make sure that he understands that. I don't see why you have to take any of your time to go up there and have them be curt with you."

This was about as honest as Claire felt she could be! She hoped Julia Mae appreciated it. She hoped she knew exactly what she had meant when she used the word "curt". She didn't doubt that Julia Mae would be treated dismissively if they would even agree to see her at all at Arlington High. She was hoping to spare her that. While she could appreciate Julia Mae's instincts as a mother, she also knew that the administration at Arlington High would see her as a Negress whose son really didn't belong at the school in the first place and that she had no standing to be arguing anything!

"It is better for you to see it this way, Julia Mae," Claire stated trying to bring the phone call to an end. "It is also better for Junior to put this behind him and move on. I will do what I can to make sure that his records are good," Claire notified Julia Mae. "Okay, dear, I'm glad we had the chance to talk and you take good care," she offered as pacification to Julia Mae.

"Thanks for calling, Mrs Peterson," Julia Mae said in return. "Let me know what I can do for you in the future."

"Bye dear, and of course, I will." Those were the words last said into the phone by Claire Peterson, but Julia Mae didn't really hear them. She was replaying the conversation in her head and trying to contain her disappointment at the way she felt her concerns had been sidelined. Her mind was full, and her heart was fuller at the end of that conversation. So many thoughts were co-mingling in her head and all the noise in her thoughts actually drowned out some of her anger. Though standing the entire time of the phone conversation with Claire Peterson, Julia Mae was now sitting down on the seat that was attached to the gossip bench where the phone rested.

She ran her right hand across her forehead and dragged it down her face as if that would erase the signs of disgust, disappointment and disbelief that she was certain were imprinted there for anyone to see. "Lord today," she said to herself as she rose from the phone bench to go upstairs to take off the clothes she had put on for her trip to Arlington Heights. The makeup on her face would come off too. However, taking the makeup off might be delayed a bit, Julia Mae decided. She was not ready to see the look on her face right now. It was the very makeup, she considered, that covered the ugliness of the reality of the situation!

"Hi Junior, I'm happy to see you," Cliff proclaimed that Wednesday late afternoon when they met in South Arlington. It was a mild day, especially for April. Cliff wore a short-sleeved plaid shirt with a pair of blue jeans, cuffed at the bottom, with white socks and his brown penny loafers. He also wore a bright smile, one that almost matched the sunlight that was now beginning to wane just a bit but had been in full force earlier in the day.

"Hey, Cliffy," Junior beamed in reply to the enthusiastic greeting, reaching to shake his hand under the leafy green trees that stood tall and plentiful on the median strip that ran the length of Mason Drive, offering the shade of its branches and leaves on hot summer days and also adumbration from any assignations that might occur on that long stretch of greenspace that ran between the white and colored sections of Arlington, right there in the industrial area, close to the workers who held jobs as machinists, mechanics, repairmen or did other hard or manual labor. Junior was also smiling and happy to see Cliff after so long, to be near him and to be able to look into his face even though he dared not touch it out in the open on Mason Drive. It wasn't odd that they would meet there since residents, both colored and white used that corridor to get to and from their homes to their jobs.

Junior wore a burgundy and navy-blue tee shirt with horizontal stripes and also a pair of blue jeans rolled up at the cuff. While he liked penny loafers too, he had put on his white high-top All-Star sneakers to meet Cliff. Cliff always liked him in these sneakers saying he looked a lot like Wilt Chamberlain. It wasn't so much that Cliff knew sports figures, but Wilt Chamberlain was often on television since he played center for the Philadelphia Warriors. Mostly, it was the Chuck Taylor sneakers that made Cliff make the connection to Wilt Chamberlain. He had told Junior once or twice that he thought Chamberlain was a nice-looking colored man.

"I'm glad you got the note I sent through Thomasine," Cliff said, still with a smile on his face standing in front of Junior. Cars were whizzing by and people were busy leaving their shops as it was rush hour and everyone was headed home or to work for the evening shift. But no one paid any particular attention to the two boys standing there smiling at each other. The two boys who seemed so affixed on each other that they wouldn't have noticed whether anyone was noticing them or not, however.

"No, I thought it was neat that you did that," Junior answered. "Thomasine is friends with both of us, so why not."

"I'm sorry that you're not at school any more but I want you to know that I defended you and told everyone that we were just talking about schoolwork and stuff."

"I knew you probably said that, Cliff," said Junior. "Anyway, no one knows what was going on and that's what's important. I didn't think we were being watched but I guess we were," he lamented, his eyes falling to the ground and away from Cliff for the first time since they had reconnected.

"It was that jerk Will Glenn who told Rakowski about us in the park after Thanksgiving. I think he was mad that I didn't invite him to my birthday party, so he ratted about that," Cliff explained. "Rakowski then began following us, I guess," he conjectured.

"Wow, I guess he heard that man yell at me to stay away from his wife and told Mr Rakowski that too," Junior figured. "That man thought I was the colored kid who worked at the grocery store delivering packages, I guess."

"Yea, I guess," Cliff replied. "Anyway, I'm real sorry all this happened to you. I miss having you around. Are you going to the colored high school?" Cliff asked. "Maybe I could come there," he joshed with a smile on his face.

"Ha, ha," replied Junior, "wouldn't that just be something? No, I'm not going to school anywhere just yet. My mother wants me to go to school in the District and my father thinks I should go to Mercer. I should be going somewhere by next week, after Easter break. School will be out for summer soon, so I don't have much time."

Not even ten minutes had passed at this point, but it seemed much longer to the two boys who hadn't been near each other in almost two weeks. Junior knew that his father would be home soon, and Cliff knew that his mother would expect him home as well. Since this was the Easter vacation week, he had a little bit more latitude in which to circulate.

"I hope we can continue to see each other," he confessed to Junior, his face blushing as he said it.

"Yes, that would be nice," came the reply he expected. "You can send me messages through Thomasine," Junior instructed. "I don't think I should call your house because your mother might answer," he told Cliff.

"Perhaps we can meet here or at Fat Jacks," Cliff offered." Junior had never taken Cliff to Fat Jacks, but other white boys went to the colored hamburger shop not far from Junior's house with their friends on occasion. But Junior didn't feel comfortable going there with him. They certainly wouldn't meet in North Arlington at any establishments so that left few choices. "My parents are going to a White House dinner for President De Gaulle of France on Friday night, so maybe you can come over then and we can talk," Cliff suggested, again blushing. They both knew what happened when they talked!

"I'm not sure about Friday," Junior acknowledged, "but if I can, how will I let you know?"

Cliff suggested that Junior ask Thomasine to give him a call at home since they wouldn't be at school that week. "I would like to see you soon, though, and not here on Mason Drive either." They both smiled at this and would have wanted to touch each other if circumstances would have been more conducive. Instead, they shook hands again and Cliff grabbed Junior's arm, just above the palm before he let go of his hand. Junior responded by jabbing Cliff on the shoulder lightly and then rubbed it a little very gently as if it were his face which he would have preferred to rub.

As Cliff was turning to go, he had to take a bus up Mason Drive that would take him past Columbia Pike up to North Arlington, he asked Cliff if he had heard the new song by the Flamingos, knowing full well he had and it wasn't even that new anymore. "I don't know if we're in a garden... or on a crowded avenue..." Cliff began singing quietly so as not to attract attention.

"You are here and so am I, maybe millions of people go by..." Junior picked up the lyrics and smiled broadly as he repeated them. By now, Cliff had turned away and was running for the bus which was headed westbound on the other side of Mason Drive. Both boys knew the chorus to the song and would probably be going over it in their heads once they had left each other.

After watching Cliff get on the bus, Junior turned away and walked slowly in the direction of Hilldale, about six or seven blocks away. He was glad he had seen Cliff. It was the highlight of his last two weeks. He couldn't tell anyone about it but maybe the joy that filled his whole body at that moment also showed on his face so that anyone could see it?

I only have eyes for you... He repeated over and over in his head as he walked those few blocks home! After a full day of being high in the sky, the sun was beginning to settle down. But not Junior! After his meeting with Cliff, he was on the rise!

Chapter 34

"Son, I got that light switch fixed for you," Wynn announced from the kitchen after he heard the door slam shut indicating to him that his son had come in the house. He knew it was Junior because Jeanne was already home and Julia Mae wasn't expected until about 7:30, another two hours away. "It won't flicker any more now, so you can see more better," he proclaimed, a can of Coca Cola in his hand. Wynn had just gotten home from work and wanted to finish the job he had put off for a little over a week. Junior had told him the light in his bedroom was flickering in and out which prevented him from reading at night which is when he mostly read.

Now that he was not doing schoolwork downstairs at the kitchen table where he had mostly done his homework, he did most of his reading alone up in his room. He did have a desk in his bedroom, as did Jeanne in hers, but Junior preferred to be downstairs because it was more open and also because he liked to snack while doing homework. Julia Mae wasn't fond of her children eating in their room. Eating should be done with your family and friends, she would always say.

"Thanks, Pop," Junior replied. "Glad you got it fixed. Did you just get home?" Junior asked. It seemed to him that Wynn had arrived earlier than usual, but he then surmised that maybe it was because he was normally home when his dad arrived from his job at the Pentagon. He had never really noticed at what time his father drove in. Now that he wasn't going to school, he was usually at home reading or maybe helping Jeanne with an assignment. Rarely was he out of the house as he was today when Wynn arrived home from work.

"I've been here for about ten minutes, sir," Wynn answered his son back. "Do I need to call you when I'm on my way home from now on?" He knew his father was joking. Wynn loved to play around with his kids.

That was the way he showed his love.

"No, sir, you don't," Junior shot back. "Just ring the doorbell when you get here so I know you're outside the door." Both Horry men smiled at each other after Junior's wisenheimer comment. Wynn and Julia Mae weren't the kind of parents who forbade any "back talk", as long as it didn't exceed the limits that Junior and Jeanne understood.

"So, son, I wanted to talk to you about this school thing," Wynn declared, changing the flippant conversation, into something more staid. Junior still hadn't made it upstairs to test the light that his father had allegedly fixed. He was now sitting on the middle step leading to the bedrooms and one bath upstairs, while his father stood in front of him, one arm leaning on the hand rest at the base of the banister on the staircase, and his right foot on the second step from the bottom. "I know that your mama has been set on you going to that West End High in the District and she has been over there with Nellie to get you enrolled. I think that you really ought to go to Mercer right here, at least for the last few months of the school year," Wynn went on. "I told your mama that we can see about you getting into another school for the next school year in September. You know her and how when she makes up her mind on something, that's all she thinks about."

"I know, Pop, I know," Junior retorted. "I want to go to West End too, but I don't think that even with using Aunt Nellie's address it will work out right now."

"I agree, Son," Wynn acknowledged! "I think we should focus on you getting back in school and not waiting around for some white person's help to get you into a white school somewhere. It was the white people who got you out of the one you were in!" Junior knew that it wasn't so easy for his father to have this discussion with him. First of all, Wynn had tried not to go against Julia Mae's wishes as to where Junior went to school even though he didn't necessarily agree with her that he should continue in a white school. "I think you can get a good enough education at Mercer," he told his son. "Being around your own people helps you to grow in ways that you never could at Arlington High or at that school in the District. Being around colored people will straighten your shoulders and lift your head because you will get a better sense of yourself and how you stack up against your own people," he professed.

Junior paid as much attention to his father's eyes as he did his words. He could see in them the earnestness with which he expressed those comments. He knew that his father had grown up in a Negro world up until the time he got into the military. Even though he was still in a colored platoon during WWII, he came into contact with whites much more often than he had in Spartanburg, South Carolina. He had told his family many times that those encounters with whites in the military actually diminished the fear that he had held of white people for all his life. He then learned that many of them were as unsure of themselves as he and that many of them were not as smart and capable as he.

"Being around white people is like having a bright light turned on for the first time," he had always joked. "You get to see just how beautiful your blackness is and you suddenly look much better, reflected against their light," he would add, usually with a snicker! Yes, they have it much better than us and there is much that we can get from them," Wynn explained. "But what we can get from them should come on top of what we get from our own and not in place of it." Junior sat rapt, without moving a muscle as his father went on to explain that he had never wanted his son to feel as though white people had the only things of value to offer. "What we get from being colored comes harder and deeper and therefore it stays with us longer and we can never forget it. It doesn't cost anything to be white, it just pays a lot," Wynn professed. "You will never be white, so you can't put that change in your pocket, so it's best for you to know how to get by with what you do have to use to get what you need!"

This wasn't what he thought he was walking into when he got home! Junior and Wynn hardly ever had this kind of conversation. He was surprised at his father but not in an unpleasant way. He knew that Wynn wasn't a thoughtless man who didn't have any awareness of what was going on around him. It's just that he didn't usually talk about it. Yet there he was, his one foot on the step and arm on the banister, leaning over his son and sharing with him vignettes of his younger life and what it has meant to grow up as a colored man. After more than an hour of this, Junior had learned many things about his father that he had never known. As if he were standing in front of a window revealing the bright sunshine, Wynn was suddenly presented to his son in a different light.

"You need to be prepared for a lot, Son," he was explaining as the front door slammed open and Julia Mae thundered in! Suddenly both Junior and Wynn turned toward the door and immediately the thoughts that had been occupying their minds had evacuated!

"What's the matter, Momma?" Junior asked. Wynn was still silent, but his face spoke for him. He was clearly in shock because this wasn't how his wife normally acted and certainly not as she walked in the front door!

"Did someone come at you on the way home?" he asked her as she was taking off her shoes and her headscarf, still shaking her head and mumbling to herself.

"I'm sorry, honey," she finally said, after taking a long exhale and swallowing hard as if she was drowning the angst that had swollen up in her long before she got home. "Hi, baby," she greeted Junior, summoning a smile to her face for the first time since she had come into the house. By now, Jeanne was coming down the steps. She too had heard the door slam and was just as shocked and curious as her father and brother who had actually witnessed it.

"You OK, Momma?" she blurted down the steps as she descended to be near her mother.

"Yes, y'all, I'm fine," Julia Mae revealed. "Sorry to scare y'all, I just had a hard afternoon dealing with that woman!"

"What woman?" they all asked almost in unison, but Wynn realized she must be talking about her boss at Horrschorns.

"What has she done now?" he asked his wife. Then, without allowing her to answer, he explained that he and Junior had been talking about the school issue and what was best going forward. Everyone was silent for a moment. It was clear that Wynn had wanted his wife to have the next word.

"Well, we don't need to talk about this now, anyway," Julia Mae finally stated.

"I want to make sure you're all right, Ma," Junior spoke up, "that's important too." Smiling and going over to her son for a kiss on the forehead that started with him and then made its way to her husband and then her daughter, Julia Mae assured her family that she was OK and that she had put all the discussion with Bama Lady behind her.

"So what did you decide about where Junior should go to school, Mr Horry?" she asked her husband facetiously.

"We didn't decide anything," he replied with an equal amount of flippancy in his voice. "But as you know, I do have an opinion about it."

"I think I know your opinion, unless something has changed," Julia Mae imparted, turning toward the kitchen where she would put her apron on over her dress and heat up the dinner that she had prepared that morning before going to work. "I know you want Junior to go to Mercer and although it doesn't look like it may happen, I still want him in a white high school because I know he will learn better," said Julia Mae, partly from the kitchen where she was moving foil-covered food from the refrigerator to the stove and taking Pyrex dishes with cooked items that had been left at room temperature and bringing them to the fire!

"And I want Junior to learn to respect and appreciate who he is instead of constantly trying to defend himself," his father argued sternly. Julia Mae was still silent but although she was focused on the dinner preparations, it was clear that she had heard what Wynn said. "I don't want him to have to always apologize for being colored," Wynn added.

"I don't think that standing up for yourself as I had to do today," Julia Mae acknowledged, "is the same as defending yourself. Getting a good education is not apologizing for anything," Julia Mae countered, "if anything it saves you from having to apologize." Wynn didn't want to get into a back and forth with his wife. What he wanted was to eat his dinner, in fact, that's what they all wanted. But nevertheless, he had to make sure he got his point across.

"Do you know any better education than growing up Negro and dealing with other Negroes?" Wynn asked. "If you don't learn about life that way, then ain't nothin' can teach you!" Julia Mae couldn't help but giggle at this and her children chuckled at the statement too.

"You know what I'm talkin' 'bout," Julia Mae chided, cutting her eye at Wynn and then leaning down to take a baked ham out of the oven. But there was no denying Wynn was right. The education colored people got, just from learning to deal with each other, was priceless!

Chapter 35

"This will be our premiere performance," Claire had joked to her parents and to Peter. This was the first time she and Chester had ever been invited to the White House for a State Dinner. Chester was not yet a senior Foreign Service Officer, but he was on the way up! Their friendship with the family who had just returned from a post at the US Embassy in Paris had been paying off. They were the ones who got the Petersons on the guest list for the dinner in honor of newly elected French President Charles De Gaulle and his wife. Claire knew that their daughter had a crush on her eldest son, but it was not kismet that the two teens would one day become a diplomatic couple as the girl might have dreamed! However, she wouldn't allow that to keep her away from her Gigi moment with Dwight and Marie Geneva and Charles and Yvonne!

"This is a reward for all our years trudging around in Africa and other off-the-map places that not many would want to go to and yet there we were," Claire declared on the phone with her mother that Friday, hours before they were to take a taxi from North Arlington to the White House on Pennsylvania Avenue.

"Isn't he in favor of granting independence to all these little colonies in Africa?" her mother asked.

"Yes," Claire responded, "De Gaulle has favored granting them independence. That is what will keep Chester in a job," she joked. "We need to personally thank him for helping my husband become an ambassador to one of those little colonies!"

"Well, okay, dear, I won't deny employment to anyone," her mother parried back.

"Will you wear something you got in New York or a little thing your colored woman made for you since you will be honoring the Africans?" she went on. Claire knew that her mother was jesting with her. They had gone out shopping together while both were in New York over Christmas when Claire had seen in a shop window on 5th Avenue a periwinkle evening gown with matching satin cape that she had to have. The gown had much of the back cut out and the shoulders had a bit of a pouf. Below the waist it flared out and Claire looked as good in it as the model who donned it for her at the 5th Avenue showroom, once she had tried it on herself. Claire knew immediately that it would be a hit in Washington. At the time she just didn't know when or where! But a diplomat's wife needed always to be prepared.

Up until that Friday afternoon, Junior hadn't decided if he would go to Cliff's house later that evening, or not. It was a warm, summerlike day and his parents had wanted to have a fish fry with Nellie and Talley in Georgetown. His aunt and uncle had invited some of their neighbors too. A warm evening in spring was a good time for the first fish fry of the year, everyone had agreed. While there was no doubt that he would have enjoyed the dinner that Nellie and her neighbors prepared, probably fried trout, cornbread, collard greens, potato salad and some kind of pie like peach or apple, that is, if it was like most of the fish frys they had, he had so longed for time alone with Cliff!

But there was no certainty that they could really be alone together the way they both wanted to; after all, Robby was there as far as Junior knew. How could he and Cliff get their arms around each other and let their hands explore if Robby was wandering around the house? Besides, wouldn't he mention to his parents that Junior had been there? Junior figured his name hadn't been mentioned much at the Peterson house since he was put out of Arlington High. Robby had noticed that Cliff hadn't been playing his rhythm and blues records so much in the last few weeks. Not that Robby cared at all, or paid that much attention to Cliff, but certain things he would notice!

"I'm gonna be starting back at school on Monday and I wanna have some fun with my friends on Friday night," Junior had decided to tell Wynn and Julia Mae. He knew his father would probably not have a problem with this. After all, he had decided that he would go to Mercer High. Actually, it was decided for him, but he was on board with it! Julia Mae had done all she could to get him into the high school near

Georgetown, an effort that Nellie and Talley had been in cahoots with because Junior would need to use their address. But no school would let him transfer that late in the school year, except for Mercer. West End High, a formerly all-white school, had told them to try back in September. "I almost lost my job trying to get you in a school," Julia Mae had informed her son. "I still may lose it because I don't know how much longer I can take that old white woman," she had said during the conversation of where Junior would start school again, those two weeks after being expelled.

"Where will you be going?" she asked when Junior made this announcement to her and Wynn. "Will you be out with Carolyn?" Junior couldn't tell them that he was going to see Cliff. He had to make up something because he dared not say he was to be with anyone that his family knew, certainly not Carolyn Stanley. They had seen each other a few times since he had been expelled and she had urged him to come to Mercer, in fact. The fact that she was there had created a bit of stress for him, however. It would more than likely mean that he was expected to spend more time with her. There would be no excuse for them not to be together now. He liked Carolyn a lot, thought she was beautiful, sweet, talented and would make someone a great wife one day. But he just didn't think he wanted to be that one! Junior wrestled with these feelings, had struggled with them for a while, but at least since last summer they had maintained less of a stranglehold on him. He thought himself on the way to becoming free of these feelings. It was a freedom he couldn't loudly proclaim. But nevertheless, it felt good inside! He had Cliff to thank for that!

He was lost in his thoughts about Cliff; many of his thoughts were of Cliff since they had finally seen each other after nearly two weeks of disassociation. He almost didn't hear the phone ringing. The phone was in the living room and he was upstairs in his bedroom and although the door was open, it was almost inaudible since his thoughts of long-delayed pleasure were so heightened that they drowned everything else out!

"Hello?"

"Hi, Junior, it's me," said the voice on the other end. "I just invited Thomasine and Pamela to come over this evening also, that way it won't just be us."

Junior wasn't sure how to respond to this disclosure, but he was proud of Cliff for plotting and planning. "We can still find a way to be alone but at least we won't be in the house by ourselves," Cliff went on, clearly a little nervous as he mouthed the words into the phone.

"Yes, I agree," Junior was finally able to say; after all, he was nervous too, and his heart was beating fast, as he heard Cliff speak the words, we can still be alone! "But I don't want it to turn into a party," he added. "I just wanted to be alone with you!" Now they had both said it! There could be no denying that the words had been uttered.

"We will be, but it will look normal this way," Cliff replied, before both of them hung up. Junior was feeling quite high after the call and sank into the sofa next to the phone with a big smile on his face!

"I'm so glad you will be going back to school on Monday," Julia Mae imparted shortly after she walked into the house and saw her son, still sitting on the sofa that he had perched on during the phone call with Cliff. Her entry had apparently jostled him awake. He sat up to discover that *The Adventures of Rin Tin Tin* was now being broadcast on the television that he had remembered turning on right after falling into the sofa. It was not one of his favorite shows. But soon, the evening news would be on. Wynn would be coming downstairs after his bath to watch it while Julia Mae and Jeanne were getting ready to go to Georgetown.

Junior could tell that his mother was once again vexed. There she was shaking her head back and forth and looking toward the floor as she replayed the day in her mind. "That woman just won't let me be, about the days I took off trying to get you enrolled in West End High."

"It ain't like there was nobody there to do the work," she contended, "and besides, there ain't even that much going on now that Easter is over." But that didn't make any particular difference to Bama Lady, as the three colored seamstresses continued to call her. "She just has to let us know that she's the boss and that she has say over our comings and goings. I am so sick of dealing with this and ain't had much peace at work since she got there," Julia Mae lamented!

In fact, this woman had decided to decrease Julia Mae's hours which was the reason she was getting home earlier for the last week. It really amounted to only an hour less of work. She had asked her to start work at 10:00 am instead of her long-standing 11:00 am and she was now off by 5:00 pm instead of 7:00 pm. Julia Mae actually preferred this time change because it allowed her to arrive home earlier. But also, it meant that she had less time to start dinner in the morning before she left. She knew, however, that it was a way for Bama Lady to punish her for the two full days and one half-day she had missed trying to re-enroll Junior in school. "You must not need this job, girl," the woman had said to Julia Mae after the second full day.

"Don't worry about it, Ma," said Junior attempting to propitiate Julia Mae. "You will get over to Aunt Nellie's and Uncle Talley's this evening and forget all about it." Junior was, of course, looking himself to the powers of mollification later that day! So, he was certain that that was what his mother needed also.

"And what will you be doing?" she asked her wily son.

"I am meeting some friends later," Junior reported. "Thomasine will be there too."

"Thomasine and not Carolyn?" Julia Mae queried. "Is that a smart decision?" she jokingly asked him.

"Aww Ma, it's just some friends getting together."

"Where will you be?" she asked. Junior thought about his answer before spilling it out. He wanted to make sure he didn't say anything that could later be disputed.

"We are not really sure yet, but we may be going up north to hang out with some kids." Julia Mae understood this to be the colored section of North Arlington as Junior had intended her to.

The plan was that Cliff would call Junior's house and he and Thomasine would head up to Arlington Heights once his folks had gone off in a taxi to the White House for the State Dinner. Of course, Robby was at home but that didn't stop him from having friends over. "Pamela and Richard might come over this evening," Claire and Chester had been apprised. "We will be listening to records and stuff," Cliff had informed his parents. Junior and Thomasine were not mentioned in this accounting. Cliff had thought to disclose that Thomasine was invited but he was certain that his parents would have then concluded that Junior might have been coming too since they were never invited without the other, at least not unless Junior was there to cut the grass and the Petersons had decided between themselves that it was best to hire a lawn service for the summer.

They hadn't told Cliff that yet, though.

"You look great in those khakis, husband," said Julia Mae, as she admired Wynn in the new slacks she had bought for him. He was wearing them with a plaid long-sleeved Arrow brand casual shirt. It was part of their *getaway* collection, designed for the man on the go! Wynn thanked his wife and returned the compliment. Julia Mae did look very pretty in a baby blue poplin dress with a starched white color, three-quarter sleeves and a tight white belt at the waist. Her waistline looked smaller since the dress flared out as much as it did. She wore the dress with a pair of yellow flats with a navy-blue bow. Unusual for Julia Mae, her hair was in a band that started at the back of her head and ended on the front peeking out between the top curls and bangs combed out over her forehead. On her arm was a navy-blue handbag. The sweater that she would probably have taken over her shoulders was left to adorn the bedroom chair since it was such a warm evening.

Even though her brother was not going with them, Jeanne wouldn't miss the time to spend with Aunt Nellie. Although she wanted to wear a pair of jeans and a shirt, Julia Mae implored her to wear a skirt and a blouse instead. "You are a young lady now and you should dress like one," her mother pleaded. Both Julia Mae and Wynn smiled when their daughter came downstairs in a dress instead, one similar to the one Julia Mae wore except it buttoned down the front and was of a plum color with a white collar. It too had a belt and a skirt semi-full and pleated like her mother's.

As he watched his family drive off to Georgetown, about the time the sun was beginning to flee from its high perch in the sky, Junior breathed a sigh of relief! All in his world was good at this moment! First of all, no one had found out his secret! Secondly, he was about to start school again in three days, although not the school he had assumed he would be going to.

But Monday would come soon enough, when he would begin his lessons again. This was Friday night, and he would be spending it in Cliff Peterson's company. In the words of Jerry Lee Lewis, goodness gracious great balls of fire!

Chapter 36

"So what's going on with you and Carolyn?" Thomasine asked when Junior showed up at her house. They had agreed to meet there before going up to Arlington Heights. Anytime he went anywhere with Thomasine it was always in one of her father's cabs. She knew how to drive but didn't yet have a driver's license. Junior knew how to drive also and did sometimes drive his father's car for short trips, even though he didn't yet have a license either but that would come as soon as he was 16 which was only a few months off.

"What do you mean what's going on with me and Carolyn?" Junior asked from the backseat of the cab as they rode up Glebe Road. His eyes darted about as he looked out the window as they drove. In one sense he cared about the answer to his question and in another, he really didn't at all. But for certain he couldn't help but feel a little bit guilty. All this scheming and plotting to be with Cliff and there was Carolyn Stanley who was the one he was supposed to be spending his time with. But, according to this news he was now getting from Thomasine, Carolyn wasn't necessarily sitting alone.

"There's this guy at Mercer that has been hanging around her," Thomasine explained. "He lives near me and he told my brother that they had been doing things together. Apparently, they talk to each other at lunch and leave school together sometimes," Seeny revealed.

"Well, I'm sure he's just a friend," Junior responded. "She has a right to have friends."

"Of course, she does," Seeny replied. "But it's just that you're not around, so…" It was clear that Thomasine was trying to send him a message. But he already knew that he was the great pretender! When he thought of his relationship with Carolyn, if he could even call it a relationship, his mind kept going back to the Platters song, which had come out a few years earlier but was still popular and probably Julia Mae's favorite song ever! "Too real is this feeling of make believe, too real when I feel what my heart can't conceal!"

"Oh yes, I'm the great pretender, just laughing and gay like a clown, I seem to be what I'm not you see!" So, while Junior was lost in a world of his own maybe Carolyn had moved on to a real life boyfriend. "Anyway, I'll be at Mercer starting on Monday and Carolyn and I will get back on track." Junior knew he had to say this to Thomasine to assuage his feelings of guilt about all but abandoning Carolyn since he started going to Arlington High and, more importantly, began his friendship with Cliff Peterson, whose house they were now near. His quickened heartbeat served as a kind of Cliff detector! His excitement and nervousness always acted as a divining rod and it was always Cliff at the other end! Thomasine didn't know it, but she and Pamela were only a ruse for the two of them to be alone together, if only for just a few minutes. So maybe someone else's arms would be around Carolyn Stanley on that warm April Friday night. But he would be pressed against Cliff and in no particular hurry to get away!

"Just becaaauuse my composure sorta slips the moment that your lips meet mine, chances are you think my heart's your Valentine!" Pamela and Cliff were laughing and drinking while they listened to records when Thomasine and Junior rang the Petersons' doorbell. They were drinking that new soda called Sprite and seemed to be enjoying it. At her brother Peter's suggestion, Claire had bought the new fresh-tasting soda, something like ginger ale but with lemons instead of ginger. After Cliff opened the door the two new arrivals could hear the Johnny Mathis record that was whirling about on the Telefunken stereo in the dining room of the Peterson house. *"Guess you feel you'll always be the one and only one for me, and if you think you could, chances are your chances are, awfully good..."*

It had been several months since he was in the Peterson house, last summer, in fact. At that time, the furniture seemed aloft and matched his own feelings of floating on a cloud. But since then, with all that had transpired, everything had come crashing back down to earth! But he was now hoping he could put all that behind him! Right now, he was only a few feet away from the source of his elation; there was no doubt in

Junior's mind that his excitement would lift him up again.

Junior knew that Cliff and his family liked Johnny Mathis. Many white people did, but not so many colored people, were his fans. True, he had a fine tender tenor voice that sweetly wafted into the air, but for most Negroes it left a sour note. But Pamela and Cliff seemed to be enjoying the music and the soft drinks. "Hi, Cliff, hi, Pamela," Thomasine greeted upon entering, the cab that she and Junior had ridden in now dispatched with instructions to come back for her an hour and a half later.

"Hello," both said back to Thomasine, and Cliff's smile and attention then turned to Junior who had entered behind Thomasine.

"Hi, Junior," he said, the smile growing brighter every minute that he looked his way.

"Hi, Cliff, how are you doing?" Junior replied smiling and glowing back at him.

"Would you two like some soda and cupcakes?" Pamela asked, acting as the hostess of the evening. It was clear to Thomasine that Pamela might have considered herself to be Cliff's girlfriend although she had a hard time seeing that to be the case. Cliff had struck her as one of those boys who didn't see his way to having a girlfriend but rather friends who were girls.

"Save some of those cupcakes for your mother and daddy," said the maid coming into the living room from the kitchen. "Hello, Junior and Thomasine." She greeted them in her usual, high-pitched voice always loaded with an extra helping of enthusiasm.

"Hi, Gussie," Seeny and Junior offered back. Her main reason for being there was to prepare dinner for Cliff and Robby since Claire and Chester had to busy themselves that evening, for their State Dinner at the White House. She would be leaving shortly after dinner had been consumed, the dishes washed and kitchen cleaned. She also had the task of putting the house back together after the slight disarray it had been thrust into by activity involved in getting ready for a White House feast.

"I doubt that Mother and Dad will want any cupcakes after the tarte tartin or the crème caramels that they are probably having at the White House," Cliff joshed to Pamela. She laughed back and posited that maybe they might be having Baked Alaska instead. By this time, Thomasine and

Junior had made their way over to the cupcakes that Gussie had placed on the pale green Formica counter and against this backdrop, the lemon frosted cupcake that Junior went for really stood out. Thomasine chose a chocolate topped yellow cupcake which some might have taken as a metaphor for her closeness to Junior.

"Well, y'all enjoy while I go check on Robby outside," Gussie implored. Robby had already enjoyed one or two cupcakes and had gone outside to toss his baseball back and forth to the boy who lived next door. He had no particular interest in being inside with Cliff and his friends. Of Cliff's friends, Robby did like Richard a little bit. He thought him an odd boy and even being six or so years younger, he felt superior to him. But Richard was unable to come that night.

"What other records do you have?" Thomasine asked after the third Johnny Mathis recording. "I'm kind of tired of hearing him," she admitted. *It's Not for Me to Say* had already played and the beguiling sounds of *A Certain Smile* were beginning to fade on the Telefunken.

"Well, my parents bought the soundtrack album *to A Summer Place*," Cliff noted. "We can listen to that."

"Oh wow, I like that music," Pamela exclaimed, "but only the theme song."

"That's true, I guess," noted Cliff. "There's really not that much to listen to there. I have some other records in my room, records that I know Junior likes." Cliff looked over at Junior as he said this, as if to send him a message.

"You mean the records you played at your birthday party?" Thomasine asked.

"Yes, some of them are at least," he answered.

"Cool!" Thomasine exclaimed, "let's hear some of them!"

"Okay," Cliff replied, just as Robby and his friend had run into the kitchen to snatch the last two cupcakes from the platter on the counter. Junior had had his eye on a chocolate cupcake with vanilla frosting, but it was now too late. The boy from next door had plucked it from the plate.

"Junior, come with me to get some records," Cliff suggested. "You can help me choose the best ones." By now the two young boys had left to go back outside. Cliff and Junior soon followed their path out of the kitchen towards Cliff's bedroom, leaving the two girls alone to talk about

241

school, fashion, movies or perhaps boys! "Gee, isn't this soda pretty good?" Cliff asked, referring to the Sprite that they were drinking, both of them with a bottle in their hands as they walked out of the kitchen.

"Yeah, it's pretty good," Junior agreed. "I haven't really heard about it before but is so different from Coca Cola," he added.

"Yes, I like the lemony taste," Cliff stated. "My uncle Peter in Chicago worked on the advertising in the US," he added. "The soda comes from Germany and his firm was hired to get Americans to buy and like it."

"Well, is it his firm that makes me like it or is it the taste?" Junior asked laughing. "I think I just like it on my own!"

Now alone in the bedroom and out of earshot of the girls who were still downstairs in the kitchen, Cliff turned to Junior, putting his bottle of Sprite down on a nightstand. He then took that now free left hand and put it on Junior's waist and proceeded to rub the back of his head with the other. "Yes, it makes me feel good inside," he said, as if he were in a commercial! Both boys then laughed and Junior quickly followed suit and, moving in closer to Cliff, put both hands around Cliff's waist as he pressed his slightly quivering body against his sandy-haired host whose heart was pounding so loudly it seemed as though it might explode all over Junior! The two hadn't been in each other's embrace for weeks and it was hard to believe that they were now right up on each other right there in Cliff's bedroom where they had not been in such a position since the previous summer when Robby had almost seen them slow dancing together. Remembering this close call caused Junior to suggest that they move further away from the bedroom door which was still slightly ajar and make some noise every now and then that would mimic the sound of thumbing through records. After all, that is what they had come up to do.

But instead of riffling through records, the two boys were moving to the beat of each other's hearts as they hadn't had the opportunity to do since their clandestine closet carrying-on had been countermanded at Arlington High. Junior looked into Cliff's eyes the way a man who hadn't eaten for two weeks looks at a piece of steak put before him and Cliff looked back at him like a cat who hadn't been stroked in weeks looks at its master who has just taken it into his arms!! Cliff had his hands on just a little too much, but it wasn't Ricky Nelson's record, which was hiding somewhere in the pile. Also in that pile was Sam Cooke's You Send Me, and that was the way Junior was feeling with Cliff's hands exploring him the way they were!

"Are you two coming?" they could hear Pamela's voice call up from downstairs. They realized that they had been up long enough to have at least picked three or four records to play at that point. But it was hard for them to tear away from each other.

"We are on the way," Cliff shouted back, lifting his face away from Junior's neck long enough to reply to his friend, and with a slightly shaky voice at that! Both hearts were beating fast and it might have come across in Cliff's voice but it was too late at that point.

His arms still around Cliff's lower waist and making their way down to his buttocks, Junior blurted, "What about the Lil Richard, Bobby Darin and Dinah Washington along with the ones you picked out?"

"That sounds good," Cliff retorted, his hands still buried in Junior's treasure!

At that point, standing deep in Cliff's bedroom away from the door that was still open half-way, they thought they heard footsteps on the stairwell coming upstairs. Everything else faded into the background when they were close up on each other, so they couldn't be sure of what had precipitated the sounds they heard. Both boys, startled, turned their heads toward the door to see if it was either Pamela or Thomasine inviting themselves upstairs or perhaps the maid coming into Cliff's room for some reason. Both hearts were still pounding wildly, and neither would have been able to utter a word as they would have been rendered speechless if either of the girls or the maid had suddenly peered into the room and seen them enmeshed the way they were! As the two boys finally broke apart to reassemble themselves as well as their clothes which had been released from their bodies to various extents, they looked at each other with nervous and uneven smiles. Suddenly, another, more decisive set of footsteps was heard on the steps but this time it was clear that someone was running downstairs!

Only one person in the house actually ran down the steps from his bedroom to the kitchen, living room, dining room or outside to play and that was Robby, Cliff knew. He didn't realize Robby had even come upstairs but that apparently explained the steps on the stairs he was certain he had heard earlier. Perhaps he had come up to get something out of his room, Cliff concluded. At any rate, he and Junior were now going down. They were about to get back to the girls.

"After all that time you two found only four records?" Thomasine queried.

"We decided on two each, but we had to make sure we made the right decision on which two," Junior laughed. Cliff joined in the laughter and added that there were so many records to choose from, but it was important to make sure they gave it their best shot at picking something everyone would like.

"What were you two doing while we were upstairs?" Cliff then asked.

"We were talking with Gussie about her cupcake recipe and we also went outside in the garden. It's so nice outside and we have run out of cupcakes and Sprite," Pamela pointed out, "We thought about walking to the market to get more soda before it closes. Robby came upstairs to ask you if it was okay to walk with us to the market," Pamela went on.

"Robby didn't ask me anything," Cliff countered.

"He said he changed his mind once he got upstairs," claimed Pamela.

"Where *is* Robby?" Cliff asked, nervously.

"He asked me if he could go next door with his lil friend *Martian*," the maid piped in. Martian's real name was Martin, but due to fanaticism over little green men, all the kids called him Martian. "They went to get his baseball glove and bat," the maid continued. She had been nearby the entire time, still tidying up the kitchen and living room in advance of Claire and Chester's return home. "I told him to ask you but he said he didn't want to go back upstairs."

244

Chapter 37

Saturday afternoons at Horrschorns were always abuzz with activity! It would seem that nothing at all was going on in Georgetown, Cleveland Park or Woodley Park, Kalorama or Chevy Chase because all the folks who lived in those areas were downtown at the mainstay department store shopping or socializing! Many of the ladies from Alexandria, Arlington, Falls Church and Bethesda joined them as they met for lunch or an afternoon snack after trying on clothes or shopping for their husbands. And despite the fact that the store's customers comprised Washington's "genteel society", Saturday afternoons in the tearoom were often anything but polite and cordial and apparently this Saturday was no different.

Shortly after he arrived at work at the restaurant, located on the top floor of the grand building in downtown, Junior heard a raucous exchange between some patrons and the manager, but he wasn't exactly sure what it was about. The dishwashing staff never went into the dining room, so he would have no way of knowing or seeing what was going on. As it happened, his favorite waiter friend whom he hadn't seen that much lately, was working that Saturday afternoon. He knew that because he had seen him come into the kitchen to speak with someone. The waiter didn't speak to him but acknowledged Junior with his eyes.

"You can cancel the orders," he overheard the waiter say, realizing that he had never learned his name. "They all left, so just kill the three plates," the waiter reaffirmed before turning around to leave. He had on his usual uniform of black pants, white shirt and white bowtie and wore a look of disgust on his face. Whatever was happening or had happened outside had seemed to have an effect on him. At any rate, Junior had his pile of dishes to attend to in that long white porcelain sink that stretched nearly four feet long and had many spouts of hot water pouring into it.

Whatever had happened outside didn't involve him, and there was nothing he could do about it unless there was a mess of dirty dishes that he would be left to clean up.

Shortly after he had put his full attention toward the dirty dishes sitting in the sudsy sink below him, Junior could hear the manager who was talking in a loud voice, so loud it could be heard all the way in the kitchen. He couldn't make out all that was being said with all the noise inside the kitchen, but he could tell that he was in a heated discussion with a woman. The woman was talking very excitedly and that along with her southern accent made what she was saying that much more difficult to understand. The conversation within earshot didn't last that long but it was clear that it had already been going on for some time before it got near the kitchen door. It seemed to be ending now and he was able to discern that the manger had said, "I'm sorry this has happened, but it has been resolved." Probably some older lady who was complaining about the condition of the lettuce on her salad or that the iced tea wasn't sweet enough, Junior thought, based on the accent and the type of women who usually came to the tearoom on Saturday afternoon.

Things had finally quietened down enough that he had forgotten about the fracas, preferring instead to think about his Friday night with Cliff. They hadn't spoken since, but he was still charged up! His thoughts about Cliff and their friendship had been more on his mind of late.

After about an hour and a half of his five-hour shift it was time for his first 15-minute break. He usually went outside for his break, especially if the weather was nice alfresco. Junior wasn't as turned off by the heat as his father or sister, so the fact that the outside temperatures were in the 80s didn't so much bother him. The kitchen was air-cooled although it wasn't yet turned on in April. Instead, the fans were going full force and that kept it cool enough for him. But, as there were many cooks, managers and dishwashers in the kitchen, it was definitely hot from just the bodies alone. When he walked through a part of the kitchen near the dining room to get to the stairwell leading downstairs to the store's loading area, where most of the kitchen or receiving staff took their break, he could hear or see no residue of the earlier confrontation. In fact, his waiter friend wasn't even in sight.

The restaurant seemed normal. That is, as much as he would know "normal" for this place. He had never really set foot in it much. But he knew it was reasonably large, although there were smaller areas as well that most of the crowd seemed to occupy on Saturday afternoons. They were with round tables, pink and white cloth table coverings, mirrored walls and sconces with some Impressionist artwork. Beautiful chandeliers dangled above shining down light on patrons working in tandem with the broad and tall windows framed in gold leaf. Although, soft, sheer curtains shielded the room from getting too much of the Saturday afternoon sun.

On the way downstairs he heard the door slam, the one he had just walked through. The direction of the footsteps on the stairwell suggested that whoever had come through the door was also walking downstairs behind him. "Hey, you," said the voice. "Haven't seen you around much." With a smile on his face, Junior turned his head around and focused his eyes upward and met those of his waiter friend who was now standing about five steps above him and staring down at him with an equally warm smile. "Too bad about what happened this morning," said the waiter, "that should never have happened."

Now stopped, Junior waited for his friend to catch up before asking what had in fact happened. "I heard a lot of chatter and saw some commotion but have no idea what was going on," he said, a blank look on his face.

The waiter, now standing right next to Junior, clearly wanted to re-tell the story. He brushed back the top of his Brylcreemed blond hair; the crown had come undone and was flopping a bit while he was running down the stairs. It was clear that *the little dab didn't do* on that steamy Saturday afternoon! "There were two colored ladies at a table with a white woman, apparently they were all college friends or worked at a college, something like that," the waiter recounted. "This woman that comes in regularly, some Arlington County hostess, had come in with some of her friends and noticed them and almost lost her breath! But she managed to regain her composure and had me summon the maître d'.
They were sitting at or near the table that she sits at regularly with her friends from Arlington and she was upset that they were near her." The waiter stopped to catch his breath for a minute and hearing another door

slam above them on the stairwell, they decided to continue their downward walk while the witness continued his testimony on the way down. "The maître d' offered to reseat the ladies, but all the open tables were at the back of the restaurant near the kitchen and they refused to sit there. 'We usually sit at that particular table,' she argued, 'and generally we sit near people that we know or recognize,' she added. One of the other ladies in her party decided to chime in that 'the tearoom has always been a safe place to come but now it looks like that has changed and that's too bad. Washington is going to hell,' she huffed and looked to her peck of partisans for approval."

The waiter seemed embarrassed to recount this story. He was blushing and clearly saddened to be sharing it with Junior. His young friend seemed not to know what to say. It wasn't a surprise to him that any of this would happen. What was surprising was that any colored women would even bother to show up at the tearoom in the first place, which was officially known as the Blossom Room, with wallpaper of beautiful cherry blossoms of which some of the tables had a spectacular view from the high windows, when the blossoms popped each spring.

"The two colored women and white woman kept quiet and said nothing the entire time, while the women from Virginia continued to complain and tried to get other tables to complain too." Junior just kept his head down and continued to walk down the stairs toward the light of day.

"Did the colored ladies leave?" he finally asked.

"Well, not at first," came the reply. "But then the three of them did walk out. I had taken their orders, but the manager made me serve other tables first because he wanted to see if anyone would complain about their being there. Finally, after all the fuss from the other table and the stares they were getting, the three of them just left. What else would you expect them to do?" he asked solemnly.

By now they were outside, and the air was still warm and stuffy. Junior wasn't sure if it had gotten clammier as a result of the story he had just been told or if it was purely the weather on its own. Perhaps it was a combination of both, he concluded. "I'm sure the three of them found someplace else to go," he said. "After all, there's plenty of places in Washington. They can take the streetcar to Union Station or go up to 13th

Street to the White Tower hotel. They serve tea there too." Junior had remembered hearing his mother and Aunt Nellie talking about that place and how fancy it was. It tended to cater to light-skinned colored people, though. If the two colored ladies were light skinned, then they would be served courteously. The decor probably wasn't as nice as Horrschorns tearoom but at least they could visit with each other in peace! "I'm sure they looked nice and had the money," he added. The waiter had no reply to this.

"Anyway, my name is Wally," the waiter said, "I don't think we ever introduced ourselves."

"I'm Junior, no, we haven't," Wally heard in reply.

"You are in high school, right?" Wally asked. Junior replied that he was and that he lived in Arlington. He decided not to go into the full story about "high school". There were a few other employees outside as well scattered around, some smoking, others drinking soda from bottles and a few chatting with each other. There were few places to sit, a wall here or a ledge there but no actual seats. Few wanted to get their uniforms dirty, especially those who might directly work with customers. For that reason, no one would sit up on the loading dock itself. Wally had walked over to someone who was smoking to ask if he could bum a cigarette.

"Are you in college?" Junior asked him when he came back.

"Yes, I go to George Washington University," Wally answered. "It's close to the department store so easy for me to work here during the week if I'm in school."

"Do you live with other students?" Junior wanted to know. After a drag on his cigarette, it was about time for both to head back upstairs since break was over; Wally told Junior that he lived with another student but not from George Washington University.

"We get involved in lots of things," Wally revealed as they walked back upstairs. "Maybe some of it might interest you."

"What kinds of things do you do?" Junior queried, raising his eyebrows as high as his curiosity.

"We try to help stir things up," Wally asserted with a smile. His response seemed vague to Junior but perhaps that was the way it was meant to be.

At any rate, it was time to get back to the dishes. He had a little less than four hours to go until he would head to Georgetown where he would spend the night with his aunt and uncle. Saturday evenings after dinner were a time for a bit of television and a lot of getting ready for church the next day. If he could swing it, he would watch the *Dick Clark Saturday Night Show* with Nellie and Talley. No doubt Julia Mae, Wynn and Jeanne would be watching it too back at his house. Billy Bland was scheduled to be on the show that night. Julia Mae and Wynn were more familiar with Bland's music, but he had a song currently playing on the radio that was hot at the moment. Bland would be sure to sing Let the Little Girl Dance on Saturday night. Everyone Junior knew would be watching! Years earlier, when Bland sang with a group called the Bees, they released a song called My-ding-aling and that is what Julia Mae and Wynn remembered about Bland most. They had played the record a few times at parties when Junior was younger. He had always thought it an odd song and didn't quite understand what was meant by "ding-aling".

As he got older, he had begun to figure it out with the help of other boys in the neighborhood whose parents played the record. They all laughed about it and grabbed the front of their pants as they laughed and joked with each other. No one grabbed anyone else's pants but once or twice Junior wondered what would have happened if someone had! He remembered feeling a little flushed when this thought came to his head.

That Sunday was the hottest day of the year up to that point! But it was after they had returned from church that things would really heat up at the Horry household!

Julia Mae, Wynn and Jeanne were ready for Mount Calvary that Sunday morning. Junior, who was still a bit apprehensive about starting at Mercer High on Monday, decided to go to church with his aunt and uncle in DC. He wanted to defer any interactions with his new classmates until Monday. Julia Mae wouldn't have entertained the notion of him not going to church at all, so this was his next best option. His mother felt she had to be in church on that bright, hot Sunday morning because she owed God a thank you for finally bringing to an end the nettlesome school transfer business. It was hard enough to accept the fact that Junior had been tossed out of Arlington High, a place she had worked so hard to get him into, but now she had to lick her wounds, already slow to heal, to get him into another school! "Lord, this has to come to an end before

I do," she would lament, shaking her head as usual after such orisons.

So now, the end was near and she, her son and the rest of her family, had lived through it! God needed to be given his proper thanks for that and not only for that, but also the fact that it seemed that things would now settle down for her at work since she was no longer taking time away from the alterations room to get Junior enrolled in school. "Peace be still," was the other thing Julia Mae would say every time she thought about all that had been going on for the last several weeks, even though at times, it seemed like much, much longer.

"The Race for Space Takes the Long and High Road!" read the black metal signboard out front on the grounds of Mount Calvary Baptist Church on that hot Sunday morning. The last Sunday of April was the beginning of Revival at Mount Calvary Baptist. That was the time that the church called upon members, and even visitors, to renew their faith in God and to commit to doing his work here on Earth! Wynn chuckled at the sign as they were walking into the front door of the church that morning, dabbing at his forehead with the crisp folded white handkerchief lifted from his breast pocket. "Hopefully it's cooler up there in space than it is down here on Earth," he jived.

"God needs you, our people need you and our church needs you," the minister had been preaching in the weeks leading up to Easter and Revival. Despite the surprising heat for April, the church was still fairly crowded, and ushers were passing out hand fans as fast as they could. The fans at Calvary, just like those at all other Negro churches in the area or anywhere else in the country, advertised the local colored businesses, like funeral homes, cab companies or restaurants. There were even seam-stresses and drapery makers who advertised. Colored businesses generally got a good deal for their advertising dollar. They didn't need to pay the higher costs of television or radio advertising, to the extent that either of these media was open to them. And besides, they got their product into the hands of consumers way more easily and for much, much longer than the thirty or sixty-second advertising spot on TV or radio. They just gave them to the local churches and their ads were "aired" for hours every Sunday.

After the singing and the announcements and the greeting of the guests, the pastor knelt in prayer before giving his morning Revival sermon. The organ rolled as if to announce the arrival of God! The hard and strong punches the organist invoked on the keys with his fingers made it clear that God would have a resounding message that morning! The organ solo went on for about a minute, building up the anticipation of just what Jesus had to say to the faithful at Mount Calvary.

Coming off his knees, his eyes were closed, and he was silent and solemn looking. What message had God given the pastor today, many were surely thinking? Would he continue on his colored people empowerment kick, as many had begun to refer to it? Or would he give a more "traditional" sermon, especially since this was the beginning of Revival? No matter what he said next, no one would have trouble hearing him because now that the organ solo had crescendoed, the church was still and all eyes and ears were locked on the pulpit and the man who stood in the center underneath the large wooden cross that hung in front of the giant stained-glass window that brought in so much light through its colors of blue, yellow, red, gold and green that it invoked the same joy that seeing a rainbow across a sunny sky brought, especially after a long, hard rain!

"Good morning, church," he started out! "What on earth are you doing?" he asked. "How many times have you heard someone ask that question?" the pastor queried. The question implies a certain code of propriety that we all understand and basically agree to, he went on. "It helps us feel *safe* and don't we all just love the feeling of *safety*?" he asked. "But I want to tell you, Mount Calvary, this is not the time to cling to familiar ground while we should be reaching for the stars and marching into the unknown," he bellowed out. "Socrates said, that 'man must rise above the Earth to the top of the atmosphere and beyond, for only thus will he fully understand the world in which he lives.' Now that's what the great Greek philosopher said thousands of years ago," the pastor explained.

"At the same time, we can't be so blinded by the celestial bright lights that we don't see the darkness, injustice or mistreatment that is going on in front of our very eyes! The American author, James Thurber, now an old man, once said *let us not look back in anger, nor forward in fear, but around in awareness*! I don't mean to be talking out of both sides of my mouth," he continued with a smile on his face. "We can reach while we stay in place, church. God is calling on us to be heavenly right here on earth!" At this point, it was clear to the congregation that the pastor was still on his drive to get the colored race on the road to a better future. If there was a fast lane they could access, well, all the better!

"It seems that some want to go to the stars and the moon and to Mars and Venus or wherever else, in order to escape the problems right here or to conquer new worlds with the same mindset they have in this one," the minister preached on. "But remember, children of God, what the Lord said! 'I will punish the world for its evil, and the wicked for their iniquity, I will put an end to the pomp of the arrogant and lay low the pompous pride of the ruthless.' That is Isaiah, 13th chapter, 11th verse. And in Isaiah 10th chapter, 1st verse, 'Woe to those who enact evil statutes and to those who constantly record unjust decisions.'

"In this season of Revival, we must remember what God calls us to do," the pastor instructed his flock. "We must look to the heavens where our Savior dwells as we make sure his work is done and his Kingdom is realized right here on Earth where we dwell! That young preacher in Birmingham, Martin Luther King, Jr is trying to do just that, not only for colored people but for all the world's people," the pastor brayed, hands raised and head turned toward the sky! "'Then I saw a new heaven and a new earth, for the first heaven and the first earth had passed away, and the sea was no more,'" he maintained from the pulpit, quoting Revelation, twenty-first chapter and first verse.

"Young Reverend King understands," the minister stated. "He understands what many of us around the nation understand and that is that now is the time for us to reach for things that may not have seemed to be in our grasp! But in reality, if we reach high enough, we will realize how within our grasp these things actually are. However, if we keep our hands at our sides, we will never know the power of our reach!

"'Set your minds on things that are above, not on things that are on earth', according to Colossians third chapter, second verse," the preacher instructed. "But, at the same time, we must keep our feet on the ground and stand tall and proud while we do it. Young Reverend King has been showing us the way to do this, but we can all do it, and we must all do it if we expect to make heaven right here on Earth until God calls us home among the stars!

"Our space, our future, our salvation and our conquest is right here on Earth, not on Mars or Venus," argued the pastor, now beginning to conclude the morning sermon. "Let others launch a rocket ship into space and try to conquer creatures on other planets," he stated. "That is what some of these others do." Sounds of laughter and cackling filled the church after this comment.

"You know that's how they are," shouted many in the congregation which was followed by more laughter and clapping!

"But let us find our peace and our place right here," the pastor continued once things started to quiet down. "Let us make a place for ourselves right here on the ground and rejoice in the peace in the Garden.

"But always remember, congregation, the words of the Bible in First Peter third chapter, 14th verse: 'But even if you should suffer for the sake of righteousness, you are blessed and DO NOT FEAR THEIR INTIMIDATION, AND DO NOT BE TROUBLED!'" Trembling, the pastor sat down in his wooden chair with the purple velvet lining, situated underneath the cross. His head was bowed down but held up by both hands and sweat was running from his head as if it had been banished like a devil, from Heaven!

"What power did the word give us today?" asked the head deaconess, coming to the lectern at the end of sermon. "What joy it brings to know that we have the right to a fine and happy life right here just like anyone else, and that we don't have to go to Heaven to live in joy and peace!" Julia Mae held up her right hand, palm open and head bowed slightly down. This was the way that she and many around the church signaled their agreement that they had just got a good and solid message from God on that Sunday afternoon. She was happy to be at church because she heard exactly what she needed to hear going into the new week.

There would be challenges for both her and her son at his new school. But hearing the word was akin to putting on a shield! God would protect her and her family no matter what they had to walk through as they trod along! She walked sprightly out of Mount Calvary although Wynn waned a little bit behind as he tried to delay walking out into the spring heat wearing a medium gray suit, white shirt buttoned up to the top and trimmed with a burgundy necktie. Jeanne fell in between the two of them coming out of the two-hour service as they headed to the car. The two Horry women were both in short-sleeved dresses with collars that took to the sky with the first light breeze. Julia Mae, for one, definitely felt uplifted!

"Is Junior coming back home or going straight to Aunt Nellie's for dinner?" Jeanne asked.

"I'm sure he will go home with them," her mother replied. "No point in him coming back over here!"

"I just hope the house won't be too hot with all that cooking," Wynn confided. "You know how hot it gets over there in the summer even with those fans going." Julia Mae, still on a high from the pastor's sermon, was in no place to let anything make her hot under the collar.

"I'm sure it will be fine, honey," she said. "We make do every summer and it isn't nearly that hot today."

Chapter 38

Sunday afternoons were often the same at the Horry house. That period between church, when they went to church which was most Sundays, and dinner at Nellie and Talley's was spent with a little relaxation and talking on the phone to Leeta and Brown in Charlotte. So that, when the phone rang about an hour after they had returned home, Julia Mae and Wynn naturally thought that it was the Brown family calling, even though it was a little bit earlier than they usually rang.

"Hello," Julia Mae greeted into the phone thinking she would recognize the "hello" that shot back through the other end. While she did recognize the female voice, it wasn't that of her sister-in-law.

"Julia Mae," said the interloping voice, "I'm sorry to interrupt your afternoon but I have to tell you that I was surprised to hear that your son was in my house the other day. I thought we had agreed that it was best for him and my son not to be in touch with each other." As surprised to get this information as she was to hear this voice on the other end of the phone, Julia Mae stood in silence for what seemed like close to a minute before responding.

"Mrs Peterson, good afternoon, I didn't realize that Junior had gone to your house! He certainly didn't tell us he was going there. I hope no trouble was caused," she said, in an effort to mollify her concerned caller.

"It just isn't good for the two of them to be together," Claire Peterson clamored. "It really is best for them to stay away from each other! We had decided to use a lawn service this summer anyway and since they don't go to school together any more, I can't see a reason for them to socialize," she went on.

"Yes, I understand," answered Julia Mae. "In fact, we had mentioned to Junior that it might be better not to expect to cut your grass this summer, so I completely agree," Julia Mae tried to impress upon Claire.

"I will speak to him and make sure it doesn't happen again, Mrs Peterson."

"Please do make sure that it doesn't happen again," Claire responded in the sternest voice that she had ever used to Julia Mae, in fact that she had used with anyone in quite some time. "I don't think there's any good reason for them to be with each other after all that has happened, and I think that you and I should make sure they understand that," Claire insisted!

"Yes, yes, I agree," Julia Mae stammered. "After all that has happened it is definitely best for them to stay away from each other, although I don't think my boy means any harm. I think he is just being friendly as I know he can be," she went on in defense of Junior. "He means no harm, but it is better for them to walk away clean from each other. Goodbye, Mrs Peterson, and I'm sorry you had to trouble yourself with the call," Julia Mae said just before hanging up the phone. "I will definitely speak to my son."

By now, both Wynn and Jeanne were surrounding Julia Mae. They had stayed nearby thinking that the ringing phone might have been Leeta calling as usual, but then became curious and concerned, first by Julia Mae's stupor and then by the deduction that Junior had done something that would come as such a shock to his doting mother!

"What the heck is wrong with that boy?" Julia Mae hollered to no one in particular.

"What did he do?" demanded Wynn. "Did he go see that boy again?" Were they smoking something or what, he wanted to know?

"She didn't say anything about any smoking but it sounded like something happened that she didn't want to go into," Julia Mae concluded. "What is it that's going on with those two?"

The air was already hot, but it had steamed up even more since the phone call! Nevertheless, Wynn, wearing a look of anguish on his face, walked around in circles for a minute and then took a deep breath before he said anything else, all the while noting the tension that his wife had now begun to display. The uplifting religious experience she had just encountered now seemed to have been trampled down and sullied. "It ain't nothin' to worry about," Wynn finally said, hoping to console his wife. "They are just curious about each other."

Julia Mae turned to her husband with a quizzical look on her face. He knew that meant she wanted him to expound on what he was trying to say to her.

"I've seen this happen in the military when colored boys and white boys got around each other for the first time. They just wanted to find out about each other. They would poke the other one to see if and how they bleed," he explained, "I think that's exactly what it is!"

"Well, I don't want my son bleeding for anybody," Julia Mae quickly responded, although she knew her husband had made the claim metaphorically. "I feel like going to Washington right now to sit him down and find out what went on at that house and why he was there in the first place."

Wynn had no more to say to her, but it seemed as though he was having a private conversation in his head.

Chapter 39

Claire and Chester Peterson, Claire in particular, had been on a roller-coaster ride all weekend! They hadn't gone to an amusement park, although Glen Echo across the river over in Maryland had just added the Satellite Jet that Robby was anxious to try! Ever since coming home from the White House dinner and being told that Junior had been at their house while they dined with the First Family and the President of France and his wife, they were stunned. The intensity that the shock left on her must have come out in her call to Julia Mae, she had no doubt!

It wasn't Cliff who told them and Gussie had left by the time they returned. In fact, by the time they got back, no one was at home except Cliff and Robby, who were, of course, expected to be there. Claire kept replaying the evening in her head. After returning home she had asked Cliff how things went. She remembered that he delayed at first, wanting to hear all about their evening at the White House dinner. "It was splendid," Claire had said. "The food was divine, and we got to see many of your father's colleagues and had some good conversations also." Cliff asked if they got to sit with the Eisenhowers and the DeGaulles and was told no, that they didn't get terribly close to them.

"But nevertheless, we enjoyed it and were quite pleased to be there for the evening," his father crowed!

"How was your party?" Chester had asked, "It doesn't look like the house has suffered any damage."

"No damage done," his oldest son replied, "and we just had sodas and cupcakes and played records," Cliff reported. Claire wanted to know who came and when she heard Cliff's reply her soft smile had abandoned her face, a still powdered face with a subtle pale red blush rubbed on. But now, her pale white face had become flushed naturally.

"Junior was here?" she asked, her body going stiff as she leaned against the Danish Modern sofa.

Yes, Cliff affirmed. "He came with Thomasine. He always comes with Thomasine, as you know. You always like her here," he added, as if to justify the presence of the boy he had had his hands all over and face and other parts up against.

"You didn't mention that he would be coming," his father pointed out. Cliff had been prepared for this and, even though he hated to lie to his parents, nevertheless told them that he didn't actually know in advance that Junior was coming.

"He just sprang up on me," Cliff had said. Of course, they had no way of knowing whether this was true or not. They didn't know that the two of them had plotted this tryst in advance. This was their only way of being alone together. Alone, while together with the two girls, downstairs.

That was the Petersons' brief but fairly strained conversation on Friday night with Cliff. It wasn't until Saturday that they heard from Robby! By Sunday afternoon, just before Claire made her phone call to Julia Mae, the Peterson house was as still and quiet as a courtroom. It appears as though Robby had been the star witness. Was Cliff going on trial for an unspeakable crime?

What Robby had seen must have been so shocking that he couldn't even speak about it, or else he couldn't put into words what he actually witnessed. The result was that he was too tongue-tied to give much testimony! This meant that Claire and Chester had no actual misconduct to charge Cliff with; however, they were certain they knew the nature of his transgressions!

"We don't want you seeing that boy again and that's final," Chester decreed. Chester rarely spoke so firmly to his sons, so there was no doubt in Cliff's mind that he meant what he said. But what Cliff wasn't sure about was what they knew about that evening. It wore on him ever since his parents had confronted him on Saturday evening just before they were to sit down to dinner.

Apparently, they had heard something from Robby. Had he seen them together finally? After the other narrow escapes being discovered entangled together, had Robby finally seen him and Junior intertwined? The thought sent shivers all through Cliff and almost sent him into mild cardiac arrest! We were never near the door, he reminded himself. We would have heard if Robby or anyone else was close by, he further thought. But then Cliff recalled that Robby or someone, most likely Robby, had come upstairs at one point. Otherwise, how could the steps running downstairs be explained? Maybe he did look in the door and see something, Cliff finally admitted to himself. That would explain why Robby had acted particularly distant and uncommunicative all weekend. They generally never had too much interaction, but all weekend? Robby hadn't even looked at him!

He must have told them what he had seen. That's the only conclusion Cliff could come to, sitting there on the Arne Jacobsen egg chair, rocking back and forth and feeling as if whatever standing he had with his parents was now debased. If he had been a priceless porcelain figurine on their étagère, it was clear that there was now a crack that could never be repaired.

Shortly after they had returned home from Florida Avenue Baptist, Nellie was in her apron in the kitchen. That she was still singing In Times Like These You Need an Anchor was the only sign that she had been to church at all. But that song, a new gospel offering making its way around Negro churches to help bolster those who felt embattled by circumstances around them, was like a jolt!

She had removed her hat, her hairpiece, the one with the upswept bun that made her look like Sophia Loren from behind, the earrings she had worn as well as the necklace, and of course her dress, heels, gloves and handbag. There might have been a trace of her perfume if you got near enough. But right now, she was close only to the pots and pans that would soon contain the food that, once cooked, would have its own aroma capable of drowning out the fragrance sprayed on her neck, wrist and behind her ear, with its own pleasant and enticing smell.

"Junior, you and your uncle go on out and buy your school supplies now before your folks get here," Nellie yelled out from the kitchen to her nephew and Talley. They will probably be here by 5:00 or so. By the time they returned from church it was already after 3:00. Five and dime stores would be closed in a couple of hours and Junior wanted to change clothes before his parents got there. He had brought some over when his father dropped him off at his aunt and uncle's house on Saturday late morning before his shift at Horrschorns was to start.

"Yes, ma'am, I'm just changing my clothes," he yelled back loud enough to be heard all the way in the kitchen downstairs.

No one knew how much school notebooks, pencils and paper would be available in late April, but perhaps there would be enough for Junior to find enough for his new classwork at Mercer. He didn't want to discard his school notes from all the classes at Arlington High; he figured they would come in handy, plus he also figured that they would be more advanced than the lessons for the same grade at Mercer. But at the same time, he wanted to start fresh at his new school. It was his way of giving Mercer a chance. Let it be a fresh start and let me not go in there with hand me down notes, he joked to himself. It was almost guaranteed that the books used at Mercer were already well enough used. In fact, there was little doubt that many might have come from Arlington High and the other white high schools from past years. That was the way it worked. *Something old, nothing new, something tattered, smudged too*, was what the colored teachers and students would say at the beginning of each new school year!

It had been a little more than two hours since the phone call from Claire Peterson, but Julia Mae Horry was still holding onto some irritation, both with the caller and even more, with her son, the subject of the call! Her sister-in-law Leeta had, in fact, called as usual, about 40 minutes after the irritating call and Julia Mae let Wynn and Jeanne do most of the talking because she couldn't get her mind off the preceding call. "How are things going with the protests?" she remembered asking.

"They are still continuing the sit-ins and so far, no one has been hurt," she recalled Leeta responding. "But nothing has changed. We still can't eat at those counters and I don't know if that will ever be the case and I don't even know if I care," Leeta went on.

Coming at the time it did, a time when she was up to her neck with white people in the first place, all Julia Mae could say was, "Well, you know those crackas don't change." Even though they may wear sheep's clothing, they're still wolves".

Chapter 40

By the time she arrived at her sister's house, she had tried hard to put all that behind her because she didn't want to lash out at Junior in front of the family. "Hey, Momma and Daddy," Junior had said after opening the door for them at Nellie's suggestion while she was still in the kitchen getting dinner. Talley too was busy, filling up ice trays he had just bought while out shopping with Junior, in order to make sure they had enough ice to make it through the evening. As usual, cold, iced tea was on the menu.

"Hello, son, how was church today?" Julia Mae asked, seeing the smile on her son's face.

"Yes, we had a good service today," he responded. "How was Mount Calvary?" he asked after greeting his father and sister.

"It was a good service today, as usual," his mother told him. "The pastor is continuing to challenge us to be better."

"Speaking of which," Wynn interrupted, "your mother wanted to ask you about something." Julia Mae turned to her husband with a surprised look on her face. She was glad that he had mentioned to Junior that she wanted to discuss something with him but also surprised because that wasn't something that Wynn would normally do.

"What did you want to talk about, Momma?" Junior inquired.

"Oh, we can go outside and talk," she said, not wanting to get in the way of her sister's dinner preparations. By now Nellie was out of the kitchen and instead of handling the baked chicken, she was hugging her sister and brother-in-law. Talley too was done with filling the ice trays and was now offering glasses of iced tea to the guests, Jeanne first.

Julia Mae knew that she couldn't go through a whole dinner with her concerns on her mind. She had to find some time to talk with her son about them. Now that everyone had a glass of iced tea and the rest of the family were seated in the King Louis living room underneath the fan and rehashing their respective church experiences, Julia Mae and Junior went out to the small backyard to talk. There wasn't much shade back there but fortunately, the earlier heat had begun to wane, and the sun had ceased its stronghold. Seated on two of the plastic folding chairs that populated the backyard, their iced teas in hand, Junior began to freeze up. He wasn't sure what his mother wanted to talk about. He figured she was at least happy that he was starting back at school the next day, although not the school she wanted him to attend. Did she want to continue her quest to get him into a white school on the eve of his going to Mercer, he wondered?

"Why did you go to the Peterson house on Friday to see that boy?" Immediately, the two of them could see the surprise on each other's face once Julia Mae had allowed this question she had been holding inside for hours, to escape from her lips. She was shocked that she had blurted it out so directly and Junior was surprised that she even knew! From the look on his face, Julia Mae knew that her son wasn't expecting her to know that he had gone to Arlington Heights the previous Friday. This made her even more uneasy. And also, the fact that it was taking a squirming Junior more time than usual to respond, her concerns became heightened.

"I was there with Seeny, Momma. Cliff invited both of us over for soda and snacks and we just listened to music," he testified. Julia Mae knew immediately that talking about this made her son anxious. She could always tell when he was anxious because he would talk faster and often beads of sweat would form on the top of his head. Both of these things were happening in tandem while they sat out in the backyard. Yes, it was hot but suddenly things seemed to be getting hotter by the moment!

"Don't you think it's better for you not to see that boy, after all that has happened with you and him?" his mother asked earnestly. She leaned toward him as if to whisper the question even though there was no one around to hear either of them speak. "Hasn't enough damage been done and they haven't taken any responsibility for anything?" she protested. "Everything has fallen on you... you have had to pay the price for everything." Finally, she asked, "Why is Cliff still so important to you that you want to be in his company?" Junior had had time to gather his composure as well as his thoughts by the time Julia Mae had finished her statement-question combination.

"We are friends, Momma," he told Julia Mae. "You wanted me to have friends and you wanted me and Cliff to get to know each other," he continued. "Well, we became friends!"

Julia Mae looked at her son with the eyes of a mother who loved the child she was focused on, but nevertheless was chafed by that child's choices. "Some people you just can't be friends with," she tried to explain. "Some friendships just aren't meant to be!"

"Are you asking me never to spend any more time with Cliff?" Junior wondered.

"I think it's best if you don't," Julia Mae replied. "You will meet other kids at Mercer and you already have friends from there," she continued. "Besides, who knows who you will meet when you start school in September, wherever it is that you go?" Julia Mae continued her appeal to her son by pointing out that he would meet new boys wherever he went and there would be none of the baggage that knowing Cliff Peterson carried.

Junior looked a little forlorn at his mother! But still, he didn't blame her for anything she said. He knew she was just being a good mother and was responding the way practically any mother he knew would. Certainly, his Aunt Nellie would say the same thing and she wasn't even a mother, only a second mother! He realized that Julia Mae didn't understand how things really were. How could she? This, neither she nor anyone else could *ever* understand! And it didn't help that neither he nor Cliff could ever explain it to any of them either!

They sat in silence for a few minutes after this backyard summit, both stealing an occasional smile at each other, both knowing that the other loved and cherished them deeply! Before either could say another word, Wynn had come outside to see what was going on. "What are you two doing out here so long?" he asked with lightness in his voice. "Aunt Nellie is 'bout to bring out her delicacies and if you're not careful, the rest of us will eat everything up!"

"Aww come on, Pop, you don't even eat that much," Junior shot taking his father's lead to lighten the moment.

"We just got some things straight," Julia Mae reported. "I think we understand each other better about that situation that came to our attention this afternoon," she concluded.

"Well good, good, good," Wynn replied. "Too many new friends out there to make to chase behind people that don't want you," he stated, shaking his head as if it gave his protestation more heft. Junior nodded his head in agreement in order to bring the discussion to a close. He knew that was what his parents wanted. He also knew that his father wasn't speaking from first-hand knowledge when he implied that Cliff didn't want him. He knew that nothing could be further from the truth. Cliff obviously wanted him and was eager to show him how much every chance he got. But this he would have to keep under wraps as always!

"You go on in honey," Wynn advised his wife. "I just wanted to have a little father-son chat with Junior."

"Oh, now it's your turn?" Julia Mae inquired, more making a statement than asking a question. "Well good, you two have your chat, see you inside in a minute."

Wynn stood directly across from Junior, a bit uneasy and at first silent as if gathering his thoughts while looking off into the distance. But then he steered his eyes forward and parked them on his son who looked back at him a bit apprehensively!

"Son, I know what the friendship with that boy means to you!" Wynn started off, clearing his throat, speaking in a voice a notch above a murmur. I just want you to know that you may see things differently one day. Even if you don't, you will probably find a friendship like that when you are older that you can maintain without all this stress and strain. Whether you want us to know about your friendship or not, it won't be such a burden for you and we won't feel the need to bother you about it!"

With that, Wynn put his left hand on Junior's shoulder and rested it there for a minute. With his eyes fixed to the ground, he breathed deeply again and then gently ushered his son out of the dark into the house. He, at least, felt lighter, having let all this come out!

Back inside and washing up for dinner, neither Wynn, Julia Mae nor Junior had anything more to say about what had been discussed in either conversation during those collective twenty or so minutes on the back patio. Although Julia Mae was curious about what her husband had to say to their son, she didn't ask.

Junior wouldn't have been able to tell her anyway. He wasn't quite sure himself what it was his father was saying to him! But like having been discovered in the janitor's closet with Cliff, Junior once again felt exposed! Did his father somehow know what he wanted so bad to keep hidden away? Had Old Papa pulled Wynn aside and told him what kind of son he really had?

One thing was clear. Other folks were out in their backyards too because they could hear laughing, and the sounds of dishes being moved about, backdoor springs making noise from the pressure of opening and closing and also the sounds of music, some from records and some coming from the radio. Colored stations had switched from gospel music to jazz and rhythm and blues by that time of day, so much of what they heard was the wafting of Sarah Vaughan, Dinah Washington, Nat Cole, Sam Cooke and a few doo-wop groups every now and then. But back inside, it was the aroma of Nellie's dinner that caught their attention. She had brought just about everything to the table from the kitchen and was ready for everyone to dig in.

"Is everything okay between you two?" she asked smiling. "I wouldn't want to have my only sister and my favorite nephew not on speaking terms," she joked. "I would probably have to choose sides and that would be a hard one for me!" After everyone had snickered, Nellie loudest among them, she turned a bit more serious!

"I never told y'all this, but that woman I work for had the nerve to tell me that it was too bad about Junior leaving Arlington High but that it was for the best!" Julia Mae looked over at her sister with a scowl on her face but said nothing as Nellie continued to speak. "She said, with all that juvenile delinquency stuff going on in '57 and afterwards, it is just not the time to be bringing colored kids into white schools!" Nellie was rolling her eyes as she reported this. No one at the table knew exactly how to respond to this, at first. Considering the silence at the table, Nellie was unsure if she should say more but she decided she would fill the silence with more details of the prior conversation with her lady. "President Eisenhower just signed that Civil Rights bill for colored people so you can see that things are changing for them but it will take time, she told me."

Finally, Julia Mae spoke up. "Why would she even say anything about Junior?" she asked. Nellie explained that the woman had finally figured out that Junior was the colored boy who got expelled from the school.

"She asked me what had happened, and I told her that it was all a mistake, and we were sorry it ever happened. I had to say something," Nellie attested, "I couldn't tell her to mind her business and stay the heck out of it like I wanted to."

"After all, I've already had one or two job offers from her friends just to be their cook," she shared. "I could get the same money too, so she had better watch herself." This elicited a good laugh from everyone even though they had heard this revelation before and knew that Nellie could find another place of employment if she wanted.

"That Civil Rights bill she's talking 'bout is just a way to get colored folks to vote for Nixon in November, Pastor preached back in March when Eisenhower signed it," Julia Mae argued. "Of course, they want to make sure Negroes can vote without problems so they can vote for them!"

"How did she find out it was Junior?" Wynn wanted to know, getting back to the main conversation.

"Well, I guess the way I shot outta her house that day saying that I had to see about my nephew, I guess she figured it out," Nellie acknowledged.

"Besides, you know they all talk," Julia Mae piped in. "They don't have much else to do except sit around and talk about things they know nothing about!"

Nellie was feeling a tad guilty about bringing this up, but Wynn had confided to her while his wife and son were out back that their conversation had to do with his connection to the white boy he was hiding in the closet with at Arlington High.

"Well, I didn't mean to add salt to old wounds, y'all," she felt obligated to say. "I was just reminded about how tense the whole thing is and how it brings out folks' true colors," Nellie lamented. "She also added one more thing," Nellie shared. "Right now, people are focused on our scientific achievements and advancements and this is no time for us to be taking our full attention off what is going to make our country great." Nellie delivered this last part with a dusting of sarcasm.

"Oh well, they can have their school," Julia Mae imparted. "My son is out but I'm sure it won't stop there. It's not about being near white people, it's about having access to the opportunities and advantages denied to colored people," Julia Mae proclaimed. "They don't understand that, or don't want to understand it," she concluded. "All I want is for my son to have all the advantages he's entitled to and capable of using to his best advantage." She then turned to look at Jeanne, and with a smile on her face, said, "My daughter too."

"Well," said Wynn with gusto in his voice, "you know how I feel about that!"

Like the baked chicken on their plates, that particular conversation at this point was well done! They went on to discuss Sunday church sermons and starting at a new school just a little over a month before school would be out for summer. "Well, I sure wish I was at Griffith this afternoon," Wynn announced. He knew that his son wasn't much of a baseball fan but perhaps he would catch the irony of seeing Pumpsie Green play ball over on Florida Avenue.

"I agree with that," Talley averred. His mouth was full of baked chicken at the time, but he couldn't let the moment go by without showing his support for what his brother-in-law had said. "The crowds were coming in as we were leaving church," he noted. "It took us much longer to get out of there than it should have." Griffith Stadium was only a stone's throw from Florida Avenue Baptist.

"Who is Pumpsie Green?" Jeanne asked, much to Junior's relief, even though she didn't realize it. He had heard his father go on and on about Pumpsie ever since he got to run bases as a Boston Red Sox infielder for the first time in a game against the Chicago White Sox out in the Windy City in the summer just before he enrolled at Arlington High. It was one of those big moments for colored sports fans in '59 because Pumpsie finally broke the Red Sox's color barrier. Since they were the last major league baseball team to allow a Negro to play, it was considered baseball's last strike out for Jim Crow!

"Pumpsie is the last colored boy, to join the major leagues, princess! Every team now has one of us playing," he explained. "Junior was a first and Pumpsie was a last but both of those are good things in the long run," he chuckled looking at his son. "That means that the story will end somewhere good!"

"Can you find out the score of that game, brother?" Wynn asked Talley. "With all the yelling I heard outside a few minutes ago, I would say the Senators won that game," he disclosed, in a way answering his own question. "Let me turn on the radio and find out," Talley offered, looking at his wife as he was about to get up.

"Don't you dare turn that radio on while we having dinner, husband, or I will hit you with that roasting pan sitting in the sink." Everyone chucked and Talley sat back down.

"Well, I'm sure they won but we will find out later." As it turned out, the Senators had won the Sunday afternoon game 11-10.

"You know the White Sox are coming on May 7," Wynn informed anyone who was listening. "I will get me and Junior a ticket since we missed today's game."

"Can you get me a ticket too, better yet, I will get us three tickets unless anybody else wants to go," Talley chimed on.

"Thanks, brother-in-law," Wynn beamed. "If anybody else wants to go let her speak now before Talley buys the tickets this week," he declared.

"We will let you boys go by yourselves," Julia Mae demurred. "Besides, I have some dresses to work on and your princess has to help me."

"Thanks, Pop," Junior finally interjected. "I may have to work at the store on Saturday, but I can probably switch shifts for Friday evening." He would have at least a week's notice to find someone to replace him on his Saturday afternoon shift so that he could go to the game.

Working on a Friday night would mean that Junior would miss dinner with the family but at least he would not risk losing his job. Horrschorns tearoom didn't easily tolerate absences from its waiting or dishwashing staff. Washington's high society had to be sustained, especially on a Friday evening in spring, and dishes had to be washed! The tearoom closed at 7pm every night of the week. Most society ladies without husbands or children, and bachelors without a cook to prepare them dinner, had usually taken their light meals by then. Junior would make it home in time for the *Twilight Zone*.

Despite the fact that she preferred she didn't have to, on that Monday morning, Julia Mae made it to the DC Transit bus stop where she would wait for the express bus to take her across the Potomac River to the sewing machines at Horrschorns downtown, where she would make alterations on her mood if she were to make it through the day. These days, the trip was too quick. As much as she loved her work, lately she didn't much love the place where she did it! Her boss, the Bama lady had been continuing to make work life miserable. One of the other ladies in the alterations room had overheard a conversation between her and a shopper whom the supervisor apparently knew well.

It came to be mentioned in the conversation, according to Julia Mae's co-worker, that Julia Mae had done some work for a neighbor of hers in Arlington. The lady who had been Julia Mae's customer let slip that her clothing maker worked at one of the downtown department stores full time. When questioned, she divulged that it was Horrschorns department store but never actually gave Julia Mae's name, apparently. Doing her best Nancy Drew, the alterations room supervisor thought that she had figured out who it was based on where Julia Mae lived and also because she knew how good a seamstress she is. "I'm sure it's that gal who works under me," Bama lady boasted to her friend, according to the recounting. "I'm sure she fancies herself as a colored Coco Chanel," she declared in her Alabama drawl; the woman cackled in her telling.

"Oh well, she can think what she wants to," Julia Mae responded after this had been revealed. "She doesn't know my business and doesn't need to."

"That ain't no lie," the co-worker responded, "but she can make it hard for you! I notice that she has already cut your hours back a little and who knows what she will do next," the woman pointed out.

"Don't worry," Julia Mae intonated, "I see what's going on and I'm getting myself prepared for whatever happens."

The co-worker smiled at her, put her hand on her shoulder and shook her head. "Well, God be with you, chile! I know you have been through a lot with your son and now you got to deal with this!"

Just as they were ending their conversation, the boss lady walked in with a rack of clothing, mostly dresses, women's suits and a few men's suits as well. "As usual, these have their instructions and due date slips

271

on them so y'all get started," she instructed her staff. Prior to her coming to Horrschorns, Julia Mae would have been the one to dole out the work. She knew who was quickest and who was good at what. She would always keep the most difficult work for herself. The new boss had not taken the time to learn the particular skills of the three ladies that now worked under her, but it was clear, as she had been told at the outset by her superiors, Julia Mae Horry was the best! Despite what she thought of her, getting the work of the alterations room done well and timely would be difficult without her! And besides, the other two ladies still looked to "JH" as they affectionately called her, to guide them and steer the appropriate work their way.

Chapter 41

After all that had been mulled over, there was still uncertainty in Arlington Heights that morning. "I think you should ask him about it immediately," Claire announced to her husband as she was preparing to serve him coffee and toast and eggs.

"I will see if he brings it up first," answered Chester. "I think I should give him the opportunity to further explain himself and what he was thinking." This conversation had started upstairs in the bedroom long before the two of them had arrived downstairs in the kitchen. Now dressed in his dark gray suit and blue and yellow rep tie, Chester was ready to put this topic to rest. His way of doing that was to focus on his coffee, toast and eggs while Claire sat across from him in a checkered dress, a simple one that a woman could wear around the house, sipping her coffee and glancing at Chester as he glanced at the front page of the *Washington Post*.

Claire had brought the latest issue of *Look* magazine to the table to read as she ate her breakfast, which never happened until after she had got Chester off to work and Cliff and Robby off to school. The boys were about to come downstairs for their own breakfast of cereal and toast which was already awaiting them. Even though she had preferred to get some confirmation from her husband about the conversation she deemed of utmost importance, she decided to let it go; after all, Cliff and Robby were due downstairs any minute.

Sixty pages on the big parties, the big wheels, the beauty and the meaning of democracy's hometown, read the cover of the April 26 *Look* magazine. "How bittersweet," Claire uttered in a low voice, a wistful look on her face.

"What is?" asked her husband sitting in front of her still glancing at the morning newspaper although finishing his coffee and munching on the last few bites of toast. Claire turned the front cover of the issue to his face. The cover, an image of the Lincoln Memorial with the Reflecting Pool in view was even more poignant because the direction of the image showed Arlington in the background.

"Oh, nice cover," Chester acknowledged, "I will have to read that."

"There's also an article here on someone you know at State," Claire shared. "Isn't that ironic?"

Just then, she heard footsteps coming down the steps and immediately realized it was Robby. He always walked faster and more determined than his older brother. "Goodbye, Dad," he said, holding out his hand to his father for their customary morning handshake.

"Bye, son, have a good day at school," Chester imparted as he was on his way out the door to the family car. "Tell Cliff goodbye for me."

Normally Cliff would be downstairs by now too. But since his conversation with his family on Sunday, he had felt like the odd man out! It was hard for him to come face to face with them, especially Robby. Although nothing was said, things had been awkward ever since Saturday night, really. He still didn't know what they knew, but it was clear that Robby had shared something about what was going on in his bedroom with Junior. Cliff's face had worn a deep red all weekend and it got redder every time he thought about it. Perhaps it was a mistake for him to have worn that red and black checked Arrow shirt to school that day. It almost looked as though the shirt had a turtle-neck sweater underneath that pulled up to his face as the hue on his face matched the red in the shirt. But he was now coming downstairs after he had heard his father leave. That would be one less person to see and one less conversation to have.

Later at school he saw Thomasine and also Pamela although not together. They were hardly ever together except at his house on those few occasions. "How was the rest of your weekend?" Thomasine asked. Needless to say, Cliff could not tell her how things had really gone in the aftermath of Junior and him being discovered in his room. Instead, he smiled, a very ruddy smile, and said it was fun.

"I will have a note for you to give to Junior later on," he told his friend. "I will see you in class and give it to you then."

Chapter 42

Over at Mercer High, Junior felt as if he had just moved to a new town, even though he lived near many of the other students and knew quite a few of them. His homeroom teacher had explained that he had joined them after leaving Arlington High as one of the Arlington Five. "He should be applauded for his bravery and his efforts to make progress," proclaimed the teacher. "At the same time, we are happy to have him with us and I want everyone to welcome Mr Wynn Horry, Jr graciously," she added.

"Hey, Junior, we knew you would be back," one boy shouted out, gaining laughter in the aftermath of the comment. "Pretty soon the Five will be Zero," he went on. This comment elicited a new round of laughter but Junior still said nothing. He only smiled and looked straight ahead at the homeroom teacher.

"None of this is anything to joke about," she finally felt obliged to say amidst the laughter. "We need to be supportive of each other, not take opportunities to make jokes."

Carolyn Stanley had walked him to school that morning. That was his mother's suggestion. Julia Mae didn't want him to walk into school alone. She knew how apprehensive he was about going there in the first place and she shared his concerns. "Don't let them needle you too much," she had admonished him before he left. "Hardly any of them could have done what you did, and you remember that. Whatever they say to you, just keep in mind that much of it may come from jealousy," his mother instructed. He knew that his mother was, as always, in his corner. He did wonder where she would stand if she had known the full story, though. It seemed clear to him that if anyone *did* know it, they hadn't shared it with Julia Mae Horry.

But, as much as he could allow himself to even fathom his parents knowing what had gone on in the bedroom on Friday night, and what had gone on many, many times before between him and Cliff, and in many different places, he believed deep down that they would not have abandoned him. He suddenly recalled a story that his Aunt Nellie had shared with the family a few years back when he was about ten. A Senate colleague of her congressman boss had committed suicide in office. The story was that he had become despondent over his health but Nellie, who was always listening, had heard it was because his son was about to be exposed for being *funny*! Apparently, the son had tried to pick up a cop for sex in a park across from the White House. Other members of the Senate had found out about it and held it over the father's head. This had happened during the McCarthy witch hunts as many referred to them, and hardly anyone was safe!

Junior wasn't exactly sure at the time why this story stuck in his head or what it even meant. But somehow, he had associated with it and retained it even at that early age. Now, six years later as it came back to him, he thought about his own parents and how they would handle the situation if they had known about what went on with Cliff. He just couldn't imagine them killing themselves over it. He realized he couldn't speak for Cliff's parents, though. Perhaps they had more to lose. But regardless, nothing would come to that, it was pretty clear to him.

"I'm glad you are here, Junior," said Carolyn as she leaned over to kiss him in a quiet spot once they had arrived at Mercer. No one could see them where they were standing, awfully close to each other.

"I'm glad I'm here too," he responded. They then parted and went to their respective homerooms. She with a smile on her face and he with a look of confusion and a pit in his stomach!

Mercer didn't look anything like Arlington High. Of course, they both had chalkboards, classrooms, windows, desks and hallways, but that was pretty much where it ended. Arlington was a much bigger school yet it seemed empty compared to Mercer which had more students per class than Arlington. The classrooms were smaller, darker and the desks were older and definitely more worn. One thing that was certain was that the atmosphere at Mercer was more friendly and easygoing. Junior wasn't sure if it was because a colored boy at a white high school would naturally not be as warmly received as at a colored school. But he quickly concluded that among colored people it probably was just a more relaxed atmosphere in general. He knew enough about the differences between Negroes and whites to know that Negroes had more fun with each other than white people did. They were just more informal and that was one thing he did like about his race.

All in all, he missed Arlington High. Not so much because of Cliff but because there he had entered a completely new world, one that was many times superior to the one that he had lived in for all his life up to that point. Ever since he had entered this new world, going back to the old one had felt like a punishment. It was akin to offering a treat to a newborn baby and then, once he was happily enjoying it, snatching it away! That was just cruel!

Not at the top of the list of things he missed, but Cliff was not at the bottom either! True, he had many friends at Mercer, most he had known since grade school, but Cliff was more than that. Cliff had allowed him access! Now that he was in this new world, nothing else would ever be satisfactory. Cliff had been his chaperon through this world and had eased his connection to it. Yet, all that aside, he was determined to make the most of his few weeks at Mercer. Whether he would want to stay for another school year or not was an unwritten story. Many of the teachers were people he knew and respected. They were members of the church or leaders in the community and people looked up to them. There was no doubt that they cared about him more than the teachers at Arlington High.

One of those teachers, Miss Bridges, was a church member and was always doing things in the community. She was one of the organizers of the Winter Cotillion and was continuously encouraging the teenagers and younger kids to put their best foot forward and their best outfits on so they could show the world how beautiful they were. No one at Arlington High thought of him as beautiful, except perhaps some of the cafeteria workers and maybe some of the custodians, although none of them would have used that word! Junior also thought about how much Cliff might have missed him too. He knew that Cliff was often unsure of himself and benefitted from Junior's confidence and strength. Surely these days he must be missing that. It was certainly obvious the previous Friday night how much Cliff had missed him. His enthusiasm for having his colored friend so close seemed to grow every minute he was near!

But once again he had to try to put Cliff out of his mind. Junior looked around the classroom at Mercer and tried to smile at the students who were joshing about his having been run out of Arlington High and about how they would fear being so close to white people because the hatred of these people might rub off on them and *they* "might start to hate niggers themselves"! Like all the other similar comments, this one elicited much laughter. Amid all the laughter and joking around he realized that there was a kind of pride! He and the others had learned to stand up tall and strong, even while they were jonin on each other! It was a rite of passage that they put each other through to help them survive the world they had to live in. This was not the place for Cliff to be occupying space in his head. He had to put him away in order to get through these days.

His mother was right, Junior had begun to understand over the course of the first week at his new school. She had often said that he would get a better education at the white school. Junior realized for sure that what he had been taught at Arlington High was more advanced than what the students were learning at Mercer. Most of the teachers knew the subject matter well enough, although not all. However, many of the students didn't come to the subject matter as prepared and often the teachers weren't able to nurture a consistent amount of enthusiasm for what was being taught. But what he was getting that was different was the *take* on many subjects. The colored teachers often urged students to think about things differently. History, civics and English particularly, were courses presented in a different way than at Arlington High. These teachers tailored the same facts to better fit their students. Students needed to be armed with an education that would better enable them to maneuver through the world as the world allowed them to. This wasn't an issue at Arlington High, or any of the other white schools.

The boy who was talking the most about Junior being kicked out of Arlington High, it turns out, was the boy that had been spending time with Carolyn Stanley. And he definitely wasn't someone that Junior knew. The three of them were in the same civics class and Carolyn was talking with him when Junior entered the classroom. Junior recognized him from his homeroom and apparently the boy had known about Junior before he even arrived at Mercer.

"Junior, do you two know each other?" Carolyn asked.

"No, not really," he replied. "I think I've seen him in my homeroom, though."

"Yea, man, we're in the same homeroom, cat. My name is Kiro." Surprised to hear the boy's unconventional name, Junior asked if it was the same name as the capital of Egypt.

"It is," Kiro explained, "but spelled K-i-r-o. Almost like the syrup and just as sweet!" The boy he had just been introduced to looked at Carolyn in a sly way when he made the comment referring to Karo syrup.

"OK," Junior said, adding that he thought it was an interesting name, deciding to ignore the suspect comment. "Do you two know each other well?" Junior asked Carolyn, figuring that she might not have been aware that he had heard about the two of them. Carolyn pulled on one end of the scarf that she was wearing around her neck and then ran that same hand down the front of her light blue skirt as if in doing so the appropriate answer to Junior's question would be let loose. After a few more seconds, she acknowledged that they had gotten to know each other at school, even though they had seen each other around the neighborhood.

"He doesn't live that far away from me and he's always got some kind of noise going," Carolyn giggled.

Kiro was about as tall as Junior but definitely skinnier. He was a dark-skinned boy also, but with a rounder face, although attractive. He wore his low-cut hair parted on the right side. He had full brownish-pink lips and Junior wondered if Carolyn knew what it was like to kiss them as she had kissed his. This was obviously the boy that Seeny had told him about. The one that she reported that Carolyn had been spending so much time with. He appeared to be a popular kid as many in their homeroom class seemed to follow his lead and laugh at his jokes, many of which Junior had to admit, were funny. But why hadn't he met him before either at Frederick Douglass Junior High or in the neighborhood, he wondered?

"You didn't go to Douglass, did you?" Junior decided to just come out and ask. Kiro replied no and explained that he had just moved to Arlington in the late summer before school started. "Where did you move here from?" Junior was curious to know. This boy seemed different from most of the kids he had grown up with. Not different in a bad or good way, just different. It wasn't surprising to him that he was from someplace else. When Kiro divulged that he had moved from Chicago, for some reason things made more sense to Junior. He had never been to Chicago, didn't know anyone well who had ever lived there but he had images of the city. Talley drove through Chicago or at least around it, to get his congressman boss and his family home and back to Washington. Often, he would stop over in the Windy City, as he often referred to it, on the way home. He talked about shopping in some of the city's great department stores to buy a gift for Nellie. There was one on the Southside that catered mostly to Negroes and it was big and grand, he would boast.

Why anyone would want to leave Chicago to come to Arlington was beyond Junior. He figured that Kiro must have got into some kind of trouble and that is why he was now in Arlington. Junior imagined that Chicago wasn't the kind of town that could offer much succor to kids in trouble, particularly colored ones. He wondered if Carolyn knew anything about Kiro's past. Did she question as to whether or not he was running from something, from some bad past? Did she ever think that he might have caused someone harm or did something so terrible that a city as big as Chicago didn't have strong enough shoulders to prop him up or enfold him?

One thing that was certain was that Kiro was new and probably exciting to a lot of the kids because he was from Chicago. He even dressed differently from most. He wore pressed slacks to school and his shirts were of bright colors with more designs and patterns than that of the other boys. Junior came to the conclusion that Kiro was just more colorful all around. He wore his hair a little higher on top and cut close on the sides. Junior wondered how long he would have lasted at Arlington High. He didn't seem like the kind of colored boy that would have been chosen to go to a white school in the first place, nor did he appear to be one who would have gone had he been chosen. He made that clear by the things he said. "If I'm from the first people on Earth, why do I feel like I'm last all the time?" he had heard him ask in civics class during one lesson. Teachers at Mercer would actually take the time to respond to a question like that usually, and not just ignore it as would happen at Arlington for a question or comment that didn't seem related to the subject matter at hand.

It had come as a surprise to Junior, and certainly to Carolyn too, that he and Kiro were actually becoming friendly. Kiro was indeed curious about his time at Arlington High but seemed to accept that Junior was smart and that was why he was allowed to go to the school. Kiro wasn't a dumb student either and he even understood the concept of integration but felt that white people needed to accept Negroes for who they were first and not expect them to change to suit them! He was clear about that in his conversations with Junior, and Junior was actually surprised at how much he had thought his viewpoints out. He explained that, with very few exceptions, in Chicago, schools were almost always segregated by neighborhood pattern. The school he had left was all Negro and the closest whites to his neighborhood lived in an all-white community and the junior high school reflected that.

"Since you're from Chicago and might feel homesick, would you want to go with me and my pop and uncle to a White Sox game Saturday after next?" Junior found himself proffering when talking to Kiro in homeroom during the middle of the week.

"Hmm, who are they playing?" Kiro inquired.

"They are playing in DC against the Senators," Junior informed him. "My dad loves Floyd Robinson and can watch Minnie Miñoso play any day. He told me I could invite someone if I wanted to." It was true that Wynn revered the Chicago White Sox. They were a good team first and foremost. But, Good Lord, he couldn't get over the fact that they also had the most Negro players of any team in major league baseball. While most teams had one colored player, and many brought that one on grudgingly, the White Sox had four. And it was almost ten years since Minnie Miñoso had signed on.

While his father hadn't actually said that it was OK for Junior to invite a friend, he knew it would be fine. He also knew that his dad would actually be proud of him for making a new friend at Mercer so quickly. The fact that Kiro also played softball was an added bonus. He had learned this information during one of their conversations. He was the type of fella Wynn wanted his son to be around. In fact, Kiro was the type of fella he wanted his son to be!

"I will ask my grandparents if I can come but I doubt it will be a problem," Kiro confirmed. "No doubt the Cuban Comet and his team

281

will kick Washington's butt right in its own home field," he added confidently. Junior was happy and hopeful that Kiro could join him and his father and uncle for the game that first weekend in May. He had decided that it was better too for him to be friends with Kiro than enemies. If he, Carolyn and Kiro were friends, it would be less likely that Kiro would go after Carolyn which would, of course, make him look weak in the eyes of all their classmates who were mostly also the neighborhood kids. This was his strategy, at least. Besides, there were many other girls who wanted to get close to Kiro. Not many of them were as pretty as Carolyn Stanley but there were those who would do what it took to get his attention.

Claire was still after Chester to get to the bottom of what she knew was important to the future of their family. It had been nearly two weeks since they had heard this news and yet Chester still hadn't done what she thought was his due diligence. He had vowed that he would bring the conversation up again before the week was over. Truth be told, he had broached the subject of a possible post in Luxembourg with the State Department official who had first brought it up at the White House State dinner in late April, but things hadn't been finalized yet. He had told Claire this, but she thought he was dragging his feet on pinning the official down for the appointment.

"I feel it better for us not to go to Africa after all, even though taking a post in Europe would not be as advantageous to your career as going to a new African nation as a head of mission," she had concluded. "We might sacrifice something in the short term," she had argued, "but in the long term, this is better for our family."

But on the very afternoon he thought he would visit his colleague who would help make the decision on who got the post in Luxembourg, a basically lateral position, the news that was being reported had dominated the attention of everyone at State. "Soviets Down American Plane; US Says it was Weathercraft; Khrushchev Sees Summit Blow," reported the *New York Times* that had just arrived in his office after lunch. The news was also on the radio and many around State had been talking about it even before the newspaper headlines. These people were senior enough to always be in the know. "What will this mean for the upcoming Paris Summit?" many of his colleagues were asking. Some had been planning to be in the French capital for the meeting between the two superpowers and France and Great Britain scheduled for just one week away.

Apparently, according to what was being reported, the American astronaut had parachuted out of the plane which flew high above the Soviet Union after it had been torpedoed by Russian missiles. The astronaut was captured by the Soviets. It was a known secret by many that the US had been spying on the Soviets to gain information on their military ability for years. But the President was contending that the U-2 plane was not a spy plane, rather one that was gaining information on the weather.

Regardless, this was not the day to bring up a potentially stormy topic like this new post in western Europe. Many were vying for the post and most had been in the running long before Chester Peterson who didn't even know there would be an opening before the State Dinner in April. If he had learned anything in his twenty-one years at State, it was that when it came to jostling for a posting, one needed to let one's interest be known but not appear to be overly hungry or eager. Claire had been a State Department wife long enough to know that.

But she was motivated by something else. His wife was clearly determined to get their family away from Washington and he knew what it was that she was trying to escape. This incident with Cliff had changed almost everything in the Peterson household. Something had to happen and happen quick; Claire had made it clear! "Cliff needs to be in a different environment," she had stated. While he didn't disagree with that, Chester wasn't certain that stifling his career by going to Luxembourg was the best answer. However, he wasn't dismissing his wife's concerns.

As expected, later that evening, Claire brought up the subject of whether Chester had had the conversation at work that day. "Today was not the day," he protested, hoping to shut off any long discussion.

"I know that everyone was probably focused on the news but that made me think," she told her husband. "I think we should send Cliff to astronaut camp right after school ends in a few weeks. There's one outside Rochester and we can send both him and Robby there for a couple of months since we wanted them to spend some time with my parents anyway. If we are going to move, that would be great timing," she added. "They would get back just before we pack up the house to ship it overseas."

"There was some interesting local news today too," Claire decided to reveal. She held up the front page of the *Northside Story,* the new North Arlington community weekly that had recently started to circulate. It had been lying on the dining room table. "Another Negro Student Expelled from Arlington High," the headline read. Chester eyed the paper but neither said anything about the front-page lead story.

"Astronaut camps might be seeing an increase in interest right now since the Russians blasted at our aircraft," Chester commented. "Everyone's thinking we gotta get back at 'em somehow!" But his joshing aside, he took his wife seriously and agreed it might be good for the boys. The Peterson family needed to move on!

Chapter 43

Junior was surprised at how busy Horrschorns tearoom was on a Friday night. He had never worked during the week before. He expected it to be busy on Saturday afternoons when he usually worked but figured that not so many people would be in the restaurant on a Friday night. But, as Wally, his friend the waiter pointed out, there were many widows and bachelors in Washington, and this was usually how many of them spent their Friday evening. Wally had become accustomed to the attention he received from the widows and many of the bachelors who frequented or were regulars on Friday nights. He was sure that many of them looked forward to seeing him and a few of the other waiters, each week. It didn't bother him. In fact, the tips that came his way as a result more than made up for any uncomfortable staring or suggestive questions or comments that may have come from his tables. Often some of the men and women would ask if he could come to their home or apartment to help them with this or with that but he always refused and said that he was usually too busy with his college work. But for many, that made him even more interesting. The idea of a college man in their grasp really whetted their appetite!

"Would you like to come over to my apartment this evening to talk about an effort to make some changes that my roommate and I are working on?" Wally asked Junior when they got the first opportunity to talk on their break that Friday evening.

"What kind of changes?" Junior asked.

"Just some of the progressive efforts that I mentioned to you before," Wally explained.

"If I can't come tonight how about tomorrow evening?" Junior wondered.

"Well, that could work but we have a meeting scheduled for tonight with others and I think it might be something you'd be interested in," Wally noted. "Why can't you come tonight?" he asked.

Junior explained that it might be kind of late once he got off and he had to get back to Virginia because his folks would be waiting for him. He didn't want to acknowledge that he and his family watched *Twilight Zone* on Friday nights.

"Why can't you tell me now, what you're talking about?" Junior asked Wally.

"I don't want to discuss it here," Wally replied. "Plus, my roommate is really the one behind the planning, so he should be the one to explain it."

Junior promised that he would visit on Saturday. He told them that he would already be in the city anyway for a baseball game and he could come then. In honesty, he wasn't sure that it would fly since he would be with his father and uncle. But especially if Kiro was with him, it would be easier to come up with an excuse to break away from his family. Wally wrote down his address on the back of a patron check form, and also added his phone number. "Call me if you have any questions or have trouble finding me," Wally instructed. "I will be working an early shift tomorrow, so I should be home around four."

That Saturday was a warm and pleasant day in Washington, and everyone had enjoyed watching baseball. Kiro's spirits were especially high! After a nearly three-hour game at Griffith Stadium, the Chicago White Sox had beaten the Washington Senators 6-4 and the game helped them maintain their position as first place in the American League so far for the season. With their defeat of the Senators, the White Sox had won 11 games since the start of the season. The Senators were way down in 6th place in the league and it wasn't expected that they would defeat the Chicago ball players. Minnie Miñoso and the other colored players on the Chicago team, as always, got loud cheers and applause from colored fans at the game, even though it was a Washington crowd. Negro fans usually sat in a particular section of the stadium even though they didn't have to. That meant it was always obvious where the cheers or jeers were coming from when it was the Negro fans making them.

"We are going to stay in town for a little while," Junior announced to Wynn as they were making their way out of the stadium after the game had ended. It was about time that Wally would be home, and Junior could soon make it over to the apartment he shared with his roommate. Junior hadn't yet mentioned any of these plans with his friend, but he hoped Kiro would want to come along too. If he didn't, he would probably have to leave him by himself in a city that he didn't know well, although Kiro wasn't one to be defenseless, it was clear.

Regardless, he knew he could use Kiro as a reason to stay in the city because the new boy hadn't had too many opportunities to get into the District on his own. His grandparents were old-time Arlington residents and didn't have much use for Washington. Therefore, it was rare that his grandfather would drive into the city unless he came to pick up supplies or do the occasional handyman job. His grandmother was a housekeeper at a hotel in the old part of Alexandria and almost never came into the city. Surely Kiro would be excited at the opportunity to spend some time out and about on a Saturday afternoon when the temperatures suited most tastes and the White Sox had just made the day even sweeter for a boy from Chicago!

"What are y'all planning to do?" Wynn asked his son, looking alternately at him and at Kiro.

"We are just going to get a milk shake around here and maybe meet up with some people I know from work," Junior told his father. He quickly followed up by assuring his father that he would be home by 6:30 that evening. The Horrys usually ate dinner around 7 or 7:30 on Saturdays which was about the time they ate during the week. Junior was usually home by then from his afternoon shift at Horrschorns. They generally waited for him to eat.

"Why don't we get some liquor instead?" Kiro suggested, looking at Junior slyly. Of course, he waited until after Wynn and Talley had walked off to put this question to his friend.

"Where are we gonna get liquor?" Junior replied, raising his eyebrows as he turned toward Kiro.

"Aren't there any bars around here?" Kiro asked. "Anyway, man, I'm just kidding. I can get as much liquor as I want at my grandparents' place," Kiro confided. "They don't keep a close watch and my granddaddy will take a drink every chance he can get."

"Well, lucky you," Junior retorted. He acknowledged to this new boy who he was continuing to find out new things about that it wasn't like that at his house. "My folks would know if I did that and I don't want to hear the noise." Kiro shook his head, patted Junior's back and said that's the way it is living with Big Daddy and Big Momma. "They're just too old and too tired to worry about every little thing," he concluded with a chuckle. "So what do you wanna do after we get this milkshake?"

"This Joe I work with is having a meeting at his apartment that he asked me to attend," Junior shared. "He's a white cat and he and his roommate work on issues that make things better for people. That's all they told me about it."

"Makes what things better and for what people?" Kiro asked as Junior had expected he would. After all, he would have asked the same question after such a nebulous statement. Junior, someone who preferred to be as exact as possible, was sorry he didn't have more information. But that is exactly why he wanted to go to 16th Street up near Crestwood to find out.

"My friend will be home soon, so we can hang out a bit and then take the streetcar to his place."

Kiro wanted to know if the group would be a bunch of white people. "You are the one who hangs out with the pasty faces, not me," he assailed. "I don't know, man, but I don't think so."

"Anyway, we can go over there and if we don't like what we see and hear, we can split," Junior promised.

"I hope that boy isn't planning on meeting that white boy somewhere," Wynn disclosed to his brother-in-law.

"You think that's what he's planning to do?" Talley wondered.

"No, I don't really think so, but I know his mother would pull her hair out if he did. No telling what she would do to him if she finds out that was what this is all about. I'd be disappointed too after the chat we had at your house the other night," Wynn acknowledged, a wistful look on his face.

"I doubt that," Talley said attempting to reassure a concerned father. "That boy he's with doesn't seem like anyone who spends too much time hanging around white people." Both laughed at this because it did seem obvious from just the three hours that they spent with the two of them, most of it with at least three sets of eyes glued to what was happening on the baseball diamond.

"Hey Talley, brother, did you just witness that ass whupping?" said someone calling out from behind them as they were walking down Georgia Avenue toward Florida Avenue where they would continue forward until Georgia had turned into 7th Street. They had parked their car near 7th and Q.

Turning around, Talley realized he knew who the voice belonged to even before looking over his shoulder. "Hey, Broadman, are you still here trying to buy Griffith Stadium, you old tycoon?" Talley asked in jest.

"One day, one day," this man, Broadman, responded with a smile on his face. "Gee, I haven't seen you in quite a little while, brother, how you been?" Broadman asked. He was a round-faced, yellow-skinned man of about 55 with a broad belly. He wasn't as light skinned as Talley, but he was guarding against getting any darker that sunny Saturday afternoon by wearing a straw fedora with a blue band around it. It was not quite summer yet but both Wynn and Talley had on straw fedoras as well. No one wanted to wear a felt or wool hat or cap to a baseball game. It just didn't seem right. Broadman pulled off his dark Ray Bans and slipped them into his shirt pocket, one arm hanging down, before he offered his hand to Talley to shake.

"Good to see you, man," said Talley as he shook his hand. "This is my brother-in-law Wynn Horry. We just brought his son to the game." Wynn shook the man's hand and told him it was nice to make his acquaintance. He asked how he enjoyed the game and what team he rooted for.

"Well, it's like this," said the man, "I grew up in Washington, and spent most of my life here except for my time in the Pacific during the War, so I'm definitely a homeboy but still I always got to go with my White Sox!"

"I know that's right, man," Wynn returned, "Can't go wrong with the White Sox. I pulled for the Dodgers to win the Series last year but it was hard because I love those Sox almost the same," he added.

"Well, I get it, cat, old brothers like you and me just have that attachment to the Dodgers that we can't shake."

"You know it, you know it," Talley commented, interjecting himself into the conversation. "So how is the real estate business going for you?"

he asked. "I bet you own almost every property in Shaw by now, except for Griffith Stadium, right?"

"Ha, well noo," answered Broadman, "not quite. In fact, I'm looking to sell a few places right now," he pointed out. "Can't buy anything new, until I sell one or two I already got," he admitted. "You know anyone interested in a nice lil storefront with a residence above?" Broadman asked.

Before anyone could answer he told the two men that he was in fact headed to the property at that very moment as he was expecting to meet a prospective buyer there. "It's a nice lil place just off 9th Street not too far from Shiloh. If you're headed in that direction, let me show you the place," Broadman suggested. "Talley, maybe your man might want it." Mr Broadman knew that Talley's Congressman boss had owned several properties around Washington and a few of them were apartment houses in the Negro parts of town. Actually, it was the Congressman's wife's family that owned the properties. She had grown up in Maryland and her father had bought lots of property in Baltimore and DC as she was growing up. Now that he was dead, she had inherited the buildings. Talley had worked as the handyman for a few of them and he and Nellie had managed to scrape up the money to buy a rundown property themselves which he quickly turned into a two-family home. It was located within walking distance of where they now were, but closer to North Capitol Street.

"Sure, always curious to see what's on the market," Talley answered, "so long as it's okay with my ride home," he chuckled, turning to Wynn.

"No problem with me, man, let's go," Wynn responded. There were plenty of people out walking the streets of Shaw that late afternoon, as people usually do in nice weather. They were going to movies, restaurants, some going in and out of bars, playgrounds and some just strolling with no particular place to go. This is what he and Julia Mae always said they missed by living in Arlington. The number of people in the streets and the many places they could go. This was not the way life was in Arlington. But that was the reason they moved there in the first place.

Shortly after Junior was born the two decided that they wanted to raise their kids in a quieter atmosphere where people weren't so close together. Neither of them had grown up in a big city with people on top of each other and both wanted their kids to have space too. But now that both Junior and Jeanne were as old as they were, every time he was in the city, he realized how nice it was to be nearer to so much activity. Besides, colored people in Washington looked better, dressed better and lived better. It was just more fun!

Finally, they were at the house that Broadman wanted to show them. It was a fine smaller property, and actually, not that little. The stucco house was painted white with a yellow trim around the door and windows. Wynn didn't so much like the yellow, but he did like the patch of grass that grew on both sides of the door. It was on a quiet street but not far from a main intersection. There was a business space downstairs with two bay windows on either side of the center door. The three fairly wide and tall windows on each side were perfect for display. There was only one front door, but Wynn had assumed that once inside the front door, there was another door that would lead to separate parts of the building.

One door, he assumed, would lead to the ground floor commercial space and another would lead upstairs to a residence. "Would you all be interested in seeing inside since we're here?" Broadman asked.

"Yea, sure," said Talley, "may as well." Once inside, Wynn realized his hunch was off. The downstairs space was much nicer and larger than he had envisioned. It had shiny slat wood floors, probably Georgia pine he figured, and ample room to display whatever one wanted to display. In the back of the space was a bathroom and a supply closet along with another very large room which seemed as if it might once have been an office or workroom. From this area which had several windows, they could see a backyard which looked ample enough. It wasn't as big as their current yard space but there was also a paved spot for a car, which they did not have in Arlington. But it was also a contained space. No door led to the upstairs, although there was apparently a basement too and a door led down to it.

"Nice space," Talley proclaimed. "Now I'm curious to see the upstairs."

"Well, that's the next stop on the tour," Broadman reported. "Let's go," he told them. "My appointment is due here in about ten minutes, so

I can show you quickly." As they came out of the downstairs space, they actually went back out of the front door and walked around to the right of the property where there was a second door that led upstairs.

Wynn asked what had been in the building prior. "It was a candy store," Broadman reported. "But I'm pretty sure it doubled as a numbers place also." He explained that card games almost always went on in the large room in the back.

"Anyway, after about four years, things got bad."

"Did people stop buying candy?" Talley asked in jest, "Because I'm sure the numbers racket didn't fall off," he added, now laughing.

"No, I'm sure," Wynn piped in, "colored folk will play their numbers!"

"No, the husband took sick, went in the hospital and later died," Broadman explained. "The wife couldn't carry things on by herself. I felt bad for them," he acknowledged, hoping it made him sound less like a greedy, uncaring landlord. "But I have to keep the mortgage payments going nevertheless."

The upstairs had the same beautiful floors that shone brightly because of the light that came in from the front room. Once they got upstairs, they could make a right turn to the living room with large bay windows which brought in considerable light with an equally large dining room right across the hall. Both rooms, in addition to being bright, were larger than the ones in Arlington. "The dining room could be used as a bedroom," Broadman pointed out, drawing privacy from the pocket doors that met in the middle when closed. Otherwise, there were three bedrooms, all with closets, all about the same size, a bathroom and a kitchen at the back which was quite large and could easily fit their dining room table, with a back porch beyond it. "Not a bad place," proclaimed Broadman.

"No, not at all," Wynn agreed. He liked the fact that the bedrooms weren't all so close to each other and that the kitchen was huge. It was definitely a roomier house than they currently lived in. By now, all could see that Broadman's appointment had arrived. There was this well-dressed colored couple waiting outside. They must be the ones coming to look at the house!

"I wonder how Julia Mae would like this place," he pondered as he and Talley walked back to the car after they had said goodbye to Broadman. "So much more space than we have now, plus she would have room to make her clothes and to display them."

"That's true," Talley agreed. "And you would be closer to us. No more bridges to cross," Talley laughed.

Wynn couldn't help but chortle too. He wasn't exactly sure about Julia Mae but he definitely liked what he had seen. "This place would be a homerun all around," he concluded.

Chapter 44

The streetcar going north on 16th Street toward Wally's apartment was full of passengers. Many who got on at the corner of 16th and U where he and Kiro boarded were coming from Griffith Stadium as well. But many who were already on the streetcar had clearly been downtown. There were shopping bags all around including a few from Horrschorns and other downtown stores. It was such a busy late afternoon in Washington and apparently the sun had decided to work overtime!

Once the two boys alighted from the streetcar across the street from the apartment house that Wally lived in with his roommate, Junior noticed how different the area looked from where they had been in Shaw. Certainly, it bore no resemblance to Hilldale or even Arlington Heights. Instead of homes, most of the residences were apartment buildings, some large and some more medium sized. Many of them were about thirty or more years old as their Art Deco architecture betrayed. Junior didn't know the term Art Deco, but he knew these structures were older than he was. But there were some much larger and very modern newer buildings along that stretch of 16th Street also, and there were also others on the way as construction sites here and there suggested. Of course, no one was working at them because it was a Saturday.

"Hello, you made it," said Wally as he greeted Junior at the apartment door. He had had to buzz them upstairs, so, of course, he knew beforehand that they had arrived.

"This is my friend Kiro," said Junior as he turned to acknowledge his friend.

"Nice to meet you, Kiro," Wally responded, offering his hand to Kiro who was slow to raise his own for a handshake. "A few others have also arrived, but I want you to meet Laurence, the one who is organizing things," Wally stated. "Laurence is a divinity student at Howard and the others here are students from Howard, George Washington, Georgetown and other schools in the area."

Once they had made it into the living room they saw quite a few young people who looked to be of college age. Most of them were young men but quite a few females had come out as well. While many of them were Negro, there were about five white males in addition to Wally and three white females. Kiro looked at Junior as if to say who are these people and why would they want us to be here. As near as they both could tell, they were the youngest ones there. Junior, and probably the same for Kiro, had never been in a room where Negro and white adults comingled so easily. That alone was enough to hold Junior's attention. So much so that he didn't notice the look of disquiet on Kiro's face.

"This is my roommate Laurence," Wally announced as he escorted Junior and Kiro over to his friend who was standing in the middle of a group of men and explaining something as they all listened intently. Laurence was one of those Negroes who talked with his hands like white people do, Kiro thought to himself. Junior had not anticipated that Laurence would be colored but as he thought about it more, he wasn't surprised at all. Wally definitely came across as one of those white people who were comfortable around Negroes.

"Hello, Laurence," Junior said while offering his hand. Kiro followed suit although still a bit tentative about who this Laurence was and what he was about.

"Glad you could make it," Laurence shared. "I have heard about you, Junior, and I was hoping you would be interested in joining us especially since you live in Arlington."

"My friend lives in Arlington too," Junior offered, still not sure what his denizen ship had to do with anything.

"Great," Laurence responded. "Come on in and get to know everyone and I will end the suspense over what this is all about in a few minutes. Many of these folks were here last night when we first discussed it, but many are also new like you two." With that, Laurence went off and found Wally who was just coming back from the kitchen with more potato chips and peanuts. Both boys noticed that after Wally had put the snacks in their respective bowls that were becoming depleted, Laurence took hold of Wally's elbow as they walked off toward the kitchen together.

The two boys then made their way toward the snacks and Junior noticed that Sprite was also on the table, along with Coke and Ginger Ale. "I had this before," he announced to Kiro. "You should try it," he told him.

"Where is the booze or the beer?" Kiro asked, showing little interest in the Sprite or anything else on the table.

"I don't think this is that kind of party," Junior explained. Kiro shrugged his shoulders and reached into the potato chip bowl, grabbing a handful of the Lays chips and then stuffing his mouth as though the ingredients in potato chips gave him extra powers! Junior had taken a seat on one of the lounge chairs in the apartment, one that had become vacant when someone got up to follow Laurence and Wally out of the room. Junior had already noticed that the furniture was modern like at Cliff's house, at least most of it was.

The sofa that the girls were sitting on didn't have the same look, but the chairs tables and lamps did. Also, the art on the wall was reminiscent of the Peterson house and there was a great deal of African-looking art or masks either on the wall or in the form of statuettes on tables. There was a large credenza that sat in the middle of the room that reminded him of what he had seen at Cliff's house with its beautiful walnut brown wood and three-dimensional relief, but nowhere near as nice. He thought this appropriate given that the two who lived there were young and represented so much that was new!

The chair on which he sat had a square frame and black metal legs that angled out. The upholstery was a solid color wool and the chair was amazingly comfortable. It struck him that this piece of furniture he was sitting on was both soft and inviting with its plush back and seat cushions and ample armrests. But it was also strong and secure with its wrought iron legs that splayed out like those of a spaceship. Could sitting in one of these chairs have been the inspiration for Laurence's desire to open up this new world he was headed toward with this action he hoped to launch, Junior wondered?

Before he could take in all there was to see in the apartment and outside, where there was also a balcony too with rattan chairs that looked like flying saucers, he noticed that someone was walking over to him.

Before he knew it, this person was already upon him. "Hi, I'm Fenn," said the guy, a tall, slender white man with dark blond hair. He wore tortoise shell glasses along with a blue and white plaid short-sleeved shirt with a white tee underneath. His khaki slacks were a bit too wide for his waist, evidenced by the fact that the brown belt which cinched his waist caused the slacks to fold around his midsection.

Kiro had turned his attention to one of the colored girls in the group who he had offered a Coca Cola to. This made Junior more at ease as he chatted with Fenn. In the conversation, he learned that Fenn had grown up in a small town in Minnesota, was a freshman at Georgetown and was not much older than him. Something about Fenn reminded him of Cliff but it wasn't his looks. He didn't consider Fenn to be as handsome as Cliff, but he did observe that he was also shy and seemed smart. He had entered college at seventeen and would soon turn eighteen. Junior himself would soon be sixteen. Knowing that someone else was close to his age aside from Kiro was somewhat comforting.

Junior wasn't sure why Fenn had come over to talk with him when he probably knew most of the other, older guys in the assembled group. Anyway, he had now someone to converse with, especially since Kiro was off talking to the girls. Several more minutes into the conversation, he knew more details about Fenn. He had come to Georgetown to study religion, and he had never been to the east coast prior to moving to Washington. Junior had begun to notice that Fenn spoke differently from the other white people he had become acquainted with. He had come to learn since being at Arlington High that not all white people talked the same, although he hadn't heard this particular accent before. This must be how they talk in Minnesota, Junior figured.

As Junior shared more about himself, he found it difficult to tell the full story about his high school transfer so he would just say that his parents thought it was best. Laurence called everyone to attention. "By now you have all heard about the students in Greensboro doing the sit-in at the Woolworth lunch counter," he said loudly, hoping to halt all side conversations. Junior, curious to hear what he would say next about this protest, decided not to acknowledge that his own cousin was involved in those sit-ins, the ones in Charlotte, at least.

"Many of us have stated how extremely proud we are of our brothers and sisters in North Carolina who are carrying this out," Laurence went on. "The question has arisen several times as to what we can do here to try to bring about the same kind of change. Lunch counters in DC are open and in nearby Maryland, the same thing," he told the group, most of whom were aware and nodded in agreement.

"Virginia," Wally yelled out from across the room, facing Laurence.

"That's right," Laurence shouted in agreement. "We need to turn our attention to Virginia. I have been thinking about Arlington and I believe this is a good time to launch this campaign."

All this caught Junior by surprise. But he realized then why Laurence had made the statement that he was happy that Junior showed up since he lived in Arlington. Junior looked over at Kiro to see what reaction he had and Kiro looked back at him before they once again turned their attention to Laurence.

"Last year, Arlington integrated its school system, or more accurately, three schools let in a few colored students, but lunch counters and some other public facilities are still segregated," Laurence told the group. "He didn't know I would put him on the spot, and perhaps I shouldn't, but we have one of the soldiers of integration among us tonight," Laurence declared. One of the two young men who joined us was among the Negro students to integrate Arlington High, he revealed. At that point, all eyes turned to him and Kiro. Junior realized that Wally had shared some of what they had discussed during their break conversations with his roommate. But it didn't anger him. Many in the room had begun to clap as they looked at the two boys, most not knowing who exactly Laurence was referring to. However, as Fenn was still standing next to Junior and he was looking at him and smiling as he clapped, all seemed to quickly catch on as to who the organizer was singling out.

"So, what is your plan?" Wally yelled out again.

"I want to implement a peaceful sit-in in Arlington in June," Laurence unveiled on cue. "I first want to hear reactions to it and see who would be interested in participating and who else you might know who would be interested. This is just the second meeting of many to come but I am hoping to do this within the next month." Laurence explained that it had to happen quickly before too many people could come up with reasons as to why it shouldn't and also, before most local college students took off for summer break.

The difference between Arlington and Greensboro, Laurence explained, is that there are several locations that students can sit in as opposed to the single location in Greensboro. "That is why this needs to be an orchestrated effort and why we need as many interested and committed people as we can get." Looking around the room once Laurence had finished his appeal, Junior had come to the conclusion that most, if not all seemed interested and willing to affect more change in Arlington. As the evening wore on, Junior felt that this was something he could do and wanted to do. Fenn was in and told Junior he was hoping they could talk more about it away from Laurence and Wally's apartment.

"So what do you think about what we heard?" Junior asked Kiro when they were on the streetcar headed downtown to where they could pick up the bus to go back to Arlington.

"I'm not sure," Kiro answered. "I don't know what sitting at the counter is supposed to do. As far as I know, those brothers and sisters in Carolina still haven't ate!" It was banter, but Junior realized the point he was making. "But he is definitely right about one thing, Kiro added, "with all our brothers and sisters beginning to stand on their own two feet in Africa this spring, we can definitely stand on ours over here."

"Or sit," Junior joked, He confided to Kiro that his cousin Asha was among those students in North Carolina and that she felt that their actions were having an impact.

"Just the attention their actions are getting all around the country and around the world is making a difference," he argued. Kiro countered that he was glad they felt as if they were making a difference, but he wasn't sure that those white folks felt that way.

"Anyway, I prefer to be part of the pickets rather than sitting at a counter," Kiro concluded. Junior had been hearing at Mercer that efforts were being stepped up for a student-led picket of shops on Arlington Boulevard, Lee Highway and other shopping destinations to protest the firing of the boy who had gone to Arlington High that was falsely accused of rape, and the general treatment of Negro shoppers from time to time. Plus, they had also stepped up their demands since he had first heard about the plans the year before. The organizers, spurred on by some of the colored teachers, wanted to put pressure on stores to hire colored sales clerks as well. They had even planned to offer rides to stores in Washington while the strike was on. Thomasine's father had been approached to offer one or two of his cabs, or freedom ferries as they were being nicknamed. They wanted these store owners to know for certain that colored shoppers were serious about their demands and that they were prepared to wait it out.

They were just waiting for school to be over in order to get the protests started. Many teachers had planned to join them. "I don't know what I might do if some whitey takes his fist to my head while I'm sitting peacefully at the counter and can't hit him back," Kiro spouted. "I have already threatened a white man's life and I don't want to go through that again!"

Chapter 45

Julia Mae had had her hands full all weekend. She was so focused on getting her dressmaking finished that she hardly paid attention later that evening when Wynn told her about the baseball game. She did notice, though, that Junior did not arrive at home with him. As any good mother would, she asked her husband where their son was. Once she had learned that he was hanging with a friend in the city, a friend who wasn't Cliff, her mind was back at ease and she continued to focus on little else but her work. She scarcely even noticed when Wynn told her about the great little house he had toured, the one that had a shop downstairs with beautiful bays that could showcase her fabulous frocks!

Jeanne had proven to be invaluable. Julia Mae had been able to tackle more of the work with her daughter's help. Jeanne handled the weekend housework, which freed her mother up for her clothes making. She wasn't so happy, though, that she had to forgo her work at the hospital to help her mother. She would have preferred to be wearing her candy striper uniform and helping to make the recovery for Carver patients a little sweeter. Instead, she was in an old dress and headwrap — she referred to it as her Aunt Jemima uniform — as she worked to do away with a week's worth of dust and dirt.

May was the month for proms, cotillions and big parties among the people she sewed for and there was always a tremendous amount of work to do for them. In fact, she was so busy and tired that she decided not to go to church on Sunday in order to get as much done at home before her work week started on Monday. She felt guilty about not going to Mount Calvary, but she figured the Lord understood. "He has sent me these customers and he knows what I need to do for them, so he must understand," she would joke when her outside work kept her away from the 6th pew from the front on the left side of the pulpit, where the Horrys sat every Sunday. She still wanted Wynn to take the kids to church, though. There was nothing keeping any of them from going, although he had wanted to make sure he was home to hear the Dodgers vs. Phillies game, later that evening. They were playing in L.A. so the game wouldn't be on the radio until after he had got home from church.

Junior was daydreaming over his own Sunday plans and hoping they would become reality. He had given a note to Seeny on Friday morning for her to give to Cliff. He had dropped it off at her house on the way to Mercer. By the time he had returned from work on Friday evening, Cliff had replied with his own note which Junior picked up from Seeny's house on the way home from Horrschorns. *I will try to meet you on Sunday at that place on George Mason Drive but I'm not sure I can. If I can, I will be there at 3:00. Please don't be mad if I can't come. Cliffy.*

Junior had re-read the short note several times that late afternoon. He had hoped it would give him solace. He had waited for about 45 minutes at the strip along the drive where they had met before, but Cliff was apparently not able to come. He couldn't stay any longer because it was about time for him to get back home so they could all head over to Georgetown for dinner with Aunt Nellie and Uncle Talley. But Junior was heavyhearted that he didn't get to see his friend. He hadn't seen him since that Friday night a week before. That fateful Friday when they were apparently spotted in Cliff's room doing what they normally did behind doors that were firmly closed. Although, it was now apparent that closed doors didn't keep their secrets safe! Despite that the forbidden had now been uncovered, his longing for Cliff remained potent!

He knew Cliff needed him to help process what had happened. It was easier for Junior because his family didn't fully know what had gone on in the Peterson house. He imagined that Cliff was disappointed as well that they had not been able to meet. But there would be other times. They had always found a way to be with each other. Junior then turned his thoughts to what he would say when asked where he had run off to. Both Julia Mae and even Wynn were more watchful of him ever since the call from Claire Peterson. He decided that he would go by Kiro's house although he knew he wouldn't be at home. At least he could say that he had gone over there.

Kiro had fascinated Junior all the more since he had explained to him how threatening the life of the white man who had assaulted his mother had led her to send him to Virginia to live with his grandparents for his own safety and for hers too. Junior was certain that no one in Arlington knew this, except for the grandparents, of course. He figured if had told his own parents, Kiro would be one more friend who would be blacklisted. Carolyn didn't know, he was sure, and he wouldn't tell her unless it became necessary! Necessary that is, to help him preserve his dignity as *the Great Pretender*!

"I didn't know we had a poet among us," Miss Bridges boasted later that week at the start of English class. A week before, she had given the assignment to the class to express their feelings about what was going on socially and politically in America, through creative writing. She knew the students were talking about the burgeoning student-led sit-ins in the south as well as the actions of Dr Martin Luther King, Jr. She also realized that many were hearing about the upcoming Presidential election at home from parents who were trying to weigh the two candidates on who might be better on Civil Rights issues. "One good way to process your thoughts on these issues is through creative writing," she had told the class, which included both Junior and Kiro.

"Kiro, would you like to come and read your poem before the class?" she appealed to him from her desk in front. Kiro was certainly not a shy boy but he hesitated to come before the class at first. Junior figured it might be because he didn't want anyone to know that he had been dabbling at poetry for a while. Junior had learned that over their few weeks of getting to know each other. But now he was on his feet and heading toward the front of the class. The teacher handed him the paper on which he had written the poem. She had added "A" in red ink and wrote "short but powerful poem" in that same red ink.

White isn't the only color with might! Yellow is bold and not afraid to fight! Red is strong proud and able! And brown sits at the power table! But black, for some the least favorite of all, eclipses those others and isn't afraid to fall! It remains true that all colors may flatter! But since time began, black continues to matter!

Yes, white sits at the top of the heap! And yellow has been known to weep! Red has had much taken away! But black will receive its due one day!

The pigment itself does not make the claim! It's the power we give it that brings praise or shame!

Junior could see Kiro's hands shaking just a little by the time he had finished reading his poem and held his head up to face the class. A round of applause broke out among the students and Kiro, making jokes here and there, took a bow before sitting down. Miss Bridges announced that there were other good works as well but that no one else had written poetry except for Kiro, whose poem was called "Color Wield". She then passed around a few other examples of the best work to the class to read and Junior's brief essay, kind of a poem as well, but not a rhyming one, was among them.

The blood of the slaughtered provides the power for our future achievement. It is not dried up and wasted. It energizes our overcoming. It is not spilled in vain. The tears that have been watered are not a pool of stagnant water. They have become a mighty river that flows throughout this land and continues to sustain the thirsty, the parched and the seeds that will one day grow into a beautiful flower. The white gleam we see should not blind our eyes or provoke fear but rather it should light our path as we follow the bright star that directs us upward, upward, upward!

Though beaten, beaten, beaten, we are not broken and still rise upward toward the sky even when we cannot see the sunlight because of the tears clouding our eyes. But always we feel the healing warmth on our shoulders. Our dark shoulders that glisten in the light and become big, that become strong! Pride and determination keep us on the path and we don't stray because even in the darkest times we can see the white gleam of that bright star!

He too had received an "A" and Miss Bridges had written "Excellent" on his paper. "I love the way you have interpreted Lift Every Voice and Sing," the teacher added!

Later that day when he arrived home Junior had received another note that brought a smile to his face. Seeny had dropped off a letter from Cliff. As expected, he had apologized for not being able to make it that Sunday afternoon. Things have been busy at my house and my mom got sick, so I had to help around the house. I still want to see you, the note read. I hope that maybe we can try again this weekend. I can meet you in the city after work on Saturday if you can make it. Please let me know. Actually, Junior preferred this plan. This way, he wouldn't have to come up with an excuse to leave the house to meet Cliff somewhere. Since he would already be down there, they could meet downtown and get lost in the crowd!

Chapter 46

"Hey g'morning, JH, how you feeling this morning?" was the question put to Julia Mae on the phone from a voice she recognized. It caught her by surprise that her co-worker would be calling her at home early in the morning when she was soon to leave for the department store. "I wanted to grab you before you get in 'cos I know you have a meeting with boss lady today. Don't say you heard it from me but it was Edna who told on you about the outside business."

Right then and there, Julia Mae's heart almost stopped and even though her co-worker couldn't hear it through the phone, she almost choked on the orange juice she was drinking when she received the news!

"I know she told you it was some white woman who mentioned it to boss lady, but it was her! I overheard her telling it when she didn't even realize I had come back into the alterations room while she had gone up into the office to tattle! I didn't wanna tell you." The co-worker went on, "because I was hoping that it wouldn't come to nothing."

Julia Mae was finally able to summon her voice enough to speak. "Well, thank you for telling me, she said. "Don't worry, I won't say anything about it, and I will act like I don't even know what that snake did."

"All righty honey," her co-worker said into the phone, "I will see you when you get to work and don't let either of them snatch your joy!" Julia Mae laughed, as best she could. She expected a comment like this from her God-fearing co-worker.

"They didn't give it to me, they can't take it away," she countered.

As disappointing as this revelation was, it was still good for her to know. Edna would become second fiddle if Julia Mae should leave and she would also get a little bit more pay. The former boss had seen to it that Julia Mae received more pay than the others because she was good and also fast. It never fails that one of your own will try to pull you down, Julia Mae contemplated, with a sigh. She smiled in my face and tried to stab me in the back, but at least now I know!

With this information, Julia Mae finished her orange juice. Then she checked herself in the mirror to make sure that no disgust or dismay showed on her face but afterwards did something she normally would never do before going to work. Going upstairs in hurried steps, she made a B-line for the bedroom she shared with Wynn and went straight to the jewelry box she kept in the second drawer of her dresser. Back behind her blouses and scarves she pulled it out, opened it and gently lifted out her single strand of gleaming white cultured pearls, the ones she only wore to church, funerals, weddings or other special occasions.

Taking off the gold pendant that she had been wearing originally that morning, Julia Mae replaced it with the white band of beads that she strung around her neck holding her head high! She loved the way they shone against her dark neck hanging there just slightly below her collarbone. These pearls made her feel big-ticket and gave her a sense of what it must be like to be one of the women she sewed for. That was the way she wanted to feel that morning! Suddenly she noticed something! Since she was so focused on donning that necklace, she had forgotten that she still had on the gold earrings that perfectly matched the now discarded gold pendant. Back inside the jewelry box, she found first one, then with a bit more rifling, the second pearl earring that would sink into her pierced ears and make her feel even more regal! No matter what the day would bring, she would remember that her value was high every time she touched her pearl earring or rubbed that necklace that announced itself the same as that of any woman shopping at Horrschorns!

"I understand that you have a side-business and that is not allowed as long as you work at this store," said the woman who had been installed as her supervisor.

"I do on occasion do some work for friends or people I know," Julia Mae responded, her hands folded as she sat on the chair in front of boss lady's desk.

"Well, if you want to keep this job, you will need to give that up, I just want you to know." Julia Mae was glad that this exchange didn't come until the end of the workday. She figured that it was because boss lady wanted to make sure she had done all the work that was slated to be finished for the day instead of walking out when she was told that it was either the side business or Horrschorns. Coming face to face with this late in the day also meant that she had those pretty, shimmering pearls blinding anyone who looked at her all day!

"OK, ma'am, I understand what you mean, and I will do what is necessary," Julia Mae informed the woman. That seemed at the time to be the most appropriate thing to say. She wasn't exactly sure at that point what was necessary, but she realized she was on the way to finding out whether she wanted to or not. This situation was about to take care of itself somehow, some way. But as for today, she had too much work to do both at Horrschorns and back at home. Julia Mae had managed to get through the entire day without letting on to "Edna Judas" as she had been referring to her since the revelation, that she knew she was a turncoat.

They all carried on as usual in the alterations room and Julia Mae made sure that Edna noticed she was wearing her pearls. Every chance she got to be near Edna's sewing table she made it a point to finger them or found a reason to bend her head over so that they would dangle, like looking at her shoes or straightening out her uniform. Now the day was over, and she would soon be home with her family, which was the most solace she could ever expect. She was proud that she had survived the day. The fact that both of them seemed to be against her was interesting in and of itself. Boss lady had no more use for Edna than she did for her. But, if Edna could bring her information she could use, well they could be bedfellows for a minute or two. For Edna, she wasn't naive about gaining any closer relationship with her supervisor, but she could at least revel in the fact that her closet rival had been brought down a notch or two. Folks were like that. Everyone knew it and everyone accepted it. The fact that this happened was no reason not to go on living!

"Guess what, Momma," Jeanne implored after Julia Mae had disrobed, de-jeweled and donned her apron, trading the kitchen for the alterations room. Wynn had arrived home and was enjoying his scotch on the rocks while watching the *Huntley-Brinkley Report* when she arrived. Junior was helping his sister with an assignment at the kitchen table. Everyone else had already heard the news that Jeanne was so anxious to share with Julia Mae it was obvious.

"What is it, dear?" Julia Mae asked.

"You need to sit down for this one," Wynn interjected before Jeanne had the chance to reply. Jeanne looked at her father sideways but then added the smile back on her face before revealing the news to her mother.

"Virginia is getting married!" At first Julia Mae's face registered surprise as if she couldn't possibly have heard Jeanne say what she thought she said.

"Who is she marrying?" she asked, still incredulous.

"She's marrying Perry Cocceli," Jeanne answered, "and the wedding is in the middle of September!"

"The white boy?" Julia Mae queried.

"Yessss, the father of her baby," Wynn answered back!

"Do they hope to get the baby back that she gave up for adoption?" Julia Mae asked.

"That baby has gone to a new family, Ma," Jeanne explained.

After what seemed like several minutes of silence, Julia Mae replied that she was in fact shocked and very happy for Virginia. "What a surprise!" she proclaimed. "Where will the wedding be?" she then wondered, "They can't get married around here."

"Perry rented an apartment in Washington where they have been staying together and they will get married there," Jeanne confided.

"Ain't that a kick in the butt?" Wynn asked. He was in his own state of disbelief but still, he was happy for Virginia as well. He had always thought she was a nice girl and was happy that she was getting away from her family and out on her own. And she had snagged her white man to everyone's disbelief!

"I wonder if she will be wearing a wedding dress?" Julia Mae asked.

"Are you looking for a new customer, Ma?" Jeanne responded with a smirk.

"No," said Julia Mae, "not really, although I'm happy to do whatever I can for her. But I was just wondering if she had planned to be in a traditional wedding gown, a white one," Julia Mae questioned of no one in particular.

"Yes, I believe she will," answered Jeanne. "At least that's what she seemed to think when she was telling me about her plans," she added. Julia Mae and Wynn looked at each other and both smiled, more with their eyes than with their mouths. They understood each other. A woman who had already had a baby shouldn't be wearing a white dress even if she did end up getting married since she was no longer considered pure!

"Oh well, just when you think you know everything," Wynn professed, shaking his head back and forth.

"Well, that's the best news I have heard all day," his wife acknowledged, now with a full-faced smile. "What do you know, some things DO change!"

Chapter 47

During the past couple of weeks, Cliff had been getting home from school about an hour later than usual because he had picked up a paper route in his neighborhood, delivering the *Evening Star*. Still embarrassed and ill at ease about what had gone on in the house with Junior, he wanted to be away from home more, but he also wanted to have an excuse in case he went to South Arlington to meet up with Junior. He could always say the evening newspapers got delivered late or that he ended up having a long chat with one of his subscribers, which could very well happen in his neighborhood of older retired people who often longed for a young person to talk to.

But on this particular Wednesday, two weeks before the start of summer vacation, Cliff heard a familiar and always welcomed voice as he entered his house. As far as he was concerned, he could hear this voice every day but wasn't exactly expecting to hear it at the house on that day! "Uncle Peter, what are you doing here?" Cliff shouted, sincerely surprised to see his favorite uncle sitting on the sofa having a cocktail with his mother. Robby wasn't there, which meant he must have been out playing softball with his friends in Adams Park, so Cliff had Peter all to himself, although he had to share him with Claire at the moment.

"I came out to see my two favorite nephews," Peter said, "and also to help you celebrate your good news and to share my own news with you all."

"What good news do you have?" Cliff asked. "Are you about to get married or have you already done so?"

"Oh no, nothing as dramatic as that," Peter answered, laughing so hard that he had to put down on the teak surfboard cocktail table the curved low ball cocktail glass with the harlequin design that held his gin and tonic with the two cubes of ice. He feared that the thought of him getting married might cause the glass to shatter right there in his hand!

"No, Cliffy, I'm moving to New York with my firm to head a department there. I flew out to pick up a friend in DC and we're driving up there for me to look at apartments," Peter announced.

"Oh wow," Cliff replied, "congratulations! Mom didn't say you were coming out," he went on, looking at Claire as he spoke.

"I asked her not to," Peter admitted. "I wanted it to be a surprise. I don't even think your father knows yet. Where is he, by the way?" Peter asked. "I thought those State Department men basically had banker's hours."

"He should be home soon," Claire interjected, "as should Robby." "I'm sure they'll both be happy to see you!"

"So, the Petersons are moving to Luxembourg, I hear," said Peter.

"Looks like it, whether we want to or not," Cliff replied and Peter wasn't sure if he was being sarcastic or just sad about the fact that he was leaving Virginia and the United States.

"Don't you want to go?" Peter asked. Cliff replied that he would go wherever his family went. "I was all resolved for you to go somewhere in Africa and then my sister tells me that you are going to Luxembourg. Well, that's practically like going to Paris or Berlin, so I'm all for it," his uncle said with a laugh and a stir of his nearly devoured cocktail.

"Well, I think it's a better move for us at this time," Claire imparted. "It will help us get our priorities straight and keep up with all the progress being made at home," she further explained. Peter, wearing a puzzled look, asked his sister what priorities they needed to get straight, but Claire just offered back a slight smile and took a big sip of her cocktail.

"It will be a busy summer for us," Cliff told his uncle. "I start astronaut camp up near Rochester in two weeks," Cliff revealed, using the more official term for it rather than the colloquial one that the kids used, thinking his uncle might not be familiar.

"And you were just getting used to your paper route I bet," chimed Peter.

"Well, I was only a three-week fill-in in the first place," Cliff confided. "I was just substituting for my friend Richard whose father passed away and his family is now in Dublin."

"Space camp should be fun," Peter commented. "There must be tons of boys these days who are interested in becoming astronauts. I'm sure astronaut camp is as good as having one foot in the stratosphere already," he chuckled. "Is Robby going too?"

"He will go as well and actually I think he might enjoy it more than Cliff," their mother interjected. "But after that, they get to spend some time with Mother and Dad and I think that will be good before we head to Luxembourg City. This time, though," she added, "I know you all will actually come visit us while we're overseas."

"I know I will," Peter proclaimed.

"Isn't it about time for dinner?" Peter questioned, "And where is that other son of yours?"

"Gussie is broiling a prime rib and roasting some potatoes and vegetables just for you," Claire announced, "We will be eating in about an hour. Chester and Robby will be home by then," she stated.

"They normally come home together because Dad drives by the softball field and picks him up on the way home," Cliff explained.

"So, who is this friend you are going to New York with?" Cliff questioned his uncle. By now, Peter had finished his cocktail and was currently puffing a cigarette, having opened up a new pack of Marlboro! It had been his favorite cigarette for a long time, even though his firm lost the account to make the cigarette more appealing to men. It had always been considered a woman's cigarette since it was first rolled out. Leo Burnett's creation of the Marlboro Man a few years earlier had done the trick and Peter had so wished his firm had won the account because that would have been exactly the concept that he would have devised. After all, he knew many Marlboro men!

In between puffs, he told his nephew and Claire who also seemed particularly interested in what he had to say, that his friend was someone he had met when he last visited them in November for Thanksgiving. "He's an artist and lives over in Dupont Circle," he explained. "He has a great eye for design and in fact he used to live in Greenwich Village, so he has a better sense of New York than even I do. I will stay over there tonight, in fact, so we can get an early start on the drive in the morning," said Peter. Claire said nothing and Cliff smiled and commented that it would be fun to have someone to look at apartments with.

As Claire was about to go into the kitchen to check on dinner,

Chester and Robby walked in the house laughing. Apparently, something funny had happened either on the softball field or some private joke was shared in the car on the way home. Upon noticing that his uncle was sitting on the daybed, Peter having switched over to the daybed after he was done making a second cocktail to go along with his cigarette, Robby ran over to give him a hug. "Hey, Uncle Peter," he said, "why are you here?" Peter reprised his story of wanting to help them celebrate their move to Europe and also to drive up to New York to look for an apartment owing to a job transfer. While Robby didn't have any follow up questions on this (all he said was, "Oh cool"), Chester certainly did.

"Moving to New York are you," he uttered, more a statement than a question. "Why?" he asked. "I thought you liked Chicago."

"I love Chicago but New York, well, that needs no justification!" Peter proclaimed. "The apple is big and tasty and when you bite it it bites back!"

"Ha," Chester replied, loosening his tie and walking over to the bar to make his own cocktail. "Just the kind of pithy remark I expect from an ad man... or a movie starlet!"

"Well, I hope never to disappoint on either count," Peter shot back, just as Claire walked into the room to announce that they needn't let anything get cold!

"Dinner is ready," she reported.

"Shall we dig in?" Chester asked.

Chapter 48

As things were moving forward for the sit-ins in Arlington, more college students were getting involved. Wally had invited Junior to more meetings, most of them sit-in training sessions, all held on Saturday afternoon. This happened to be the most convenient time for him since he was already in the city, and also for other students, who were free from classes and final exams on the weekend. More students were coming on board and they now had more than enough bodies to sit at counters at several sites in Arlington, including the People's Drug Store that Junior had decided to demonstrate at, but also a Drug Fair and a few other five and dime stores.

Word had spread to other parts of Virginia through a student network that Laurence had worked to develop in towns and cities on the coast, near the North Carolina border and throughout the state, that young people, mostly Negro but some whites too, wanted to bring peaceful action for change to their town. Laurence, Wally, Fenn and the others had decided to launch a team they were naming the Student Peaceful Assembly Committee to Educate. This team would spend the summer traveling to these towns to train students to do peaceful protest actions like sit-ins. They had asked Junior to join them for about a month and a half to help recruit other high school aged students to participate. Junior was surprised by this! He had never seen himself doing anything like this and was pretty certain that Julia Mae and Wynn would not so easily see him doing it either!

As for the Arlington sit-ins, Fenn would be with him at the counter at People's. They had, in fact, become more acquainted with each other over the weeks since the first meeting. It seemed that the "day of action", as they were calling it, would be sometime during the second week of June. The date was kept under wraps so as not to allow anyone who might have sided with the businesses to tip anyone off to what was being planned. All that most knew was to be prepared to "act" sometime in June.

There was no meeting on the afternoon that Junior was to meet Cliff downtown, fortunately. Cliff had taken the bus from South Arlington into downtown Washington as Junior had instructed him to. He waited outside the store until Junior came out. Wally happened to be on break and standing outside the store when Junior came out to meet Cliff. Junior introduced the two of them and Wally smiled at both of them. As they walked off to get the streetcar up to Georgetown where they would find privacy in a deserted area somewhere near the canal, Cliff asked Junior who Wally was.

"He's a waiter in the tearoom and we have become friends," Junior acknowledged. He told him how Wally's roommate, a Howard University divinity student, was organizing an event similar to the sit-ins in Greensboro and Charlotte, for some Arlington businesses.

"Really," replied Cliff, astonished that this civil rights action that everyone around the country was now becoming aware of over the last few months, was about to happen in Arlington. The television news had been reporting for the past few weeks the plight of the colored students in Baton Rouge who had been arrested and jailed for participating in similar sit-ins. Although the idea of sit-ins was catching fire all over the south, the Southern Code was by no means broken! Be that as it may, no one would have expected such a horrid response to this kind of demonstration in Arlington as occurred in Baton Rouge and other places.

"Will you participate?" Cliff asked Junior as they stood together on the crowded streetcar headed up Pennsylvania Avenue toward Georgetown.

"Yes, I will," Junior replied. "Will you join us?" he inquired of Cliff.

"I would definitely join you," answered Cliff. "My mother knows the store manager at that drug store well, and I don't think he will be hard to deal with," Cliff forecasted. "But I will be leaving for camp the first week of June, right after school is out, I wanted to tell you." He confided to Junior, looking at him and then looking away, his head down. "Then, we are moving to Luxembourg in early September. My dad has been posted there for two years!"

"Wow," Junior replied. He couldn't quite find any more words to say right then.

"I won't even be here for your birthday," Cliff conceded. "But I have something I want to give you before I leave, anyway."

"You don't have to do that," Junior responded, although still reeling from what he had just had to process. But he knew when saying it that he couldn't talk Cliff out of this gesture. "So, we get to see each other before you leave for camp, then," Junior confirmed. He was doing his best to assuage himself and also to put a positive spin on what had just been revealed. Junior had decided not to tell Cliff about the proposition he had been made, to spend some time traveling through Virginia to train high schoolers in peaceful protest actions. It had been occupying a lot of room in his mind since Laurence first mentioned it to him. But now, he was pretty sure he knew what he wanted to do.

Consumed with their own load of thoughts and anxiousness, both boys were quiet on that cloudy but warm Saturday early evening. The day seemed sullen and that appeared to match the current mood. They seemed not to notice the many people, young and old, colored and white, male and female, out and about around them as they sought out a safe and quiet place to be free! To be liberated from all the eyes on them and from the, at times, disquieting ideation going on in their heads, was what they wanted most! Junior and Cliff were both apprehensive about what lay before each of them during those upcoming weeks, as anyone would be. But now they had each other to turn to for relief. It was beginning to get dark, so wherever they decided to stop along the canal as they walked would be a place that would shield them from whoever might be looking. They could comfort each other in whatever way they wanted and needed to.

"Will there be any colored boys at the camp you go to?" Junior asked once they had found a quiet and shady, grassy area to park themselves. Cliff never answered the question but then it didn't even matter. Other things became more pressing!

Chapter 49

Those next few weeks at Horrschorns had all blended into each other. Julia Mae was basically just there to do the work she had to do. Her spirit had pretty much abandoned her body and she was only going through the motions, although still doing it well. Of course, she hadn't quit doing the outside work which was about as busy as the work waiting for her at the department store. But she never once again discussed it with the two ladies she worked with. The boss lady had decided not to say any more about it either, but it was clear that nothing had changed between the two of them. The air was spoilt, as Nellie would say! Making it through those hours at work was about all that Julia Mae could focus on even though when she got home, she still had a job to do being a mother and a wife.

"How are things going with getting ready for your final exams?" she asked both Jeanne and Junior. Of course, she knew that her children were not likely to have any concerns when it came to their schoolwork. They were both smart and capable and she knew they would both pass all their classes and go on to the next grade in the fall. Jeanne had been pestering Wynn to teach her to drive even though she couldn't get a license for another two years. "That's my daughter," she told Nellie who laughed and joked that Jeanne would probably never need a man but was pretty enough to get "all the men she wanted". The consensus of all was that she was, and she probably would.

"Do you think you will want to stay at Mercer next year?" Julia Mae asked Junior the weekend before the school year was to end. "Now that you have your new friend and you are nearer to Carolyn, do you feel more like you are settled now?" she wanted to know. Of course, neither she nor Wynn knew anything about the plans to sit in at the drug stores and dime stores in Arlington nor the exact plans to begin protesting outside certain Arlington stores in the upcoming weeks.

"I'm not sure, Momma," Junior answered. He was surprised in a way that she would even ask him because he was certain she had wanted him to go to West End High in the District in September. Junior was sure that he probably wouldn't want to stay at Mercer in the fall, but it was true that he was getting something out of it that he couldn't get from Arlington High, or any of the other white schools. The fact that Cliff would be gone overseas made it easier for him to put Arlington in his past. "I have decided that I don't want to cut grass this summer, though," he confirmed.

"Will you stay at Horrschorns all summer then?" Julia Mae wondered.

"No, I don't want to wash dishes there either!" Junior was surprised at how quickly and confidently those words shot from his lips. It was obvious that Julia Mae was too, from the expression on her face right after he had fired that salvo!

"Come on, Julia Mae, let's get ready to leave," Wynn had shouted loudly as he walked back in the house from washing the car.

"All right, I'm ready," she said. "Let's go see this house with the dress shop downstairs again, that you can't get off your mind. I'm surprised it's still available after all these weeks," she expressed.

"Well, if those last people had been able to come up with the money, it wouldn't be," Wynn retorted. "You might even say the fact that it's still available means it is meant for us," he concluded. Junior could see that his mother's face was beginning to show excitement again. But he knew she would soon recall their conversation and he would have to explain himself and his intentions for the summer.

The fact was that all the Horrys did like the house. Wynn had gotten back in contact with the owner about a week and a half after first seeing it and drove the kids over to DC after work where they picked up Julia Mae downtown and drove up to see the place on Q Street. "Wow, that is a cute little white house and look at those bay windows!" Julia Mae exclaimed upon seeing the place. By the time Broadman had taken the family through the house all had fallen in love with it! There were questions that needed to be answered, like could they sell the house in Arlington for enough money to buy this place and what would it be like trading Arlington for DC, but they did like the place and Julia adored the shop and workroom downstairs. "I could call my shop Whitehouse Dressmakers," she joked.

Wynn had come to the conclusion that they could make it work, especially with Nellie and Talley's help. He knew they would help as much as they could. "If Broadman is willing to take a down payment and understand that we will have more money once we sell our house," he told the family, "I think we can swing it." So here they were, on the way to meet the owner to make their offer.

"I feel good about this," Julia Mae beamed as she got in the car. "This is right for us, I just know it."

"We won't need to lie about our address if Junior decides to go to school in DC, either," she stated, smiling. "Also, our princess will be able to walk to Carver Hospital for her candy strip work," she added, looking over her shoulder at her daughter in the back seat.

"That's right, Momma," Jeanne concurred. "I won't have to wait for Daddy to drive me to the hospital on Saturdays and I'd be able to work after school sometimes as well."

"I thought every princess wanted to have her very own chariot," her father supposed, looking into the rearview mirror. Jeanne repaid him with the smile he had hoped to elicit.

"Speaking of Junior," said Wynn, "it would be a nice birthday present for him also." Junior would turn 16 on the weekend after the sit-in at People's Drugs, the "action" that his parents were still in the dark about; however, it was now out in the open as to when this action would happen. It would be the following Thursday, the second one of the month. All the college students were now done with classes and so was he, the high schooler who had just completed his freshman year and would in three months be a high school junior somewhere.

That is, if something bad didn't happen that would require Julia Mae and Wynn to know what he was involved in. The training sessions over the preceding weeks had, after all, attempted to prepare participants for all kinds of reactions from those who didn't take well to what they were doing. No one minced words about the possibly dire consequences of this action. But Junior knew this better than all the others. He was perhaps the most qualified to take a seat where no one of his race had sat before. And he knew that he could imbue that feeling of pride in any young colored person he encountered throughout the state if he was a part of the Student Peaceful Assembly Committee Education team.

Kiro hadn't changed his mind, however. He would not be joining the sit-in but he would be on the forefront of the demonstrations outside certain stores the following week. No one had told him about the education team, Junior was certain, because they thought he might be too volatile for it. Not even the colored boy, the former Arlington High student who lost his job over the rape allegations, would be there. He and his family had moved across the river to Washington.

For all his capricious behavior, Kiro was always saying things that caused Junior to think! Perhaps it was because of it, Junior had begun to consider. But recently, when they were talking about the upcoming sit-ins and protests, he had made one comment in particular that stuck.

"Why doesn't your group stir up some action outside Arlington High School once the new school year starts, to call attention to the fact that they have been throwing the Blacks out of the school about five minutes after they get there!?"

Junior was quite surprised at this comment coming from his new, much more bellicose friend. "I didn't think you wanted us to be there with them in the first place," Junior pointed out.

"I never said *that*," Kiro replied. "All I know is that I don't think it would work for me to be in that environment. That's not the same thing as saying that no Negroes should be doing it," he added. "As long as those people feel they can do whatever they want to us and nobody will stand up and say 'no', they will continue to do it. Why do you think I'm joining the protests?" Kiro quizzed.

As far as Junior knew, no one else had suggested protesting on behalf of the two colored boys, expelled from Arlington High. But he couldn't help but wonder what effect any more colored housecleaning at Arlington's newly integrated schools might have on the Negro community and perhaps even the newspaper, television and radio reporters. Up 'til then, not a word about it had come on the television or radio news. Even though many had heard that about a week before Junior's dismissal, a colored boy had also been put out of the junior high that had been integrated. This information was still percolating in the community. But it hadn't reached the boiling point yet.

Nevertheless, all this helped drive Junior to his decision about how he would spend the first month or so of the summer vacation. All that remained was to deliver this news to Wynn and Julia Mae later in the weekend. Perhaps after another one of the pastor's colored people's empowerment sermons, would be the right time! Surely there would be one again on the upcoming Sunday.

With his wife and daughter piled in the car to come to DC, Wynn turned on the radio just after shifting into gear. The colored station he usually listened to was playing *High Hopes* by Frank Sinatra, or at least that's what he thought at first. But it was not his recent hit song, it became clear, but a re-recorded version done for the John Kennedy Presidential campaign. *Everyone wants to back Jack, Jack is on the right track!* Sinatra had gone on record for his support of Kennedy for President. *He's got high hopes. Nineteen Sixty's the year for his high hopes. Come on and vote for Kennedy.*

Chapter 50

That afternoon Junior had planned to end his shift at Horrschorns about an hour earlier than usual so he could meet Cliffy one last time before his parents pulled up to go to what might turn out to be their new house. As decided, Cliff would meet him outside the store but this time in the dock area where the employees took their cigarette breaks. Junior had told him how to get out there. He had come downstairs, early, his face and hands washed, in his street clothes and ready to meet Cliff for the last time before he was sent off to space camp.

"I brought you something," Cliff said walking over to him with a big smile on his face! "Happy Birthday, Junior," Cliff blushed, handing Junior a gift-wrapped square package that was the size of a record album, which left no doubt as to what was hidden underneath the brightly colored paper that said "Sweet Sixteen". Junior blushed at the wrapping paper, although it wasn't exactly obvious that he was blushing, and then quickly tore it off before anyone else would see it.

"Oh wow, Johnny Mathis' Greatest Hits and More Greatest Hits," he laughed. "You know I'm not a big fan of his," Junior reminded Cliff, smiling as he said it.

"I know you're not, but he can grow on you," Cliff smirked. "On the second album there's a song called A Certain Smile," Cliff told Junior. "I want you to play it and think of me!"

"I will," Junior quickly replied, "but it won't take a Johnny Mathis song for that to happen," he added.

"I will be thinking of you on your birthday," Cliff wanted Junior to know. "What will you do to celebrate your 16th?" he asked. Junior replied that he would be with his family, of course, and that his Aunt Nellie would make him his favorite cake.

"She said she was making a chocolate cake for me and also one for

Senator Kennedy at the same time, to take to his house in Georgetown to remind him of what he must do for colored people if he wins the election in November." Both boys laughed but Junior still wasn't quite sure whether or not his aunt actually meant it. After all, the Kennedys didn't live that far from her house. Their place was just six or so blocks away across Wisconsin Avenue. And no one who knew Nellie Lester would put it past her to do something like that.

"Then I will have a party with my friends," Junior noted. However, he didn't mention that his new friend Fenn had invited him out for some food to help him celebrate, as well. "I'm looking forward to turning 16," he told Cliff. "Maybe I can drive up to Rochester to the space camp." The two boys wanted to hug each other but knew they couldn't right out there in the open. Junior asked Cliff to follow him into the gentlemen's room, where he hoped they'd have some privacy.

The washroom appeared empty and they locked themselves in a far stall where Junior pressed Cliff against the wall, their bodies sealed together. Junior could feel Cliff's heavy breathing on his neck, his strong heartbeat against his own and his sweaty hands running up and down his body. Anyone who would have entered the men's room could probably have seen the two pairs of calves clad in blue jeans rolled up at the ankles both exposing white high top sneakers intertwined underneath the stall door, as Cliff had started wearing the same sneakers he so liked on Junior. That is, if someone entering had looked in that direction. But that didn't seem to matter to the two of them, fervently finding their joy in the john. The flood of emotion and desire they felt at that moment drowned out reason. The two of them had thought about being together like this for so long! They were now two medium fires, the flames of which could be doused only by smothering each other's body! Although, like rubbing two sticks together, the sparks created by the contact only caused the flames to grow!

During the embrace, Cliff lifted his head off Junior's shoulder and actually rested his lips on Junior's intentionally for the first time. They had brushed their lips against each other's before, but never really kissed. Up 'til this moment, Junior had resisted taking the bait!

With their lips spontaneously pressed together, as if they were glued onto each other's the two boys abruptly broke away on impulse when they heard the door to the washroom about to open. Junior, his heart racing, fled from the stall almost immediately! Fortunately, this time no clothes had come undone or completely removed!

It was the washroom attendant, an old colored man, coming back from his break to once again pass out the hand soap and hand towels to those who wished to clean up after conducting what business they had to conduct. Neither boy had realized there was an attendant on duty and the elderly Negro man seemed stunned to encounter Junior, a colored teenager, in the public gentlemen's room. As Junior hurried past him on the way out, the old man's mouth was still agape as he watched the teen reach for the gold-plated door handle that led him to his escape. Cliff had stalled a bit before making his own exit. Perhaps his eyesight is bad, and he didn't really notice anything, Junior hoped, wondering what might be going through the old man's mind.

Despite the close call, both of them felt lucky that they had had the bathroom to themselves for those few minutes. Outside the bathroom Junior and Cliff smiled nervously at each other as both made sure that any hard evidence of their stolen moments had been concealed. Cliff handed Junior the Johnny Mathis records that he had abandoned in the stall as he absconded. Both smiled as Junior tucked the records under his arm. "You can't ditch Johnny that easily," Cliff quipped. Junior laughed and each then walked out of the nearest exit which poured into F Street. Junior went first and then a minute or two later, Cliff followed. It would be less conspicuous if he lingered in the store longer.

Meeting up with each other outside the store, the two boys walked around the corner so that Junior's parents wouldn't see them together if they came early. They were more at ease now. He was no longer worried about being found out in the stifling men's room now that he was out in the open air. Neither was he worried about explaining the albums.

"I will write to you once a week from space," Cliff joked. He knew to send any letters to Thomasine's house, although Junior hadn't mentioned to him that his family might be moving to DC. The two boys then shook hands as Cliff turned away to go back to Horrschorns, explaining that he wanted to buy something for his grandmother with the money he had made from the paper route, before heading back to Arlington for his babysitting job. "I have to keep an eye on my little brother because my folks are going to see *Romeo and Juliet* over at the National Theater. They love that play!" Cliff was smiling hard at Junior and trying to take as much of him in as possible before turning away to join the foot traffic headed toward Horrschorns.

Junior watched Cliff as he walked off toward the entrance to the store. He was still for a moment, filled with emotion and many countervailing thoughts. Yet, he joked to himself that maybe he too should go back into the store with the paycheck that he had just picked up, to buy Julia Mae a gift that he could hand her to occupy her hands and keep her from choking him when he told her that he really wanted to go to towns in Virginia to help liberate the captives, so to speak. He knew she realized there was a war going on! She had been living through it all her life, after all. How could she and Wynn not want their son to help bring freedom to others longing for it?

But he was never serious about going back into Horrschorns. He had washed his hands of that place! Instead, he strode slowly toward the south-east corner of 14th Street, cattycorner from the store, where his family would soon pick him up. He thought about receiving those letters from "space" as Cliff had referred to them realizing how far away Cliff already was. Undoubtedly, they would stay in contact, at least for a while but probably the space that would soon separate them would get filled up by something or someone that would hold it more certainly! He thought back to what his father said to him weeks before in Nellie's back yard, still not quite sure what he meant but… strangely, there was comfort in the not knowing!

But now he was sullen! His lips, a minute ago, warm, lush, and tingling from the bait, were now puckered and pouting!

Somehow through this funk and mind rambling and undoubtedly in an effort to rouse himself, he thought of Bolle Jackson! Bolle was the colored boxer from a recent episode of the Twilight Zone. It was a memorable episode because it was the first one of the series with an all-Negro cast. Bolle had been knocked out in a match and lay cold and stiff on the mat. Miraculously he got back on his feet. He didn't know how he did it. But, in the end, he was the one with fists clinched in the air celebrating the victory!

With his Johnny Mathis records under his arm, Junior's lips

managed to convert to a smile. The power of the bait? Or maybe, the magic of Mathis which he had been unaware of all this time! Maybe he had absorbed the strength of Bolle? Or maybe it was Brick Springfield, his own creation proving to be his alter ego. Brick, the one whose talents and gifts were heralded and no one questioned his abilities.

Standing across the street from Horrschorns, looking left, he realized he had never studied the store from that vantage point. There it was, washed in tea-time sunlight! In the afternoon glare, he could see that the luster of the old structure was beginning to fade. Time and the forces of nature had thrown the stalwart a blow! It looked a bit vulnerable as if defending its place against the glass and steel skyscrapers rising around it!

Mark F. Johnson, 2021